"The captured Earth girl is the key to locating the Kur agent," I said. "That is why she must not see our faces nor know in whose power she has been."

"Precisely," said Samos.

"It is also known that her ship was taken by a Port Kar captain. She cannot be simply released and allowed to proceed on her secret mission. All would then suspect that she had become our decoy, a lure to bring forth the Others' agents."

"Still," said Samos, "we must attempt to regain the ring, or at all costs to prevent it falling into the hands of the Kurii."

"When the other women prisoners are put upon the slave block, let her be put there with them," I replied. "I will attend the sale in disguise to see who buys her. And then I shall follow where they lead even to the heart of the unexplored jungle. . . ."

JOHN NORMAN

books available from DAW:

HUNTERS OF GOR
MARAUDERS OF GOR
TRIBESMEN OF GOR
SLAVE GIRL OF GOR
BEASTS OF GOR
EXPLORERS OF GOR
TIME SLAVE
IMAGINATIVE SEX

EXPLORERS OF GOR

John Norman

DAW BOOKS, INC.
DONALD A. WOLLHEIM, PUBLISHER
1633 Broadway
New York, N.Y. 10019

FIRST PRINTING, MARCH 1979

PRINTED IN U.S.A.

4   5   6   7   8   9   10   11   12
PRINTED IN U.S.A.

Contents

1

I TALK WITH SAMOS

She was quite beautiful.

She knelt near the small, low table, behind which, cross-legged, in the hall of Samos, I sat. At this table, too, cross-legged, sat Samos. He faced me. It was early evening in Port Kar, and I had supped with Samos, first captain in the council of captains, that congress of captains sovereign in Port Kar. The hall was lit with burning torches. It contained the great map mosaic.

We had been served our supper by the collared slave, who knelt near us.

I glanced at her. She wore a one-piece tunic of rep-cloth, cut high at the thighs, to better reveal them, her steel collar, which was a lock collar, and her brand. The brand was the common Kajira mark of Gor, the first letter, about an inch and a half in height and a half inch in width, in cursive script, of the expression 'Kajira', which is the most common expression in Gorean for a female slave. It is a simple mark, and rather floral, a staff, with two, upturned, frondlike curls, joined where they touch the staff on its right. It bears a distant resemblance to the printed letter 'K' in several of the Western alphabets of Earth, and I suspect, in spite of several differences, it may owe its origin to that letter. The Gorean alphabet has twenty-eight characters, all of which, I suspect, owe their origin to one or another of the alphabets of Earth. Several show a clear-cut resemblance to Greek letters, for example. 'Sidge', on the other hand, could be cuneiform, and 'Tun' and 'Val' are probably calligraphically drifted from demotic. At least six letters suggest influence by the classical Roman alphabet, and seven do, if we count 'Kef', the first letter in 'Kajira'. 'Shu' is represented by a sign which seems clearly oriental in origin and 'Homan', I speculate, may derive from Cretan. Many Gorean letters have a variety of pronunciations, depending on their linguistic context. Certain scribes have recommended adding to the Gorean alphabet new letters, to independently represent some of these sounds which, now, require alternative pronunciations, context-de-

9

pendent, of given letters. Their recommendations, it seems, are unlikely to be incorporated into formal Gorean.

In matters such as those of the alphabet conservatism seems unshakable. For example, there is not likely to be additions or deletions to the alphabets of Earth, regardless of the rationality of such an alteration in given cases. An example of the conservatism in such matters is that Goreans, and, indeed, many of those of the Earth, are taught their alphabets in an order which bears no rational relation whatsoever to the occurrence pattern of the letters. That children should be taught the alphabet in an order which reflects the frequency of the occurrence of the letters in the language, and thus would expedite their learning, appears to be too radical and offensive an idea to become acceptable. Consider, too, for example, the opposition to an arithmetically convenient system of measurement in certain quarters on Earth, apparently because of the unwillingness to surrender the techniques of tradition, so painfully acquired so long ago.

"Do Masters desire aught else of Linda?" asked the girl.

"No," said Samos.

She put her small hand on the table, as though to reach to him, to beg his touch.

"No," said Samos.

She withdrew, head down. She picked up the small tray from the stand near the table. On it was the small vessel containing a thick, sweet liqueur from distant Turia, the Ar of the south, and the two tiny glasses from which we had sipped it. On the tray, too, was the metal vessel which had contained the black wine, steaming and bitter, from far Thentis, famed for its tarn flocks, the small yellow-enameled cups from which we had drunk the black wine, its spoons and sugars, a tiny bowl of mint sticks, and the softened, dampened cloths on which we had wiped our fingers.

I had eaten well.

She stood up. She held the tray. The gleaming collar, snug and locked, was very beautiful on her throat.

I remembered her from several months ago when I had first seen her, when she had had about her throat only a simple collar of iron, curved about her throat by the blows of a metal worker's hammer.

She looked at Samos, her lip trembled.

She had been the girl who had brought to the house of Samos the message of the scytale. The scytale had been a marked hair ribbon. Wrapped about the shaft of a spear, thus

10

aligning the marks, the message had appeared. It had been to me, from Zarendargar, or Half-Ear, a war general of the Kurii, inviting me to meet him at the "world's end." My speculation that this referred to the pole of the Gorean northern hemisphere had proved correct. I had met Half-Ear there, in a vast northern complex, an enormous supply depot intended to arm and fuel, and otherwise logistically support, the projected invasion of Gor, the Counter-Earth. I think it likely that Half-Ear perished in the destruction of the complex. The body, however, was never recovered.

The girl who had served us this night, slender and blond, blue-eyed, of Earth origin, had delivered to us the scytale. She had not, originally, even understood it to contain a message.

How different she seemed now from what she had then been. She had been brought to the house of Samos still in the inexplicable and barbarous garments of Earth, in particular, in the imitation-boy costume, the denim trousers and flannel shirt of the contemporary Earth girl, pathologically conditioned, for economic and historical reasons, to deny and subvert the richness of her unique sexuality. Culture decides what is truth, but truth, unfortunately for culture, is unaware of this. Cultures, mad and blind, can die upon the rocks of truth. Why can truth not be the foundation of culture, rather than its nemesis? Can one not build upon the stone cliffs of reality rather than dash one's head against them? But how few human beings can think, how few dare to inquire, how few can honestly question. How can one know the answer to a question which one fears to ask?

Samos, of course, immediately recognized the ribbon as a scytale. As for the girl, he had promptly, to her horror, had her clothing removed and had had her put in a brief rep-cloth slave tunic and a rude neck-ring of curved iron, that she would not escape and, anywhere, could be recognized as a slave. Shortly thereafter I had been invited to his house and had received the message. I had also questioned the girl, who had, at that time, spoken only English. I recalled how arrogant and peremptory she had been, until she had learned that she was no longer among men such as those of Earth. Samos had had her taken below and branded, and used for the sport of the guards, and then penned. I had thought that he would have sold her, but he had not. She had been kept in his own house, and taught the meaning of her collar, fully.

I saw the brand on her thigh. Although the brand was the

11

first letter, in cursive Gorean script, of the most common Gorean expression for a slave girl, 'Kajira', its symbolism, I think, is much richer than this. For example, in the slave brand, the 'Kef', though clearly a Kef and in cursive script, is more floral, in the extended, upturned, frondlike curls, than would be the common cursive Kef. This tends to make the mark very feminine. It is at this point that the symbolism of the brand becomes more clear. The two frondlike curls indicate femininity and beauty; the staff, in its uncompromising severity, indicates that the femininity is subject to discipline; the upturned curves on the frondlike curls indicate total openness and vulnerability. It is a very simple, lovely brand, simple, as befits a slave, lovely, as befits a woman.

Incidentally, there are many brands on Gor. Two that almost never occur on Gor, by the way, are those of the moons and collar, and of the chain and claw. The first of these commonly occurs in certain of the Gorean enclaves on Earth, which serve as headquarters for agents of Priest-Kings; the second tends to occur in the lairs of Kurii agents on Earth; the first brand consists of a locked collar and, ascending diagonally above it, extending to the right, three quarter moons; this brand indicates the girl is subject to Gorean discipline; the chain-and-claw brand signifies, of course, slavery and subjection within the compass of the Kur yoke. It is apparently difficult to recruit Goreans for service on Earth, either for Priest-Kings or Kurii. Accordingly, usually native Earthlings are used. Glandularly sufficient men, strong, lustful, and vital, without their slave girls, would find Earth a very dismal place, a miserable and unhappy sexual desert. Strong men simply need women. This will never be understood by weak men. A strong man needs a woman at his feet, who is truly his. Anything else is less than his fulfillment. When a man has once eaten of the meat of gods he will never again chew on the straw of fools.

"You may withdraw," said Samos to the girl.

"Master," she begged him, tears in her eyes. "Please, Master."

A few months ago she had not been able to speak Gorean. She now spoke the language subtly and fluently. Girls learn swiftly to speak the language of their masters.

Samos looked up at her. She stood there, lovely, holding the tray before her, on which reposed the vessels, the tiny cups and glasses, the bowls, the spoons, the soft, dampened

12

cloths on which we had wiped our hands. She had served well, beautifully, effacing herself, as a serving slave.

"Master," she whispered.

"Return the things to the kitchen," he said. I saw, from her eyes, that she was more than a serving slave. It is interesting, the power that a man may hold over a woman.

"Yes, Master," she said. When she had knelt facing Samos, she had knelt in the position of the pleasure slave. When she had knelt facing me, she had knelt in the position of the serving slave. Samos, it was said, was the first to have brought her to slave orgasm. It had happened six days after she had first been brought to his house. It is said that a woman who has experienced slave orgasm can never thereafter be anything but a man's slave. She then knows what men can do to her, and what she herself is, a woman. Never thereafter can she be anything else.

"Linda begs Master's touch," she said. The name 'Linda' had been her original Earth name. Samos had, after it had been removed from her, in her reduction to slavery, put it on her again, but this time as a slave name, by his will. Sometimes a girl is given her own name as a slave name; sometimes she is given another name; it depends on the master's will. She spoke freely before me of her need for his touch. She was no longer an inhibited, negatively conditioned Earth girl. She was now open and honest, and beautifully clean, in her slavery, in her confession of her female truths.

Seeing the eyes of Samos on her she quickly went to the door, to leave, but, at the door, unable to help herself, she turned about. There were tears in her eyes.

"After you have returned the things to the kitchen—" said Samos.

"Yes, Master," she said softly, excitedly. The small, yellow-enameled cups moved slightly on the tray. She trembled. The torchlight glinted from her collar.

"Go to your kennel," said Samos, "and ask to be locked within."

"Yes, Master," she said, putting her head down. I thought she shook with a sob.

"I hear from the chain master," said Samos, "that you have learned the tile dance creditably."

The tiny cups and glasses shook on the tray. "I am pleased," she said, "if Krobus should think so."

The tile dance is commonly performed on red tiles, usually beneath the slave ring of the master's couch. The girl per-

13

forms the dance on her back, her stomach and sides. Usually her neck is chained to the slave ring. The dance signifies the restlessness, the misery, of a love-starved slave girl. It is a premise of the dance that the girl moves and twists, and squirms, in her need, as if she is completely alone, as if her need is known only to herself; then, supposedly, the master surprises her, and she attempts to suppress the helplessness and torment of her needs; then, failing this, surrendering her pride in its final shred, she writhes openly, piteously, before him, begging him to deign to touch her. Needless to say, the entire dance is observed by the master, and this, in fact, of course, is known to both the dancer and her audience, the master. The tile dance, for simple psychological and behavioral reasons, having to do with the submission context and the motions of the body, can piteously arouse even a captured, cold free woman; in the case of a slave, of course, it can make her scream and sob with need.

"I hear that you have worked hard to perfect the tile dance," said Samos.

"I am only a poor slave," she said.

"The last five times you have performed this dance," said Samos, "Krobus tells me that he could not restrain himself from raping you."

She put down her head. "Yes, Master," she said, smiling.

"After you have been locked in your kennel," said Samos, "ask for a vessel of warm water, oils and a cloth, and perfume. Bathe and perfume yourself. I may summon you later to my chamber."

"Yes, Master," she said, delightedly. "Yes, Master!"

"Slave!" he said.

"Yes, Master," she said, turning quickly.

"I am less easy to please than Krobus," he said.

"Yes, Master," she said, and then turned and fled, swiftly, from the room.

"She is a pretty thing," I said.

Samos ran his tongue over his lips. "Yes," he said.

"I think you like her," I said.

"Nonsense," he said. "She is only a slave."

"Perhaps Samos has found a love slave," I said.

"An Earth girl?" laughed Samos.

"Perhaps," I said.

"Preposterous," said Samos. "She is only a slave, only a thing to serve, and to beat and abuse, if it should please me."

"But is not any slave," I asked, "even a love slave?"

14

"That is true," said Samos, smiling. Gorean men are not easy with their slaves, even those for whom they care deeply.

"I think Samos, first slaver of Port Kar, first captain of the council of captains, has grown fond of a blond Earth girl."

Samos looked at me, angrily. Then he shrugged. "She is the first girl I have felt in this fashion toward," he said. "It is interesting. It is a strange feeling."

"I note that you did not sell her," I said.

"Perhaps I shall," he said.

"I see," I said.

"The first time, even, that I took her in my arms," said Samos, "she was in some way piteously helpless, different even from the others."

"Is not any slave piteously helpelss in the arms of her master?" I asked.

"Yes," said Samos. "But she seemed somehow different, incredibly so, vulnerably so."

"Perhaps she knew herself, in your touch, as her love master," I said.

"She felt good in my hands," he said.

"Be strong, Samos," I smiled.

"I shall," he said.

I did not doubt his word. Samos was one of the hardest of Gorean men. The blond Earth girl had found a strong, uncompromising master.

"But let us not speak of slaves," I said, "girls who serve for our diversion or recreation, but of serious matters, of the concerns of men."

"Agreed," said he.

There was a time for slaves, and a time for matters of importance.

"Yet there is little to report," said he, "in the affairs of worlds."

"The Kurii are quiet," I said.

"Yes," said he.

"Beware of a silent enemy," I smiled.

"Of course," said Samos.

"It is unusual that you should invite me to your house," I said, "to inform me that you have nothing to report."

"Do you think you are the only one upon Gor who labors occasionally in the cause of Priest-Kings?" asked Samos.

"I suppose not," I said. "Why?" I asked. I did not understand the question.

"How little we know of our world," sighed Samos.

"I do not understand," I said.

"Tell me what you know of the Cartius," he said.

"It is an important subequatorial waterway," I said. "It flows west by northwest, entering the rain forests and emptying into Lake Ushindi, which lake is drained by the Kamba and the Nyoka rivers. The Kamba flows directly into Thassa. The Nyoka flows into Schendi harbor, which is the harbor of the port of Schendi, and moves thence to Thassa." Schendi was an equatorial free port, well known on Gor. It is also the home port of the League of Black Slavers.

"It was, at one time, conjectured," said Samos, "that the Cartius proper was a tributary of the Vosk."

"I had been taught that," I said.

"We now know that the Thassa Cartius and the subequatorial Cartius are not the same river."

"It had been thought, and shown on many maps," I said, "that the subequatorial Cartius not only flowed into Lake Ushindi, but emerged northward, traversing the sloping western flatlands to join the Vosk at Turmus." Turmus was the last major river port on the Vosk before the almost impassable marshes of the delta.

"Calculations performed by the black geographer, Ramani, of the island of Anango, suggested that given the elevations involved the two rivers could not be the same. His pupil, Shaba, was the first civilized man to circumnavigate Lake Ushindi. He discovered that the Cartius, as was known, enters Lake Ushindi, but that only two rivers flow out of Ushindi, the Kamba and Nyoka. The actual source of the tributary to the Vosk, now called the Thassa Cartius, as you know, was found five years later by the explorer, Ramus of Tabor, who, with a small expedition, over a period of nine months, fought and bartered his way through the river tribes, beyond the six cataracts, to the Ven highlands. The Thassa Cartius, with its own tributaries, drains the highlands and the descending plains."

"That has been known to me for over a year," I said. "Why do you speak of it now?"

"We are ignorant of so many things," mused Samos.

I shrugged. Much of Gor was *terra incognita*. Few knew well the lands on the east of the Voltai and Thentis ranges, for example, or what lay west of the farther islands, near Cos and Tyros. It was more irritating, of course, to realize that even considerable areas of territory above Schendi, south of the Vosk, and west of Ar, were unknown. "There was good reason to speculate that the Cartius entered the Vosk, by way of Lake Ushindi," I said.

"I know," said Samos, "tradition, and the directions and flow of the rivers. Who would have understood, of the cities, that they were not the same?"

"Even the bargemen of the Cartius proper, the subequatorial Cartius, and those of the Thassa Cartius, far to the north, thought the rivers to be but one waterway."

"Yes," said Samos. "And until the calculations of Ramani, and the expeditions of Shaba and Ramus, who had reason to believe otherwise?"

"The rain forests closed the Cartius proper for most civilized persons from the south," I said, "and what trading took place tended to be confined to the ubarates of the southern shore of Lake Ushindi. It was convenient then, for trading purposes, to make use of either the Kamba or the Nyoka to reach Thassa."

"That precluded the need to find a northwest passage from Ushindi," said Samos.

"Particularly since it was known of the hostility of the river tribes on what is now called the Thassa Cartius."

"Yes," said Samos.

"But surely, before the expedition of Shaba," I said, "others must have searched for the exit of the Cartius from Ushindi."

"It seems likely they were slain by the tribes of the northern shores of Ushindi," said Samos.

"How is it that the expedition of Shaba was successful?" I asked.

"Have you heard of Bila Huruma?" asked Samos.

"A little," I said.

"He is a black Ubar," said Samos, "bloody and brilliant, a man of vision and power, who has united the six ubarates of the southern shores of Ushindi, united them by the knife and the stabbing spear, and has extended his hegemony to the northern shores, where he exacts tribute, kailiauk tusks and women, from the confederacy of the hundred villages. Shaba's nine boats had fixed at their masts the tufted shields of the officialdom of Bila Huruma."

"That guaranteed their safety," I said.

"They were attacked, several times," said Samos, "but they survived. I think it true, however, had it not been for the authority of Bila Huruma, Ubar of Ushindi, they could not have completed their work."

17

"The hegemony of Bila Huruma over the northern shores, then, is substantial but incomplete," I said.

"Surely the hegemony is resented," said Samos, "as would seem borne out by the fact that some attacks did take place on the expedition of Shaba."

"He must be a brave man," I said.

"He brought six of his boats through, and most of his men," said Samos.

"I find it impressive," I said, "that a man such as Bila Huruma would be interested in supporting a geographical expedition."

"He was interested in finding the northwest passage from Ushindi," said Samos. "It could mean the opening up of a considerable number of new markets, the enhancement of trade, the discovery of a valuable commercial avenue for the merchandise of the north and the products of the south."

"It might avoid, too, the dangers of shipment upon Thassa," I said, "and provide, as well, a road to conquest and the acquisition of new territory."

"Yes," said Samos. "You think like a warrior," he said.

"But Shaba's work," I said, "as I understand it, demonstrated that no such passage exists."

"Yes," said Samos, "that is a consequence of his expedition. But surely, even if you are not familiar with the role of Bila Huruma in these things, you have heard of the further discoveries of Shaba."

"To the west of Lake Ushindi," I said, "there are floodlands, marshes and bogs, through which a considerable amount of water drains into the lake. With considerable hardship, limiting himself to forty men, and temporarily abandoning all but two boats, which were half dragged and thrust through the marshes eastward, after two months, Shaba reached the western shore of what we now know as Lake Ngao."

"Yes," said Samos.

"It is fully as large as Lake Ushindi, if not larger," I said, "the second of the great equatorial lakes."

"Yes," said Samos.

I conjectured that it must have been a marvelous moment when Shaba and his men, toiling with ropes and poles, wading and shoveling, brought their two craft to the clear vista of vast, deep Lake Ngao. They had returned then, exhausted, to the balance of their party and boats, which had been waiting for them at the eastern shore of Ushindi.

18

"Shaba then continued the circumnavigation of Lake Ushindi," said Samos. "He charted accurately, for the first time, the entry of the Cartius proper, the subequatorial Cartius, into Ushindi. He then continued west until he reached the six ubarates and the heartland of Bila Huruma."

"He was doubtless welcomed as a hero," I said.

"Yes," said Samos. "And well he should have been."

"The next year," I said, "he mounted a new expedition, with eleven boats and a thousand men, an expedition financed, I now suppose, by Bila Huruma, to explore Lake Ngao, to circumnavigate it as he had Ushindi."

"Precisely," said Samos.

"And it was there that he discovered that Lake Ngao was fed, incredibly enough, by only one major river, as its eastern extremity, a river vast enough to challenge even the Vosk in its breadth and might, a river which he called the Ua."

"Yes," said Samos.

"It is impassable," I said, "because of various falls and cataracts."

"The extent of these obstacles, and the availability of portages, the possibility of roads, the possibility of side canals, are not known," said Samos.

"Shaba himself, with his men and boats, pursued the river for only a hundred pasangs," I said, "when they were turned back by some falls and cataracts."

"The falls and cataracts of Bila Huruma, as he named them," said Samos.

"The size of his boats made portage difficult or impossible," I said.

"They had not been built to be sectioned," said Samos. 'And the steepness of the portage, the jungle, the hostility, as it turned out, of interior tribes, made retreat advisable."

"The expedition of Shaba returned then," I said, "to Lake Ngao, completed its circumnavigation and returned later, via the swamps, to Lake Ushindi and the six ubarates."

"Yes," said Samos.

"A most remarkable man," I said.

"Surely one of the foremost geographers and explorers of Gor," said Samos. "And a highly trusted man."

"Trusted?" I asked.

"Shaba is an agent of Priest-Kings," said Samos.

"I did not know that," I said.

"Surely you suspected others, too, served, at least upon occasion, in the cause of Priest-Kings."

19

"I had supposed that," I said. But I had never pressed Samos on the matter. It seemed to be better that I not know of many agents of Priest-Kings. Our work was, in general, unknown to one another. This was an elementary security precaution. If one of us were captured and tortured, he could not, if broken, reveal what he did not know. Most agents, I did know, were primarily engaged in the work of surveillance and intelligence. The house of Samos was a headquarters to which most of these agents, directly or indirectly, reported. From it the activities of many agents were directed and coordinated. It was a clearing house, too, for information, which, processed, was forwarded to the Sardar.

"Why do you tell me this?" I asked.

"Come with me," said Samos, getting up.

He led the way from the room. I followed him. We passed guards outside the door to the great hall. Samos did not speak to me. For several minutes I followed him. He strode through various halls, and then began to descend ramps and staircases. At various points, and before various portals, signs and countersigns were exchanged. The thick walls became damp. We continued to descend, through various levels, sometimes treading catwalks over cages. The fair occupants of these cages looked up at us, frightened. In one long corridor we passed two girls, naked, on their hands and knees, with brushes and water, scrubbing the stones of the corridor floor. A guard, with a whip, stood over them. They fell to their bellies as we passed, and then, when we had passed, rose to their hands and knees, to resume their work. The pens were generally quiet now, for it was time for sleeping. We passed barred alcoves, and tiers of kennels, and rooms for processing, training and disciplining slaves. The chamber of irons was empty, but coals glowed softly in the brazier, from which two handles protruded. An iron is always ready in a slaver's house. One does not know when a new girl may be brought in. In another room I saw, on the walls, arranged by size, collars, chains, wrist and ankle rings. An inventory of such things is kept in a slaver's house. Each collar, each link of chain, is accounted for. We passed, too, rooms in which tunics, slave silks, cosmetics and jewelries were kept. Normally in the pens girls are kept naked, but such things are used in their training. There were also facilities for cooking and the storage of food; and medical facilities as well. As we passed one cell a girl reached forth. "Masters," she whimpered. Then we were beyond her. We also passed pens of male slaves. These, usually criminals and debtors, or prisoners taken in wars, then enslaved, are commonly sold cheaply and used for heavy labor.

We continued to descend through various levels. The smell and the dampness, never pleasant in the lower levels of the pens, now became obtrusive. Here and there lamps and torches burned. These mitigated to some extent the dampness. We passed a guards' room, in which there were several slaver's men, off duty. I glanced within, for I heard from within the clash of slave bells and the bright sound of zills, or finger cymbals. In a bit of yellow slave silk, backed into a corner, belled and barefoot, a collared girl danced, swaying slowly before the five men who loomed about her, scarcely a yard away. Then her back touched the stone wall, startling her, and they seized her, and threw her to a blanket for their pleasure. I saw her gasping, and, half fighting, half kissing at them, squirming in their arms. Then her arms and legs were held, widely separated, each of her limbs, her small wrists and belled ankles, held in the two hands of a captor. The leader was first to have her. She put her head back, helpless, crying out with pleasure, subdued.

We were soon on the lowest level of the pens, in an area of maximum security. There were trickles of water at the walls here and, in places, water between the stones of the floor. An urt slipped between two rocks in the wall.

Samos stopped before a heavy iron door; a narrow steel panel slipped back. Samos uttered the sign for the evening, and was answered by the countersign. The door opened. There were two guards behind it.

We stopped before the eighth cell on the left. Samos signaled to the two guards. They came forward. There were some ropes and hooks, and heavy pieces of meat, to one side.

"Do not speak within," said Samos to me. He handed me a hood, with holes cut in it for the eyes.

"Is this house, or its men, known to the prisoner?" I asked.

"No," said Samos

I donned the hood, and Samos, too, donned such a hood. The two guards donned such hoods as well. They then slid back the observation panel in the solid iron door and, after looking through, unlocked the door, and swung it open. It opened inward. I waited with Samos. The two guards then, reaching upward, with some chains, attached above the door, lowered a heavy, wooden walkway to the surface of the water. The room, within, to the level of the door, contained

21

water. It was murky and dark. I was aware of a rustling in the water. The walkway then, floating, but steadied by its four chains, rested on the water. On its sides the walkway had metal ridges, some six inches in height, above the water. I heard tiny scratchings at the metal, small movements against the metal, as though by numerous tiny bodies, each perhaps no more than a few ounces in weight.

Samos stood near the door and lifted a torch. The two guards went out on the walkway. It was some twenty feet in length. The flooded cell was circular, and perhaps some forty-five feet in diameter. In the center of the cell was a wooden, metal-sheathed pole, some four inches in diameter. This pole rose, straight, some four feet out of the water. About this pole, encircling it, and supported by it, was a narrow, circular, wooden, metal-sheathed platform. It was some ten inches on all sides, from the circumference of the pole to the edge of the platform. The platform itself was lifted about seven or eight inches out of the water.

One of the guards, carrying a long, wooden pole, thrust it down, into the water. The water, judging by the pole, must have been about eight feet deep. The other guard, then, thrusting a heavy piece of meat on one of the hooks, to which a rope was attached, held the meat away from the platform and half submerged in the water. Almost instantly there was a frenzy in the water near the meat, a thrashing and turbulence in the murky liquid. I felt water splashed on my legs, even standing back as I was. Then the guard lifted the roped hook from the water. The meat was gone. Tiny tharlarion, similar to those in the swamp forest south of Ar, dropped, snapping, from the bared hook. Such tiny, swift tharlarion, in their thousands, can take the meat from a kail-iauk in an Ehn.

The girl on the platform, naked, kneeling, a metal collar hammered about her neck, the metal pole between her legs, grasping it with both arms, threw back her head and screamed piteously.

The two guards then withdrew. Samos, hooded, walked out on the floating walkway, steadied by its chains. I, similarly hooded, followed him. He lifted the torch.

The platform's front edge was about a yard from the tiny, wooden, metal-sheathed, circular platform, mounted on the wooden, metal-sheathed pole, that tiny platform on which the girl knelt, that narrow, tiny platform which held her but inches from the tharlarion-filled water.

She looked up at us, piteously, blinking against the light of the torch.

She clutched the pole helplessly. She could not have been bound to it more closely if she had been fastened in close chains.

The small eyes of numerous tharlarion, perhaps some two or three hundred of them, ranging from four to ten inches in length, watching her, nostrils and eyes at the water level, reflected the light of the torch.

She clutched the pole even more closely.

She looked up at us, tears in her eyes. "Please, please, please, please, please," she said.

She had spoken in English.

She, like Samos' Earth girl, Linda, had blue eyes and blond hair. She was slightly more slender than Linda. She had good ankles. They would take an ankle ring nicely. I noted that she had not yet been branded.

"Please," she whimpered.

Samos indicated that we should leave. I turned about, and preceded him from the walkway. The guards, behind us, raised the walkway, secured it in place, and swung shut the door. They slid shut the observation panel. They locked the door.

Samos, outside, returned his torch to its ring. We removed the hoods. I followed Samos from the lower level, and then from the pens, back to his hall.

"I do not understand what the meaning of all this is, Samos," I told him.

"There are deep matters here," said Samos, "matters in which I am troubled as well as you."

"Why did you show me the girl in the cell?" I asked.

"What do you make of her?" asked Samos.

"I would say about five copper tarsks, in a fourth-class market, perhaps even an item in a group sale. She is beautiful, but not particularly beautiful, as female slaves go. She is obviously ignorant and untrained. She does have good ankles."

"She speaks the Earth language English, does she not?" asked Samos.

"Apparently," I said. "Do you wish me to question her?"

"No," said Samos.

"Does she speak Gorean?" I asked.

"No more than a few words," said Samos.

There are ways of determining, of course, if one speaks a

23

given language. One utters phrases significant in the language. There are, when cognition takes place, physiological responses which are difficult or impossible to conceal, such things as an increase in the pulse rate, and the dilation of the pupils.

"The matter then seems reasonably clear," I said.

"Give me your thoughts," said Samos.

"She is a simple wench brought to Gor by Kur slavers, collar meat."

"You would think so?" he asked.

"It seems likely," I said. "Women trained as Kur agents are usually well versed in Gorean."

"But she is not as beautiful as the average imported slave from Earth, is she?" asked Samos.

"That matter is rather subjective, I would say," I smiled. "I think she is quite lovely. Whether she is up to the normal standards of their merchandise is another question."

"Perhaps she was with a girl who was abducted for enslavement," said Samos, "and was simply, as it was convenient, put in a double tie with her and brought along."

"Perhaps," I shrugged. "I would not know. It would be my speculation, however, that she had deep potential for slavery."

"Does not any woman?" asked Samos.

"Yes," I said, "but some are slaves among slaves." I smiled at Samos. "I have great respect for the taste and discrimination of Kur slavers," I said. "I think they can recognize the slave in a woman at a glance. I have never known them to make a mistake."

"Even their Kur agents who are female," said Samos, "seem to have been selected for their potential for ultimate slavery in mind, such as the slaves Pepita, Elicia and Arlene."

"They were doubtless intended to be ultimately awarded as gifts and prizes to Kur agents who were human males," I said.

"They are ours now," said Samos, "or theirs to whom we would give or sell them."

"Yes," I said.

"What of the slave, Vella?" he asked.

"She was never, in my mind," I said, "strictly an agent of Kurii."

"She betrayed Priest-Kings," he said, "and served Kurii agents in the Tahari."

"That is true," I admitted.

24

"Give her to me," said Samos. "I want to bind her hand and foot and hurl her naked to the urts in the canals."

"She is mine," I said. "If she is to be bound hand and foot and hurled naked to the urts in the canals, it is I who will do so."

"As you wish," said Samos.

"It is my speculation," I said, "that the girl below in the pens, in the tharlarion cell, in spite of the fact that she is, though beautiful, less stunning than many slaves, is simple collar meat, that she was brought to Gor for straightforward disposition to a slaver, perhaps in a contract lot."

"Your speculation, given her failures in Gorean, is intelligent," said Samos, "but it is, as it happens, incorrect."

"Speak to me," I said.

"You would suppose, would you not," asked Samos, "that such a girl would have been discovered on some chain, after having passed through the hands of one or more masters, and simply bought off the chain, or purchased at auction."

"Of course," I said. "Yet she is not yet branded," I mused. Kur slavers do not, usually, brand their girls. Usually it is their first Gorean master who puts the brand on them.

"That is a perceptive observation," said Samos.

"How did you come by her?" I asked.

"Quite by accident," said Samos. "Have you heard of the captain, Bejar?"

"Of course," I said. "He is a member of the council. He was with us on the 25th of Se'Kara." This was the date of a naval battle which took place in the first year of the sovereignty of the Council of Captains in Port Kar. It had been, also, the year 10,120 C.A., Contasta Ar, from the founding of Ar. It was, currently, Year 7 in the Sovereignty of the Council of Captains, that year, in the chronology of Ar, which was 10,126 C.A. On the 25th of Se'Kara, in the first year of the Sovereignty of the Council of Captains, in the naval battle which had taken place on that date, the joint fleets of Cos and Tyros had been turned back from Port Kar. Bejar, and Samos, and I, and many others, as well, had been there. It was in that same year, incidentally, that Port Kar had first had a Home Stone.

"Bejar," said Samos, "in an action at sea, overtook a ship of Cos."

I listened. Cos and Tyros, uneasy allies, one island ubarate under large-eyed Chendar, the Sea Sleen, and the other under gross Lurius, of Jad, were nominally at war with Port Kar.

25

There had been, however, no major engagements in several years. Cos, for some years, had been preoccupied with struggles on the Vosk. These had to do with competitive spheres of influence on the Vosk itself and in its basin and adjacent tributary-containing valleys. The products and markets of these areas are quite important commercially. Whereas most towns on the river are, in effect, free states, few are strong enough to ignore powers such as Cos and its major rival in these territories, the city of Ar. Cos and Ar compete with one another to gain treaties with these river towns, control the traffic, and dominate the commerce of the river to their respective advantages. Ar has no navy, being an inland power, but it has developed a fleet of river ships and these, often, skirmish with the river ships of Cos, usually built in Cos, transported to the continent and carried overland to the river. The delta of the Vosk, for most practical purposes, a vast marsh, an area of thousands of square pasangs, where the Vosk washes down to the sea, is closed to shipping. It is trackless and treacherous, and the habitat of marsh tharlarion and the predatory Ul, a winged lizard with wing-spans of several feet. It is also inhabited by the rencers, who live upon rence islands, woven of the rence reed, masters of the long bow, usually obtained in trade with peasants to the east of the delta. They are banded together under the nominal governance of the marsh Ubar, Ho-Hak. They are suspicious of strangers, as are Goreans generally. In Gorean the same expression is used for 'stranger' and 'enemy'. The situation on the Vosk is further complicated by the presence of Vosk pirates and the rivalries of the river towns themselves.

"The engagement was sharp," said Samos, "but the ship, its crew, passengers and cargo, fell to Bejar as prize."

"I see now," I said, "the girl was slave cargo on the ship which fell to Bejar."

Samos smiled.

"It was not a slave ship, I gather," I said, "else it is likely her head and body hair would have been shaved, to reduce the degree of infestation by ship lice in the hold." I looked at him. "She could have been, of course, in a deck cage," I said. These are small cages, fastened on deck. At night and in rough weather they are usually covered with a tarpaulin. This tends to prevent rust.

"It was not a slave ship," said Samos.

I shrugged. "Her thigh was as yet bare of the brand," I

26

said, "which is interesting." I looked at Samos. "Whose collar did she wear?" I asked.

"She wore no collar," said Samos.

"I do not understand," I said. I was genuinely puzzled.

"She was clothed as a free woman and was among the passengers," said Samos. "She was not stripped until she stood on the deck of the ship of Bejar and was put in chains with the other captured women."

"She was a passenger," I said.

"Yes," said Samos, "a passenger."

"Her passage papers were in order?" I asked.

"Yes," he said.

"Interesting," I said.

"I thought so," said Samos.

"Why would an Earth girl, almost totally ignorant of Gorean, unbranded, free, be traveling on a ship of Cos?"

"I think, clearly, it has has something to do with the Others, the Kurii," said Samos.

"That seems likely," I said.

"Bejar," said Samos, "one well known to me, discerning that she was both unbranded and barbarian, and ignorant of Gorean, and knowing my interest in such matters, called her to my attention. I had her, hooded, brought here from his pens."

"It is an interesting mystery," I said. "Are you certain you do not wish me to question her in her own language?"

"No," said Samos. "Or certainly not at present."

"As you wish," I said.

"Sit down," said Samos. He gestured to a place behind the small table on which we had had supper.

I sat down, cross-legged, behind the table, and he sat down, cross-legged, across from me.

"Do you recognize this?" asked Samos. He reached into his robes and drew forth a small leather packet, which he unfolded. From this he took a large ring, but too large for the finger of a human, and placed it on the table.

"Of course," I said, "it is the ring which I obtained in the Tahari, that ring which projects the light diversion field, which renders its wearer invisible in the normal visible range of the spectrum."

"Is it?" asked Samos.

I looked at the ring. I picked it up. It was heavy, golden, with a silver plate. On the outside of the ring, opposite the bezel, was a recessed, circular switch. When a Kur wore the

27

ring on a digit of his left paw, and turned the bezel inward, the switch would be exposed. He could then depress it with a digit of his right paw. The left hemisphere of the Kur brain, like the left hemisphere of the human brain, tends to be dominant. Most Kurii, like most men, as a consequence of this dominance of the left hemisphere, tend to be "right pawed," or right handed, so to speak. One press on the switch on the Tahari ring had activated the field, a second press had resulted in its deactivation. Within the invisibility shield the spectum is shifted, permitting one to see outward, though in a reddish light.

"I would suppose so," I said.

I looked at the ring. I had given the Tahari ring to Samos, long ago, shortly after returning from the Tahari, that he might send it to the Sardar for analysis. I thought such a device might be of use to agents of Priest-Kings. I was puzzled that it was not used more often by Kurii. I had heard nothing more of the ring.

"Are you absolutely sure," asked Samos, "that this is the ring which you gave me to send to the Sardar?"

"It certainly seems much like it," I said.

"Is it the same ring?" he asked.

"No," I said. I looked at it more closely. "No," I said, "it is not the same ring. The Tahari ring had a minute scratch at the corner of the silver plate."

"I did not think it was," said Samos.

"If this is an invisibility ring, we are fortunate to have it fall into our grasp," I said.

"Do you think such a ring would be entrusted to a human agent?" asked Samos.

"It is not likely," I said.

"It is my belief that this ring does not cast the invisibility shield," said Samos.

"I see," I said.

"Take care not to press the switch," said Samos.

"I will," I said. I put the ring down.

"Let me speak to you of the five rings," said Samos. "This is information which I have received but recently from the Sardar, but it is based on an intelligence thousands of years old, obtained then from a delirious Kur commander, and confirmed by documents obtained in various wreckages, the most recent of which dates from some four hundred years ago. Long ago, perhaps as long as forty thousand years ago, the Kurii possessed a technology far beyond what they now

28

maintain. The technology which now makes them so dangerous, and so advanced, is but the remnants of a technology
mostly destroyed in their internecine struggles, those which
culminated in the destruction of their world. The invisibility
rings were the product of a great Kur scientist, one we may
refer to in human phonemes, for our convenience, as Prasdak
of the Cliff of Karrash. He was a secretive craftsman and, before he died, he destroyed his plans and papers. He left behind him, however, five rings. In the sacking of his city,
which took place some two years after his death, the rings
were found."

"What became of the rings?" I asked.

"Two were destroyed in the course of Kur history," said
Samos. "One was temporarily lost upon the planet Earth
some three to four thousand years ago, it being taken from a
slain Kur commander by a man named Gyges, a herdsman,
who used its power to usurp the throne of a country called
Lydia, a country which then existed on Earth."

I nodded. Lydia, I recalled, had fallen to the Persians in
the Sixth Century B.C., to utilize one of the Earth chronolo-
gies. That would, of course, have been long after the time of
Gyges.

"One is reminded of the name of the river port at the
mouth of the Laurius," said Samos.

"Yes," I said. The name of that port was Lydius.

"Perhaps there is some connection," speculated Samos.

"Perhaps," I said. "Perhaps not." It was often difficult to
know whether isolated phonetic similarities indicated a historical relationship or not. In this case I thought it unlikely,
given the latitude and style of life of Lydius. On the other
hand, men of Lydia might possibly have been involved in its
founding. The Voyages of Acquisition, of Priest-Kings, I
knew, had been of great antiquity. These voyages now, as I
understood it, following the Nest War, had been discontin-
ued.

"Kurii came later for the ring," said Samos. "Gyges was
slain. The ring itself, somehow, was shortly thereafter
destroyed in an explosion."

"Interesting," I said.

"That left two rings," said Samos.

"One of them was doubtless the Tahari ring," I said.

"Doubtless," said Samos.

I looked at the ring on the table. "Do you think this is the
fifth ring?" I asked.

"No," said Samos. "I think the fifth ring would be too precious to be taken from the steel world on which it resides. I do not think it would be risked on Gor."

"Perhaps they have now learned how to duplicate the rings," I ventured.

"That seems to me unlikely for two reasons," said Samos. "First, if the ring could be duplicated, surely in the course of Kur history, particularly before the substantial loss of their technology and their retreat to the steel worlds, it would have been. Secondly, given the secretive nature of the rings' inventor, Prasdak of the Cliff of Karrash, I suspect there is an additional reason which mitigates against the dismantlement of the ring and its consequent reproduction."

"The secret, doubtless, could be unraveled by those of the Sardar," I said. "What progress have they made with the ring from the Tahari?"

"The Tahari ring never reached the Sardar," said Samos. "I learned this only a month ago."

I did not speak. I sat behind the table, stunned.

"To whom," I then asked, "did you entrust the delivery of the ring to the Sardar."

"To one of our most trusted agents," said Samos.

"Who?" I asked.

"Shaba, the geographer of Anango, the explorer of Lake Ushindi, the discoverer of Lake Ngao and the Ua River," said Samos.

"Doubtless he met with foul play," I said.

"I do not think so," said Samos.

"I do not understand," I said.

"This ring," said Samos, indicating the ring on the table, "was found among the belongings of the girl in the tharlarion cell below. It was with her when her ship was captured by Bejar."

"It surely, then, is not the fifth ring," I said.

"But what is its purport?" asked Samos.

I shrugged. "I do not know," I said.

"Look," said Samos. He reached to one side of the table, to a flat, black box, of the sort in which papers are sometimes kept. In the box, too, there is an inkwell, at its top, and a place for quilled pens. He opened the box, below the portion containing the inkwell and concave surfaces for pens.

He withdrew from the box several folded papers, letters. He had broken the seal on them.

"These papers, too, were found among the belongings of our fair captive below," said Samos.

"What is their nature?" I asked.

"There are passage papers here," he said, "and a declaration of Cosian citizenship, which is doubtless forged. Too, most importantly, there are letters of introduction here, and the notes for a fortune, to be drawn on various banks in Schendi's Street of Coins."

"To whom are the letters of introduction," I asked, "and to whom are made out the notes?"

"One is to a man named Msaliti," said Samos, "and the other is to Shaba."

"And the notes for the fortunes?" I asked.

"They are made out to Shaba," said Samos.

"It seems then," I said, "that Shaba intends to surrender the ring to agents of Kurii, receive fees for this, and then carry to the Sardar this ring we have before us."

"Yes," said Samos.

"But Priest-Kings could surely determine, as soon as the switch was depressed, that the ring was false," I said. "Ah, yes," I said.

"I fear so," said Samos. "I suspect the depression of the switch, presumably to be accomplished in the Sardar, will initiate an explosion."

"It is probable then," I said, "that the ring is a bomb."

Samos nodded. He, through my discussions with him, and his work with the Sardar, was familiar with certain technological possibilities. He had himself, however, like most Goreans, never witnessed, first-hand, an explosion.

"I think it would be like lightning," he said, picking his words slowly.

"Priest-Kings might be killed," I said.

"Distrust and dissension might be spread then between men and Priest-Kings," said Samos.

"And in the meantime, the Kurii would have regained the ring and Shaba would be a rich man."

"It seems so," said Samos.

"The ship, of course, was bound for Schendi?" I asked.

"Of course," he said.

"Do you think the girl below knows much of this?"

"No," said Samos. "I think she was carefully chosen, to do little more than convey the notes and the ring. Probably there are more expert Kur agents in Schendi to receive the ring once it is delivered."

31

"Perhaps even Kurii themselves," I said.

"The climate would be cruel upon Kurii," he said, "but it is not impossible."

"Shaba is doubtless in hiding," I said. "I do not think it likely I could locate him by simply voyaging to Schendi."

"Probably he can be reached through Msaliti," said Samos.

"It could be a very delicate matter," I said.

Samos nodded. "Shaba is a very intelligent man," he said. "Msaliti probably does not know where he is. If Shaba, whom we may suppose contacts Msaliti, rather than the opposite, suspects anything is amiss, he will presumably not come forth."

"The girl is then the key to locating Shaba," I said. "That is why you did not wish me to question her. That is why she must not even know she has been in your power."

"Precisely," said Samos. "She must remain totally ignorant of the true nature of her current captivity."

"It is known, or would soon be known, that her ship was taken by Bejar," I said. "It is doubtless moored prize at his wharfage even now. She cannot be simply released and sent upon her way. None would believe this. All would suspect she was a decoy of some sort, a lure to draw forth Shaba."

"We must attempt to regain the ring," said Samos, "or, at worst, prevent it from falling into the hands of the Kurii."

"Shaba will want the notes for the fortunes," I said. "Kurii will want the false ring. I think he, or they, or both, will be very interested in striking up an acquaintance with our lovely prisoner below."

"My thoughts, too," said Samos.

"It is known, or will soon be known, she was taken by Bejar," I said. "When his other women prisoners are put upon the block, let her be put there with them, only another woman to be sold."

"They will be sold as slaves," said Samos.

"Of course," I said, "let her, too, be sold as a slave."

"I will have the iron ring removed from her throat," said Samos, "and have her, tied in a slave sack, sent to Bejar."

"I will attend her sale, in disguise," I said. "I will see who buys her."

"It could be anyone," said Samos. "Perhaps she will be bought by an urt hunter or an oar maker. What then?"

"Then she is owned by an oar maker or an urt hunter," I said. "And we shall consider a new plan."

Urt hunters swim slave girls, ropes on their necks, beside

their boats in the dark, cool water of the canals, as bait for urts, which, as they rise to attack the girl, are speared. Urt hunters help to keep the urt population in the canals manageable.

"Agreed," said Samos.

He handed me the ring on the table and the letters of introduction, and notes.

"You may need these," he said, "in case you encounter Shaba. Perhaps you could pose as a Kur agent, for he does not know you, and obtain the true ring for the Kurii notes. The Sardar could then be warned to intercept Shaba with the false ring and deal as they will with him."

"Excellent," I said. "These things will increase our store of possible strategies." I placed the ring and the papers in my robes.

"I am optimistic," said Samos.

"I, too," I said.

"But beware of Shaba," he said. "He is a brilliant man. He will not be easily fooled."

Samos and I stood up.

"It is curious," I said, "that the rings were never duplicated."

"Doubtless there is a reason," said Samos.

I nodded. That was doubtless true.

We went toward the door of his hall, but stopped before we reached the heavy door.

Samos wished to speak.

"Captain," said he.

"Yes, Captain," said I.

"Do not go into the interior, beyond Schendi," said Samos. "That is the country of Bila Huruma."

"I understand him to be a great ubar," I said.

"He is also a very dangerous man," said Samos, "and these are difficult times."

"He is a man of vision," I said.

"And pitiless greed," said Samos.

"But a man of vision," I reminded him. "Is he not intending to join the Ushindi and Ngao with a canal, cut through the marshes, which, then, might be drained?"

"Work on such a project is already proceeding," said Samos.

"That is vision," I said, "and ambition."

"Of course," said Samos. "Such a canal would be an inestimable commercial and military achievement. The Ua, hold-

33

ing the secret of the interior, flows into the Ngao, which, by a canal, would be joined with Ushindi. Into Ushindi flows the Cartius proper, the subequatorial Cartius. Out of Ushindi flow the Kamba and the Nyoka, and those flow to Thassa."

"It would be an incredible achievement," I marveled.

"Beware of Bila Huruma," said Samos.

"I expect to have no dealings with him," I said.

"The pole and platform below, on which is held prisoner our lovely guest," said Samos, "was suggested to me by a peacekeeping device of Bila Huruma. In Lake Ushindi, in certain areas frequented by tharlarion, there are high poles. Criminals, political prisoners, and such are rowed to these poles and left there, clinging to them. There are no platforms on the poles."

"I understand," I said.

"But I think you have nothing to fear," said Samos, "if you remain within the borders of Schendi itself."

I nodded. Schendi was a free port, administered by black merchants, members of the caste of merchants. It was also the home port of the League of Black Slavers but their predations were commonly restricted to the high seas and coastal towns well north and south of Schendi. Like most large-scale slaving operations they had the good sense to spare their own environs.

"Good luck, Captain," said Samos.

We clasped hands.

As we exited from his hall, Samos spoke to one of the guards outside the huge double doors. "Linda," he said.

"Yes, Captain," said the guard, and left, moving down the hall. The Earth slave, Linda, was not kept in the pens. She was kept in the kennels off the kitchens. In spite of this she wore only the common house collar. Too, she was allotted a full share of domestic duties. Samos did not pamper his slaves, even those he knelt often at his slave ring.

I thought of the girl below, imprisoned on the tiny platform in the tharlarion cell. She would have the ring on her neck removed and then be placed in a slave sack and taken to the house of Bejar. I supposed that Bejar, or the slaver to whom he sold her, and the others, would mark her slave.

How piteously and helplessly she had clung to the pole. She had already begun to learn that Gor was not Earth.

"I wish you well, Captain," I said to Samos.

"I wish you well, Captain," said he to me. Again we clasped hands and then I strode from him, down the hallway toward the double gates leading from his house. At the first of the two gates, the one which consists of bars, while awaiting its opening, I glanced back.

Samos was no longer in sight, having gone to his chambers. A guard was in the hallway, with his spear.

The gate of bars was unlocked and I slipped through. It closed and locked, and I waited for the outer gate, that of iron-sheathed wood, to be opened.

I glanced back again and I saw the slave, Linda, naked, on a leash, being led to her master. She saw me, and looked down, shyly.

I exited then through the second gate of the house of Samos.

I had heard that she did the tile dance exquisitely. I almost envied Samos. I decided I would have the dance taught to my own slaves. I would be curious to learn which of them could perform it well, and which brilliantly.

"Greetings, Captain," said Thurnock, from the boat.

"Greetings, Thurnock," I said. I stepped down into the boat and took the tiller. The boat was thrust off into the dark water, and, in moments, we were rowing quietly toward my house.

2

I ATTEND THE MARKET OF VART

The girl screamed, fighting the sales collar and the position chain.

She tried to pull it from her throat.

The two male slaves, to the right, turned the crank of the windlass and she was drawn, in her turn, struggling, before the men.

The men in the crowd regarded her, curiously. Had she never been sold before?

She tried to turn away, and cover herself, her feet in the damp sawdust. The inside of her left thigh was stained yellow, as she had lost water in her terror.

The auctioneer did not strike her with his whip. He merely took her arms and lifted them, so that the position chain, attached to each side of the sales collar, lay across her upper

35

arms. Then he had her clasp her hands behind the back of her neck, so that the chain, on each side of the collar, was in the crook of her arms, and she was exposed in such a way that she could be properly exhibited.

In a higher class market girls are usually fed a cathartic a few hours before the sale, and forced to relieve themselves shortly before their sale, a kettle passed down the line. In the current market such niceties, especially in large sales, were seldom observed.

By the hair the auctioneer pulled her head up and back so that her features might be observed by the men.

"Another loot girl taken by our noble Captain, Bejar, in his brilliant capture of the *Blossoms of Telnus*," called the auctioneer. He was also the slaver, Vart, once Publius Quintus of Ar, banished from that city, and nearly impaled, for falsifying slave data. He had advertised a girl as a trained pleasure slave who, as it turned out, did not even know the eleven kisses. The Vart is a small, sharp-toothed winged mammal, carnivorous, which commonly flies in flocks.

"A blond-haired, blue-eyed barbarian," called the auctioneer, "who speaks little or no Gorean, untrained, formerly free, a purse not yet rent, a thigh not yet kissed by the iron. What am I offered?"

"A copper tarsk," called a man from the floor, a fellow who rented chains of work girls.

"I hear one tarsk," called the auctioneer. "Do I hear more?"

"Let us have the next girl!" called a man. The slaves at the windlass tensed, but the auctioneer did not tell them to move the chain, removing the blond girl and bringing forth the next item on the chain.

"Surely I hear more?" called the auctioneer. "Do I hear two tarsks?" I suppose he may have paid two or three tarsks for her himself, to Bejar.

The girl was beautiful, but not as beautiful, it was true, as most Gorean slave girls. I did not think she would bring a high price. Unfortunately, then, almost anyone might buy her. I looked about. It seemed a common, motley crowd for the house of Vart, where men came generally to buy cheap girls, sometimes in lots, at bargain prices. His establishment was located in a warehouse near the docks. I conjectured there were some two hundred buyers and onlookers present. I wore the tunic, and leather apron and cap, of the metal worker.

36

"Look at her," said the man beside me. "How ugly she is, what a she-tarsk."

"A true she-tarsk," agreed another.

They had seen, I gathered, few Earth girls. They did not understand the effects of years of insidious, pervasive, anti-biological conditioning. Their own culture, perhaps because of the limitations imposed on it by Priest-Kings, who did not wish to be threatened or destroyed by an animal with which they shared a world, had taken different turnings. They would not understand a world in which dirty jokes had point, a world in which a woman's attractiveness was supposedly a function of the utilization of certain commercial products, or a world in which men and women were taught that they were the same, and in which they attempted to believe it, and would hysterically insist it was true, bravely ignoring the evidence of their reason, senses and experience. Civilization may be predicated upon the denial of human nature; it may also be predicated upon its fulfillment. The first word that an Earth baby learns is usually, "No." The first word that a Gorean baby learns is commonly, "Yes." The machine and the flower, I suspect, will never understand one another.

"Let us see another girl!" called yet another man.

"A new girl!" cried others.

Many women, of course, once under the helpless condition of slavery, increase considerably in beauty. This has to do primarily I think with psychological factors, in particular with the destruction of neurotic patterns, inculcated in the Earth female, of male-imitation, and the concurrent necessity imposed upon her by the whip, if necessary, to reveal and manifest her deeper self, that of a female. On the other hand, doubtless, the dieting, exercise, instruction in cosmetics and adornment, and the various forms of slave training, are also not without their effect.

"Do I hear two tarsks?" asked the auctioneer.

If a woman truly is, in her secret heart, a man's slave, how can any female who is not a man's slave be truly a woman? And how can any woman who is not truly a woman be happy?

Can a woman be free only when she is a slave? Is this not the paradox of the collar?

"Come Masters, Kind Sirs," called the auctioneer. "Can you not see the promise of this slender, blond, barbarian beauty?"

There was laughter from the floor.

37

"What a cheap, slovenly man of business is our friend, Vart," said the fellow next to me. "Look, he has not even had her branded."

"Add that into her price," grumbled another.

"At least you do not have to worry about that," said a man, to me.

I wore the garb of a metal worker. Usually girls, if not marked by a slaver, are marked in the shop of a metal worker.

I smiled.

The auctioneer was now calling off her measurements, and her collar, and wrist and ankle-ring size. He had jotted these down on her back with a red-grease marking stick.

"Will not an urt hunter give me at least two tarsks for her?" called out the auctioneer good-humoredly, but with some understandable exasperation.

I wished that either Bejar or Vart had had her branded. It would be easier to keep track of her that way.

"She is not worth tying at the end of a rope and using in the water as a bait for urts," called out a man, the fellow who had first suggested that she be removed from the sales position.

There was laughter.

"Perhaps you are right," called out the auctioneer, agreeably.

"Would an urt want her?" asked another man.

There was more laughter.

"Perhaps an urt!" laughed a man.

"Go down to the canals," said another man. "See if you can get two tarsks from the urts!"

There was again general laughter. The auctioneer, too, seemed amused. He apparently recognized that it was futile, and a bit amusing, to be attempting to get an interesting price on this particular bit of slave meat.

There were tears now, and bitterness, in the girl's eyes. I knew, from her general attitudes and responses, that she understood very little of what was transpiring, and yet, clearly, she must understand that she was the butt of the laughter of the men, who held her in contempt and scorned her, who were not interested in her, who had not bid hardly upon her, who obviously wished her to be taken from their sight. She was a poor slave. She stood there, in the collar, with the position chain attached to each side of it, the chain, on each side,

38

over an upper arm, held in the crook of her arms, her hands clasped behind her neck.

"I hate you," she cried, suddenly, to them, in English. "I hate you!"

They, of course, did not understand her. The hostility of her mien, however, was clear.

The auctioneer took handfuls of her long blond hair, from the right side of her head, rolled it into a ball between his palms, and thrust it in her mouth. She stood there. She knew she must not spit out the hair. She knew she was not then to speak.

"I am afraid that you are almost worthless, my dear," said the auctioneer to her, in Gorean.

She looked down, bitterly. I knew this type of response. The woman who fears she cannot please men then sometimes tends to feel hostility toward them, perhaps turning her own rage and inward disappointment outward, laying the blame upon them, and developing the obvious defensive reactions of belittling sexuality and its significance, and attempting, interestingly, to become manlike herself, to be one with them, though in an aggressive, competitive manner, often attempting to best them, as though one of themselves. Since she was not found desirable as a woman she attempts to become a more successful man than the men who failed to note her attractiveness. This type of response, however, however natural on Earth in such a situation, would not be feasible on Gor in a slave. Gorean free women, of course, may do what they wish. The slave girl, on the other hand, does not compete with the master, but serves him. The blond-haired girl might or might not hate men, but on Gor, as a slave, she would serve them, and serve them well. The woman who fears that she is unattractive to men, of course, is generally mistaken. She need only learn to please men. A woman who pleases men, and pleases them on their own terms, would, on Earth, be a startling rarity, an incredibly unusual treasure. On Gor, of course, she would be only another of hundreds of thousands of delicious slaves. On Gor a readiness to please men, and an intention to do so, and on their own terms, is expected in any girl one buys. Should a girl prove sluggish in any respect, it is simple to put her under discipline. Eventually, of course, a woman learns that to please a man on his own terms is the only thing that can, ultimately, fulfill her own deepest needs, those of the owned, submitting love slave.

"I am afraid you are almost worthless, my blue-eyed,

blond-haired prize," said the auctioneer to the girl. She looked out, dully, bitterly, at the crowd, her hands clasped behind her neck, hair from the right side of her head looping up to her mouth.

I had little fear for her, however. Her neurotic responses, functions of her Earth conditioning, would have little place on Gor.

They cannot be maintained on Gor.

They would be broken.

She would learn slavery well, like any woman.

The crowd watched the auctioneer, who stood close by the girl.

I was curious, however, that Kurii had brought her to Gor. She did not seem, objectively, of quite the same high quality of beauty as most of the wenches brought by Kurii to Gor, either as agents or as simple, immediate slaves.

The auctioneer made certain her hands were clasped tightly behind the back of her neck. He actually took her hands in his and thrust them closely together. She looked at him, puzzled, slightly frightened. He stepped behind her.

I smiled.

She suddenly screamed, and sobbed and gasped, her hair, wet, expelled from her mouth. She looked at the auctioneer, in terror, but dared not release her hands from the back of her neck. He, with one hand, wadded together her hair, and thrust it again in her mouth. She must not cry out, or speak. In his right hand, coiled, he held the whip which he had removed from his belt a moment before. He had administered to her the slaver's caress with the heavy coils. She shook her head, wildly. She tried to draw back, but his left hand, behind the small of her back, held her in place.

She threw back her head, shaking it wildly, negatively. Then there was a spasm. Then she sobbed, shuddering, tensing herself. The auctioneer then, holding her, brought the coils near her again. She put her head back, her eyes closed. But he did not touch her then. She opened her eyes, looking up at the ceiling of the warehouse in which she was being sold. Still he did not touch her. She whimpered. Then I saw her legs tense and move, slight muscles in the thighs and calves. She half rose on her toes. Still he did not touch her. Then I saw her, with a sob, thrust herself toward the coils. But still he did not touch her. Then, as she looked at him, tears in her eyes, he, looking at her, deigned to lift the coils against her piteous, arched, pleading body. She then writhed

40

at the chain, sobbing, her hands clenched behind her neck, her teeth clenched on her own hair. She tried to hold the whip between her thighs. He then withdrew the whip, and turned to the crowd, smiling. He fastened the whip at his belt.

"What am I bid?" he asked.

The girl whimpered piteously. He turned about and, with his right hand, open, cuffed her, as one cuffs a slave. Her head was struck upward and to the left. There was a bit of blood at her lip, which began to swell. There were tears in her eyes. She looked at him. She was silent.

"What am I bid?" asked the auctioneer.

"Four tarsks," said a man.

"Six," said another.

"Fifteen," called out another.

"Sixteen," said a man.

The girl, shuddering, standing as she had, her hair in her mouth, her hands behind her head, put her head down, miserably. She did not dare to look even at the bidders, who might own her. She knew that her needs had betrayed her.

I smiled to myself. The selection of this woman for service in the Kurii cause now seemed clearer than it had before. She, like others, doubtless, when their political duties were finished, would have been collared and silked, and set to the task of learning to please masters. I thought she would make, in time, a good slave. She was already adequately beautiful and, in time, in bondage, might become incredibly beautiful. Her responsiveness, though not unusual for a slave girl, was surely impressive for an unmarked Earth girl in her first sale. Responsiveness, of course, is something that can increase and deepen in a woman, and under the proper tutelage and discipline, does so. The female slave, in the fullness of her womanhood, and helplessness, attains heights of passion from which the free woman, in her pride and dignity, is forever barred. She is not a man's slave.

"Twenty-two tarsks," called a man in the crowd.

"Twenty-four!" called another.

Yes, the responsiveness of the girl on sale had been impressive. In some months, in the proper collar, and at the right slave ring, I suspected she would become paga hot, hot enough to serve even in the paga taverns of Gor.

Her head was down.

"Twenty-seven tarsks," called a man.

How shamed she was. Why was she so ashamed that she

41

had sexual needs and was sensuously alive? Of course, I reminded myself, of course, she was an Earth girl.

"Twenty-eight tarsks," called a man.

The girl's body shook with an uncontrollable sob. Her secret, doubtless long hidden on Earth, that she had a deep, latent sexuality, had been ruthlessly and publicly exposed in a Gorean market. She had writhed, and as a naked slave.

"Twenty-nine tarsks," called a man.

She had writhed not only as a woman, but as a slave.

Her head was down. Her body shook.

For a moment I almost felt moved to pity. Then I laughed, looking at her. Her responses had revealed her as a slave.

"Forty tarsks," said a voice, triumphantly. It was the voice of Procopius Minor, or Little Procopius, who owned the Four Chains, a tavern near Pier Sixteen, to be distinguished from Procopius Major, or Big Procopius, who owned several such taverns throughout the city. The Four Chains was a dingy tavern, located between two warehouses. Procopius Minor owned about twenty girls. His establishment had a reputation for brawls, cheap paga and hot slaves. His girls served nude and chained. Each ankle and wrist ring had two staples. Each girl's wrists were joined by about eighteen inches of chain, and similarly for her ankles. Further each girl's left wrist was chained to her left ankle, and her right wrist to her right ankle. This arrangement, lovely on a girl, produces the "four chains," from which the establishment took its name. The four-chain chaining arrangement, of course, and variations upon it, is well known upon Gor. Four other paga taverns in Port Kar alone used it. They could not, of course, given the registration of the name by Procopius Minor with the league of taverners, use a reference to it in designating their own places of business. These four taverns, if it is of interest, are the Veminium, the Kailiauk, the Slaves of Ar and the Silver of Tharna.

"Forty tarsks," repeated Procopius Minor, Little Procopius. He was little, it might be mentioned, only in commercial significance, compared to Procopius Major, or Big Procopius. Big Procopius was one of the foremost merchants in Port Kar. Paga taverns were only one of his numerous interests. He was also involved in hardware, paper, wool and salt. Little Procopius was not little physically. He was a large, portly fellow. To be sure, however, Procopius Major was a bit larger, even physically.

The girl looked up now, sensing the cessation in the bidding, the repeating of a bid, the tone of the voice of Procopius Minor.

Her hands were still behind the back of her neck. She had not been given permission to remove them. She looked out at Procopius Minor. She shuddered. She realized that he might soon own her, totally.

"I have heard a bid of forty tarsks," said the auctioneer, Vart. I supposed it would be good for the girl to serve for a time in a low paga house. It is not a bad place for a girl to begin to learn something of the meaning of her collar. "Do I hear another bid, a higher bid?" called Vart. Yes, she would look well in chains, kneeling to masters in a paga tavern. "My hand is open," called Vart. "Shall I close my hand? Shall I close my hand?"

He looked about, well pleased. He had never counted on getting as much as forty tarsks for the blond barbarian.

"I will now close my hand!" he called.

"Do not close your hand," said a voice.

All eyes turned toward the back. A tall man stood there, lean and black. He wore a closely woven seaman's aba, red, striped with white, which fell from his shoulders; this was worn over an ankle-length, white tobe, loosely sleeved, embroidered with gold, with a golden sash. In the sash was thrust a curved dagger. On his head he wore a cap on which were fixed the two golden tassels of Schendi.

"Who is he?" asked the man next to me.

"I do not know," I said.

"Yes, Master?" asked the auctioneer. "Is there another bid?"

"Yes," said the man.

"Yes, Master?" asked the auctioneer.

"I take him to be a merchant captain," said a man near me.

I nodded. The conjecture was intelligent. The fellow wore the white and gold of the merchant, beneath a seaman's aba. It was not likely that a merchant would wear that garment unless he were entitled to it. Goreans are particular about such matters. Doubtless he owned and captained his own vessel.

"What is his name and ship?" I asked.

"I do not know," said the man.

"What is Master's bid?" asked the auctioneer.

There was silence.

We looked at the man. The girl, too, in the sales collar and position chain, her hands behind her neck, looked at him.

"What is Master's bid?" asked the auctioneer.

"One tarsk," said the man.

We looked at one another. There was some uneasy laughter. Then there was again silence.

"Forgive me, Master," then said the auctioneer. "Master came late to the bidding. We have already on the floor a bid of forty tarsks."

Procopius turned about, smiling.

"One silver tarsk," said the man.

"Aiii!" cried a man.

"A silver tarsk?" asked the auctioneer.

Procopius turned about again, suddenly, to regard the fellow in the back, incredulously.

"Yes," he said, "a silver tarsk."

I smiled to myself. The slave on sale was not a silver-tarsk girl. There would be no more bidding.

"I have a bid for a silver tarsk," said Vart. "Is there a higher bid?" There was silence. He looked to Procopius. Procopius shrugged. "No," he said.

"I shall close my hand," said the auctioneer. He held his right hand open, and then he closed it.

The girl had been sold.

The girl looked at the closed fist of the auctioneer with horror. It was not hard to understand its import.

The auctioneer went to her and pulled the hair from her mouth, then threw it back over her right shoulder. He smoothed her hair then, on both sides and in the back. He might have been a clerk adjusting merchandise on a counter. She seemed scarcely conscious of what he was doing. She looked out, fearfully, on the man who had bought her.

The auctioneer turned to the buyer. "With whom has the house the honor of doing business?" he asked.

"I am Ulafi," said the man, "captain of the *Palms of Schendi*."

"We are truly honored," said the auctioneer.

I knew Ulafi of Schendi only by reputation, as a shrewd merchant and captain. I had never seen him before. He was said to have a good ship.

"Deliver the girl to my ship," said Ulafi, "at the Pier of the Red Urt, by dawn. We will depart with the tide."

He threw a silver tarsk to the auctioneer, who caught it expertly, and slipped it into his pouch.

"It will be done, Master," promised the auctioneer.

The tall black then turned and left the warehouse, which was the market of Vart.

Suddenly the girl, her hands still behind the back of her neck, threw back her head and screamed in misery. I think it was only then that her consciousness had become fully cognizant of the import of what had been done to her.

She had been sold.

Vart gestured to the slaves at the windlass and they turned its large, two-man crank, and the girl who had been sold was drawn from the sales area. The next girl was a comely wench from Tyros, dark-haired and shapely. At a word from Vart she stood with her hands behind her neck, arching her body proudly for the buyers. I could see she had been sold before.

3

WHAT OCCURRED ON THE WAY TO THE PIER OF THE RED URT; I HEAR THE RINGING OF AN ALARM BAR

It was near the fifth hour.

It was still dark along the canals. Port Kar seems a lonely place at such an hour. I trod a walkway beside a canal, my sea bag over my shoulder. The air was damp. Here and there small lamps, set in niches, high in stone walls, or lanterns, hung on iron projections, shed small pools of light on the sides of buildings and illuminated, too, in their secondary ambience, the stones of the sloping walkway on which I trod, one of many leading down to the wharves. I could smell Thassa, the sea.

Two guardsmen, passing me, lifted their lanterns.

"Tal," I said to them, and continued on my way.

I wore, as I had the night before, the garb of a metal worker.

I heard an urt splash softly into the water, ahead of me and to my left.

I passed iron doors, narrow, in the walls. These doors usually had a tiny observation panel in them, which could be slid back. The walls were sheer. They were generally windowless until some fifteen feet above the ground. Yards, and gardens and courts, if they exist, are generally within the house, not outside it. This is very general in Gorean architecture. But there were few gardens or courts in Port Kar. It was a crowded city, built up from the marshes themselves, in the Vosk's delta, and space was scarce and precious.

There were pilings along the walkway, to which, here and there, small boats were moored. The walkway itself varied from some five feet to a yard in width.

I had stayed at the sales in the warehouse of Vart for a time after the sale of the blond barbarian. I had not wished to leave immediately after her sale, for that might have indicated, had there been a curious observer present, that that sale had been the one in which I had been interested.

The dark-haired, shapely girl from Tyros had gone for twenty-nine tarsks. She had proved, under Vart's touch, a hot, helpless slave and the bidding then had been quick and meaningful. She had been purchased by Procopius Minor for the Four Chains. He seemed well pleased with the buy. She was hot and she had cost him not forty but only twenty-nine tarsks. He had then, I conjectured, forgotten the blond barbarian. Tyros is a city enemy to Port Kar. Many men in Port Kar would enjoy having a girl of Tyros weep herself slave in their arms. She would make good money for Procopius Minor. She had been an excellent buy, a superb bargain. He might even enjoy using her himself. Who was the girl who had been previously sold? Ah, yes, the blond barbarian, purchased by Ulafi of Schendi.

The next two women sold had been a mother and daughter from Cos. They were sold to separate buyers, as pot girls. The mother brought sixteen tarsks and the daughter fourteen. They were among the eleven women, including the blond barbarian, who had been sold by Bejar to Vart. They had been taken in the capture of the *Blossoms of Telnus*. The crew and male passengers of the *Blossoms of Telnus* had also been sold by Bejar to Vart, but these had been auctioned by Vart in the morning, on the wharf blocks, as work slaves.

I had then stayed for only two more sales, and had then left, those of a peasant girl, blond, from southwest of Ar, and a merchant's daughter from Asperiche. The peasant girl brought eight tarsks; the merchant's daughter, to her indignation, brought only six. She had not yet learned slave heat. A strong master would teach it to her. She would learn it, or die. Frigidity is accepted by Goreans only in free women. Slave fires, of course, lurk in every woman. It is only a question of arousing them. Once the slave discovers her sexuality, a venture in which the humiliated slave, to her dismay, is forced to participate to the fullest, she can never again ignore it. Once she has begun to learn the orgasms of the slave girl she can never again be contented with anything less. She is then a master's girl. "I beg for your touch, Master," she whispers. Perhaps he will satisfy her; perhaps he will not. It is his whim. He is the master.

I stopped on the walkway. Ahead, some yards, was a girl dark-haired, lying on her belly on the walkway, reaching with her hand down to the canal, to fish out edible garbage. She was barefoot, and wore a brief, brown rag. I did not think she was a slave. Some free girls, runaways, vagabonds, girls of no family or position, live about port cities, scavenging as they can, begging, stealing, sleeping at night in crates and under bridges and piers. They are called the she-urts of the wharves. Every once in a while there is a move to have them rounded up and collared but it seldom comes to anything.

I was not worried about the girl. I was more alert to the fact that, moments before, two guardsmen had passed. The rounds of guardsmen are generally randomized, usually by the tossing of coins, different combinations corresponding to different schedulings. One of the most practical strategies for those who would avoid guardsmen, of course, is to follow them in their rounds. I was very aware of the fact that I carried, in my sea bag, the ring which the blond barbarian had had on the *Blossoms of Telnus* and the notes, bearing the signatures and seals of Schendi bankers, who had been made out to Shaba, the geographer of Anango, the explorer of Lake Ushindi, and the discoverer of Lake Ngao and the mysterious Ua River. I thought these might bring him out of hiding, with the Tahari ring, if I could not locate him by means of the blond Earth girl who had been purchased by Ulafi, captain of the *Palms of Schendi,* merchant, too, of that city.

The girl, hearing my approach, drew her legs up quickly under her, and rose to her feet, turning to meet me. She smiled, brightly. She was pretty.

"Tal," said she.

"Tal," said I.

"You are strong," she said.

47

We were in the vicinity of the pier of the Red Urt. It is not a desirable district.

I put down my sea bag.

She looked up at me.

"It is dangerous for you here," I said. "You should be home."

"I have no home," she said.

She traced an idle pattern on my left shoulder with her finger tip.

"Who would want to hurt a little she-urt," she said.

"What do you want?" I asked. I was alert to the tiny sound behind me.

"I will please you for a tarsk bit," she said.

I did not speak.

She suddenly knelt before me. "I will please you as a slave girl, if you wish," she said.

"When I want a slave girl," I said, "I will have a real slave girl, not a free woman pretending to be a slave girl."

She looked up at me, angrily.

"On your feet, free woman," I said.

She got up angrily. She was not a slave. Why should I accord her the privilege of kneeling at my feet?

"I'm hot and I'm pretty," she said. "Try me."

I touched her flanks. They were good. I then took her by the upper arms. I looked into her eyes. She lifted her lips to mine.

"No!" she screamed, wild-eyed, as I suddenly lifted her from her feet and spun about, she knowing herself lifted helplessly into the path of the blow. I dropped her inert body to one side.

"You should take your breath," I told him, "before you approach. Too, you should have your arm raised early, that the movement of the sleeve not be audible. Too, you should have the girl, in her diversion, keep her eyes closed. That could be natural enough, and, in that way, you would not be reflected in the mirror of her eyes." It had not been difficult to detect his approach, even apart from the more obvious clues I had called to his attention. The senses of a warrior are trained. His life may depend on it.

With a cry of rage the man attacked. I caught the club hand, which was clumsy, and, twisting it, dashed his face first into the walkway. I then took him by the hair and thrust the side of his head into the wall. He slumped down, unconscious. I took binding fiber from my sea bag and tied his

48

wrists together behind his back, and crossed and tied his ankles. I then turned to the girl. I tied her hands behind her back, and then took her by the ankles and held her upside down, thrusting her head and shoulders, and upper body, under the cold waters of the canal. In a few seconds I pulled her up, sputtering, and sat her, tied, against the wall across from me. She gasped for air; she tried to clear water from her eyes. She choked. Her hair and the rag she wore were wet. She backed further against the wall, drawing her legs up, pressing her knees closely together. She looked at me, frightened. "Please, let me go," she said. Dawn would be well glistening now over the marshes to the east. It was still rather dark in the canal streets with the buildings on each side. There was fog visible on the canals.

"Please, let me go," she said. "It will mean the collar for me."

"Do you recall what you said to me," I asked, "shortly before I turned you about?"

"No," she said.

"Oh?" I asked.

"Yes, yes!" she said.

"Say it, again," I told her.

"Please," she begged.

"Say it," I said.

"I'm hot and I'm pretty," she stammered. "Try me," she said. She swallowed hard.

"Very well," I said.

I drew her to me by the ankles.

"Please let me go," she said. "It will mean the collar for me. Oh, oh."

Then in moments she moaned and wept.

I forced her to yield well, to the very limits of the free woman. Then I was finished with her.

She looked up at me. "Have I pleased you?" she asked, tears in her eyes.

"Yes," I said.

"Let me go," she said.

I took her ankles, crossed and tied them. Then I threw her beside the man, her head to his feet. I tied her neck to his feet, and her feet to his neck. They would wait, thus, for the guardsmen.

"They will banish him and collar me," she said.

"Yes," I said.

I knelt down on one knee beside her. I took a tarsk bit

49

from my pouch, and thrust it in her mouth. She was a free woman. Since I had no intent of enslaving her myself, it seemed fit that I should pay her for her use. She had asked, as I recalled, for a tarsk bit. Had I intended to keep her, I might have simply raped her, and then put the collar on her. A slave has no recourse.

I rose to my feet, and, shouldering my sea bag, whistling, continued on toward the pier of the Red Urt, where Ulafi's ship, the *Palms of Schendi*, was moored.

I soon hurried my steps, for an alarm bar had begun to ring.

I heard steps running behind me, too, and I turned about. A black seaman ran past me, he, too, heading toward the wharves. I followed him toward the pier of the Red Urt.

4

I RECAPTURE AN ESCAPED SLAVE; I BOOK PASSAGE ON A SHIP FOR SCHENDI

"How long has she been missing?" I asked.

"Over an Ahn," said a man. "But only now have they rung the bar."

We stood in the vicinity of the high desk of the wharf praetor.

"There seemed no reason to ring it earlier," said the man. "It was thought she would be soon picked up, by guardsmen, or the crew of the *Palms of Schendi*."

"She was to be shipped on that craft?" I asked.

"Yes," said the man. "I suppose now her feet must be cut off."

"Is it her first attempt to escape?" asked another man.

"I do not know," said another.

"Why is there this bother about an escaped slave," demanded a man, his clothing torn and blood at his ear. "I have been robbed! What are you doing about this?"

"Be patient," said the wharf praetor. "We know the pair. We have been searching for them for weeks." The praetor handed a sheet of paper to one of his guardsmen. People were gathered around. Another guardsman stopped ringing the alarm bar. It hung from a projection on a pole, the pole fixed upright on the roof of a nearby warehouse.

"Be on the watch for an escaped female slave," called the guardsman. "She is blond-haired and blue-eyed. She is barbarian. When last seen she was naked."

I did not think it would take them long to apprehend her. She was a fool to try to escape. There was no escape for such as she. Yet she was unmarked and uncollared. It might not prove easy to retake her immediately.

"How did she escape?" I asked a fellow.

"Vart's man," said he, "delivered her to the wharf, where he knelt her among the cargo to be loaded on the *Palms of Schendi*. He obtained his receipt for her and then left."

"He did not leave her tied, hand and foot, among the bales and crates for loading?" I asked.

"No," said the man. "But who, either Vart's man, or those of the *Palms of Schendi*, would have thought it necessary?"

I nodded. There was reason in what he said. Inwardly I smiled. She had simply left the loading area, when no one was watching, simply slipping away. Had she been less ignorant of Gor she would not have dared to escape. She did not yet fully understand that she was a slave girl. She did not yet understand that escape was not permitted to such as she.

"Return the girl to the praetor's station on this pier," said the guardsman.

"What of those who robbed me!" cried the fellow with the torn clothing and the blood behind his ear.

"You are not the first," said the praetor, looking down at him from the high desk. "They stand under a general warrant."

"Who robbed you?" I asked the man.

"I think there were two," said the man. "There was a dark-haired she-urt in a brown tunic. I was struck from behind. Apparently there is a male confederate."

"She approached you, engaging your attention," I asked, "and then you, when diverted, were struck from behind?"

"Yes," said the fellow, sourly.

"I saw two individuals, who may be your friends," I said, "on the north walkway of the Rim canal, leading to the vicinity of this very pier."

"We shall send two guardsmen to investigate," said the praetor. "Thank you, Citizen, for this information."

51

"They will be gone now," said the man with the blood behind his ear.

"Perhaps not," I said.

The praetor dispatched a pair of guardsmen, who moved swiftly toward the Rim canal.

"Be on the watch for an escaped female slave," repeated the guardsman with the paper. He spoke loudly, calling out, over the crowd. I heard him adding to the available information. New data had been furnished to him from a wharf runner, who had her sales information in hand, brought from the records of the house of Vart. This included, however, little more than her measurements and the sizes of the collar, and wrist and ankle rings that would well fit her.

I went over to the edge of the pier, some hundred yards or so away, to where the *Palms of Schendi* was moored. Longshoremen, bales and crates on their shoulders, were filling her hold. They were being supervised by the second officer. It was now grayishly light, a few Ehn past dawn. I could not yet see the golden rim of Tor-tu-Gor, Light Upon the Home Stone, rising in the east over the city.

"Are you bound for Schendi?" I called to the officer.

"Yes," said he, looking up from his lading list.

"I would take passage with you," I said.

"We do not carry passengers," said he.

"I can pay as much as a silver tarsk," I said. It did not seem well to suggest that I could afford more. If worse came to worse I could book passage on another vessel. It would not be wise to hire a ship, for this would surely provoke suspicion. Similarly, it would not be wise to take one of my own ships, say, the *Dorna* or the *Tesephone*, south. They might be recognized. Gorean seamen recognize ships with the same ease that they recognize faces. This is common, of course, among seamen anywhere.

"We do not carry passengers," said the second officer.

I shrugged, and turned away. I would prefer, of course, to have passage on this ship, for it would be on this ship that the girl, when apprehended, would be transported. I did not wish to risk losing track of her.

I looked up to the stern castle of the *Palms of Schendi*. There I saw her captain, Ulafi, engaged in conversation with one whom I took to be the first officer. They did not look at me.

I stood there for a few moments, regarding the lines of the *Palms of Schendi*. She was a medium-class round ship, with a keel-to-beam ratio of about six to one; that of the long ship is usually about eight to one. She had ten oars to a side, two rudders, and two, permanent, lateen-rigged masts. Most Gorean ships were double ruddered. The masts of round ships are usually permanently fixed; those of long ships, usually single-masted, are removed before battle; most Gorean ships are lateen-rigged; this permits sailing closer to the wind. The long, triangular sail, incidentally, is very beautiful.

I turned away from the ship. I did not wish to be observed looking at it too closely. I wore the garb of the metal workers.

According to the tide tables the first tide would be full at six Ehn past the seventh Ahn.

I wondered if Ulafi would sail without the blond-haired barbarian. I did not think so. I hoped that he had not put out a silver tarsk for her simply because she had struck his fancy. That would indeed be infuriating. I was certain that he would wait until she was regained. If he missed the tide, however, I did not think he would be pleased.

There seemed to be something going on now at the post of the wharf praetor, so I returned to that area.

"It is she!" said the fellow in the torn tunic with the blood behind his ear, pointing at the small, dark-haired girl. She stood before the high desk of the praetor, her wrists tied behind her back. Beside her, his hands, too, bound behind him, stood the fellow who had been her accomplice. They were fastened together by the neck, by a guardsman's neck strap. The girl, interestingly, was stripped, the brief, brown tunic having been taken from her. I had not removed it. I had only thrust it up, over her hips. It did not seem likely to me that the guardsman, either, would have removed it, as she was, I presumed, a free woman. Yet it was gone, and she was naked.

"We found them both trussed like vulos," laughed a guardsman.

"Who could do such a thing?" asked a man.

"It was not guardsmen," said a guardsman. "We would have brought them in."

"It seems they picked the wrong fellow to waylay," said a man.

"It is she," said the fellow with the blood behind his ear. "She is the one who diverted me, while her fellow, he, I suppose, struck me." He pointed then to the man.

53

The girl shook her head, negatively. It seemed she wanted to speak.

"What do you have in your mouth, Girl?" asked the praetor.

One of the guardsmen opened her mouth, not gently, and retrieved the coin, a rather large one, a tarsk bit. Ten such coins make a copper tarsk. A hundred copper tarsks make a silver tarks.

The praetor placed the coin on his desk, the surface of which was some seven feet high, below the low, solid wooden bar The height of the praetor's desk, he on the high stool behind it, permits him to see a goodly way up and down the wharves. Also, of course, one standing before the desk must look up to see the praetor, which, psychologically, tends to induce a feeling of fear for the power of the law. The wooden bar before the desk's front edge makes it impossible to see what evidence or papers the praetor has at his disposal as he considers your case. Thus, you do not know for certain how much he knows. Similarly, you cannot tell what he writes on your papers.

"Give me back my coin!" said the girl.

"Be silent," said a guardsman.

"She is the one who cooperated in the attack upon you?" asked the praetor, indicating the bound girl.

"Yes," said the man with blood behind his ear.

"No!" cried the girl. "I have never seen him before in my life!"

"I see," said the praetor. He apparently was not unfamiliar with the girl.

"Ha!" snorted the man who had accused her.

"How did you come to be helpless and tied beside the canal?" inquired the praetor.

The girl looked about, wildly. "We were set upon by brigands, robbed, and left tied," she said.

There was laughter.

"You must believe me," she said. "I am a free woman!"

"Examine the pouch of the man," said the praetor.

It was opened by a guardsman, who sifted his hands through coins.

The girl looked, startled, at the pouch. She had apparently not understood that it had contained as much as it did. Her small hands pulled futilely, angrily, at the binding fiber which restrained them.

"It seems that the fellow who robbed you," smiled the praetor, "neglected to take your pouch."

The bound man said nothing. He glared sullenly downward.

"He also left you a tarsk bit," said the praetor, to the girl.

"It was all I could save," she said, lamely.

There was more laughter.

"I was not robbed," said the bound man. "But I was unaccountably, from behind, struck down. I was then tied to this little she-urt. Her guilt is well known, I gather, on the wharves. Clearly enemies have intended to unjustly link me to her guilt."

"Turgus!" she cried.

"I have never seen her before in my life," he said.

"Turgus!" she cried. "No, Turgus!"

"Did you see me strike you?" asked the fellow who had been addressed as Turgus.

"No," said the fellow who had been struck. "No, I did not."

"It was not I," said the bound man. "Unbind me," said he then to the praetor. "Set me free, for I am innocent. It is clear I am the victim of a plot."

"He told me what to do!" she said. "He told me what to do!"

"Who are you, you little slut?" asked the bound man. "It is obvious," he said, to the praetor, "that this she-urt, whoever she is, wishes to implicate me in her guilt, that it will go easier on her."

"I assure you," smiled the praetor, "it will not go easier on her."

"My thanks, Officer," said the man.

The girl, crying out with rage, tried to kick at the man tied beside her. A guardsman struck her on the right thigh with the butt of his spear and she cried out in pain.

"If you should attempt to do that again, my dear," said the praetor, "your ankles will be tied, and you will hear the rest of the proceedings while lying on your belly before the tribunal."

"Yes, Officer," she said.

"What is your name?" asked the praetor of the girl.

"Sasi," she said.

"Lady Sasi?" he asked.

"Yes," she said, "I am free!"

There was laughter. She looked about, angrily, bound. I

55

did not think she would need be worried much longer about her freedom.

"Usually," smiled the praetor, "a free woman wears more than binding fiber and a neck strap."

"My gown was taken, when I was tied," she said. "It was torn from me."

"Who took it," asked the praetor, "a casual male, curious to see your body?"

"A girl took it," she cried, angrily, "a blond girl. She was naked. Then she took my garment. Then I was naked! Find her, if you wish to be busy with matters of the law! I was the victim of theft! It was stolen from me, my garment! You should be hunting her, the little thief, not holding me here. I am an honest citizen!"

There was more laughter.

"May I be freed, my officer?" asked the bound man. "A mistake has been made."

The praetor turned to two guardsmen. "Go to where you found these two tied," he said. "I think our missing slave will be found in the garment of the she-urt."

Two guardsmen left immediately. I thought the praetor's conjecture was a sound one. On the other hand, obviously, the girl would not be likely to linger in the place where she had stolen the she-urt's brief, miserable rag. Still, perhaps her trail could be found in that area.

"I demand justice," said the girl.

"You will receive it, Lady Sasi," said the praetor.

She turned white.

"At least she will not have to be stripped for the iron," said a fellow near me, grinning.

The girl moaned.

The praetor then addressed himself to the fellow who had the dried blood caked behind his left ear. It was dried in his hair, too, on the left side of his head.

"Is this female, identified as the Lady Sasi, she who detained you, when you were attacked?" asked the praetor.

"It is she," he said.

"I never saw him before," she wept.

"It is she," he repeated.

"I only wanted to beg a tarsk bit," she said. "I did not know he was going to strike you."

"Why did you not warn him of the man's approach behind him?" asked the praetor.

"I didn't see the man approaching," she said, desperately.

"But you said you didn't know he was going to strike him," said the praetor. "Therefore, you must have seen him."

"Please let me go," she said.

"I was not seen to strike the man," said the fellow whom the girl had identified as Turgus. "I claim innocence. There is no evidence against me. Do what you will with the little slut. But set me free."

The girl put down her head, miserably. "Please let me go," she begged.

"I was robbed of a golden tarn," said the fellow with the blood at the side of his head.

"There is a golden tarn in the pouch," said a guardsman.

"On the golden tarn taken from me," said the man, "I had scratched my initials, Ba-Ta Shu, Bem Shandar, and, on the reverse of the coin, the drum of Tabor."

The guardsman lifted the coin to the praetor. "It is so," said the praetor.

The bound man, suddenly, irrationally, struggled. He tried to throw off his bonds. The girl cried out in misery, jerked choking from her feet. Then two guardsmen held the fellow by the arms. "He is strong," said one of the guardsmen. The girl, gasping, regained her feet. Then she stood again necklinked to him, beside him, his fellow prisoner.

"The coin was planted in my pouch," he said. "It is a plot!"

"You are an urt, Turgus," she said to him, "an urt!"

"It is you who are the she-urt!" he snarled.

"You have both been caught," said the praetor, beginning to fill out some papers. "We have been looking for you both for a long time."

"I am innocent," said the bound man.

"How do you refer to yourself?" asked the praetor.

"Turgus," he said.

The praetor entered that name in the papers. He then signed the papers.

He looked down at Turgus. "How did you come to be tied?" he asked.

"Several men set upon me," he said. "I was struck from behind. I was subdued."

"It does not appear that you were struck from behind," smiled the praetor.

The face of Turgus was not a pretty sight, as I had dashed it into the stones, and had then struck the side of his head against the nearby wall.

"Is the binding fiber on their wrists from their original bonds, as you found them?" asked the praetor of one of the guardsmen.

"It is," he said.

"Examine the knots," said the praetor.

"They are capture knots," said the guardsman, smiling.

"You made a poor choice of one to detain, my friends," said the praetor.

They looked at one another, miserably. Their paths had crossed that of a warrior.

They now stood bound before the praetor.

"Turgus, of Port Kar," said the praetor, "in virtue of what we have here today established, and in virtue of the general warrant outstanding upon you, you are sentenced to banishment. If you are found within the limits of the city after sunset this day you will be impaled."

The face of Turgus was impassive.

"Free him," he said.

Turgus was cut free, and turned about, moving through the crowd. He thrust men aside.

Suddenly he saw me. His face turned white, and he spun about, and fled.

I saw one of the black seamen, the one who had passed me on the north walkway of the Rim canal, when I had been descending toward the pier, looking at me, curiously.

The girl looked up at the praetor. The neck strap, now that Turgus was freed of it, looped gracefully up to her throat, held in the hand of a guardsman. Her small wrists were still bound behind her back.

She seemed very small and helpless before the high desk.

"Please let me go," she said. "I will be good."

"The Lady Sasi, of Port Kar," said the praetor, "in virtue of what we have here today established, and in virtue of the general warrant outstanding upon her, must come under sentence."

"Please, my officer," she begged.

"I am now going to sentence you," he said.

"Please," she cried. "Sentence me only to a penal brothel!"

"The penal brothel is too good for you," said the praetor.

"Show me mercy," she begged.

"You will be shown no mercy," he said.

She looked up at him, with horror.

"You are sentenced to slavery," he said.

"No, no!" she screamed.

58

One of the guards cuffed her across the mouth, snapping her head back.

There were tears in her eyes and blood at her lip.

"Were you given permission to speak?" asked the praetor.

"No, no," she wept, stammering. "Forgive me—Master."

"Let her be taken to the nearest metal shop and branded," said the praetor. "Then let her be placed on sale outside the shop for five Ehn, to be sold to the first buyer for the cost of her branding. If she is not sold in five Ehn then take her to the public market shelves and chain her there, taking the best offer which equals or exceeds the cost of her branding."

The girl looked up at the praetor. The strap, in the hand of the guardsman, grew taut at her throat.

"This tarsk bit," said the praetor, lifting the coin which had been taken from her mouth earlier, "is now confiscated, and becomes the property of the port." This was appropriate. Slaves own nothing. It is, rather, they who are owned.

The girl, the new slave, was then dragged stumbling away from the tribunal.

I noted that Ulafi, captain of the *Palms of Schendi*, and his first officer, were now standing near me in the crowd. They were looking at me.

I made my way toward them.

"I would book passage on the *Palms of Schendi*," I told them.

"You are not a metal worker," said Ulafi to me, quietly.

I shrugged. "I would book passage," I said.

"We do not carry passengers," he said. Then he, and his first officer, turned away. I watched them go.

The praetor was now conversing with the fellow, Bem Shandar, from Tabor. Papers were being filled in; these had to do with the claims Bem Shandar was making to recover his stolen money.

"Captain!" I called to Ulafi.

He turned. The crowd was dispersing.

"I could pay a silver tarsk for passage," I told him.

"You seem desperate to leave Port Kar," said he.

"Perhaps," I told him.

"We do not carry passengers," said he. He turned away. His first officer followed him.

I went to a guardsman, near the praetor station. "What efforts are being made to recover the lost slave?" I asked.

"Are you with the *Palms of Schendi*?" he asked.

"I hope to book passage on that ship," I said. "I fear the

captain will delay his departure until she is recovered." I was sure this was the case.

"We are conducting a search," said the guardsman.

"She may be wearing the garment of a she-urt," I said.

"That is known to us, Citizen," said he.

"I myself," said a nearby guardsman, "stopped a girl answering the description, one in the torn rag of a she-urt, but when I forced her to reveal her thighs, she was unmarked."

"Where did you find such a girl?" I asked.

"Near the Spice Pier," he said.

"My thanks, Guardsman," said I.

It seemed to me that the blond girl might well consider various strategies for eluding capture. I did not think she would be likely to flee east along the canal walkways, for these were relatively narrow and, on them, between the buildings and the canal, she might be easily trapped. Also, though this would not figure in her thinking, she could, on the north, east and south, be trapped against the delta walls or at the marsh gates. I did not think it likely she would risk stealing a boat. Even if she could handle a small craft, which I doubted, for she was an Earth girl, probably from an urban area, the risk of discovery would be too great. Also, though she did not know it, a she-urt in a boat would surely provoke instant suspicion. Where would such a girl obtain a boat, if she had not stolen it. Too, it would, given the construction of the buildings of Port Kar, be difficult to attain the roof of one from the outside of the building. I did not think she would try to gain admittance to a building. She would probably then, in my opinion, try to find her way to markets or stay about the wharves. The markets were, for the most part, save the wharf markets, deeper in the city. I did not think she would reach them, or know how to find them. She was then, probably, in the vicinity of the wharves. Here she would, presumably, attempt to conceal herself. She might hide in various ways. Obvious ways of hiding would be to conceal herself among the boxes and bales at the wharves, to creep into a crate, or barrel, or to cover herself with sheets of sail canvas or with heavy coils of mooring rope. Guardsmen, I was certain, would examine such possibilities systematically. Too, a she-urt found in such a place, it not being night, would surely be viewed as a girl in hiding. She would presumably then be tied and taken to the praetor. Perhaps she is wanted for something.

I was now in the vicinity of the Spice Pier.

I did not think my quarry would elect an obvious way of hiding, one in which she, if found, would be immediately exposed as a fugitive. She was doubtless highly intelligent. She had been chosen as a Kur agent.

I seized a dark-haired she-urt by the arm. "Let me go," she screamed. "I have done nothing!"

"Where do the she-urts band?" I asked.

"Let me go!" she cried.

I shook her. "Oh, oh," she cried.

I then stopped shaking her. I held her by the arms, her toes barely touching the ground. She was then quiet, looking up at me. Her eyes were frightened. I saw she was ready to be obedient.

"There are some girls behind the paga taverns, on the northern shore of the Ribbon's alley," she said.

I released her and she sank to her knees, gasping.

The Ribbon is one of Port Kar's better-known canals. A narrower canal, somewhat south of it, is called the Ribbon's alley. It was a bit past dawn and the paga taverns backing on the smaller canal would be throwing out their garbage from the preceding night. She-urts sometimes gather at such places for their pick of the remnants of feasts.

It would be less than an Ahn until the fullness of the tide. I quickly crossed two bridges, leading over canals, each joining the sea. Then I walked eastward, and took a left and a right, and crossed another small bridge. I was then on the northern shore of the Ribbon's alley. The Ribbon's alley, like most small canals, and many of the larger canals, does not join the sea directly but only by means of linkages with other canals. The larger canals in Port Kar, incidentally, have few bridges, and those they have are commonly swing bridges, which may be floated back against the canal's side. This makes it possible for merchant ships, round ships, with permanently fixed masts, to move within the city, and, from the military point of view, makes it possible to block canals and also, when drawn back, isolate given areas of the city by the canals which function then as moats. The swing bridges are normally fastened back, except from the eighth to the tenth Ahn and from the fifteenth to the seventeenth Ahn. Most families in Port Kar own their own boats. These boats are generally shallow-drafted, narrow and single-oared, the one oar being used to both propel and guide the boat. Even children use these boats. There are, of course, a variety of types of craft in the canals, ranging from ramships harbored in the courts of captains to the coracles of the poor, like leather tubs, propelled by the thrusting of a pole. Along the sides of the major canals there are commonly hundreds of boats moored. These are usually covered at night.

I saw her with several other girls, behind the rear court of the Silver Collar. They were fishing through wire trash containers. These had been left outside until, later, when the girls had finished with them, when the residues would be thrown into the canals. It was not an act of pure kindness on the part of the attendants at the paga tavern that the garbage had not been flung directly into the canals.

I looked at the girls. They were all comely. There were seven of them there, not including the one in whom I was interested. They wore rags of various sorts and colors; they had good legs; they were all barefoot.

I saw the blond-haired barbarian standing back. She, apparently, was repulsed by the garbage. She did not wish to touch it. The other girls paid her no attention.

Except for her failure to exhibit interest in the garbage she might have been only one she-urt among the others. She was as pretty, and as dirty, as the rest.

Suddenly she saw me. For an instant I saw she was frightened. Then she doubtless reassured herself that I could not know her. She was, after all, only another she-urt. Her thighs were unmarked.

She went then, as not noticing me, to the basket of garbage. She tried to saunter as a she-urt. Steeling herself she thrust her hand into the fresh, wet garbage. She looked up at me. She saw I was still watching her. In her hand there was a half of a yellow Gorean pear, the remains of a half moon of verr cheese imbedded in it. She, watching me, lifted it toward her mouth. I did not think it would taste badly. I saw she was ready to vomit.

Suddenly her wrist was seized by the girl, a tall, lovely girl, some four inches taller than she, in a brief white rag, who stood with her at the basket. "Who are you?" demanded the girl in the white rag. "You are not one with us." She took the pear from her, with the verr cheese in it. "You have not laid with the paga attendants for your garbage," she said. "Get out!" Any woman, even a free woman, if she is hungry enough, will do anything. The paga attendants knew this. "Get out!" said the girl in the white rag.

Not unrelieved, though I do not think she understood much of what was said to her, the blond barbarian backed

62

away. She reacted then, despite herself, with momentary horror, as the girl in the white rag bit thoughtlessly into the pear with verr cheese. Then, remembering herself, she tried to look disappointed. "Get out," said the girl in the white rag. "This is our territory." The other girls now, too, belligerently, began to gather around. "Get out," said the girl in the white rag, "or we will tie you and throw you into the canal."

The blond-haired barbarian backed away, not challenging them. The girls then returned to the garbage. The blond-haired girl looked at me. She did not know which way to go. She did not wish to pass me, but yet, on the other hand, she did not wish to leave a vicinity where the she-urts were common.

The buildings were on one side, the canal on the other. Then she began to walk toward me, to pass me. She tried to walk as a she-urt. She came closer and closer. She tried not to look at me. Then when she was quite close to me, she looked into my eyes. Then she looked down. I think she was not used to seeing how Gorean men looked at women, at least slaves and low women, such as she-urts, assessing them for the furs and the collar. Then she looked boldly up at me, brazenly, trying to pretend to be bored and casual. Then she tossed her head and walked past me. I watched her walk past me. Yes, I thought, she would make a good slave.

I began to follow her, some twenty or thirty feet behind her. Surely this made her nervous, for she was clearly aware of my continued nearness. Surely she must have suspected, and fearfully, that I knew who she was. But she could not know this for certain.

Behind us we heard two girls squabbling over garbage, contesting desirable scraps from the wire basket.

I would let her continue on her way. She was going in the direction which I would take her.

In a few moments, beside one of the canals leading down to the wharves, in the vicinity of the Spice Pier, we came on four she-urts. They were on their bellies beside the canal, fishing for garbage.

The blond-haired girl joined them. Her legs and ankles were very nice.

I knew she was intensely aware of my presence. Boldly she reached out into the water and picked up the edible rind of a larma. She looked at me. Then she bit into it, and then, tiny bite by tiny bite, she forced herself to chew and eat it. She swallowed the last bit of it. I had wanted her to eat garbage out of the canal. It would help her to learn that she was no longer on Earth.

I would now capture her. I wished Ulafi, if possible, to sail with the tide.

I busied myself in the sea bag and, not obviously, drew forth a small strip of binding fiber; then I drew the bag shut by its cords.

The girl had risen to her feet and, looking at me, and tossing her head, turned away.

I caught up with her quickly, took her by the back of the neck and, shoving, thrust her, stumbling, running obliquely, against the wall to my right. I tossed the sea bag to her left. As I had thrown her to the wall it would be most natural for her to bolt to the left. She stumbled over the sea bag and half fell. Then I had her left ankle in my left hand and her right ankle in my right hand. I dragged her back, towards me, on her belly. I then knelt across her body and jerked her small hands behind her. I tied them there.

A small fist struck me. "Let her go!" cried a girl. I felt hands scratching at me. Small fists pounded at me. The four girls who had been fishing for garbage in the canal leaped upon me. "Let her go!" cried one. "You can't simply take us!" cried another. "We are free! Free!" cried another.

I stood up, throwing them off me. I cuffed two back and two others crouched, ready to leap again to attack.

I stood over the blond girl, one leg on each side of her. She lay on her belly, her hands tied behind her.

Another girl leaped toward me and I struck her to one side with the back of my hand. She reeled away and sank to her knees, looking at me. I think she had never been struck that hard before. Her hand was at her mouth, blood between the fingers.

The other girl who, too, had been ready to attack, backed now uneasily away. She did not wish to come within reach of my arm.

"Let her go!" said the leader of the four girls. "You can't just take us! We are free! Free!"

"We will call a guardsman!" cried another.

I grinned. How delightful are women. How weak they are. How fit they are to be made slaves.

"I am sorry I struck you as hard as I did," I told the girl I had last struck. "I lost my patience," I said. "I am sorry." She, after all, was not a slave. She was a free woman. Slaves,

64

of course, may be struck as long and as hard as one wishes. The girl between my feet, a slave, would learn that.

"Free her," said the leader of the girls, pointing to the blond-haired barbarian helpless between my feet.

"You cannot just take her," said another girl. "She is a free woman."

"Do not fret your heads about her, my pretty, little she-urts," I said. "She is not a free woman. She is an unmarked slave, escaped from Ulafi of Schendi."

"Is it true?" asked the leader of the she-urts.

"Yes," I said. "Follow me, if you will, to the praetor station, where this fact may be made clear to you."

"Are you a slave?" asked the leader of the girls to the girl between my feet.

"She does not speak Gorean," I said, "or much of it. I do not think she understands you."

The girl between my feet was crying.

"If she is a slave," said one of the girls, "she had best learn Gorean quickly."

I thought that was true.

"I hope for your sake," said the leader of the she-urts to the girl, "that you are not a slave." Then she said to the other girls, "Find pieces of rope."

"Are we going to the praetor station?" asked one of the girls, uneasily.

"Of course," said the leader.

"I do not want to go to the praetor station," said one of the girls.

"We have done nothing," said the leader. "We have nothing to fear."

"There are men there," said one of the girls.

"We have men to fear," said another.

"We are going," said the leader, determinedly.

I picked up the Earth-girl slave, and threw her over my shoulder. She squirmed helplessly, crying. I picked up my sea bag then, and, the girl on my shoulder, the sea bag in my left hand, made my way toward the pier of the Red Urt.

"Are her thighs marked?" asked the praetor.

"No," said a guardsman. He had already made this determination.

The girl stood, her hands bound behind her, in the brief rag of the she-urt, before the tribunal of the praetor. The neck strap of a guardsman was on her throat.

"Is this your slave?" asked the praetor of Ulafi of Schendi.

"Yes," said he.

"How do I know she is a slave?" asked the praetor. "Her body, her movements, do not suggest that she is a slave. She seems too tight, too cold, too rigid, to be a slave."

"She was free, captured by Bejar, in his seizure of the *Blossoms of Telnus*," said Ulafi. "She is new to her condition."

"Is Bejar present?" asked the praetor.

"No," said a man. Bejar had left the port yesterday, to again try his luck upon gleaming Thassa, the sea.

"Her measurements, exactly, fit those of the slave," said a guardsman. He lifted the tape measure, marked in horts, which had been applied, but moments before, to the girl's body.

The praetor nodded. This was excellent evidence. The girl's height, ankles, wrists, throat, hips, waist and bust had been measured. She had even been thrown on a grain scale and weighed.

The praetor looked down at the girl. He pointed to her. "Kajira?" he asked. "Kajira?"

She shook her head vigorously. That much Gorean she at least understood. She denied being a slave girl.

The praetor made a small sign to one of the guardsmen.

"Leash!" said the fellow, suddenly, harshly, behind the girl, in Gorean.

She jumped, startled, and cried out, frightened, but she did not, as a reflex, lift her head, turning it to the left, nor did the muscles in her upper arms suddenly move as though thrusting her wrists behind her, to await the two snaps of the slave bracelets.

"Nadu!" snapped the guard. But the girl had not, involuntarily, begun to kneel.

"I have her slave papers here," said Ulafi, "delivered with her this morning by Vart's man."

He handed them to the praetor.

"She does not respond as a slave because she has not yet learned her slavery," said Ulafi. "She has not yet learned the collar and the whip."

The praetor examined the papers. In Ar slaves are often fingerprinted. The prints are contained in the papers.

"Does anyone know if this is Ulafi's slave?" asked the praetor.

I did not wish to speak, for I would, then, have revealed

66

myself as having been at the sale. I preferred for this to be unknown.

The four she-urts, with which the blond-haired barbarian had fished for garbage in the canal, stood about.

"She should have been marked," said the praetor. "She should have been collared."

"I have a collar here," said Ulafi, lifting a steel slave collar. It was a shipping collar. It had five palms on it, and the sign of Schendi, the shackle and scimitar. The girl who wore it would be clearly identified as a portion of Ulafi's cargo.

"I wish to sail with the tide," said Ulafi. "In less than half an Ahn it will be full."

"I am sorry," said the praetor.

"Has not Vart been sent for," asked Ulafi, "to confirm my words?"

"He has been sent for," said the praetor.

From some eighty or so yards away, from the tiny shop of a metal worker, I heard a girl scream. I knew the sound. A girl had been marked. She who had been the Lady Sasi, the little she-urt who had been the accomplice of Turgus of Port Kar, had been branded.

"I am afraid we must release this woman," said the praetor, looking down at the girl. "It is unfortunate, as she is attractive."

"Test her for slave heat," suggested a man.

"That is not appropriate," said the praetor, "if she is free."

"Make her squirm," said the man. "See if she is slave hot."

"No," said the praetor.

The praetor looked at the girl. He looked at Ulafi.

"I am afraid I must order her release," he said.

"No!" said Ulafi.

"Wait," said a man. "It is Vart!"

The girl shrank back, miserably, her hands tied behind her back, the neck strap on her throat, before Vart, who had pushed through the crowd.

"Do you know this girl?" asked the praetor of Vart.

"Of course," said Vart. "She is a slave, sold last night to this captain." He indicated Ulafi of Schendi. "I got a silver tarsk for her."

The praetor nodded to a guardsman. He thrust the girl down to her knees. She was in the presence of free men. With the neck strap he pulled her head down and tied it down, fastening it to her ankles by means of the neck strap; the leather between her neck and ankles, which were now crossed and bound, was short and taut. Her rag, the brown, torn tunic of the she-urt, stolen from she who had been Sasi, was then cut from her. She knelt bound then, and naked, in one of several Gorean submission positions.

"The slave is awarded to Ulafi of Schendi," ruled the praetor.

There were cheers from the men present, and Gorean applause, the striking of the left shoulder with the right hand.

"My thanks, Praetor," said Ulafi, receiving back the slave papers from the magistrate.

"Slave! Slave!" screamed the leader of the she-urts to the bound girl. "Slave! Slave!" they cried.

"To think we let you fish garbage with us, when you were only a slave!" cried the leader.

Then the she-urts who had accompanied me to the station of the praetor, kicking and striking with their ropes, fell upon the bound slave.

She wept, kicked and struck. "Slave! Slave!" they cried.

"Get back!" called the praetor, angrily, to them. "Get back, or we will collar you all!"

The girls, swiftly, shrank back, fearfully. But they continued to look with hatred on the slave.

The blond girl tried to make herself even smaller and more submissive, that she be not more abused. She sobbed. She had had a taste of the feelings of free women towards a slave, which she was.

"Captain Ulafi," said the praetor.

"Yes, Praetor," said Ulafi.

"Have her marked before you leave port," he said.

"Yes, Praetor," said Ulafi. He turned to his first officer. "Make ready to leave port," he said. "We have twenty Ahn."

"Yes, Captain," said the man.

"Bring an ankle rack," said Ulafi to one of the guardsmen. One was brought.

"Put her in it," said Ulafi. The guardsman removed his neck strap from her throat, freeing, too, her ankles. He untied her hands. Lifting her under the stomach he held her ankles near the rack; another guardsman placed her ankles in the semicircular openings in the bottom block and then swung shut the top block, with its matching semicircular openings, over them. He secured the top block, hinged at the left, to the bottom block, with a metal bolt on a chain, thrust through the staple on the lower block, over the hasp, swung down from the upper block.

The guardsman who had held the girl then ceased to support her. She made a little cry. The weight of her upper body was then on the palms of her hands, her arms stiff. Her ankles were locked in the rack. This helped to support her weight. Her ankles protruded behind the rack. Her feet were small and pretty. She looked about, helplessly.

"Bring the scimitar of discipline," said Ulafi. This was brought by a guardsman. Ulafi showed the heavy, curved blade to the girl. She looked at it with horror.

"You should not have run away, little white slave," he said.

"No, no!" she said, in English.

He went behind her and, gently, that he not cut her, laid the blade upon her ankles.

"No, no!" she cried. "Please, don't! Please, don't! I will be good! I will be good!"

She tried to turn her head, to look behind her. "I will not run away again!" she cried. "Please, please," she whimpered, "do not cut off my feet."

Ulafi handed the scimitar to one of the guardsmen. He then went to the girl's head, taking the dagger from his sash.

She was trembling in misery.

Ulafi pointed to the high desk of the praetor. Then he looked at her. "Kajira?" he asked.

The girl had lied before the desk of the praetor. She had denied being a Kajira, a slave girl.

She twisted her head upward, toward the praetor's desk. "Forgive me! Forgive me!" she begged.

"Kajira?" asked Ulafi.

"Yes, yes," she sobbed. Then she cried out, "La Kajira! La Kajira!" This was a bit of Gorean known to her. 'I am a slave girl.'

Ulafi, with his dagger, but not cutting her, put it first to her right ear, and then to the side of her small nose, and then to the left ear.

"Don't hurt me," she begged. "I'm sorry I lied! Forgive me, forgive me! La Kajira! La Kajira!"

Ulafi stood up, replacing the dagger in his sash. The girl had now learned that her feet might be cut off for running away, that her ears and nose might be cut from her for lying. She was still an ignorant girl, of course, but she now knew a little more of what it might be to be a slave on Gor.

"Release her from the rack," said Ulafi. The rack was opened and the girl collapsed, shuddering, on the wharf.

"Tie her hands and fasten her at a dock ring," said Ulafi, to his second officer, and two seamen, one of whom was the fellow who had passed me on the walkway of the Rim canal, on the way to the pier of the Red Urt. "Then whip her," said Ulafi. "Then bring her to the shop of the metal worker. I shall await you there. Bring, too, a pole and cage to the shop."

"Yes, Captain," said the second officer.

"Come with me, if you would," said Ulafi to me.

I followed him to the shop of the metal worker. Outside the shop, stripped, weeping, chained by the neck to a ring, freshly branded, was the girl who had been the Lady Sasi, of Port Kar. A guardsman stood near her. If she was not soon sold for the cost of her branding she would be taken and put on the public shelves, large, flat steps, leading down to the water, near where the Central canal meets Thassa, the sea. She was a cheap slave, but she was pretty. I did not think she should have attempted to inconvenience honest citizens. When she saw me she tried to cover herself and crouch small. I smiled. Did she not know she was branded?

"Heat an iron," said Ulafi to the metal worker, a brawny fellow in a leather apron.

"Tal," said the man to me.

"Tal," said I to him.

"We always keep an iron hot," said the metal worker. But he did turn to his assistant, a lad of some twelve years. "Heat the coals," said he to him. The lad took a bellows and, opening and closing it, forced air into the conical forge. The handles of some six irons, their heads and a portion of their shafts buried in the coals, could be seen.

I looked out the door of the shop. I could see the girl, about one hundred and fifty yards away, her wrists crossed and bound before her, tied by the wrists to a heavy ring at the side of the pier. She knelt. Then the first stroke of the whip hit her. She screamed. Then she could scream no more but was twisting, gasping, on her stomach, and side and back, under the blows of the whip. I think she had not understood before what it might mean, truly, to be whipped. Men passed her, going about their business. The disciplining of a slave girl on Gor is not that unusual a sight.

"I have five brands," said the metal worker, "the common Kajira brand, the Dina, the Palm, the mark of Treve, the mark of Port Kar."

"We have a common girl to brand," said Ulafi. "Let it be the common Kajira brand."

I could see that the girl had now been unbound from the ring. She could apparently not walk. One of the seamen had thrown her over his shoulder and was bringing her toward the shop. She was in shock. I think she had not realized what the whip could do to her.

Yet the beating had been merciful and brief. I doubt that she was struck more than ten or fifteen times.

I think the purpose of the whipping had been little more than to teach her what the whip could feel like. A girl who knows what the whip can feel like strives to be pleasing to the master.

I could see the lateen sails on Ulafi's ship loosened on their yards.

Men stood by the mooring ropes.

Two sailors, behind the second officer, carried a slave cage. It was supported on a pole, the ends of which rested on their shoulders.

The girl was brought into the shop and stood in the branding rack, which was then locked on her, holding her upright. The metal worker placed her wrists behind her in the wrist clamps, adjustable, each on their vertical, flat metal bar. He screwed shut the clamps. She winced. He then shackled her feet on the rotating metal platform.

"Left thigh or right thigh?" he asked.

"Left thigh," said Ulafi. Slave girls are commonly branded on the left thigh. Sometimes they are branded on the right thigh, or lower left abdomen.

The metal worker turned the apparatus, spinning the shaft, with its attached, circular metal platform. The girl's left thigh now faced us. It was an excellent thigh. It would take the mark well. The metal worker then, with a wheel, tightening it, locked the device in place, so that it could not turn.

I looked at the girl's eyes. She hardly knew what was being done to her.

The metal worker drew out an iron and looked at it. "Soon," he said, putting it back.

I looked at the girl. She had tried to run away. She had lied at the praetor's desk. Yet her feet had not been removed. Her nose and ears had not been cut from her. She had been shown incredible mercy. She had only been whipped. Her transgressions, of course, had been first offenses, and she was only an ignorant barbarian. I think now, however, she clearly

71

understood that Gorean men are not permissive, and that her second offenses in such matters would not be likely to be regarded with such lenience.

"She is in shock, or half in shock," I said.

"Yes," said the metal worker. "She should be able to feel the mark."

He took the girl by her hair and, by it, cruelly, shook her head; then he slapped her, sharply, twice. She whimpered.

"May I?" I asked. I pointed to a bucket of water nearby, used in tempering.

"Surely," said the metal worker.

I threw the cold water over the girl who, shuddering and sputtering, pulled back in the branding rack.

She looked at me, frightened. But her eyes were now clear. She twisted, wincing. She could now feel the pain of the whipping which she had endured. She sobbed. But she was no longer numb, or in shock. She was now a fully conscious slave, ready for her branding.

"The iron is ready," said the metal worker. It was a beautiful iron, and white hot.

Ulafi threw the metal worker a copper tarsk. "My friend here," said Ulafi, indicating me, "will use the iron."

I looked at him. He smiled. "You are of the metal workers, are you not?" he asked.

"Perhaps," I smiled. He had told me earlier that I was not of the metal workers.

"We are ready to sail," said Ulafi's first officer, who had come to report.

"Good," said Ulafi.

I donned leather gloves and took the iron from the metal worker, who cheerfully surrendered it. He assumed I was, because of my garb, of his caste.

Ulafi watched me, to see what I would do.

I held the iron before the girl, that she might see it. She shrank back. "No, no," she whimpered. "Please don't touch me with it."

The girl is commonly shown the iron, that she may understand its might, its heat and meaning.

"Please, no!" she cried.

I looked upon her. I did not then think of her as an agent of Kurii. I saw her only as a beautiful woman, fit for the brand.

She tried, unsuccessfully, to struggle. She could move her wrists, her upper body and feet somewhat, but she could not move her thighs, at all. They were, because of the construction of the branding rack, held perfectly immobile. They would await the kiss of the iron.

"Please, no," she whimpered.

Then I branded her.

"An excellent mark," said Ulafi.

While she still sobbed and screamed the metal worker freed her wrists of the clamps. Ulafi put her immediately in slave bracelets, braceleting her hands behind her, that she not tear at the brand. The metal worker then freed her thighs of the rack, and she sank, sobbing, to her knees. He freed her ankles of the shackles which had held them at the circular, metal platform. Ulafi then, pushing her head down, fastened the sturdy, steel shipping collar on her throat, snapping it shut behind the back of her neck. It had five palms on it, and the sign of Schendi, the shackle and scimitar.

"Put her in the cage and load her," said Ulafi.

The girl was then taken, braceleted, and thrust into the tiny slave cage, which was then locked shut. She knelt, sobbing, in the cage. The two sailors then lifted the cage on its poles, and, kneeling, she was lifted within it. I looked at her. I saw in her eyes that she had begun to suspect what it might mean to be a slave girl.

She was carried to the ship.

I did not think she would now escape. I thought now she could be used easily to help locate Shaba, the geographer of Anango, the equatorial explorer. In my sea bag were the notes for him, made out to bankers of Schendi. In my sea bag, too, was the false ring, which the girl had carried.

"I am grateful to you for having apprehended the slave," said Ulafi to me.

"It was nothing," I said.

"You also marked her superbly," he said. "Doubtless, in time, she will grow quite proud of that brand."

I shrugged.

"Captain," said I.

"Yes," said he.

"I would still like to book passage with you to Schendi," I said.

He smiled. "You are welcome to do so," he said.

"Thank you," I said.

"It will cost you a silver tarsk," he said.

"Oh," I said.

He shrugged. "I am a merchant," he explained.

I gave him a silver tarsk, and he turned about and went down to the ship.

"I wish you well," I said to the metal worker.

"I wish you well," said he to me. I was pleased that I had branded women before.

I wondered how much Ulafi knew.

I then left the shop of the metal worker.

Outside I saw the guardsman unchaining the girl who had been the she-urt, Sasi. Her hands were now bound before her body, and she already had his strap on her throat.

"You did not sell her?" I asked.

"Who would want a she-urt?" he asked. "I am going to take her now to the public shelves."

Looking at me the small, lovely, dark-haired girl drew back.

"What do you want for her?" I asked.

"It cost a copper tarsk to brand her," he said.

I looked at her. She looked at me, and trembled, and shook her head, negatively.

I threw him a copper tarsk.

"She is yours," he said.

He took his strap off her throat, and unbound her hands.

"Submit," I told her.

She knelt before me, back on her heels, arms extended, head down, between her arms, wrists crossed, as though for binding.

"I submit to you, Master," she said.

I tied her hands together; she then lowered her bound wrists; I pulled up her head. I held before her an opened collar, withdrawn from my sea bag. I had had one prepared.

"Can you read?" I asked her.

"No, Master," she said.

"It says," I said, " 'I am the girl of Tarl of Teletus.' "

"Yes, Master," she said.

I then collared her. I had thought that some wench, probably one to be purchased in Schendi, would have been a useful addition to my disguise, as an aid in establishing and confirming my pretended identity as a metal worker from the island of Teletus. This little wench though, now locked in my collar, I thought would serve the purpose well. There was no particular reason to wait to Schendi before buying a girl. Besides, the collar on her might help to convince Ulafi, who seemed to me a clever and suspicious man, that, whatever I might be, I was a reasonably straightforward and honest

74

fellow. I traveled with a girl who wore a name collar.

"Are there papers on her?" I asked the guardsman.

"No," said the guardsman. Most Gorean slaves do not have papers. The brand and collar are deemed sufficient.

I pulled the little slave to her feet, and pointed out the *Palms of Schendi*.

"Do you see that ship?" I asked.

"Yes," she said.

"Run there as fast as your little legs will carry you," I said. "And tell them to cage you."

"Yes, Master," she said, and ran, sobbing, toward the ship.

I then shouldered my sea bag and followed her. A moment after I had trod the gangplank, it was drawn up. The railing was shut and fastened.

A sailor thrust the small dark-haired slave into a small cage, and snapped shut the padlock, securing it. It was next to another cage, that which contained the blond barbarian. The dark-haired girl looked at her, startled. "You!" she said. The blond girl drew back, as she could, in her cage. "Kajira!" hissed the dark-haired girl, angrily, at her. It was the blond who had taken her garment as she had lain trussed with Turgus of Port Kar, while awaiting the arrival of the guardsmen who would take them into custody. There were tears in the eyes of the blond girl. She pulled with her wrists against the bracelets which held her hands behind her. Then she looked angrily at the dark-haired girl. "Kajira!" she said to her, angrily.

Mooring ropes were cast off.

Sailors, at the port rail, with three poles, thrust the *Palms of Schendi* away from the dock. Canvas fell from the long, sloping yards.

The two helmsmen were at their rudders.

The first officer directed the crew. The captain, Ulafi of Schendi, stood upon the stern castle.

"Ready," called the second officer.

Ten sailors, on a side, slid oars outboard.

"Stroke," called the second officer, he acting as oar master.

The long oars dipped into Thassa and rose, dripping, from the greenish sea. The vessel moved slowly outward, into wider waters. A breeze from the east, over Port Kar, swelled the sails. They lifted and billowed.

"Oars inboard!" called the second officer.

The helmsman guided the ship to the right of the line of white and red buoys.

I watched Port Kar, its low buildings, fall behind. The sky was very blue.

I went to the cage which contained the girl I had bought. She looked up at me. Her wrists were still bound.

"I do not have a name," she said. It was true. She was as nameless as a tabuk doe or a she-verr. I had bought her. I had not yet given her a name.

"You are Sasi," I told her, naming her.

"Yes, Master," she said, putting her head down. She would wear her old name, but it had now been put on her as a slave name, by my will.

The second officer, now freed of his duties as oar master, approached me. He indicated Sasi. "There is an extra charge," said he, "for the keeping and feeding of livestock. It will cost you an extra copper tarsk."

"Of course," I said. I handed him, from my pouch, a copper tarsk. He turned about, and left.

I looked down at the other cage, and the blond-haired barbarian, who had been an agent for Kurii, kneeling, naked, her wrists braceleted behind her, put her head down. I looked at the brand, fresh in her burned thigh. It was small, precise, deep, clean and sharp, a severe, lovely mark, unmistakable and clear; her thigh now well proclaimed what she was, a Gorean slave.

Ulafi, merchant and captain, stood upon the deck of the stern castle.

I stood at the rail. Canvas snapped in the wind over my head. The masts and timbers of the ship creaked. I smelled the sharp freshness of gleaming Thassa, the sea. I heard her waters lick at the strakes. A sailor began to sing a song of Schendi, and it was taken up by others.

I watched Port Kar drop behind.

5

WE PLY TOWARD SCHENDI

"Lesha," snapped the second officer to the blond girl.

She spun from facing him, and lifted her chin, turning her head to the left, placing her wrists behind her, as though for snapping them into slave bracelets.

"Nadu!" he snapped.

She swiftly turned, facing him, and dropped to her knees. She knelt back on her heels, her back straight, her hands on her thighs, her head up, her knees wide.

It was the position of the pleasure slave.

"Sula, Kajira!" said the man.

She slid her legs from under her and lay on her back, her hands at her sides, palms up, her legs open.

"Bara, Kajira!" he said.

She rolled quickly to her stomach, placing her wrists behind her, crossed, and crossing her ankles, ready to be bound.

"She is a pretty thing," said Ulafi, and turned away.

"Yes," I said.

"Sula!" said the man. "Bara! Nadu! Lesha! Nadu! Bara! Sula! Nadu!"

The girl was gasping. There were tears in her eyes, as she knelt on the deck. Once she had been struck when her transition between two of the movements had been insufficiently beautiful. Another time she had been struck when her response had been insufficiently prompt.

The trip south towards Schendi is a long one, consuming several days, even with fair winds, which we had had.

"Do you think she will make a good slave?" asked Sasi, standing beside me, eating a larma.

"Perhaps, in time," I said. "How are her lessons in Gorean coming along?"

Sasi shrugged. "I am teaching her as I can," she said. "Barbarians are so stupid."

I had had Sasi, at the invitation of Ulafi, spend several hours a day tutoring the blond girl in Gorean. Sasi enjoyed this, standing over the blond girl with a strap, striking her when she made mistakes. When she had had a good session Ulafi would sometimes, when he thought of it, throw her a bit of cake or pastry, which she would gratefully receive. She would then kneel before Ulafi and kiss his feet, clutching the bit of cake or pastry. "Thank you, Master," she would say. She would then kneel before Sasi, her teacher, and offer her the bit of cake or pastry, which Sasi would take, taking most of it and returning a portion of it to her. "Thank you, Mistress," she would say, for Sasi was first girl. She would then creep to her cage, and be locked within it. She would lie curled up in it, a lovely, helpless slave, and try to make the bit of cake or pastry last as long as possible.

When more than one slave girl stands in a relationship of

77

slave girls, as when they serve in the same shop or house, or adorn the same rich man's pleasure gardens, it is common for the master, or masters, to appoint a "first girl." Her authority is then to the other girls as is that of the master. This tends to reduce squabbling. The first girl is usually, though not always, the favorite of the master. There is usually much competition to be first girl. First girls can be cruel and petty but, commonly, they attempt to govern with intelligence and justice. They know that another girl, at the master's whim, may become first girl, and that they themselves may then be under her almost abolute power. In my own house I often rotated the position of first girl among my slaves who were native Goreans. I never made an Earth-girl slave first girl. This is fitting. Let them be always as the slaves of slaves.

I looked at the Earth girl, who had been left kneeling on the deck, the second officer having left her there. She did not move a muscle. She was being well trained.

"I hate her," said Sasi.

"Why?" I asked.

"She is so stupid and slow," said Sasi.

"Things are hard for her," I told Sasi. "Remember that she is only a barbarian."

"She is stupid," said Sasi.

"I do not think she is stupid," I said.

"She is slow," said Sasi.

"She is learning," I said.

"She will always be a pitiful, clumsy slave," said Sasi.

"Perhaps," I said. "I do not know." Frankly I did not think she was, even now, a pitiful, clumsy slave. She seemed to me to learn quickly. I felt that she would, in time, particularly if put under sex conquest, prove superb.

"Are you going to train me a little tonight, Master?" asked Sasi.

"Perhaps," I said.

I had already brought her past the limitations of the free woman's heat.

Sometimes at night I would pull her forth from her cage, the key to which had been given to me, use her, and then put her back in the cage.

After the first three or four days she had begun to grow rather fond of her collar. It is an interesting transition in a woman.

I looked at the blond-haired slave, kneeling in the position of the pleasure slave.

78

Sasi bit into the larma fruit.

The first two days the blond-haired girl could not eat. She had shrunk back in horror from the gruel of meal and fish, fit provender for slaves, thrust in its pan into her cage. She had looked at me. Compared to it the garbage of Port Kar had been *haut cuisine*. But on the third day she had finished it, thrusting it with her fingers into her mouth and licking the pan clean. Slaves are often not permitted utensils. Seeing that the pan was clean, Ulafi had then had his second officer commence her lessons. The next day Sasi, at Ulafi's request of me, had begun to improve her Gorean.

"Do you think she is pretty, Master?" asked Sasi.

"Yes," I said. I did think she was pretty. She seemed more lovely now than when we had left Port Kar. It was probably the fresh air, the exercise and the finding of herself under the absolute domination of men. The training, too, doubtless helped.

The second officer now returned to the kneeling girl and, standing behind her, loosely, with a movement of the slave whip, looped the five broad blades of the whip about her neck. He then held the loops against the whip's staff, her neck encircled by them. He then, pulling against the side of her neck, threw her to his feet.

"What are you?" he asked.

"A slave girl, Master," she said, her neck in the loops of the whip.

"What is a slave girl?" he asked.

"A girl who is owned," she said.

"Are you a slave girl?" he asked.

"Yes, Master," she said.

"Then you are owned," he said.

"Yes, Master," she said.

"Who owns you?" he asked.

"Ulafi of Schendi," she said.

"Who trains you?" he asked.

"Shoka of Schendi," she said.

"Do you have a brand?"

"Yes, Master."

"Why?"

"Because I am a slave."

"Do you wear a collar?"

"Yes, Master."

"What sort of collar do you wear?"

"A shipping collar, Master. It shows that I am a portion

79

of the cargo of the *Palms of Schendi*." I thought the girl's Gorean, though the responses were generally simple, had improved considerably in the last few days.

"What is the common purpose of a collar?"

"The collar has four common purposes, Master," she said. "First, it visibly designates me as a slave, as a brand might not, if it should be covered by clothing. Second, it impresses my slavery upon me. Thirdly, it identifies my master. Fourthly—fourthly—"

"Fourthly?" he asked.

"Fourthly," she said, "it makes it easier to leash me."

He kicked her in the side. She winced. Her response had been slow.

"Do you like being a slave girl?" he asked.

"Yes, Master," she said. She sobbed. She was again kicked.

"Yes, Master! Yes, Master!" she cried.

"What does a slave girl want more than anything?" he asked.

"To please men," she said.

"What are you?" he asked.

"A slave girl," she said.

"What do you want more than anything?" he asked.

"To please men!" she cried.

"Nadu!" he cried, loosening the whip coils on her throat.

She swiftly knelt, back on her heels, back straight, head high, hands on her thighs, knees wide.

He then left her again, and she remained kneeling. She moved no muscle.

"Is she more pretty than I, Master?" asked Sasi.

"Your beauties are quite different," I said. "I think you are both quite pretty. I think you will both make superb little slaves."

"Oh," said Sasi.

An additional utility of the collar, though it did not count as one of its four common purposes, was that it made it easier to put the girl in various ties. For example, one can use it to tie her hands before her throat, or at the sides or back of her neck. One can use it with, say, rope or chain, to fasten girls together. One can tie her feet to her collar, and so on. If the feet are tied to the collar the knot is always in the front, so that the pressure will be against the back of the girl's neck and not the front. The purpose of such a tie is to hold the slave, not choke her. Gorean men are not clumsy in their binding of women.

80

I looked at the kneeling, blond-haired girl. How miserable, superficially, she seemed in her slavery. I supposed that if she were asked, outside the context of training, where certain answers are prescribed, if she liked being a slave girl, she would have denied it vehemently, perhaps with tears. Doubtless she would have begged piteously for her freedom. Yet I recalled that when her trainer, Shoka of Schendi, had flung her to his feet by the whip coils on her neck she had fallen in a certain way, and had lain at his feet in a certain fashion. I recalled the position of her wrists and palms, and the look in her eyes, as she had looked up at him. Her hip had been turned. Both legs had been drawn back, but one more than the other. Her toes had been pointed, accentuating the turn of her calf. She had not fallen clumsily. She had not lain clumsily at his feet. She had lain at his feet, and looked at him, as a slave. She had not been trained to do that. I did not even think she was aware of this sort of thing.

"Do you like me, Master?" asked Sasi.

"Yes," I said, "particularly since you have had a bath."

"Oh, Master," she said.

I had scrubbed her the first day out from Port Kar, she kneeling in a tub, with sea water and a deck brush.

"What was the last time you had a bath?" I asked her.

"A girl pushed me in the South canal a year ago," she said.

"I see," I said.

"Is Master fastidious?" she asked.

"Not particularly," I said, "but I will expect you to keep yourself reasonably clean from now on. You are no longer a free woman."

"No, Master," she said.

"You are now a slave girl," I said.

"Yes, Master," she said. She knew that slave girls must be attentive to matters of appearance, health, cleanliness and hygiene. They are no longer free women.

Yesterday the blond-haired girl had been permitted to walk about the deck. I had stopped near her and she had, immediately, knelt, for she was in the presence of a free man. I had walked slowly about her. She was very nice. I had then stood before her, and she had, suddenly, dropped her eyes. I saw a tiny movement in her hands, on her thighs, as though she would turn them, exposing the palms to me, but then she pressed them down her thighs, hard. I crouched beside her. Then I smiled. I smelled slave heat. Then I got up and went about my business. I saw her later leaning against the main

81

mast. Later I looked at it, and saw that she had made marks in it with her nails.

"I myself prefer the training of the furs," said Sasi, biting again into the larma fruit.

The blond-haired girl still knelt in the position of the pleasure slave. For the time her trainer had forgotten about her.

"You just do not like being struck with the whip," I told her.

"Perhaps that is it," she laughed. "Master," she said.

"Yes," I said.

"If I am good, you will not whip me, will you?" she asked.

"I might," I said.

"Oh," she said.

Sometimes I had had Sasi train with the blond-haired girl, but generally I did not. Ulafi had no objection to her sharing the barbarian's training. Indeed, he had even suggested the arrangement. Graciously he had made no charge for this. On the other hand I had not charged him for the instruction which Sasi was giving the blond barbarian in Gorean. Our arrangement, thus, though tacit, was a tidy one.

Sasi, Gorean, even in the collar a few days, was already far beyond the blond-haired barbarian. It was for this reason that I had had her seldom train with the barbarian. There had simply not been much point to it. The barbarian still needed the simplest and most elementary lessons of slave training.

Shoka, recollecting her, had now returned to the vicinity of the blond-haired barbarian. She did not know he was behind her. "Bara!" he called. "Sula! Nadu! Lesha! Sula! Bara! Nadu!" Instantaneously she performed. Then she was again kneeling, as before.

"Not bad," said Sasi, chewing on the larma.

"Yes," I said. Though Sasi was well advanced beyond the blond barbarian, I suspected that the blond barbarian, moving slowly at first, might in time catch up with her, and perhaps even surpass her. The blond barbarian, I suspected, had unusual slave potential.

Shoka then, without warning, struck her with his whip. She did not break position, but she gasped. Her face was startled, her eyes were wild. She did not know why she had been struck. In a sense there had been no reason. One does not need a reason to strike a slave. But in another sense, in the training situation, there had been a reason, that she was subject to discipline, and that it could be meted out by the master purely at his whim or caprice. She tensed. She did not know, Shoka behind her, if she would be struck again.

But Shoka took her by the hair and, she, pulled to her feet, bent over, was conducted to her cage. There he released her and she fell to her hands and knees, to crawl into the cage, to be locked within.

"May I speak, Master?" she asked.

"Yes," he said.

"Why was I struck?" she asked.

"Kiss my feet," he said.

She did so.

Then she looked up at him.

"It pleased me," he said.

"Yes, Master," she said.

"Into the cage, Slave," he said.

"Yes, Master," she said.

In a moment she had been locked within. I saw her looking after him. Then she looked at me, too, and then she looked down. I saw her lie on her side in the cage, her legs drawn up. The cage is very tiny.

I looked out, over the rail. There were white clouds in the sky, and the sky was very blue. We would make Schendi, if the winds held, in four days.

"Master," said Sasi.

"Yes," I said. I turned to look at her.

She looked up at me. She smiled. "If I get to be good," she said, "may I have a garment?"

"Perhaps," I said.

"I think I would like a garment," she said, chewing on the larma fruit.

"It would give me something to tear off you," I admitted.

She looked up at me, smiling.

"The collar looks well on you, Sasi," I said. "You could have been born in a collar."

"For all practical purposes," she said, "I was."

"I do not understand," I said.

"I am a woman," she said, chewing on the fruit.

"Why are you bound for Schendi?" asked Ulafi of me. It was late evening now. I stood again by the rail.

"I have never been there," I said.

"You are not of the metal workers," he said.

"Oh?" I asked.

"Perhaps you know Chungu," said he.

"The hand on watch," I said.

"He," said Ulafi.

"By sight," I said. I did remember him quite well. He was the fellow who had passed me on the northern walkway of the Rim canal, when I had been on my way to the pier of the Red Urt. I had seen him, too, later, in the vicinity of the desk of the wharf praetor.

"Before the general alarm was permitted to sound in Port Kar, in the matter of apprising the wharves of the news of an escaped slave," said Ulafi, "we, naturally, conducted a search for her ourselves. We expected to pick her up without difficulty in a few minutes, you understand."

"Of course," I said.

"She was naked, and a barbarian," said Ulafi. "Where could she go? What could she do?"

"Of course," I said.

"Yet she was clever," said Ulafi.

"Yes," I said. She had stolen a garment and concealed herself, unmarked and uncollared, among she-urts. I had no doubt that she was a highly intelligent girl. That intelligence could now be applied, now that she was a slave, to the pleasing of masters.

"We did not wish to annoy the praetor," said Ulafi.

"It would be embarrassing, too, I suspect," I said, "for one of Schendi, and one who was a captain, too, to call public attention to the fact that he had lost a girl."

"Would you like to be thrown overboard?" asked Ulafi.

"No," I said, "I would not like that."

"Would this not have been embarrassing for anyone?" asked Ulafi.

"Of course," I said. "Forgive me, Captain."

"When we decided to enlist the aid of guardsmen, and inquire into the reports of citizens," said Ulafi, "we had the general alarm rung. One of my men, Chungu, was hunting for the girl in the vicinity of the Rim canal. In that area he saw two assailants, a man and his female accomplice, subdued by one who wore the garb of the metal workers. Further, this deed was apparently performed with dispatch, a dispatch scarcely to be expected of one who was of the metal workers. Soon the fellow who wore the garb of the metal workers had left. He had paused little longer than was necessary to awaken the girl to consciousness, rape her and tie her to the man whose accomplice she had been."

84

"Oh," I said.

"When the alarm rang," said Ulafi, "Chungu returned to the ship."

"You were the fellow in the garb of the metal workers," said Ulafi.

"Yes," I said.

"When the assailants were brought to the praetor's desk, too," said he, "it was seen that their wrists had been bound with capture knots."

"I see," I said.

"Such knots are tied by a warrior," he said.

"Perhaps," I said.

"Why are you bound for Schendi?" asked Ulafi.

"If you knew me not of the metal workers," I asked, "why did you permit me to mark the blond-haired slave?"

"I wished to see what you would do," he said.

"You risked a badly marked thigh on the girl," I said.

"The mark was perfect," said Ulafi.

"Thus you see," said I, "that I am truly of the metal workers."

"No," said Ulafi. "I knew you were not of the metal workers. Thus I saw that you were truly of the warriors."

"Should I have blurred the brand?" I asked.

"That would have been a shame," said he, smiling.

"True," I grinned. All men like a well-marked girl.

"Too," said he, "that would have shown, had you done poorly, that you were not of the metal workers."

"Might I not have been a slaver, or one who did work with them?" I asked.

"Perhaps," said Ulafi, "but that would not have well fitted in with the dispatch with which the assailants were handled, or the knotting on their wrists, or, indeed, with your general mien, how you walk and sit, and look about yourself, your eyes, how you handle yourself."

I looked out to sea. The three moons were high abeam. The sea was sparkling.

"Was it important to you to leave Port Kar when you did?" asked Ulafi.

"I think so," I said.

"Why did you choose to voyage to Schendi?" he asked.

"Are there not fortunes to be made there?" I asked.

"In Schendi," said Ulafi, "there are fortunes and there are dangers."

"Dangers?" I asked.

"Yes," said Ulafi, "even from the interior, from the ubarate of Bila Huruma."

"Schendi is a free port, administered by merchants," I said.

"We hope that it will continue to be so," he said.

"As you have suspected," I said, "I am of the warriors."

Ulafi smiled.

"Perhaps there are some in Schendi," I said, "with whom I might take service."

"Steel can always command a price," said Ulafi. He made as though to turn away.

"Captain," I said.

"Yes," said he.

I indicated the blond-haired barbarian in her cage, a few yards forward of the mainmast. It was chained, at four points, to cleats in the deck, that it not shift its position overmuch in rough weather. A folded tarpaulin lay near it, with which it could be covered. Sasi's cage had similar appointments.

The girls relieved themselves during the day, when ordered to do so.

"I am curious about the blond-haired slave," I said. "On the wharf, the slaver, Vart, said that he had gotten a silver tarsk for her." I looked at Ulafi. "Surely such a girl, a wench of only average beauty, a tense, tight girl, awkward and clumsy, one untrained, new to the collar, one who can hardly speak Gorean, a barbarian, is worth, at best, only two or three copper tarsks."

"I can get two silver tarsks for her," said Ulafi.

"Her hair and coloring is rare in Schendi?" I asked.

"Such girls, and better, are cheap in Schendi," he said. "Do not forget that Schendi is the home port of the black slavers."

"How then will you get two silver tarsks for her?" I asked.

"She is on my conditional 'want' list," said Ulafi.

"I see," I said. That seemed to me intelligent on the part of Kur agents. They must have known that she would be sailing from Cos to Schendi. This trip, particularly because of the depredations of pirates from Port Kar, is a hazardous one. It then made sense that provisions would be made to retrieve her in a Port Kar market should she be taken and enslaved. Doubtless a similar arrangement had been made with some Schendi merchants in Tyros and perhaps in Lydius or Scagnar.

"Why are you giving her slave training?" I asked.

"She is a slave," said Ulafi. "Why should she not receive slave training?"

"True," I said. I smiled. "Who is your client?" I said.

"Is it worth a copper tarsk to you?" he asked.

"Yes," I said.

"Uchafu," he said, "a slaver in Schendi."

I handed him the copper tarsk.

"Is Uchafu an important slaver?" I asked.

"No," said Ulafi. "He usually handles no more than two or three hundred slaves in an open market."

"Does it not seem strange to you," I asked, "that Uchafu should offer two tarsks for such a girl."

"Yes," he said. "Obviously he is conducting the transaction at the behest of another."

"Who?" I asked.

"I do not know," said Ulafi.

"I would pay a silver tarsk to know," I said.

"Ah," said Ulafi, "I see you have business in Schendi that you have hitherto concealed."

"A silver tarsk," I said.

"It pains me," said Ulafi, "but I must confess I do not know. I am sorry."

I looked at the girl. She was lying in the cage, on her side, turned away from us.

"She is pretty, isn't she?" asked Ulafi.

"Yes," I said.

We watched the girl. She lay there, quietly. She ran the index finger of her right hand idly, slowly, up and down, on one of the bars near her face. She seemed lost in thought.

"Yes, a pretty slave," said Ulafi.

"Look," I said.

The girl, very delicately, lifted her head a bit from the metal floor of the cage and, with her tongue, furtively, touched the bar. Then she again touched the bar, delicately, licking it, with her tongue.

"She is beginning to suspect that she may be truly a slave," said Ulafi.

"Yes," I said.

"She is beginning to learn her collar," he said.

"Yes," I said.

The girl then lay there quietly again, her head resting on her left arm, it lying, flat, elbow bent, beneath her on the sheet-metal floor of the cage. Her face, and lips, were near the bar. The small fingers of her right hand touched the bar, near its base.

"Have you not noticed the improvement in her," asked Ulafi, "since the beginning of the voyage?"

"Yes," I said. "Her movements have become less constricted. She is no longer as clumsy or tight as she was. She is becoming less inhibited. She is becoming more beautiful." These things were true. She was being taught her slavery.

"I wonder who it is who has placed her on order," he said.

"I do not know," I said. "I would like to know."

"I, too, am curious," he said.

Ulafi then turned away from me. He walked down the deck, toward the stern castle.

I again looked out to sea. I sensed then that the girl, Sasi, was near me. She knelt lightly beside me, to my left. She put her head down. I felt her tongue, soft, at my ankle. She licked and kissed at my ankle and leg for a few Ehn.

"May I speak?" she asked.

"Yes," I said.

She looked up at me. "I beg training, Master," she said.

"Crawl to my blankets, beside the sea bag," I told her.

"Yes, Master," she said. Head down, she crawled to the blankets, and lay there.

The blond-haired girl now knelt in her cage. Her fists were on the bars. She was watching me.

I joined Sasi on the two blankets. She lay there, quietly, in her collar. But as soon as I touched her she lifted her lips to mine, and squirmed and sobbed.

I was pleased. The branded she of her was mine.

"You train well, little slave," I said.

"Please do not stop touching me, Master," she begged.

"Perhaps I should whip you," I said.

"No, no," she begged. "Please let me try to be more pleasing to you."

I smiled to myself. Already, only a few days in the collar, she was slave hot.

"Perhaps you are ready for the first of the full slave orgasms," I said.

"Master?" she said.

Then, after a few Ehn, she clutched me wildly, her fingernails cutting into my arms.

"It cannot be! It cannot be!" she said.

"Shall I stop?" I asked.

"No, no," she said, intensely.

"Perhaps I shall stop," I said.

"Your slave begs you not to stop," she said. "Oh, oh," she said. "It is coming. I sense it. It is coming!"

"What do you feel like?" I asked her.

"A slave! A slave!" she cried. "I must yield to you!" she said. "I am going to yield to you!" she cried.

"As what?" I asked.

"As a slave!" she cried. She threw back her head and, wildly, weeping, sobbing, cried out the submission of her bondage.

I kissed her.

She had not done badly. Her body was growing in vitality. She showed promise for a new slave. I was pleased.

She clutched me. "Please do not leave me," she said. "Continue to hold me, if only for a time." There were tears in her eyes. "I beg it, Master," she said.

"Very well," I said.

I held her, and kissed her, and caressed her, keeping her close and warm beside me.

"Thank you, Master," she said. She looked up at me, frightened. "I did not know it could be like that," she said. "I had no idea."

I kissed her, gently.

"As a free woman," she said, "sometimes, late at night, or in my dreams, I had dimly sensed what might be the sexuality of the slave girl, but I had never remotely understood it could be anything like that, anything so overwhelming, so helpless, so total."

"It was only a rudimentary slave orgasm," I said. It had been.

"Rudimentary?" she asked.

"Yes," I said.

"You jest with a poor slave," she said.

"No," I said.

"Truly?" she asked.

"Truly," I said.

"What then lies in store for me?" she whispered.

"Slavery," I told her.

"Yes, Master," she said.

She lay beside me then, on her back. She looked up, a slave, at the stars and moons. She touched her collar. Her body, in the moonlight, was white on the dark blankets.

"After a woman has felt anything like that," she said, "how could she ever go back to being free?"

"Not many would receive the opportunity," I told her.

She laughed. It was true. Gorean men, on the whole, do not free slaves. The freeing of a girl is almost unheard of. This makes sense. They are not free women. They are belongings, valuables, slaves, treasures. Who discards precious possessions, who surrenders treasures? If the slave girl were worth less perhaps she would be freed more. She is too marvelous to free; and if she is not marvelous, she can be slain. Too, what man who has known the glory and joy of a girl at his feet is likely to wish to exchange that for the inconvenience and bother of a free woman? No, slave girls, for all practical purposes, are not freed. They will remain in one collar or another. Men will have it that way.

"I am owned," she said, her fingers touching her collar. "You own me."

"Yes," I said.

"I do not want to be free," she said.

"Do not fear," I said. "You are too pretty to free."

She kissed me.

Sometimes when a woman is freed, for one reason or another, as can happen upon rare occasions, she becomes, sometimes after an initial elation, restless, and later, miserable. She often becomes unpleasant and irritable, consequences of her frustration. Often she attempts to inflict her dissatisfaction on others. Often she tries to dominate males in her vicinity, perhaps in an attempt to punish them for their inability or cruel refusal to understand or relieve her discomfort, perhaps, too, in an attempt to provoke them into an action which will restore her to her place in nature. She has once been in that place, and she cannot fail to recollect it. Perhaps it would have been better if she had never tasted nature. It is difficult, thereafter, to be satisfied with politics. Ignorance, as always, remains myth's sturdiest bulwark. Such women often, eventually, take to walking the high bridges or frequenting exposed areas, sometimes outside the city walls. They are courting capture and the collar. They wish to kneel again, slaves, before a man.

"I have been had many times when I was a she-urt," she said. "I have lain for paga attendants, hoping to be thrown a handful of garbage. I have been raped by vagabonds. Many times did I pleasure Turgus. Yet never did I feel anything like what you did to me."

"Of the three types of experiences you have mentioned," I

said, "the nearest to what you recently felt occurred when you hoped to be thrown garbage by paga attendants."

She looked at me with wonder. "Yes," she said, "how did you know that?"

"Because in that experience you were most under the domination of a man, dependent on him even for food. Would he or would he not throw you a few scraps? Would you be sufficiently pleasing to win from him even a few shreds of garbage?"

"Yes," she said. "It is the woman in the position of submission and subordination."

"Doubtless sometimes they even ordered you to dance naked before them," I said.

"Yes," she said.

"What occurred later then," I asked, "when they had you?"

"I reached orgasm quickly," she said.

"Of course," I said. "But still you were free. If you wished you could starve for another day, or you could seek garbage elsewhere, or beg, or fish for scraps in the canals."

"Yes," she said.

"You see," I said, "you were not totally dependent on them. You were not totally helpless. You were not their slave."

"Are you going to let me eat tomorrow?" she asked, suddenly, apprehensively.

"Perhaps," I said. "I will make that decision in the morning."

"Yes, Master," she said.

"Do you begin to see what I am saying to you?" I asked.

"Yes, Master," she whispered. "I could not have earlier had the feelings you induced in me."

"Yes," I said.

"Master," she said.

"Yes," I said.

"The very nearest thing to what I recently felt occurred on the northern walkway of the Rim canal, when you, not a vagabond, but a strong, free man, who had subdued both Turgus and myself, simply took me and used me for your pleasure."

"I recall," I said. "Too, I recall that you responded well, considering that you were at that time only a free woman."

"You treated me as a slave," she chided.

"I saw the potential slave in you," I said. "Accordingly I handled you as I would have handled a slave."

91

"That is why I could not help responding to you as I did," she said.

"And yet," I said, "that did not compare with what you recently felt."

"No," she said.

"That is because before you were a free woman," I said. "You did not then truly belong to men."

"I do now," she said.

"Yes," I said. "Now you are a slave."

"That is the difference," she said.

"Yes," I said.

"The orgasm was rudimentary?" she asked.

"Yes," I said. "Just as you could not, as a free woman, attain to the heights of the rudimentary slave orgasm recently inflicted upon you so, too, you, as a new slave, cannot yet attain to the overwhelming and degrading ecstasies familiar to a girl longer in the collar."

"Yes, Master," she said.

"You have a long way to go in slavery, little Sasi," I said.

"Yes, Master," she said.

"But in a year or two," I said, "I think you will be superb. And beyond that it is just a matter of continued growth."

"Does any woman ever learn her full slavery?" she asked.

"No," I said, "I think no woman ever learns the fullness of her slavery."

"I want to be a good slave," she said.

"Men will see that you are," I said.

"Yes, Master," she said. "Master," she said.

"Yes," I said.

"May I please have my ears pierced, Master," she begged.

"Would you be so degraded a slave?" I asked. Ear piercing, on Gor, is regarded in most cities as the most degrading thing that can be done to a girl. It is commonly done only to the lowest of pleasure slaves. Compared to it, fixing a ring in a girl's nose is regarded lightly. Indeed, among the Tuchuks, one of the Wagon Peoples of Gor, even free women wear nose rings. These matters are cultural, of course.

"Yes, Master," she said.

"Why?" I asked.

"That I might be kept always a slave," she said.

"I see," I said. A girl with pierced ears on Gor might as well, for all practical purposes, give up even the slimmest of hopes, should she entertain them, of freedom. What Gorean man, seeing a woman with pierced ears, could treat her as, or accept her as, anything but a slave?

"Please, Master," she said.

"I will have it done in Schendi," I said. Usually a leather worker pierces ears. In Schendi there were many leather workers, usually engaged in the tooling of kailiauk hide, brought from the interior. Such leather, with horn, was one of the major exports of Schendi. Kailiauk are four-legged, wide-headed, lumbering, stocky ruminants. Their herds are usually found in the savannahs and plains north and south of the rain forests, but some herds frequent the forests as well. These animals are short-trunked and tawny. They commonly have brown and reddish bars on the haunches. The males, tridentlike, have three horns. These horns bristle from their foreheads. The males are usually about ten hands at the shoulders and the females about eight hands. The males average about four hundred to five hundred Gorean stone in weight, some sixteen hundred to two thousand pounds, and the females average about three to four hundred Gorean stone in weight, some twelve hundred to sixteen hundred pounds.

"Thank you, Master," she said.

She then lay quietly beside me, on the blankets. The sea bag was to my right.

"Are you going to lock me in my cage tonight, Master?" she asked.

"No," I said, "tonight you will sleep beside me."

"Thank you, Master," she said.

"At my feet," I said.

"Yes, Master," she said.

Sailors called the watch.

The wind was soft in the triangular sails. Though it was night Ulafi had not had them furled on their yards. The sea hooks, the light anchors at stem and stern, had not been thrown out. We would not lay to. Here the sea was open and the light, from the moons and stars, was more than ample. The *Palms of Schendi*, though it was night, continued to ply her way southward. Ulafi, for some reason, seemed eager to reach Schendi.

"I love being a woman," said the girl. "I love being a woman." She kissed me.

"You are a slave," I told her.

She kissed me again. "They are the same," she whispered.

I rolled over and seized her. Almost instantly, this time,

93

she attained slave orgasm. Then she looked up at me, frightened, and I touched the side of her forehead, brushing back some hair.

"I so fear the slave in me," she said.

"You so fear the woman in you," I said.

"They are the same, Master," she said. "They are the same."

"That is known to me," I said.

She lifted her lips to mine, and kissed me softly. "Yes, Master," she said.

"To my feet," I said.

"Yes, Master," she said. She crept tremblingly to my feet.

"Curl up," I told her.

"Yes, Master," she said.

I then threw the second blanket, the top blanket, over her, covering her completely. When a blanket, or cloak, or covering of any sort, is thrown over a slave like this she may not speak or rise. She must remain as she is, silent, until the master, or some free man, lifts the covering away.

I then lay on the blanket, my hands under my head, looking up at the canvas and stars. With my foot I could feel the girl. Her breathing told me that she was soon asleep.

It was the first time, since her enslavement, she had slept outside of a cage.

She was an excellent little slave. I was pleased that I had picked her up.

After a time, restless, I got up and paced the deck. Ulafi was not asleep. He was on the stern castle. Two helmsmen stood below him, on the helm deck. The only other hand awake, as far as I knew, was the lookout, some forty feet above me, on the ringed platform encircling the mainmast, the taller of the two masts.

I walked over to the cage of the blond-haired barbarian. She, I felt, was the key to the mystery, that device whereby I might locate Shaba and the fourth ring, one of the two remaining light-diversion rings, the secret of which had apparently perished long ago with Prasdak, the Kur inventor, he of the Cliff of Karrash. The fifth ring, according to Samos, was still somewhere on one of the steel worlds. It would not be risked, we speculated, on Gor or Earth. Perhaps it served to keep order on some steel world. Shielded in invisibility an excutioner could come and go as he pleased. If we could acquire once more, of course, the Tahari ring, the fourth ring, which had been brought to Gor by a Kur faction intent upon

94

preserving the planet from destruction, we could, presumably, have it duplicated in the Sardar. The use of such rings, if their use were permitted by Priest-Kings, might well make it difficult or impossible for the Kurii to function on Gor. With it their secret strongholds might be penetrated. With it one man might, in time, slaughter an army. I was pleased that the fourth ring had been brought to Gor. Without it, given to me by a dying Kur warrior, I doubted that I could have survived to prevent, some years ago, the detonation of the explosives in the steel tower, in the Tahari, explosives that were intended to destroy Gor and the Priest-Kings, that the path to Earth might be cleared for conquest. But the faction that would have been willing to destroy one world to obtain another was, we speculated, no longer in the ascendancy on the steel worlds. Half-Ear, a war general of the Kurii, whom I had met in the north, had not been of that faction. Kurii now, it seemed reasonably clear, were again intent upon the possibilities of invasion. They sensed the weakness of Priest-Kings. Why now should they think of destroying a world which, like a ripe fruit, seemed to hang almost within their grasp?

I looked at the blond-haired barbarian. I was surprised to see that she was not asleep. Usually a girl in training sleeps well. She has been worked hard and is tired. But she was not asleep. She knelt in the small cage, her fists on the bars. She was naked; I could see the moonlight on her flesh, striped by the shadows of the bars, and glinting on the shipping collar locked on her throat. She was looking up at me. I smiled to myself. Clearly she was not sleepy.

If she had been mine I would have dragged her from the cage and thrown her upon the deck.

She looked over to where Sasi lay under the blanket. She looked at her, wonderingly. Then she looked at me, again. "I heard her cry out," she said, in English, half to herself. "What did you do to her?"

She had heard, an hour ago or so, Sasi's cry, emitted in the throes of her first slave orgasm, acknowledging her surrender to me as a slave girl.

"What did you do to her?" she asked, in English. Surely she must know, or suspect, what had been done to Sasi. Would not any woman know?

"What?" I asked in Gorean. I crouched down by the cage.

She drew back from the bars. "Forgive me," she said, frightened, in English. "I was only talking to myself, really. I did not mean to bother you, Master."

95

"What?" I asked in Gorean.

She collected herself. "It is nothing, Master," she said, in Gorean. "Forgive me, Master."

Her Gorean was still terribly limited. I saw her look again to Sasi, under the blanket, and then to me.

As she knelt before me, within the cage, I saw her straighten her back and draw back her shoulders, lifting her breasts. How beautiful they were. I do not think she even realized she had done this. It was a slave's act, displaying her imbonded beauty before the gaze of a free man. Yet I do not think she was even aware of what she had done.

I looked at her ears. They had not been pierced. I had never known a female agent of Kurii who had been brought to Gor with pierced ears. That was no accident, of course. Pierced ears in a girl mean to a Gorean that she is a slave among slaves. I looked at her. If I owned her I would have her ears pierced. That would be sufficient guarantee, on Gor, that she would always be kept in a collar.

She opened her knees, slightly, before me, as she knelt. This was done unconsciously. What a naive slave she was, doubtless still priding herself on her freedom.

Some Earth girls, of course, brought to Gor as slaves, as lovely meat for the flesh markets, did have their ears pierced. Some of them did not learn for months why it was that they were treated with a roughness and contempt far beyond that of their imbonded sisters, subjected to a harsher authority and put beneath the rudest predations of a master's lust. And yet the answer was simple. They were pierced-ear girls. It is said that the ear piercing of slaves, on Gor, originated in Turia. Certainly it was practiced there. After the fall of Turia the custom spread northward. It is now relatively common on Gor, for pleasure slaves. Slavers have discovered that a pierced-ear girl commands a higher price.

I looked into the eyes of the blond girl. She had looked again at Sasi, and then had lifted her eyes to mine. Her lower lip trembled. And then she put her head down, quickly.

I saw that she wished that it had been she, and not Sasi, who had been subjected on the blankets to the pleasure of a master. But she would not, of course, admit this to herself. Sasi, a slave, had served the pleasure of a master. She, a slave, had not. Sasi had been called to the blankets; she had been left in her cage.

Ulafi had not had her thrown to the crew. He had purchased her for another. She was to be shipped intact to her buyer in Schendi, he who had placed her on order.

She lifted her head, and our eyes met. I saw her small right hand tremble. It lifted timidly from her thigh. She wanted to reach out, through the bars, to touch me. Then quickly she drew her hand back.

She put down her head.

I thought that whoever eventually owned her would be a lucky fellow. She had excellent slave potential.

I would not have minded having her in my own collar. She had grown considerably in beauty, just on the voyage.

She lifted her head again.

I looked again into her eyes. Yes, I thought, excellent slave potential.

Again she looked down. "I find you so attractive, you brute," she said, miserably, in English, much to herself. "You are so attractive to me," she said. "I hate you, you are so attractive to me," she said. "You make me weak. I hate you."

"What are you saying?" I asked her, in Gorean, as though I could not understand her.

She looked at me, boldly. But she spoke in English, which she believed I could not understand. "I do not know what is going on in me," she said. "My clothes have been taken. I am caged. I wear a collar. I have been branded. I have been whipped. I am being trained as a slave. And yet I find you attractive. I am no good. I am no good. I want to lie before you and lick your feet. I want to serve you, fully, and as a slave!" She looked away. "I hate myself," she said. "I hate you! I hate all of them! And yet something in me is beginning to sense happiness, joy, fulfillment. How terrible I am!" She sobbed. "Perhaps I am a slave, truly," she whispered. Then she shook her head, tears in her eyes. "No, no, no, no, no," she said. "I am not a slave!"

"What are you saying?" I asked her, in Gorean.

She looked at me, and brushed back her hair. "Nothing, Master," she said, in Gorean. "Forgive me, Master," she said. "It is nothing."

"Nadu," I said.

Swiftly she knelt before me, in the tiny cage, in the perfection of the position of the pleasure slave.

"Good," I said. She had assumed it instantaneously, fluidly, beautifully.

"Thank you, Master," she said.

"It is now time to sleep," I told her.

"Yes, Master," she said, and curled up on the sheet-iron square which floored her cage.

I looked at her. Her legs were drawn up. Her toes were pointed. Her belly was sucked in, slightly. Her body was a beautiful armful of slave curves. She had not been taught to do that. I looked into her eyes. She was a natural slave, I saw, as is any woman. Too, I saw that she suspected it. I then took the tarpaulin, which lay to one side. I unfolded it, and threw it over the cage, and then tied it down, fastening it to the four cleats at the corners of the cage, covering her for the night.

6

SCHENDI

"Do you smell it?" asked Ulafi.

"Yes," I said. "It is cinnamon and cloves, is it not?"

"Yes," said Ulafi, "and other spices, as well."

The sun was bright, and there was a good wind astern. The sails were full and the waters of Thassa streamed against the strakes.

It was the fourth morning after the evening conversation which Ulafi and I had had, concerning my putative caste and the transaction in Schendi awaiting the arrival of the blond-haired barbarian.

"How far are we out of Schendi?" I asked.

"Fifty pasangs," said Ulafi.

We could not yet see land.

The two girls, on their hands and knees on the deck, linked together by a gleaming neck chain, some five feet in length, attached to two steel work collars, these fitted over their regular collars, looked up. They, too, could smell the spices, even this far from land. In their right hands, grasped, were deck stones, soft, white stones, rounded, which are used to smooth and sand the boards of the deck. Earlier they had scrubbed and rinsed and, with rags, on their hands and knees, dried the deck. Later, when finished with the deck stones, they would again rinse and, again on their hands and knees, with rags, dry the deck. Had sailors been doing these things they, of course, would have dried the deck by simply mopping it down. This was not permitted to the girls, of course. They were slaves. The boards almost sparkled white. Ulafi kept a fine ship. Behind the girls stood Shoka with a whip. He would not hesitate to use it on them, if they shirked. They did not shirk.

"Those are Schendi gulls," said Ulafi, pointing to birds which circled about the mainmast. "They nest on land at night."

"I am pleased," I said. The trip had been long. I was eager to make landfall in Schendi.

I looked to the girls. Sasi looked up at me, and smiled. The blond-haired barbarian, too, had her head lifted. She smelled the spices. She knew we were now in the vicinity of land. She looked up at the birds. She had not seen them before.

Ulafi looked to the blond-haired barbarian. She looked at him, frightened. He pointed upward, at the birds. "We are approaching Schendi," he said.

"Yes, Master," she said. She put her head down, trembling. She, a slave, did not know what awaited her in Schendi.

Shoka, behind the girls, shook out the blades of the slave whip he carried. Quickly both girls, their heads down, returned to their work.

I remained at the rail, on the port side. Soon I could see a brownish stain in the water, mingling and diffusing with the green of Thassa.

I drew a deep breath, relishing the loveliness of the smell of the spices, now stronger than before.

"Half port helm!" called Ulafi to his helmsmen. Slowly the *Palms of Schendi* swung half to port, and the great yards above the deck, pulleys creaking, lines adjusted by quick sailors, swung almost parallel to the deck. The same wind which had pressed astern now sped us southeastward.

I now regarded again the brownish stains in the water. Still we could not see land. Yet I knew that land must be nigh. Already, though we were still perhaps thirty or forty pasangs at sea, one could see clearly in the water the traces of inland sediments. These would have been washed out to sea from the Kamba and Nyoka rivers. These stains extend for pasangs into Thassa. Closer to shore one could mark clearly the traces of the Kamba to the north and the Nyoka to the south, but, given our present position, we were in the fans of these washes. The Kamba, as I may have mentioned, empties directly into Thassa; the Nyoka, on the other hand, empties into Schendi harbor, which is the harbor of the port of Schendi, its waters only then moving thence to Thassa.

99

Kamba, incidentally, is an inland word, not Gorean. It means rope. Similarly the word Nyoka means serpent. Ushindi means Victory. Thus Lake Ushindi might be thought of as Lake Victory or Victory Lake. It was named for some victory over two hundred years ago won on its shores. The name of the tiny kingdom or ubarate which had won the victory is no longer remembered. Lake Ngao, which was discovered by Shaba, and named by him, was named for a shield, because of its long, oval shape. The shields in this area tend to have that shape. It is also an inland word, of course. The Ua River is, literally, the Flower River. I have chosen, however, to retain the inland words, as they are those which are commonly used. There are, of course, many languages spoken on Gor, but that language I have called Gorean, in its various dialects, is the *lingua franca* of the planet. It is spoken most everywhere, except in remote areas. One of these remote areas, of course, is the equatorial interior. The dialects of the Ushindi region I will usually refer to as the inland dialects. To some extent, of course, this is a misnomer, as there are many languages which are spoken in the equatorial interior which would not be intelligible to a native speaker of the Ushindi area. It is useful, however, to have some convenient way of referring to the linguistic modalities of the Ushindi area. Gorean, incidentally, is spoken generally in Schendi. The word Schendi, as nearly as I can determine, has no obvious, direct meaning in itself. It is generally speculated, however, that it is a phonetic corruption of the inland word Ushindi, which, long ago, was apparently used to refer to this general area. In that sense, I suppose, one might think of Schendi, though it has no real meaning of its own, as having an etiological relationship to a word meaning 'Victory'. The Gorean word for victory is "Nykus," which expression seems clearly influenced by "Nike," or "Victory," in classical Greek. Shaba usually named his discoveries, incidentally, in one or another of the inland dialects. He speaks several fluently, though his native tongue is Gorean, which is spoken standardly in Anango, his island. The inland language, or, better, one of its dialects, is, of course, the language of the court of Bila Huruma, Shaba's patron and supporter.

"Sails ho!" called the lookout. "Two points off the port bow!"

Men went to the port rail, and Ulafi climbed to the stern castle. I climbed some feet up the knotted rope, dangling by the mainmast, which led to the lookout's platform.

I could not yet see the sails. Ulafi did not put about or change his course.

I braced myself, holding my feet together on one of the knots on the rope. I steadied myself, putting one arm about the mast.

His men did not rush to the benches, slide back the thole ports or slip the great oars outboard. Sea water was not brought to the deck from over the side. Sand, in buckets, was not brought topside from the ballast in the hold. The first officer, Gudi, did not preside over the issuance of blades and lances.

I felt distinctly uneasy that the masts could not be lowered. How vulnerable seemed the ship, the masts high, with their sloping yards and billowing canvas. There was a light catapult forward, but it had not yet been erected. If Ulafi had torch arrows they were not in evidence. Too, the fire pans had not been kindled for dipping the arrows, nor had a fire been kindled beneath the oil kettle, for filling the clay globes with flaming oil, to be cast in looping trajectories from the catapult forward. If onagri or springals lay unassembled in the hold they were not yet being brought to the deck.

I looked out, past the bow, almost dead ahead. I could now see the sails. I counted eleven of them. The ships were single-masted. They were ramships. Yet I now breathed more easily. Since I, from my lower elevation, a few feet above the deck, by the mainmast, could see their canvas, I knew that their lookouts, from their superior elevations, could see the *Palms of Schendi.* Yet the ships were not taking in canvas. They were not bringing down their yards and lowering their masts. It might have been, for all its stately progression, a convoy of merchantmen. Yet the ships were single-masted, tarnships, ramships. Too, Ulafi did not seem concerned about them, or his men. They knew, apparently, what ships these would be. Perhaps the lookout, already, had made his routine identifications. I, too, now had little doubt what ships these would be, as it was the northern spring, and we were in the waters of Schendi.

"Convey our greetings to the fleet!" called Ulafi from the stern castle, putting down his glass of the builders. Flags, in colorful series, were set at the port stem castle lines.

I lowered myself now to the deck, hand by hand.

I stood near the bow, now on the starboard side. On each side of us, five on one side, six on the other, the low, lean ships, straight-keeled and shallow-drafted, single-masted, be-

101

gan to slide past us. I could see the oars lifting and dipping in unison, as they moved by.

"You do not seem concerned," I said to Shoka, Ulafi's second officer, who stood near me.

"We are of Schendi," he said.

I stood with Shoka near the rail. "Suddenly," I said, "I have this strange feeling, as though I were swimming and then, as though from nowhere, I found myself swimming with sharks, who silently passed me, not regarding me."

"It could be frightening," admitted Shoka.

"Do they never prey on ships of Schendi?" I asked.

"I do not think so," said Shoka. "If they do, I suppose the ship and its crew are destroyed at sea. One never hears of it."

"I do not find that particularly comforting," I said.

"We are in the waters of Schendi," said Shoka. "If they were to attack Schendi ships, it does not seem likely they would do so in these waters."

"That is slightly more comforting," I granted him.

The low, sleek ships continued to pass us. I could see the black faces of crew members here and there. I could not see the nearest oarsmen, for these were concealed by the structure of the rowing frame. Occasionally I glimpsed the far oarsmen, as the ship rolled in the swells. The oarsmen would be free men. One does not put slaves at the oars of warships. The wall on the rowing frame, of course, tends to protect the oarsmen against high seas and the fire of missile weapons.

I watched the ships. They were very beautiful.

Shoka indicated that the two girls should rise and come to stand by the rail, to look out and see the fleet.

"Is that wise?" I asked. "Perhaps they should be put on their bellies, under the tarpaulins, that they not attract attention." Why should one advertise that one carried two lovely slaves?

"It does not matter," said Shoka. "Let the slaves see."

"But they will be seen as well," I pointed out.

"It does not matter," said Shoka. "In two months time those ships will have hundreds of such women chained in their holds."

The two girls then stood by the rail, lovely, naked, neck-chained together, watching the passing ships, their bare feet on the smooth boards of the deck of the *Palms of Schendi*.

"I suppose you are right," I said.

"Yes," said he.

The ships, then, had slid past us. I saw Ulafi, on his stern castle, raise his hand to a black captain, some seventy yards away, on the stern castle of his own vessel. The captain had returned this salute.

"You did not even take defensive precautions," I said to Shoka.

"What good would it have done?" he asked.

I shrugged. To be sure, one merchant ship, like the *Palms of Schendi*, could have made little effective resistance to the ships which had just passed us, nor could she, though swift for a round ship, have outrun them.

"What if they had taken such action as an indication that we were hostile?" asked Shoka.

"That is true, too," I said.

"Our defense," said Shoka, "is that we are of Schendi."

"I see," I said.

"They need our port facilities," said Shoka. "Even the larl grows sometimes weary, and the tarn, upon occasion, must find a place in which to fold its wings."

I turned about, watching the ships vanish in the distance.

"Return to your work," said Shoka to the girls.

"Yes, Master," they said and, with a rustle of chain, fell again to their knees and, seizing up the deck stones, once more, Shoka near them, vigorously addressed themselves to their labors.

I turned again to watch the ships. They were now but specks on the horizon. They plied their way northward. In the northern autumn they would return, to be refitted and supplied again in Schendi, and would then, a few weeks later, in the southern spring, ply their way southward. Schendi, located in the vicinity of the Gorean equator, somewhat south of it, provides the ships with a convenient base, from which they may conduct their affairs seasonally in both hemispheres. I was pleased that I had seen the ships. I could not have conceived of a more pleasant way in which to have made their acquaintance. I had seen the passing of the fleet of the black slavers of Schendi.

The girls had been cleaned and combed. Shoka had soused perfume on them.

"Extend your wrists, crossed, for binding," said he to the blond-haired barbarian.

She, kneeling, complied. "Yes, Master," she said. The line which Shoka now tied around her crossed wrists was already strung through a large, metal, gold-painted ring, one of two, which were mounted in the huge wooden esrs of the kailiauk head which, high above the water, surmounted the prow.

We had lain to after more closely approaching the port of Schendi in the evening of the preceding day, the day in which we had seen the fleet of the black slavers of Schendi. We could see the shore now, with its sands and, behind the sand, the dense, green vegetation, junglelike, broken by occasional clearings for fields and villages. Schendi itself lay farther to the south, about the outjutting of a small peninsula, Point Schendi. The waters here were richly brown, primarily from the outflowing of the Nyoka, emptying from Lake Ushindi, some two hundred pasangs upriver.

"Extend your wrists, crossed, for binding," said Shoka to Sasi.

"Yes, Master," she said. Her wrists then were tied to another line, it strung through the gold-painted ring fixed in the right ear of the kailiauk head at the prow. I had volunteered her, at the request of Ulafi, who had his vanities. He was an important merchant and captain in Schendi. Indeed, he had not entered port yesterday evening. The *Palms of Schendi* would make her entrance in the morning, when the wharves were busy, the shops open and the traffic bustling.

I looked about. The *Palms of Schendi* sparkled. The deck was smoothed and white, ropes were neatly coiled, gear was stashed and secured, hatches were battened, and the brass and fittings were polished. Yesterday afternoon two seamen had re-enameled the kailiauk head at the prow with brown, and the eyes with white and black. The golden metal rings, too, had been repainted. The *Palms of Schendi* would enter Schendi, her home port, in style. At sea, of course, a sensible compromise must be struck between a ship which is constantly ready, so to speak, for inspection, and one which is loose. The ship must be neat but livable; there must be order but not rigidity; the ship must be one on which men are comfortable but it must also be one on which, because of its arrangements and discipline, the efficient performance of duty is encouraged. Ulafi, it seemed to me, struck this sort of balance well with his men and ship. I thought him a good captain, somewhat begrudgingly because he was of the merchants. It was hard to fault him. He ran a clean, tight ship, but with common sense.

The light anchors were raised.

Canvas was dropped from the long, sloping yards.

Oarsmen, at the command of the first officer, a tall fellow

named Gudi, he standing now on the helm deck, slid their great levers through the thole ports. Soon, to his calls, the oars drew against the brownish waters about the hull.

The girls knelt on the deck before the stem castle, their wrists bound before them, lines leading to the rings.

The *Palms of Schendi* began to negotiate its wide turn about Point Schendi.

"Are you proud?" I asked Sasi.

"Yes, Master," she said. "I am very proud."

I stood at the port rail, by the bow. I watched the green of the shore, moving slowly by. Last night we had had lanterns at stem and stern.

I looked at the blond-haired slave girl. She was very lovely, kneeling naked, in her collar, her wrists tied before her body, the line running to the golden ring. Seeing my eyes upon her, she put her head down, ashamed.

I smiled.

Last night, an Ahn after she had been put in her cage, I had once glanced upon her. She had been lying on her back in the cage, her knees drawn up. Her hands had been beside her thighs, their backs resting on the metal of the cage floor. Her head had been turned toward me. When she had seen me look at her, she had looked up, quickly, at the square of sheet metal above her.

I had gone to the side of the cage, and crouched there. "Nadu," I had said to her, and she had then knelt before me, within the cage, behind the bars, in the position of the pleasure slave. I had studied her body, and, in particular, her face, her eyes and expression. I had then reached through the bars and taken her by the upper arms. She seemed terrified, but made no sound. I drew her toward me, until I held her against the bars. I held her there for more than a minute, reading in her eyes, and in my grip of her soft upper arms, the tenseness, the softness, the confusion, the desire, the fear, of the lovely slave.

Then I had seen what I had wanted. She pressed herself against the bars. Her eyes were closed. The lower portion of her face, the bars cruel against it, thrust toward me. Her lips, soft and wet, opened to me.

"Oh, no," she had then breathed, softly, in English, and, frightened, had drawn back. I had then released her arms and she had crouched back in the cage, against the bars on the other side. I had neither kissed nor, really, refused to kiss her. It had happened, really, neither quickly nor slowly, but as it

105

had happened, she offering her lips, almost inadvertently, hesitating, and then, frightened, dismayed, drawing back. I do not think I would have kissed her, as I did not own her, but she, of course, had not known that. I had been interested, of course, in assessing the current level of her development in bondage. That could make a difference in what happened to her, and what happened to her could make a difference in the success or failure of my own mission in Schendi. If she were still too rigid or irritating to men she might even, possibly, be slain before she could lead me to the mysterious Shaba. But my small test, affirmative in its results, convinced me that she was probably slave enough already to be permitted to live at least until she were thrown naked at his feet.

I had then continued to look at the girl for a few moments. She looked at me, miserably, frightened.

"I am not a slave," she said to herself, in English, and then, suddenly, put her head in her hands, sobbing.

I smiled.

Surely she must have sensed that the mouth kiss which she had so helplessly proffered, and had proffered as a slave, was the symbolic opening of her vagina to male penetration.

"I am not a slave, I am not a slave," she wept.

How these Earth women fight the natural woman in themselves. As far as I could tell it was not wrong to be a woman, any more than it was wrong to be a man. I do not know, of course, for I am not a woman. Perhaps it is wrong to be a woman. If not, why should they fight it so? But perhaps weak men, who fear true women, have conditioned them so. It is not clear that any true man would object to a true woman. It is clear, however, that those who fear to be either will object to both. Values are interesting. How transitory and peculiar are the winds which blow over the plains of biology.

"I am not a slave," wept the girl. "I am not a slave." Then she looked at me, suddenly, angrily. "You know that I am a slave, don't you, you brute?" She asked, in English.

I said nothing to her.

"Is that why I hate you so much," she wept, "because you know that I am a slave?"

I looked at her.

"Or do I hate you so much," she asked, "because I want you as my master?"

Then she put down her head, again. "No, no," she wept. "I am not a slave. I am not a slave!"

I then withdrew. I had no objection to the girl addressing

herself to me in English, which she was confident I did not understand. I thought it healthy that she be given the opportunity to ventilate her feelings. Many Gorean masters permit a barbarian to prattle upon occasion in her native tongue. It is thought to be good for them.

A few minutes later I had joined Sasi on the blankets.

"Please touch me, Master," she had begged.

"Very well," I had said.

I glanced back once at the cage of the blond-haired barbarian. Shoka had covered it for the night.

I had seen her body and eyes proclaim her slavery, and I had heard her mouth both deny it, and affirm it, and then again deny it. The blond-haired girl was still fighting herself. She did not know yet who or what she was. Interestingly I had heard her ask herself if she hated me, because she wanted me as her master. I knew that a girl who wants a man for her master can perform wonders for him. And yet she was only an ignorant girl, a raw girl, new to the collar. What did she know of being the slave of a master? But then I recalled that she had again denied being a slave. I smiled to myself. What a little fool she was. She did not yet know, truly, that she was a slave.

"Oh, Master," said Sasi.

Then I turned my attention away from the blond-haired girl, her intended role in my plans and what might lie ahead in Schendi. I then turned my full attention to the sweet, squirming, collared Sasi, the branded, curvacious little beast from the wharves of Port Kar. What a delight she was. She had none of the problems of the blond-haired girl. But, too, she was Gorean. Almost as soon as the collar had been locked on her she had begun, happily, to blossom in her bondage. Slavery is cultural for Goreans. They know it is something a woman can be.

"You give me great pleasure, Master," she said.

"Be quiet," I told her.

"Yes, Master," she whispered.

A quarter of an Ahn later I held and kissed her, gently, letting her subside at her own rhythms. "What are you?" I asked her.

"A slave, Master," she said.

"Whose slave?" I asked.

"Yours, Master," she said.

"Are you happy?" I asked.

"Yes, Master," she whispered. "Yes, Master."

The *Palms of Schendi* had now begun to come about, about Point Schendi.

The yards swung on the masts, capitalizing on the wind. The oars dipped and lifted.

We were still some seven or eight pasangs from the buoy lines. I could see ships in the harbor.

We would come in with a buoy line on the port side. Ships, too, would leave the harbor with the line of their port side. This regulates traffic. In the open sea, similarly, ships keep one another, where possible, on their port sides, thus passing to starboard.

"What is the marking on the buoy line that will be used by Ulafi?" I asked Shoka, who stood near me, by the girls, at the bow.

"Yellow and white stripes," he said. "That will lead to the general merchant wharves. The warehouse of Ulafi is near wharf eight."

"Do you rent wharfage?" I asked.

"Yes, from the merchant council," he said.

White and gold, incidentally, are the colors of the merchants. Usually their robes are white, trimmed with gold. That the buoy line was marked in yellow and white stripes was indicative of the wharves toward which it led. I have never seen, incidentally, gold paint on a buoy. It does not show up as well as enameled yellow in the light of ships' lanterns.

I could see some forty or fifty sails in the harbor. There must then have been a great many more ships in the harbor, for most ships, naturally, take in their canvas when moored. The ships under sail must, most of them, have been entering or leaving the harbor. Most of the ships, of course, would be small ships, coasting vessels and light galleys. Also, of course, there were river ships in the harbor, used in the traffic on the Nyoka.

I had not realized the harbor at Schendi was so large. It must have been some eight pasangs wide and some two or three pasangs in depth. At its eastern end, of course, at one point, the Nyoka, channeled between stone embankments, about two hundred yards apart, flows into it. The Nyoka, because of the embankments, enters the harbor much more rapidly than it normally flows. It is generally, like the Kamba, a wide, leisurely river. Its width, however, about two pasangs above Schendi, is constricted by the embankments. This is to control the river and protect the port. A result, of course, of the narrowing, the amount of water involved being the same, is an increase in the velocity of the flow. In moving upstream from Schendi there is a bypass, rather like a lock system, which provides a calm road for shipping until the Nyoka can be joined. This is commonly used only in moving east or upstream from Schendi. The bypass, or "hook," as it is called, enters the Nyoka with rather than against its current. One then brings one's boat about and, by wind or oar, proceeds upstream.

The smell of spices, particularly cinnamon and cloves, was now quite strong. We had smelled these even at sea. One smell that I did not smell to a great degree was that of fish. Many fish in these tropical waters are poisonous to eat, a function of certain forms of seaweed on which they feed. The seaweed is harmless to the fish but it contains substances toxic to humans. The river fish on the other hand, as far as I know, are generally wholesome for humans to eat. Indeed, there are many villages along the Kamba and Nyoka, and along the shores of Lake Ushindi, in which fishing is the major source of livelihood. Not much of this fish, however, is exported from Schendi. I could smell, however, tanning fluids and dyes, from the shops and compounds of leather workers. Much kailiauk leather is processed in Schendi, brought to the port not only from inland but from north and south, from collection points, along the coast. I could also smell tars and resins, naval stores. Most perhaps, I could now smell the jungles behind Schendi. This smell, interestingly, does not carry as far out to sea as those of the more pungent spices. It was a smell of vast greeneries, steaming and damp, and of incredible flowers and immensities of rotting vegetation.

A dhow, with a red-and-white-striped sail, slipped past us on the port side.

The bow of the *Palms of Schendi* had now come about, and the peninsula of Point Schendi dropped behind us, to port. The impassive, painted eyes, white and black-pupiled, of the huge, brown kailiauk head at the prow now gazed upon the harbor of Schendi.

It lay dead ahead, some four pasangs.

The blond-haired barbarian looked across the deck to Sasi. "Mistress," she whispered to Sasi, who stood to her as first girl.

"Yes, Slave," said Sasi.

The blond lifted her bound wrists, the line running up to the golden ring in the left ear of the kailiauk head, through

109

it, and back to the deck. "Why are we bound like this?" she asked.

"Do you not know, you little fool?" asked Sasi. I smiled, for Sasi was actually a bit shorter than the blond girl. I would have guessed they would have weighed about the same. Sasi may have weighed a little more. Neither was a large girl.

"No, Mistress," said the blond girl. She was deferential to Sasi. If she had not been, she might have been whipped to within an inch of her life.

"Rejoice," said Sasi. "You have been found beautiful enough to be put at the prow."

"Oh," said the blond girl, uncertainly. Then she knelt back, on her heels. She smiled. Then she looked up, uneasily, at the ring in the ear of the kailiauk head, that proud adornment surmounting the prow of the *Palms of Schendi*, through which her wrist rope was strung.

"On your bellies," said Shoka to them, and the two girls lay on the deck.

He first crossed the blond's ankles and tied them together, and then he did the same for Sasi. This is done to improve the line of a girl's body, as she hangs at the ring.

"Up," said Shoka to them, and they again knelt. Both were now ready to be put at the rings, the blond at the left, Sasi at the right.

We were now some three pasangs from Schendi.

A light galley, two-masted, with yellow sails, was leaving the harbor, far to port.

Coming about Point Schendi, behind us, some two pasangs astern, was a round ship. She flew the colors of Asperiche. Far to starboard we saw two other ships, a medium-class round ship and a heavy galley, the latter with red masts, both of Ianda.

"What will be done with us in Schendi?" asked the blond-haired girl of Sasi.

"I do not know what will be done with me," said Sasi, "but doubtless you will be marketed."

"Sold?" asked the blond.

"Of course," said Sasi.

Uneasily the blond girl squirmed a bit in her bonds, but they held her perfectly.

"Do not fear," said Sasi. "You will learn to obey men with perfection. They will see to it."

"Yes, Mistress," said the blond. And then she glanced at

me, and then, quickly, looked away. I continued to regard her. She knelt back as she could, her small ankles roped, a bit frightened, lifting her upper body. She displayed herself well. She trembled. She, an Earth girl, knew herself now subjected to the scrutiny of a Gorean male. She did not dare not to display herself well. She did not wish to be kicked or beaten.

Yet, as I regarded her, I saw more in her body and beauty than the mere intelligence of a collared slave.

I saw something, incipiently, of the joy and pride of the slave girl, the girl who knows that though her body is being placed in bondage her womanhood, paradoxically, is being freed.

I continued to regard her. Surely, at the beginning of the voyage, it never would have occured to Ulafi to have put her at the prow. Better than that she would have been chained in the hold, to a ring, or caged on deck, the tarpaulin thrown over the cage, that she might not detract from the splendor of his entrance into his harbor. But Ulafi and Shoka had, in the voyage, accomplished much with her. She was now, incredibly enough, sufficiently beautiful to be found acceptable for the prow of the *Palms of Schendi*. What a subtle thing is a woman's beauty. How little it has to do, actually, generally, with such matters as symmetry of form and regularity of features. It eludes scales and tapes; mathematics cannot, I think, penetrate its mysterious equations. I have never understood beauty; but I am grateful that it exists.

The girl looked up at me, and then, again, looked away. She put her head down, trembling.

I smiled, remembering her eyes. They had been those of a slave. How incredible that she did not yet know that she was a slave.

I pointed ahead, toward the harbor. It was now some two and a half pasangs away. "Schendi," I said to her.

"Yes, Master," she said.

"You will be sold there," I told her.

"Yes, Master," she said.

"Men will own you," I said.

"Yes, Master," she said.

"What do you want to do more than anything?" I asked.

"To please men," she said, recalling well her training.

"Why do you wish to do that?" I asked.

She looked up at me. "Because I am a slave girl," she whispered.

"Is it true that you are a slave girl?" I asked.

111

"Yes, Master," she whispered.

"Do you desire intensely to be a slave girl?" I asked.

"Am I in training?" she asked.

"Of course," I said.

"Yes, Master," she said, "I desire intensely to be a slave girl."

"You are not now in training," I said. "Do you desire intensely to be a slave girl?"

"No, no," she wept. "No, Master. No, Master!"

"I see," I said, and turned away from her. She knelt beside me, trembling, sobbing.

We were now some two pasangs out of Schendi. The traffic was heavier.

"Yes, Master," she whispered.

I looked down at her. "What did you say?" I asked.

"Yes, Master," she said.

"Yes, what?" I asked.

She looked up at me, tears in her eyes. "Yes, Master," she said, "I do desire intensely to be a slave girl."

"You are not now in training," I told her.

"I know," she whispered. "But I do desire, intensely, to be a slave girl." She choked back a sob. Tears stained her cheeks. She bent her head to me and, delicately, softly, kissed me on the right thigh, below the tunic's hem. Then she again, timidly, looked up at me. I did not cuff her.

"Have no fear," I told her, "your wish is granted. You are completely and totally a slave girl."

"Yes, Master," she said. Then she put down her head. Her small fists clenched. "No," she said, suddenly, "I am not a slave girl.'"

"Fight the collar," I told her. "In the long run it will do you no good."

"Why?" she asked, looking up at me. "Why!"

"Because you are a slave," I told her.

"No," she said. "No!" But I saw in her eyes that she understood that I had seen the slave in her. She knew that I had recognized it. She had not been able to conceal her from me. It is very difficult for a woman when she meets a man who can see the slave in her. What then can she do? She can flee, or kneel before him.

"No," she said, "I am not a slave!"

"Be silent, Slave," I said.

"Yes, Master," she said. She knelt back. I saw her body suffuse with a subtle pleasure, that she had been ordered to

112

silence. Her protestations had not been accepted. Her immediate realities were simple. She was silent, ordered so, and kneeling. She had not wanted her protestations to be accepted, though it had been important for her to make them. Her resistance must be overcome. How else could it be clear to her that her will, truly, was subjected to that of another? Like all women, in her heart, she wished to be owned, and mastered.

She looked straight ahead, kneeling, her body held beautifully. She bit her lower lip. She tried to look angry.

I smiled to myself.

Already I could see many signs, some subtle and some quite obvious, that the secret slave, which lurks in every woman, had begun to sense, fearfully, excitedly, that she had been brought to a world on which she might perhaps be free at last to emerge; had the chains been removed; she lifted her wrists; had her small limbs now been unfettered; she looked up from the straw, up the long, narrow stairs toward the iron door; was it now ajar; since her birth a pathological culture had thrust her into the dungeon of suppression, confining her in the darkness; her very reality and existence had been ignored and hysterically denied; but at times, sometimes in dreams, or idle moments, her screams for mercy, unheeded, had been heard from the darkness below; or was it only the sound of the wind; I suspected that the blond-haired girl, uneasily, had many times heard the cries of the imprisoned slave; the slave now, her fetters struck away by Gorean men, crept toward the iron door; could it truly be ajar; had men opened it; outside the door the blond-haired girl, tremblingly, waited; the slave was going to emerge; but the slave feared to emerge; behind her the blond-haired girl heard strong men summon forth the slave; the slave would come forth; then the blond-haired girl would gasp, for she would see that it was she herself who was the slave. Then she would feel a collar being looked on her throat, and she would kneel in the sunlight at the feet of a master.

"Put them at the prow!" called Ulafi.

Two seamen came to assist Shoka.

We were now some two pasangs out of Schendi. The traffic was heavier.

Shoka lifted up the blond girl, easily, in his arms. She was frightened. The line on her wrists went to, and through, the golden ring in the left ear of the kailiauk head at the prow of the *Palms of Schendi*. It then, from the ring, returned to the

113

deck. The two seamen then held the line at the deck. Shoka then threw the girl over the bow. She cried out with misery but, in a moment, swung from the tether, through the ring, fastened to her wrists. At Shoka's direction she was drawn up until she hung, her wrists over her head, about a foot below the golden ring. One sailor held the rope then while the other secured the line to a ring on the deck. He made a loop in the line, passed the free end through the deck ring, brought the end up through the loop, about the line and down through the loop again, then tightened the knot. The girl then swung from the ring. The knot at the ring was a simple bowline, familiar to all who know the sea, brought to Gor perhaps hundreds of years ago by mariners who had once sailed the Aegean or the Mediterranean, perhaps who had once called not such ports as Schendi or Bazi their own, but Miletus or Ephesus, or Syracuse or Carthage. In a few moments Sasi, too, swung from a golden ring, she too suspended over the brownish waters outside Schendi.

A heavy galley, out of Tyros, forty oars to a side, stroked past us, her yellow lateen sails loose on their yards. Crewmen paused in their labors to examine the beauty of the displayed slaves. Her captain, lowering his glass of the builders, lifted his hand high, fist clenched, to Ulafi, greeting him, and congratulating him on his ship and the girls which hung at its prow. Ulafi, graciously, lifting his hand, palm open, acknowledged the gesture.

We were then at the mouth of the harbor and, in a moment, had brought the line of yellow-and-white-striped buoys to port. There were already two ships behind us now, and another was ahead of us. As we moved toward the wharves three ships passed us, moving toward the open sea. There are more than forty merchant wharves at Schendi, each one of which, extending into the harbor, accommodates four ships to a side. The inmost wharves tend to have lower numbers, on the starboard side of the port, as one enters the harbor.

We could see men on the docks and on the outjutting wharves. Many seemed to recognize the *Palms of Schendi* and she was well received. I had not realized that Schendi was as large or busy a port as it was. Many of the wharves were crowded and there were numerous ships moored at them. On the wharves and in the warehouses, whose great doors were generally open, I could see much merchandise. Most in evidence were spice kegs and hide bales, but much else, too, could be seen, cargos in the warehouses and on the wharves, some waiting, some being actively carried about, being embarked or disembarked. As the *Palms of Schendi*, her canvas now taken in and the long yards swung parallel with the deck, oars lifting and sweeping, moved past the wharves many men stopped working, setting down their burdens, to wave us good greetings. Men relish the sight of a fine ship. Too, the two girls at the prow did not detract from the effect. They hung as splendid ornaments, two slave beauties, dangling over the brownish waters, from rings set in the ears of a beast. We passed the high desks of two wharf praetors. I saw, too, here and there, brief-tunicked, collared slave girls; I saw, too, at one point a group of paga girls, chained together, soliciting business for their master's tavern. Many goods pass in and out of Schendi, as would be the case in any major port, such as precious metals, jewels, tapestries, rugs, silks, horn and horn products, medicines, sugars and salts, scrolls, papers, inks, lumber, stone, cloth, ointments, perfumes, dried fruit, some dried fish, many root vegetables, chains, craft tools, agricultural implements, such as hoe heads and metal flail blades, wines and pagas, colorful birds and slaves. Schendi's most significant exports are doubtless spice and hides, with kailiauk horn and horn products also being of great importance. One of her most delicious exports is palm wine. One of her most famous, and precious, exports are the small carved sapphires of Schendi. These are generally a deep blue, but some are purple and others, interestingly, white or yellow. They are usually carved in the shape of tiny panthers, but sometimes other animals are found as well, usually small animals or birds. Sometimes, however, the stone is carved to resemble a tiny kailiauk or kailiauk head. Slaves, interestingly, do not count as one of the major products in Schendi, in spite of the fact that the port is the headquarters of the League of Black Slavers. The black slavers usually sell their catches nearer the markets, both to the north and south. One of their major markets, to which they generally arrange for the shipment of girls overland, is the Sardar Fairs, in particular that of En'Kara, which is the most extensive and finest. This is not to say, of course, that Schendi does not have excellent slave markets. It is a major Gorean port. The population of Schendi is probably about a million people. The great majority of these are black. Individuals of all races, however, Schendi being a cosmopolitan port, frequent the city. Many merchant houses, from distant cities, have outlets or agents in Schendi. Similarly sailors, from hundreds of ships and numerous distant ports, are almost always within the city. The equatorial waters about Schendi, of course, are open to shipping all year around. This is one reason for the importance of the port. Schendi does not, of course, experience a winter. Being somewhat south of the equator it does have a dry season, which occurs in the period of the southern hemisphere's winter. If it were somewhat north of the equator, this dry season would occur in the period of the northern hemisphere's winter. The farmers about Schendi, as farmers in the equatorial regions generally, do their main planting at the beginning of the "dry season." From the point of view of one accustomed to Gor's northern latitudes I am not altogether happy with the geographer's concept of a "dry season." It is not really dry but actually a season of less rain. During the rains of the rainy season seeds could be torn out of the ground and fields half washed away. The equatorial farmer, incidentally, often moves his fields after two or three seasons as the soil, depleted of many minerals and nutriments by the centuries of terrible rains, is quickly exhausted by his croppage. The soil of tropical areas, contrary to popular understanding, is not one of great agricultural fertility. Jungles, which usually spring up along rivers or in the vicinity of river systems, can thrive in a soil which would not nourish fields of food grains. The farmers about Schendi are, in a sense, more gardeners than farmers. When a field is exhausted the farmer clears a new area and begins again. Villages move. This infertility of the soil is a major reason why population concentrations have not developed in the Gorean equatorial interior. The land will not support large permanent settlements. On the equator, itself, interestingly, geographers maintain that there are two dry seasons and two rainy seasons. Once again, if there is much to this, I would prefer to think of two rainy seasons and two less rainy seasons. My own observations would lead me to say that for all practical purposes there is, on the equator itself, no dry season. The reason for the great amount of rain in the equatorial regions is, I suppose, clear to all. At the equator the sun's rays are most direct. This creates greater surface heat than oblique rays would. This heating of the surface causes warm air to rise. The rising of the warm air leaves a vacuum, so to speak, or, better, an area of less pressure or density in the atmosphere. Into this less dense area, this "hole," so to speak, cooler air pours, like invisible liquid, from both the north and south. This air is heated and rises in its turn. When the warm air reaches the upper atmosphere, well above the reflecting, heated surface of the earth, it cools; as it cools, its moisture is precipitated as rain. This is, of course, a cycle. It is responsible for the incredible rains of the Gorean equatorial interior. There are often two major rains during the day, in the late afternoon, when the warm air has reached its precipitation point, and, again, in the late evening, when, due to the turning of the planet, the surface and upper atmosphere, darkened, cools. There can be rain, of course, at other times, as well, depending on the intricate interplay of air currents, pressures and temperatures.

"Oars inboard," called Gudi, who acted as oar master.

Seamen hurled mooring lines to men on the wharf. These were looped about heavy mooring cleats. Coils of rope slung over the side cushioned the strakes of the ship, lest she grate herself on the boards of the wharf. Men gathered their gear. The gangplank was run from an opening in the starboard rail, swung open, to the wharf. The number of the wharf was eight.

I saw two slavers stop at the wharf, looking up at the slaves suspended from the rings. "If you want to sell them, bring them to the market of Kovu," called one of them, an ugly fellow, his right cheek disfigured by a long scar.

Shoka lifted his hand to them, acknowledging that he had heard them.

They then continued on their way.

Beautiful slave girls, clothed and unclothed, are not that rare on Gor. That the two girls had attracted the attention of passing slavers was high praise indeed for their unconcealed charms.

Two men from the desk of the nearest wharf praetor, he handling wharves six through ten, a scribe and a physician, boarded the ship. The scribe carried a folder with him. He would check the papers of Ulafi, the registration of the ship, the arrangements for wharfage and the nature of the cargo. The physician would check the health of the crew and slaves. Plague, some years ago, had broken out in Bazi, to the north, which port had then been closed by the merchants for two years. In some eighteen months it had burned itself out, moving south and eastward. Bazi had not yet recovered from the economic blow. Schendi's merchant council, I supposed, could not be blamed for wishing to exercise due caution that a similar calamity did not befall their own port.

The scribe, with Ulafi, went about his business. I, with the crew members, submitted to the examination of the physician. He did little more than look into our eyes and examine our forearms. But our eyes were not yellowed nor was there sign of the broken pustules in our flesh.

Two slave girls, white, barefoot, in ragged brown tunics, with golden rings in their ears, one chewing on a larma, came to stand on the wharf near the prow. "How ugly you are!" called up one of them to the girls at the rings.

"Have you ever been put at the prow?" called Sasi back to them, unhesitatingly.

They did not respond.

I saw the blond-haired barbarian, suspended at her ring, suddenly shudder with understanding. And then how proud she seemed, bound there, suddenly. She looked up at her bound wrists and the large ring. Her feet moved, rubbing slightly against one another; her ankles, crossed and bound, shifted in the small encircling rope loops which held them closely together. The line of her body, suspended as she was, was very beautiful. She looked over at Sasi, and Sasi smiled at her. Then, to my amazement, the blond girl, though her wrists must have hurt her, her weight drawing against them, smiled back at Sasi. Then she looked down with contempt at the ragged girls on the wharf.

"You are both homely, poor slaves!" called up one of the girls.

"You are homely, poor slaves, not we!" said Sasi. "We are at the prow!" She looked at them, angrily. "Were you ever at the prow?"

Again they did not answer.

"Can your master not afford to give you a decent tunic?" asked Sasi. I smiled, for Sasi, herself, did not have a stitch to wear. I would have her improve her slave skills considerably before I would let her have so much as a rag. "I wager your master has you dance for male slaves!" cried Sasi.

The two girls cried out with rage and the one girl hurled the core of the larma at Sasi, stinging her on the lower right abdomen.

"Pierced-ear girls!" cried Sasi.

The two girls suddenly looked at one another and, sobbing, turned and fled from the wharf.

Sasi looked back at me, well pleased with herself. I had to admit she had handled the two girls well. I also recalled that she had, once, in the voyage, begged me to have her own ears pierced, that she might be then all the more helplessly and irrevocably a slave. I did not know if she had changed her mind on this issue, but it did not matter. I looked at her. Yes, rings would look well in her ears. I would, thus, have her ears pierced, or would do it myself. I also looked at the blond-haired girl. Her ears, too, I decided, would look well with rings in them. She would soon have pierced ears, set well with golden rings, should she come into my ownership.

The blond-haired girl looked at me, and then looked away. I was pleased. I could see how proud she was to have been found beautiful enough to be put at the prow of a Gorean ship. Perhaps for the first time she was beginning to sense how lovely she truly was.

How ignorant women are. Do they not know how beautiful they are? Do they not know how incredibly exciting they are to men? Do they not know how they are wanted, how fiercely they are desired. If only they could see themselves but once through a man's eyes, would they not be terrified to leave the house, lest they be stripped and put under the iron, and collared, by the first man who sees them? Perhaps it is well for women not to know how desirable they are. How they might fear men, if they but knew. I speak, of course, of the men of Gor and those of a Gorean nature.

And yet on Gor women who are put in collars do not long remain ignorant of their own beauty and its meaning. It is soon taught to them, for they are slaves. Perhaps it is only the slave girl, of all women, kneeling and owned, placed uncompromisingly at the mercy of men, who had some sense of her own desirability. What woman can begin to understand men, who has not been owned by one?

"Bring in the slaves," said the physician.

One seaman held Sasi's rope taut, above the deck ring. Another undid the bowline which fastened the rope to the ring. Shoka, with a hook on a pole, drew Sasi back to the rail. He put aside the pole, and, one hand about her waist, drew her to him, lifting her then over the rail. He placed her on her back on the deck, her ankles still bound, her wrists, still tied, back over her head.

The physician bent to examine her.

Shoka then retrieved the pole and extended it outward, to draw the blond-haired girl back to the rail.

She was very beautiful. Her eyes, briefly, met mine as Shoka lifted her over the rail. He placed her on her back, beside Sasi, her wrists and ankles, like those of Sasi, still tied. Her arms, like Sasi's, elbows bent, were back and over her head.

119

"Oh!" she cried, handled as a slave girl.

Curious, the physician touched her again. She whimpered, squirming. "She's a hot one," said the physician.

"Yes," said Ulafi.

The girl looked at the physician with horror, tears in her eyes. But he completed her examination, looking into her eyes, and examining the interior of her thighs, her belly, and the interior of her forearms, for marks.

Then the physician stood up. "They are clear," he said. "The ship is clear. All may disembark."

"Excellent," said Ulafi.

The scribe noted the physician's report in his papers and the physician, with a marking stick, initialed the entry.

"May I wish you good fortune in your business in Schendi," said Ulafi.

"Yes, thank you, Captain," I said. "My thanks to you, too, for a fine voyage."

He nodded. "Thanks, too," said he, "for the use of your pretty little dark-haired slave for the prow."

"It is nothing," I said.

"I wish you well," said he.

"I wish you well," said I.

I bent to Sasi's bonds, and freed her. Then I took a pair of slave bracelets from my pouch and braceleted her hands behind her back. I would have to find lodging.

"Put that one," said Ulafi to a seaman, indicating the bound, blond-haired girl, "in sirik and chain her to a ring on the wharf. We will not have her run away again, as she did in Port Kar."

"Yes, Captain," said the man.

I went and gathered up my sea bag, Sasi behind me braceleted, to my left.

I heard the blond-haired girl being locked in sirik. She was then freed of the ropes on her.

She was pulled to her feet by the chain at her throat, that attached to the sirik, collar. The sirik collar was close-fitting and would not, like a work collar, fit over the shipping collar. The shipping collar was thrust up her throat, under her chin, where it would be easy to check. The sirik collar then had been locked about her throat below it. I did not think the girl would be let out of the shipping collar until she had been delivered into the hands of the slaver, Uchafu, who was to be her buyer. Ulafi, commendably, was taking no chances with the wench. I did not think, however, that she would be likely to attempt to escape again, anyway. She had now learned something of her slavery, and she had felt the whip. Too, surely she could remember the feel of the scimitar of discipline on her ankles at Port Kar, at the desk of the wharf praetor. At a word from Ulafi her feet would have been cut off. Mercifully she had been only whipped, thereafter being identified as what she was, a slave, by brand and collar. I did not think she would wish to lose her feet. I did not think she would attempt to escape again.

Shoka pulled her down the gangplank and, near the ship, with a length of chain and a heavy padlock, running the chain through the sirik chain, fastened her to a ring.

She knelt there, on the hot boards.

She looked up at me, naked and chained.

For an instant I saw again, in her eyes, the secret slave of her. Then I saw her eyes try to deny the slave. She bit her lip, and looked down. "No, no," she whispered to herself, in English. "I am not a slave."

"Are you going to sell me in Schendi?" asked Sasi.

"Perhaps," I said. "I will, if I wish."

"Yes, Master," said Sasi.

The blond-haired girl's head was down.

I supposed the secret slave knew well that her jailer was the blond-haired girl. But I did not think the blond-haired girl realized, or fully realized, that she herself was the slave she so cruelly suppressed.

The blond-haired girl then, timidly, lifted her eyes to mine.

I looked at her.

Gorean men, despite her will, would free that slave. The blond-haired girl would have no choice but to become her deepest, fullest and most ancient self. The lies of her false civilization cast aside, the veneers of her acculturation rent and discarded, being of no interest to Gorean men, who did not share them, the deepest and most primitive female animal in her would be liberated. She would be made to be a woman.

Frightened, the blond-haired girl quickly put down her head.

She trembled. The chains moved. She seemed small.

I continued to look upon her.

Yes, she would be made to be a woman, and in the fullest sense of the word, that of a love slave to strong men.

I turned to leave.

"Master!" she cried.

I turned about, to again face her.

121

"Do not go," she said. "Please do not leave me!"

"I do not understand," I said.

"Take me with you," she begged.

"I do not understand," I said.

"Please buy me," she said. She looked up at me, tears in her eyes, lifting her chained hands to me. "Please, Please, Master, buy me!" she said.

"He already has a girl," said Sasi, angrily.

"Be silent," I said to Sasi.

"Yes, Master," she said.

"Do you beg to be purchased?" I asked the blond-haired girl.

"Yes, Master," she said.

"Only a slave begs to be purchased," I said. It is regarded as an acknowledgment of their slavery, that they can be bought and sold.

"I am a slave," she said.

"Yes," I said, "but you do not yet really know it."

She looked at me.

"You have not yet begun to learn your collar," I told her.

"Buy me," she said. "Teach it to me."

"You tempt me, lovely slut," I said.

She looked up at me.

"Kiss my feet," I told her.

She did so, in her chains, kneeling on the hot boards of the wharf at Schendi. Then again she looked up at me.

"Another will buy you," I told her. Then I turned away from her.

"We must seek lodging," I said to Sasi.

"Yes, Master," she said.

I heard the girl behind us cry out in misery. And then she screamed, though we did not turn to regard her, in English, "I hate you! I hate you, Master! And I am not a slave! I am not a slave!"

But I remembered the feel of her lips and tongue, delicate, on my feet. The feel of the caress had been unmistakable. Her lips and tongue had been those of a slave.

"I am not a slave!" she cried in English.

I thought the girl would be useful. She would lead me, inadvertently, to the geographer Shaba, explorer of Lake Ushindi, discoverer of Lake Ngao and the Ua river. She would lead me, too, not understanding it, to the Tahari ring.

It was that which I sought, and perhaps, too, the blood of Shaba, who had betrayed Priest-Kings.

122

7

THE MARKET OF UCHAFU

There are many fine slave markets in Schendi, in particular, those of Ushanga, Mkufu, Utajiri, Dhähabu, Fedha, Marashi, Hariri, Kovu and Ngoma. The market of Uchafu, on the other hand, is not numbered among these.

One can pick up pot girls and low women there. It was thus appropriate, I suppose, that the blond-haired barbarian, ignorant and untrained, scarcely able to speak Gorean, little more than raw collar meat, should have been taken there. She would attract little attention.

"May I be of assistance to Master?" asked Uchafu, hobbling toward me, supporting himself on a knobbed stick.

"Perhaps, later," I said. "I am browsing now."

"Browse as you will, Master," said Uchafu. "You will find that we have here the finest slaves in all Schendi." He had lost several teeth and was blind in one eye. His tobe was filthy, and stained with food and blood. A long knife, unsheathed, was thrust into his sash.

"Why is that girl blindfolded?" I asked, indicating a girl, kneeling with other girls, chained, under a low, palm-thatched platform.

"Why to keep her quiet, Master," said Uchafu.

I nodded. It is a device often used by slavers.

Uchafu then hobbled away.

"Buy me, Master," said a girl near me. I glanced at her, and then passed by, moving down the row.

It was muddy in the market, for it had rained yesterday afternoon and evening, after our arrival in Schendi. The air was steamy. One could smell the vegetation and jungles behind the port. Uchafu's market was back of the merchant wharves, nearer the harbor mouth. It was on a canal, called the Fish canal, leading back from the harbor. It is adjacent, on the south, to a large market where river fish are peddled for consumption in Schendi. These are brought literally through the harbor by canoes, moving among the larger ships, from the fishing villages of the Nyoka and then delivered via the canal to the market. There are also a number

123

of small shops in the vicinity. The official name of the canal is the Tangawizi canal, or Ginger canal, but it is generally called, because of the market, the Fish canal.

"Buy me, Master," said another girl, as I passed her. She was brown-skinned and sweet-legged.

There were only, by my conjecture, at the time I was in the market of Uchafu, some two hundred and fifty girls there. Uchafu was not at his full stock at that time. He handled most of his own business but was assisted by four younger men, one of whom was his brother. In spite of the fact that he was not at full inventory he crowded his girls, leaving several of the small, open-sided, palm-thatched shelters, those about the outer wall, a low, boarded wall, empty.

Most of the girls were black, as would be expected from the area, but there were some ten or fifteen white girls there, and some two girls apparently of oriental or mixed extraction.

"Master," said a red-haired girl, reaching forth her hand, timidly, not daring to touch me.

I looked at her.

Fearfully she drew back her hand.

I moved farther down the row. Two black girls shrank back. I gathered they were new to their collars.

I then shifted my attention to another of the small shelters. They are some twenty feet long and five feet deep, and four feet high. Two heavy posts are sunk deeply into the ground at each end of each shelter. A chain runs between these posts. Each girl, on her left ankle, wears an ankle ring, with a loop of chain and a lock. By means of the loop of chain and lock she is attached to the central chain. Some of the girls also wore slave bracelets or other devices, fastening their hands before or behind their bodies. One girl, lying on her shoulder in the mud, was cruelly trussed, hand and foot, with binding fiber. Perhaps she had not been fully pleasing.

I crouched down beside a thick-ankled blond girl. I pulled her to me by the hair, and turned her head to one side. I examined her collar. The legend had once read 'I am the girl of Kikombe'. The name 'Kikombe' now, however, for the most part, with a set of rough, zigzag lines, had been scratched out, and the name 'Uchafu', with a sharp tool, had been added. I smiled. Uchafu even used second-hand collars. The Kurii were clever. Surely one would not search for a valuable girl in such a market.

"Do you like her?" asked Uchafu, who had come up near

to me again. He had kept a close eye on me. "I had her from Kikombe honestly," he said.

"I do not doubt it," I said. I gathered he thought me possibly an agent tracing smuggled slaves.

It had not been for no reason that I had seemed to express interest in the thick-ankled blond.

"Do you like white girls?" asked Uchafu.

"Yes," I said.

"They make superb slaves," said Uchafu.

"Yes," I said.

"This one is a beauty," he said, indicating the girl whose collar I had just examined.

"Have you others?" I asked.

"Yes," he said.

"Have you others with hair of this sort?" I asked.

"Yes," he said. But he looked at me, suddenly, warily.

I looked about, over the shelters near us to those at the far wall, which were empty. "You have empty shelters over there," I said. "Why do you put so many girls together? Would it not be better to space them farther apart, for purposes of display?"

"It is easier to feed and clean them this way," he said. "There is less area to be covered."

"I see," I said.

"Besides," he said, "later in the month I am expecting deliveries and I will then need that space."

There were weeds and grass growing about the interior perimeter of the low board fence encircling the market. The fence was some four feet high. A small wooden hut, with a roof thatched with palm leaves, at one corner of the compound, served as house and office for Uchafu and, I suspect, dormitory for his assistants.

"You seem to have no male slaves," I observed.

"They are now scarce in Schendi," he said. "Bila Huruma, Ubar of Lake Ushindi, uses them for work on his great canal."

"He intends to join Lakes Ushindi and Ngao, I have heard," I said.

"It is a mad project," said Uchafu, "but what can one expect of the barbarians of the interior?"

"It would open the Ua river to the sea," I said.

"If it were successful," said Uchafu. "But it will never be accomplished. Thousands of men have already died. They perish in the heat, they die in the sun, they are killed by hostile tribes, they are destroyed by insects, they are eaten by tharlarion. It is a mad and hopeless venture, costly in money and wasteful in human life."

"It must be difficult to obtain so many male slaves," I said.

"Most who work on the canal are not slaves," said Uchafu. "Many are debtors or criminals. Many are simply common men, impressed into service, victims of work levies imposed on the villages. Indeed, only this year Bila Huruma has demanded quotas of men from Schendi herself."

"These have, of course, been refused," I said.

"We have strengthened our defenses," said Uchafu, "reinforcing the palisaded walls which shield Schendi from the interior, but we must not delude ourselves. Those walls were built to keep back animals and bands of brigands, not an army of thousands of men. We are not an armed city, not a fortress, not a land power. We do not even have a navy. We are only a merchant port."

"You have, of course, nonetheless refused the request of Bila Huruma for men," I said.

"If he wishes," said Uchafu, "he could enter and burn Schendi."

"Barbarians from the interior?" I asked.

"Bila Huruma has an army at his command, organized, trained, disciplined, effective," said Uchafu. "He manages a Ubarate, with districts and governors, with courts and spies and messengers."

"I did not know anything of this breadth and power existed in the south," I said.

"It is a great Ubarate," said Uchafu, "but it is little known for it is of the interior."

I said nothing.

"Schendi," said he, "is like a flower at the feet of a kailiauk."

"You have then acceded to his request for men?" I said.

"Yes," said Uchafu.

"I am sorry," I said.

Uchafu shrugged. "But do not concern yourself with our troubles," he said, "for you are not of Schendi." He then turned about. "Have you seen the red-headed girl?" he asked. "She is very nice."

"Yes," I said, "I have seen her." I looked about. "There is a blond-haired girl over there," I said, indicating the girl in the blindfold, kneeling chained, crowded together with other girls, under one of the small, thatched roofs, on its poles. She

126

was dirty. Her knees were in the mud. Her left ankle, like that of the other girls, was fastened in an ankle ring. She, like the others, was, by the loop of chain and lock, run through the chain ring on the ankle ring, attached to the central chain of her shelter, that strung between the two heavy posts, one at each end of the shelter. She, like the others, was naked. Her small hands, her wrists secured in slave bracelets, by means of a locked chain snug at her waist, were held at her belly. She could not, then, reach the blindfold. It was of black cloth. It covered most of the upper part of her head.

"Let me show you these two," said Uchafu, leading me away from the girl in the blindfold. She was the only one blindfolded in the market. Uchafu had told me, earlier, that it was to keep her quiet.

"What of these?" asked Uchafu.

Yesterday, after I had left the blond-haired barbarian at the wharf, I had taken lodging at the Cove of Schendi, a rooming house in the vicinity of wharf ten which caters to foreign sailors. The rooms were small but adequate, with a mattress, spread upon the floor; a sea chest at one side of the room; a low table; a tharlarion oil lamp; a bowl and pitcher of water; and, at the foot of the mattress, a stout slave ring. I threw my sea bag beside the sea chest, braceleted Sasi's hands before her body about the ring, left the room, locked the door, dropped the key in my pouch and made my way downstairs, to return inconspicuously to the vicinity of wharf eight, where the *Palms of Schendi* was disembarking her cargo. I did not have long to wait. Uchafu himself had soon appeared and, meeting with Ulafi, completed the brief transaction which purchased him the blond-haired barbarian. Shoka removed the shipping collar of the *Palms of Schendi* from her neck. Uchafu then snapped his own collar on her. Shoka then freed her wrists of the wrist rings of the sirik and Uchafu locked a waist chain on her and then, about this chain, running the linkage of the bracelets behind it, braceleted her hands at her belly. Uchafu then, with the black cloth, blindfolded her, and snapped a lock leash about her collar. Shoka then removed the sirik collar from her, and the ankle rings, freeing her of the sirik. He gathered up the sirik and he took, too, unlocking it, the chain and padlock which had held her, by the sirik, at the wharf ring. He then returned to the *Palms of Schendi*. Uchafu, by the leash, pulled the braceleted, blindfolded girl to her feet, and pulled her after him, leading her from the wharf. I had followed them. Uchafu, as it turned out, had not taken a direct route to his market. I think the girl, even if she had known the streets of Schendi, would have been utterly confused as to her direction or whereabouts.

"These are nice," said Uchafu, indicating a pair of white blonds. "These are sisters," he said, "from Asperiche. You may buy them together, or separately, as you please."

The blond-haired barbarian, as she knelt frightened, in the mud, with the other girls, still wore her blindfold, that which Uchafu had placed on her at wharf eight. She would have no idea of where she was. Uchafu undoubtedly, because of the prices involved, understood that she was of some importance. On the other hand, I do not think he understood the nature of that importance. Ulafi, I was sure, had not either. There was no blood that I could see on the interior of the barbarian's thighs. Ulafi, too, I recalled, had not used her nor thrown her to his crew. This tended to confirm in my mind that they did not understand the nature of her importance. Perhaps a rich man, an eccentric of some sort, desired her. Perhaps he would not be pleased, or would not pay, if she were not delivered to him white silk. I smiled to myself. If Ulafi or Uchafu truly understood the nature of the girl's importance, that it had nothing to do with her being red silk or white silk, she would doubtless, by now, have been richly and abundantly raped. More than a hundred times by now, I expected, had they but known, she would have thrashed and squirmed, gasping, held, in the arms of strong men, her slave beauty the helpless, lascivious wine on which mighty masters would slake the thirsts of their lust.

"What do you think of them?" inquired Uchafu, indicating the two blond-haired sisters from Asperiche.

Both were blue-eyed. They crouched in the mud, chained, beneath the palm-thatched roof of the tiny shelter.

"What can you do?" I asked them.

They looked at one another, frightened. One whimpered. Uchafu angrily raised the heavy, knobbed stick he carried.

"Whatever Master desires," said one of the girls.

"Whatever Master desires," said the other girl, quickly.

"What of that one over there?" I asked, casually, indicating the blond-haired barbarian in a shelter some feet away, diagonally to my left.

"These are beauties," said Uchafu, indicating the two sisters, the blonds from Asperiche. "Buy one or both," he said.

But I had begun to walk toward the blond-haired barbarian. Uchafu hurried along behind me, and seized my sleeve, stopping me.

"No," he said, "not her."

"Why?" I asked, as though puzzled.

"She has already been sold," he said.

"How much did you get?" I asked.

"Fifteen copper tarsks," he said. He had put the price a bit high for this girl and this market. That was, I supposed, to discourage me. I recalled she had had an honest bid on her once at the market of Vart, once Publius Quintus of Ar, in Port Kar, a bid from the tavern keeper, Procopius, of forty copper tarsks. She had received this bid, of course, only after her unusual heat, for a new slave, had been made clear.

"I will give you sixteen," I told him.

Uchafu looked annoyed. I did not permit myself to smile. I knew that he had not yet sold the girl, for she was still on his chain. He was waiting for his buyer. Further, I knew, from Ulafi, he would have paid two tarsks, of silver, for her. He would doubtless receive three or four silver tarsks from the awaited buyer. But then he smiled and shrugged. "Oh, misery, for a poor merchant," said he. "I could have received sixteen for her and sold her for fifteen. Misery! But I cannot now renege upon my word, sadly enough, for I am a merchant of well-known integrity. Much as I would love to sell her to you for sixteen tarsks I must let her go to a previous buyer for fifteen. Such is occasionally the sad lot of one who has made the difficult choice, and will abide by it, of dealing straightforwardly and honestly with all men, whomsoever they may be."

"I had not realized that integrity could be such a handicap," I said.

"Ah, yes," he moaned.

"But perhaps your reputation as a noble and honest merchant will yet in the long run redound to your profit as well as your honor."

"Let us hope so," he said.

"You are one of the most honest slavers I have ever met," I said.

"My thanks, Master," breathed he, bowing low.

"I wish you well," said I.

"I wish you well," said he.

I then left his market. I think then he realized that I had not bought a girl.

"We will have more in at the end of the week!" he called. "Come again!"

I waved to him, from the other side of the low board fence.

8

WHAT OCCURRED IN THE GOLDEN KAILIAUK

"Hurry! Hurry, clumsy slave!" cried the small, scarred man, crooked-backed, his right leg dragging behind him. He wore a dirty tunic; over it was a long, brown aba, torn and ragged. He was barefoot. A brown cloth, turbanlike, was twisted about his head. He seemed angry. His feet and legs, and those of the slave, were muddy and dirty, from the mud in the streets.

"Hurry!" he cried.

"Oh!" she cried, sobbing in the blindfold, driven before him, struck again by the long switch in his right hand.

"Oh! Oh!" she cried. "Please, don't hit me again, Master!"

Then she cried out again, stumbling and weeping, before him, struck twice more.

I followed at a discreet distance. I had observed her sale by means of a glass of the builders, from a roof top near Uchafu's market. I had then telescoped the glass and slipped it into my pouch. I had seen silver exchange hands. But I did not know precisely how many pieces had been paid, as the buyer's back, as he turned, was then toward me.

"Hurry!" he cried. He struck her again.

"Yes, Master!" she cried.

He was dressed as a beggar, but I did not think him of that profession. Too, beggars do not buy slave girls, or openly buy them.

I was sure the man was an agent of Kurii.

He struck her again, and again she stumbled on before him. She still wore her blindfold, that black cloth covering most of the upper portion of her head. She had never seen, I knew, Uchafu's market and she did not know where she was being driven. All she had seen of Schendi was the harbor and wharf. Then she had been blindfolded. She stumbled on,

130

miserably, before her herder. Her small hands were still secured at her belly, but now by binding fiber. Her wrists had
been crossed and bound, and then the long end of the fiber
had been taken about her body and tied again to her wrists.
This way she could not, still, reach the blindfold, and her
back was fully exposed, as was doubtless intended, for the
stroke of the herding switch. Uchafu's collar had been removed from her in the market and another collar had been
snapped on her throat. I had not, of course, had a chance to
read it.

"Please do not strike me any more, Master!" she begged,
stumbling. "I am hurrying! I am hurrying!"

Then she stumbled against a free woman, who, in fury,
screamed at her, and began to strike and kick at her.

She fell to her knees, and put her head down. "Forgive me,
Mistress!" she begged. "Forgive me!"

The free woman, angrily, continued on her way.

"Get up!" snarled the herdsman.

The girl tried to get up but her foot slipped in the mud and
she fell to her side.

Instantly the man was on her with the switch, lashing down
at her. "Get up, you worthless white slut!" he cried.

She struggled to her feet. "Yes, Master! Yes, Master!" she
wept.

"Hurry!" he cried. He struck her again.

"Which way?" she cried, disoriented. She looked about,
blindly, her feet in the mud. "Oh! Oh!" she cried, richly
struck, and then fell to her knees, sobbing, helpless. He
pulled her to her feet by the left arm and thrust her ahead of
him, down the street.

"Hurry!" he commanded. He struck her again.

"Yes, Master," she sobbed, and, again, stumbled on before
him, a blindfolded, herded slave girl.

I looked behind me occasionally, but I saw only the normal occupants and passers-by of the streets of Schendi. I
wore the garb now of a leather worker. If inquiries had been
made it would be recalled that he who had arrived in the
Palms of Schendi had been, at least ostensibly, of the metal
workers.

"In here, worthless slave," said the man, and, taking the
girl by the arm, thrust her through the doors of a paga tavern, the Golden Kailiauk.

He took her over beside a wall, across from the main door,
and close to a small side door.

"Lie down here," he told her.

She lay down on the wooden floor.

"On your side," he said. "Pull your knees up under your chin."

She then lay there, small, her knees drawn up.

He hurled his brown aba over her, covering her completely, and limped out, through the small side door.

"Does Master desire aught?" asked a black girl, kneeling before me, a paga slave of the establishment.

"Paga," I said to her. She rose to her feet and went to the vat behind the counter. I sat down, cross-legged, behind a low table, from which vantage point I could see the girl lying on the floor, she covered with the beggar's aba.

I assumed her herdsman had delivered her to this tavern, that she be picked up by someone else.

I nursed the paga, making it last.

But no one seemed to come for her.

I began to be apprehensive that perhaps some mistake had occurred. What if Ulafi had been mistaken about the girl. What if he had not, really, received two tarsks from Uchafu for her. What if the beggar had made a serious purchase of the girl on behalf of the tavern keeper? What if she were merely being delivered here to be trained as a mere paga girl? I glanced around. There was only one other white girl in the tavern, a dark-haired girl, collared, in yellow pleasure silk, she, too, apparently a paga slave, like the black girls, waiting on the tables. Perhaps the tavern keeper only wanted another white girl, to add variety for his clientele.

I looked at the blond-haired girl lying hidden under the aba. She did not dare to move.

But, no. I recalled clearly that silver had exchanged hands in her sale.

There was no mistake.

I must wait.

I ordered another cup of paga. I played a game of Kaissa with another guest of the tavern. The paga tasted a bit strange, but it was a local paga and there is variation in such pagas, generally a function of the brewer's choice of herbs and grains. From time to time I glanced at the girl under the aba. I used the Telnus Defense on the fellow, a response to his Ubara's Gambit, which I thought might be unknown in Schendi, as it had first been seen only last spring at the Fair of En'Kara, near the Sardar Mountains. He met it squarely, however, and I myself, no Centius of Cos, was soon involved in perplexing difficulties. I did manage, narrowly, to eke out a win in the endgame.

"I did not expect you would handle my response to your Ubara's Spearman to Ubara five as you did," I told him.

"You were obviously using the Telnus Defense," he said.

"You have heard of it?" I asked.

"I have read more than a hundred analyses of it," he said. "Do you think we are barbarians in Schendi?" he asked.

"No," I said.

"I congratulate you," he said. "You are quite skilled at Kaissa."

"I did not play my best game," I said.

"No one ever does," he said.

"Perhaps you are right," I said. "You are a fine player," I said. "Thank you for the game."

He shook hands, and left. He seemed a nice fellow. Those who play Kaissa are good chaps.

I glanced once more at the girl under the aba. I blinked once or twice. My eyes felt a bit strange, scratchy. My forearms, too, and belly, felt a little itchy. I scratched them.

"Master?" asked one of the girls, a black girl with high, regal cheekbones.

"More paga," I said.

"Yes, Master," she said.

In another Ahn some musicians arrived. Shortly thereafter, as the tavern grew more crowded, they began to play. My thigh felt irritated. I dug at it with my fingernails.

I watched the white-skinned, dark-haired girl, collared, serving cups to a distant table. She was nicely legged.

A skirl on a flute and a sudden pounding on twin tabors, small, hand drums, called my attention to the square of sand at the side of which sat the musicians.

I then gave my attention to the dancer, a sweetly hipped black girl in yellow beads.

She was skillful and, I suspected, from the use of the hands and beads, had been trained in Ianda, a merchant island north of Anango. Certain figures are formed with the hands and beads which have symbolic meaning, much of which was lost upon me, as I was not familiar with the conventions involved. Some, however, I had seen before, and had been explained to me. One was that of the free woman, another of the whip, another of the yielding, collared slave. Another was that of the thieving slave girl, and another that of the girl summoned, terrified, before the master. Each of these, with

133

the music and followed by its dance expression, was very well done. Women are beautiful and they make fantastic dancers. One of the figures done was that of a girl, a slave, who encounters one who is afflicted with plague. She, a slave, knows that if she should contract the disease she would, in all probability, be summarily slain. She dances her terror at this. This was followed by the figure of obedience, and that by the figure of joy.

I looked about and did not see, any longer, the white-skinned, dark-haired girl, she who had been serving paga.

I was growing irritated, and a little drunk. It seemed to me that by now, surely, the blond-haired barbarian should have been picked up.

I glanced again at the aba by the wall. I could still see, beneath it, the lusciousness of a girl's curves. What marvelous slaves they make.

Suddenly I howled with rage and threw over the small table behind which I sat. I in two strides was at the aba, and I tore it away.

"Master!" screamed the girl beneath it, looking up, frightened.

It was not the blond-haired barbarian. It was the white-skinned, dark-haired girl, collared, in her bit of pleasure silk, who had been serving paga.

I pulled her to her knees by the hair. "Where is the other girl!" I demanded. "Where!"

"What is going on here?" cried the proprietor of the tavern, who had come in earlier, and was now behind the counter, ladling out paga.

One of the paga attendants came running toward me, but, seeing my eyes; hesitated. Several men were now on their feet. The musicians had stopped playing. The dancer stood, still, on the sand, startled.

"Where is the girl who was under this aba," I demanded. "Where!"

"What girl was it?" asked the proprietor. "Whose was she?"

"She was brought in by Kunguni, when you were out," said one of the black girls.

"I gave orders that he was not again to be admitted to this tavern!" said the man.

"You were not here," moaned the girl. "We feared to tell a free man he could not enter."

"Where were you?" called the proprietor to the attendant.

"I was in the kitchen," he said. "I did not know she had been brought in by Kunguni."

Angrily I threw the girl I held from me.

"Who saw her leave, with whom?" I demanded.

Men looked at one another.

"How came you beneath the aba?" I asked the girl whom I had thrown to one side.

"A man told me to creep beneath it," she said. "I did not see him! He told me not to look around!"

"You are lying," I told her.

"Be merciful, Master," she said. "I am only a slave!"

The paga attendant, he who was closest to me of the crowd, was looking at me, intently. I did not understand this. He edged uneasily backward. I did not understand this. I had not threatened him.

"A silver tarsk to the man who can find me that girl," I said.

The black girls looked at one another. "She was only a pot girl," said one of them.

"A silver tarsk," I said, repeating my offer, "to he who can find me that slave."

"Look at his eyes," said the paga attendant, backing away another step.

She could not have been gone long. I must hunt her in the streets.

Suddenly the dancer on the sand threw her hands before her face, and screamed. Then she pointed at me.

"It is the plague!" she cried. "It is the plague!"

The paga attendant, stumbling, turned and ran. "Plague!" he cried. Men fled from the tavern. I stood alone by the wall. Tables had been overturned. Paga was spilled upon the floor.

The tavern seemed, suddenly, eerily quiet. Even the paga girls had fled.

I could hear shouting outside, in the streets, and screaming.

"Call guardsmen!" I heard.

"Kill him," I heard. "Kill him!"

I walked over to a mirror. I ran my tongue over my lips. They seemed dry. The whites of my eyes, clearly, were yellow. I rolled up the sleeve of my tunic and saw there, on the flesh of the forearm, like black blisters, broken open, erupted, a scattering of pustules.

9

I DECIDE TO CHANGE
MY LODGINGS

"Master!" cried Sasi.

"Do not fear," I said to her. "I am not ill. But we must leave this place quickly.

"Your face," she said. "It is marked!"

"It will pass," I said. I unlocked her bracelets and slipped them into my pouch.

"I fear I may be traced here," I said. "We must change lodgings."

I had left the paga tavern by a rear door and then swung myself up to a low roof, and then climbed to a higher one. I had made my way over several roofs until I had found a convenient and lonely place to descend. I had then, wrapped in the discarded aba of Kunguni, made my way through the streets to the Cove of Schendi. Outside, from the wharves and from the interior of the city, I could hear the ringing of alarm bars. "Plague!" men were crying in the streets.

"Are you not ill, Master?" asked Sasi.

"I do not think so," I said.

I knew that I had not been in a plague area. Too, the Bazi plague had burned itself out years ago. No cases to my knowledge had been reported for months. Most importantly, perhaps, I simply did not feel ill. I was slightly drunk and heated from the paga, but I did not believe myself fevered. My pulse and heartbeat, and respiration, seemed normal. I did not have difficulty catching my breath. I was neither dizzy nor nauseous, and my vision was clear. My worst physical symptoms were the irritation about my eyes and the genuinely nasty itchiness of my skin. I felt like tearing it off with my own fingernails.

"Are you of the metal workers or the leather workers?" she asked.

"Let us not bother about that now," I said, knotting the cords on the sea bag. I looked about the room. Aside from Sasi what I owned there was either on my person or in the sea bag.

"A girl likes to know the caste of her master," she said.

"Let us be on our way," I said.

"Perhaps it is the merchants," she said.

"How would you like to be whipped?" I asked her.

"I would not like that," she said.

"Let us hurry," I said.

"You do not have time to whip me now, do you?" she asked.

"No," I said, "I do not."

"I thought not," she said. "I do not think it is the peasants."

"I could always whip you later," I said.

"That is true," she agreed. "Perhaps I should best be quiet."

"That is an excellent insight on your part," I said.

"Thank you, Master," she said.

"If I am caught, and it is thought that I have the plague," I said, "you will doubtless be exterminated before I am."

"Let us not dally," she said.

We left the room.

"You have strong hands," she said. "Is it the potters?"

"No," I said.

"I thought it might be," she said.

"Be silent," I said.

"Yes, Master," she said.

10

I MAKE INQUIRIES OF KIPOFU, WHO IS UBAR OF THE BEGGARS OF SCHENDI

The blind man lifted his white, sightless eyes to me. His thin, black hand, clawlike, extended itself.

I placed a tarsk bit in his hand.

"You are Kipofu?" I asked.

I placed another tarsk bit in his hand. He put these two tiny coins in a small, shallow copper bowl before him. He was sitting, cross-legged, on a flat, rectangular stone, broad and heavy, about a foot high, at the western edge of the large

137

Utukufu, or Glory, square. The stone was his *etem*, or sitting place. He was Ubar of the beggars of Schendi.

"I am Kipofu," he said.

"It is said," I said, "that though you are blind there is little which you do not see in Schendi."

He smiled. He rubbed his nose with his thumb.

"I would obtain information," I said to him.

"I am only a poor blind man," he said. He spread his hands, apologetically.

"There is little that transpires in Schendi which can escape your notice," I told him.

"Information can be expensive," he said.

"I can pay," I told him.

"I am only a poor and ignorant man," he said.

"I can pay well," I told him.

"What do you wish to know?" he asked.

He sat on his *etem* in brown rags, a brown cloth wound about his head, to protect him from the sun. There were sores upon his body. Dirt was crusted upon his legs and arms. The peel of a larma lay by one knee. He was blind, and half naked and filthy, but I knew him to be the Ubar of the beggars of Schendi. He had been chosen by them to rule over them. Some said that he had been chosen to rule over them because only he was blind and thus could not see how repulsive they were. Before him the deformed and maimed, the disfigured and crippled, might stand as men, as subject before sovereign, to be heard with objectivity and obtain a dispassionate and honest justice, neither to be dismissed with contempt or demeaningly gratified by the indulgence of one who holds himself above them. But if there were truth in this I think there was, too, a higher truth involved. Kipofu, though avaricious and petty in many respects, had in him something of the sovereign. He was a highly intelligent man, and one who could, upon occasion, be wise as well as shrewd. He was a man of determination, and of iron will, and vision. It was he who had first effectively organized the beggars of Schendi, stabilizing their numbers and distributing and allotting their territories. None might now beg in Schendi without his permission and none might transgress the territory of another. And each, each week, paid his tax to Kipofu, the inevitable price of government. These taxes, though doubtless much went to the shrewd Kipofu, for monarchs expect to be well paid for bearing the burdens and tribulations of office, served to obtain benefits and insurances for the governed. No beggar

138

now in Schendi was truly without shelter, or medical care or needed go hungry. Each tended to look out for the others, through the functioning of the system. It was said that even members of the merchant council occasionally took Kipofu into their confidence. One consequence of the organization of the beggars, incidentally, was that Schendi did not have many beggars. Obviously the fewer beggars there are the more alms there are for each one. Unwanted beggars had the choice of having their passage paid from Schendi or concluding their simple careers in the harbor.

"I seek information," I said, "on one who seemed a beggar, who was called Kunguni."

"Pay," said Kipofu.

I put another tarsk bit into his hand.

"Pay," said Kipofu.

I put yet another tarsk bit into his hand.

"None in Schendi who begs is known as Kunguni," he said.

"Permit me to describe the man to you," I said.

"How would I know of these things?" asked Kipofu.

I drew forth a silver tarsk.

Kipofu, I knew, through the organization of the beggars, their covering of territories, and their reports, as well as his use of them as messengers and spies, was perhaps the most informed man in Schendi. He, like a clever spider in its web, was the center of an intelligence network that might have been the envy of many a Ubar. There were few tremors in Schendi which did not, sooner or later, reach Kipofu on his simple *etem* in the square.

"That is a silver tarsk," I said. I pressed it into his palm.

"Ah," he said. He weighed the coin in his hand and felt its thickness. He ran his finger about its edge to determine that it had not been shaved. He tapped it on the *etem*. And, though it was not gold, he put it in his mouth, touching its surface with his tongue, and biting against its resistance.

"It is of Port Kar," he said. He had, too, pressed his thumb against the coin, on both sides, feeling the ship, and, on the reverse, the sign of Port Kar, its initials, in the same script that occurred on her Home Stone.

"This man," I said, "is small, and has a crooked back, hunched. He has a scar on his left cheek. He limps, dragging his right leg behind him."

The blood seemed suddenly to drain from Kipofu's face.

He turned a shade paler. He stiffened. He lifted his head, listening intently.

I looked about. None were close to us.

"No one is near us," I said. I had little doubt that Kipofu, who was reputed to have extremely sharp senses, might have heard breathing within a radius of twenty feet, even in the square. I wondered at the nature of the man, the mention of whom might have caused this reaction in the shrewd Kipofu.

"His back is crooked and it is not," said Kipofu. "His back is hunched and it is not. His face is scarred and it is not. His leg is crippled and it is not."

"Do you know who this man is?" I asked him.

"Do not seek him," said Kipofu. "Forget him. Flee."

"Who is he?" I asked.

Kipofu pressed the coin back at me. "Take your tarsk," said he.

"I want to know," I said, determinedly.

Kipofu suddenly lifted his hand. "Listen," said he. "Listen!"

I listened.

"There is one about," he said.

I looked about. "No," I said. "There is not."

"There," said Kipofu, pointing, "there!"

But I saw nothing where he pointed. "There is nothing there," I said.

"There!" whispered Kipofu, pointing.

I thought him perhaps mad. But I walked in the direction which he had pointed. I encountered nothing. Then the hair on the back of my neck rose, as I realized what it might have been.

"It is gone now," said Kipofu.

I returned to the *etem* of the Ubar of the beggars. He was visibly shaken.

"Go away!" he said.

"I would know who the man is," I said.

"Go away!" said Kipofu. "Take your tarsk!" He held it out to me.

"What do you know of the Golden Kailiauk?" I asked.

"It is a paga tavern," said Kipofu.

"What do you know of a white slave girl who works within it?" I asked.

"Pembe," he said, "who is the proprietor of the tavern, has not owned a white-skinned girl in months."

"Ah!" I said.

"Take back your tarsk," said Kipofu.

"Keep it," I told him. "You have told me much of what I wanted to know."

I then turned about and strode away, taking my leave from the presence of Kipofu, that unusual Ubar of the beggars of Schendi.

11

SHABA

The girl stood at the heavy, wooden door, on the dark street, and knocked, sharply, four times, followed by a pause, and then twice. A tiny tharlarion-oil lamp burned near the door. I could see her dark hair, and high cheekbones, in the light. The yellow light, too, flickering, in the shadows, glinted on the steel collar beneath her hair. She wore a tan slave tunic, sleeveless, of knee length, rather demure for a bond girl. It did, however, have a plunging neckline, setting off the collar well.

She repeated the knock, precisely as before.

She was barefoot. In her hand, wadded up, was a tiny scrap of yellow slave silk, which had been her uniform in the tavern of Pembe.

She was not a bad looking girl. Her hair, dark-brown, was of shoulder length.

Her accent, as I had detected yesterday evening, in the Golden Kailiauk, was barbarian. Something in it, when she had cried out, or spoken to me, suggested that she might be familiar with English.

I had little doubt she had been affiliated with he who had called himself Kunguni. She had simulated the appearance of the blond-haired barbarian beneath the brown aba. Her face and body, when she had protested her innocence to me, had belied her words. I had learned from Kipofu that she was not owned by Pembe, proprietor of the Golden Kailiauk. Doubtless, for a fee, paid by her master, if she were a slave, she had been permitted to serve in his place of business. Sometimes masters do this sort of thing for their girls. It is cheaper than renting space for them in the public or private pens. Pembe would not be likely to think anything amiss.

141

I stood back in the shadows. A tiny panel in the door slid back. Then it shut. A moment later the door opened.

I saw, in the light, briefly, the scarred face, and bent back, hunched, of he who had called himself Kunguni. He looked about, but did not see me, concealed in the shadows. The girl slipped past him, and entered the door. It then shut.

I looked about, and then crossed the narrow street. I glanced at the shuttered windows. I could see cracks of light between the wooden slats.

Inside, not far from the door, I could see the girl and the man. The room, or anteroom, was dingy.

"Is he here yet?" asked the girl.

"Yes," said the man, "he is waiting inside."

"Good," she said.

"It is our hope," said the man, "that you will be more successful this evening than last."

"I can get nothing out of her, if she knows nothing," snapped the girl.

"That is true," said the man.

The girl took the bit of wadded yellow pleasure silk she carried in her hand and, straightening it a bit, slipped it on a narrow wooden rod in an open closet. "Disgusting garment," she said. "A girl might as well be naked."

"A lovely garment," said the man, "but I agree with your latter sentiment."

She looked at him, angrily.

"Did many ask for you tonight?" he asked. "Or did Pembe have to inform them that you were not for use?"

"None asked," she said, angrily.

"Interesting," he said.

"Why is it 'interesting'?" she asked, not pleasantly.

"I do not know," he said. "It just seems that your face and body would be of interest to men, but apparently they are not."

"I can be attractive, if I wish," she said.

"I doubt it," he said.

"Behold!" she said, striking a pose.

"It is fraudulent," he said. "Women such as you understand nothing of attractiveness. With you it is a matter of externals, of acting. Any true man sees through it immediately. You confuse the pretense with the truth, the artificial and imitative with the reality. You think you could become attractive but merely choose not to be so. It is a delusion, as you understand these things. This permits you to console yourself

142

with lies and, at the same time, provides you with an excuse for despising and belittling the truly attractive woman, thinking she is merely, as you would be, if you were she, acting. But it is not true. The source of a woman's attractiveness is within her. It is internal. It comes from the inside out. She is vulnerable, and desires men, and wishes to be touched and owned. This then shows in her body and movements, and in her eyes and face. That is the truly attractive woman."

"Like that she-sleen in the other room?" asked the woman.

"She has felt the whip, and known male domination," he said. "Have you?"

"No," she said.

"I took the liberty of caressing our lovely bound captive a bit before you arrived," he said. "She is quite hot."

"I hate that sort of woman," said the girl. "She is weak. She is a slave, and I am not."

I saw the man smile.

"Tonight, if she knows anything," said the girl, "I will get it out of her."

"I am sure you will," he said.

I then saw the girl, to my surprise, remove a tiny key from her tunic.

"Permit me," he said.

"Thank you, no," she said, acidly. Then she, lifting her arms, fitted the key into the lock at the back of her collar. This action lifted the line of her breasts, which was lovely, and lifted the tan slave tunic a bit higher on her thighs. She was nicely legged, as I had noted before. "You needn't look at me as I do this," she said.

"Forgive me," he said, and turned away. He smiled. He began to undo certain buckles, attached to leather straps, within his own tunic.

She removed the collar, and set it on a shelf in the closet, with the key. "A collar," she said. "How barbaric it is to put women in collars." She shuddered.

I saw to my surprise, that the man, he who had been called Kunguni, drew forth, from beneath his tunic, a sewn, padded mound of cloth, heavy, globelike, with dangling straps. He then straightened his back. He was not tall, but he stood now slim and straight. His right leg, too, now did not seem to afflict him. He stood straight upon it. With the thumb and first finger of his right hand he peeled a cunning, jagged streak of paste and ocher from his left cheek, removing what I had taken to be a scar. I recalled the words of Kipofu: "His back

143

is crooked and it is not. His back is hunched and it is not. His face is scarred and it is not. His leg is crippled and it is not." But I did not know who he might be. "Do not seek him," had said Kipofu. "Forget him. Flee."

"How long must I continue this farce of feigned service at the Golden Kailiauk?" she asked.

"Tonight," said the man, "was your last of feigned service there."

"Excellent," she said.

He smiled.

"If you would now excuse me," she said, coolly, "I would like to slip into something suitable for a woman."

He looked at her.

"More suitable than this tunic," she said.

"Slave tunic," he said.

"Yes, slave tunic," she said, irritably.

"Are all women on your former world like you?" he asked.

"Not enough," she said.

"How I pity the men of such a place," he said.

"True women will teach them how to act and be," she said.

"What piteous fools," he said.

"What did you mean, my 'former world'?" she asked. "It is still my world."

The trace of a smile moved at the corners of the mouth of the man who had been called Kunguni.

"If you will now excuse me," she said, "I would like to change."

"I shall await you with he in the other room," he said.

"Very well," she said.

"When you come," said he, "bring your whip."

"I will," she said.

The man then left the small anteroom, closing its door behind him, and the woman reached to the wooden rods in the closet, on which garments hung.

I could not see into the other room from where I stood, nor did it obviously have windows. I backed into the dark street and then, a few feet away, saw a low, sloping roof. Most of the buildings of Schendi have wooden ventilator shafts at the roof, which may be opened and closed. These are often kept open that the hot air in the room, rising, may escape. They can be closed by a rod from the floor, in the case of rain or during the swarming seasons for various insects.

In a few moments I had hoisted myself up to the low roof

144

and then, again, climbing, I eased myself onto the roof of the building in which the man and woman had been conversing. There was a ventilator shaft, or slatted grille, over the main room, as I had anticipated. There is generally one room at least in which this arrangement occurs. Otherwise indoor living in Schendi could be difficult to bear. I could look down into the room, some fifteen feet below, through the slats in the grille. I could not, from my position, see the entire room. I could not see, most importantly, the figure whom, I gathered from the conversation and glances of the man and woman, sat at the far end of the room, behind a small table. I saw upon occasion the movement of his hands, long and black, with delicate fingers.

I could see, however, the man who had been called Kunguni and the woman who had worn the tan slave tunic. I could also see, kneeling on a dark blanket, naked, her ankles tied, her hands tied to her collar, her head down, still blindfolded, the blond-haired barbarian.

"I am sorry I am late," said the girl who had worn the tan slave tunic. "Pembe kept me later than I pleased, to finish serving paga to a drunken oarsman."

"What sacrifices we must make in the prosecution of our arduous mission," mused the fellow who had been called Kunguni.

The girl looked at him, angrily. She now wore, interestingly, tight black slacks and a black, buttoned top. I could also see she wore Earth undergarments. On her feet were wooden clogs. Her clothing seemed strikingly at odds with her setting. She apparently had little sensitivity to the aesthetic incongruities involved or, perhaps, she wished merely to reassure herself by this device that she was truly of Earth and not Gor. I had thought the slave tunic and collar had made her fit in better with her surroundings. They seemed more apt, more tasteful, more appropriate. They had been, I recalled, "right" upon her. But are they not right upon any woman, in any world?

There were two other men in the room, and I gazed upon them with some astonishment. They were large fellows, strong and lean, dressed in skins and golden armlets, and feathers. They carried high, oval shields, and short, long-bladed stabbing spears. These men, I was sure, were not of Schendi. They came from somewhere, I was sure, in the interior.

The blond-haired barbarian, blindfolded, frightened, lifted her head. Her lower lip trembled.

The fellow who had been called Kunguni crouched before the girl and, quickly, jerked loose the knot which held her bound hands, which were still tied, tethered at her collar. He held her bound wrists in one hand.

"Please do not hurt me any more," she said, in English. "I have told you all I know."

With his right hand, holding the girl's tied wrists in his left, the man tossed a rope up, over a rafter. He tied it then to her bound wrists, about the cording which secured them. He then signaled to the two large fellows who stood nearby. They put aside their shields and short spears and, hauling on the rope, jerked the blond-haired barbarian to her feet.

"Please," she wept, "I've told you all I know!"

At a signal from the man near her the two large fellows drew the girl from her feet, until she hung suspended some six inches from the floor.

"Begin," said the voice of the unseen man, he behind the table. He spoke in Gorean.

The girl in the slacks and black, buttoned top swung loose the blades of the slave whip she carried. She touched the blades to the body of the suspended girl.

"Do you know what this is?" she asked.

"A slave whip, Mistress," said the girl, in English. Their conversation was conducted entirely in English. The two girls, I gathered, were the only ones in the room who spoke English. The girl in the black slacks did, however, of course, translate, here and there, what the blond-haired barbarian said. She herself, of course, inevitably communicated with the men in Gorean.

"Speak," said the girl in the black slacks.

"I have told you all I know," wept the blond-haired barbarian. "Please do not beat me again."

"Speak," said the girl in the black slacks, touching the other girl lightly with the whip.

"My name is Janice Prentiss," she said.

"Your name was Janice Prentiss," corrected the girl with the whip.

"Yes, Mistress," said the suspended girl. "I was recruited in—"

"Be silent," said the girl with the whip.

"Yes, Mistress," moaned the girl.

146

Then the girl in the black slacks, suddenly, lashed her with the whip. The blond girl cried out with misery, twisting helplessly on the rope, her toes some six inches or so from the floor.

"Speak!" said the girl in the black slacks.

"Mistress!" cried the blond girl.

She was struck again.

"Mistress!" wept the blond girl.

"Speak of important things, of the ring and the papers!" she snarled.

"Yes, Mistress! Yes, Mistress!" wept the blond.

The girl in black slacks prepared to strike her again, but he who had been called Kunguni lifted his hand, and she lowered her arm, angrily. I saw that she enjoyed punishing the blond girl. For some reason, it seemed, she hated her.

"The ring and the papers," she said, "notes of some sort, and two letters, I received in Cos from one called Belisarius. I took passage for Schendi on the *Blossoms of Telnus,* a ship of Cos. We fell to pirates on the high seas. I think they were of Port Kar. We were boarded. Fighting was fierce but brief. Our ship was then theirs. I, and other women, placed in a net, were swung to the deck of the pirate ship. On its deck we were stripped and put in chains. we were then carried below, where we were fastened to rings. I was later sold in Port Kar. I was purchased by the merchant, Ulafi, of Schendi. He brought me slave to this port."

The girl in the black slacks struck her twice with the whip, and the suspended slave, striped by the blows, dangled, shaken, sobbing, before her.

"The ring, the papers!" said the girl in the black slacks.

"I was captured," wept the girl. "I was put on another ship. I was chained in a dark hold, with other women, naked. I do not know what happened to anything. Have pity on a slave!"

The girl in the black slacks drew back her hand again, again to strike with a five-bladed lash, but he who had been called Kunguni motioned for her not to strike. He spoke, in Gorean, to the girl in the black slacks.

"What was the name of the ship which captured the *Blossoms of Telnus?*" she asked. "Who was its captain?"

"I do not know," wept the blond girl. "I do not even know in what market I was sold."

"It was the *Sleen of Port Kar*," said he who had been called Kunguni, "captained by the rogue, Bejar, of that port."

Watching through the wooden slats above, I smiled. Bejar, in my opinion, was one of the most responsible, decent and serious captains in Port Kar.

"We had this through Uchafu, the slaver, who had spoken to Ulafi," said the man.

"Ulafi should have been recruited," said the dark-haired girl. "He will do anything for gold."

"Except betray his merchant codes," said he who was called Kunguni.

I was pleased to hear this, for I was rather fond of the tall, regal Ulafi. Apparently they did not regard him as a likely fellow to be used in the purchase of stolen notes on speculation, to be resold later to their rightful owner. Many merchants, I was sure, would not have been so squeamish. Such dealings, of course, would encourage the theft of notes. It was for this reason that they were forbidden by the codes. Such notes, their loss reported, are to be canceled, and replaced with alternative notes.

"Let us send a ship to Port Kar," said the dark-haired girl, "to obtain the ring and papers from Bejar."

"Do not be a fool," said he who was called Kunguni. "By now, Bejar has doubtless disposed of the ring, which would be meaningless to him, and has sold the notes."

"Perhaps he would give them to an agent," said the girl, "to be brought to Schendi for sale to Shaba."

"He would sell them," said the man. "He would choose to realize a sure profit. An agent might betray him. Too, an agent, carrying the notes, might be dealt with in Schendi not with gold but steel."

"They are then lost," said the girl.

"But we retain the true ring," said the man. "Belisarius, in Cos, if he learns of the loss of the *Blossoms of Telnus,* will doubtless contact his superiors, who will act. A new false ring may be fabricated, and new notes prepared."

"If he learns," said the girl.

"It could take months," admitted the man. Then he turned to face the figure seated behind the low table, whom I could not see. "You could take the ring to Cos, to Belisarius," he said.

"I am not a fool," he said. "The notes must come first to Schendi."

148

"As you wish," said he who had been called Kunguni. "But," he said, shuddering, "they may come for it."

"They?" asked the seated figure.

"They who desire it," said he who had been called Kunguni.

"I do not fear them," said the seated figure.

"I have heard they are not like men," said he who had been called Kunguni.

"I do not fear them," said the man behind the table.

"Give me the ring," said he who had been called Kunguni. "I will keep it safe."

"I am not a fool," said the other. "Bring me the notes."

"What of her?" asked the girl in black slacks, gesturing with the whip to the suspended, blond slave.

"I think she has told us, willingly and helplessly, all that she knows," said he who had been called Kunguni.

"What shall we now do with her?" asked the girl in slacks.

He who had been called Kunguni looked at the suspended, blond slave. He looked at her carefully, considering her. "She is pretty," he said. "Let her live."

He signaled to the two large fellows, those clad in skins and feathers, and armlets of gold, and said something, briefly, to them. I did not understand the language in which he spoke. It was neither English nor Gorean. They lowered the blond to the floor, and took the rope from her wrists by which she had been suspended. They then took the cording from her wrists, which had tied them together, and, with the same cording, fastened them behind her back. They then threw her to her stomach, untied her ankles, and snapped shackles on them, steel shackles, with about a six-inch run of chain. They then threw her on her knees on the dark blanket on which I had originally seen her. They slipped one end of the rope by which she had been suspended under her collar and pulled it some ten feet through, roughly, at the side of her neck. This double strand they then took some two and a half feet behind her. They looped it about a slave ring, set there in the wall, one of four, about a yard above the floor, and tied it there, the long, free ends falling loose, coiling, to the floor. She, blindfolded and shackled, her wrists bound behind her, her neck tethered to a ring, was well secured.

"What a miserable, worthless thing you are," said the girl with the whip to her.

"Yes, Mistress," said the blond girl, her lip trembling.

"Observe," said he who had been called Kunguni to the dark-haired girl with the whip. Then, to the blond, he said, sharply, "Nadu!"

Immediately, as she could, the girl assumed the position of the pleasure slave. Her hands, of course, were tied behind her.

"Despicable slave!" said the dark-haired girl.

"Yes, Mistress," wept the blond.

The dark-haired girl then drew back the whip to strike her, but he who had been called Kunguni caught her wrist, in the black sleeve of her blouse. "No," he said. "The whip will be used later."

He then released her wrist.

"Excellent," she said. "I shall look forward to it."

"And I, as well," said he.

The girl looked with hatred at the blond.

I smiled to myself. I did not think they had need any longer of the services of the dark-haired girl. Her translations, I must admit, had been fluent and accurate.

I then slipped back from the wooden slats, moved back on the roof and, quietly, lowered myself to the first roof, a low one, and, from there, down to the street.

I spun about.

I faced the short, stabbing spears of the two huge blacks. They had slipped out the front door, to receive me.

The door opened again and, in the light, I saw the face of he who had been called Kunguni. "Come in," said he, "we have been expecting you."

I straightened up. "I bear in my tunic," I said, "two letters, which should make my business clear to you."

"Move carefully," suggested he who had been called Kunguni.

Slowly, watching the points of the two stabbing spears, I drew forth the two letters. I had not carried with me, of course, either the ring or the notes.

I handed the two letters to the man at the door. He glanced at them.

"One of them," I said, "is for a man named Msaliti."

"I am Msaliti," said the man who had been called Kunguni. "Come in," he said.

I followed him into the building, through the small anteroom and into the larger room, which I had seen through the wooden grille in the ceiling. The two large fellows, in skins and feathers, with golden armlets, entered behind me.

150

Inside I saw, to one side, the blindfolded, whipped slave. She had revealed eagerly, helplessly, sobbing, all she knew. She still knelt beautifully, in the position of the pleasure slave. She had not been given permission to break position. The other girl, the dark-haired girl with the whip, seemed startled at my entrance. She had not expected me. The men, I understood, had not taken her into their confidence. I did not greet her. She was the sort of woman who is best greeted by throwing her upon her back and raping her.

I looked at the man who sat, cross-legged, behind the table. He was a large, tall man. He had long, thin hands, with delicate fingers. His face seemed refined, but his eyes were hard, and piercing. I did not think he was of the warriors but I had little doubt he was familiar with the uses of steel. I had seldom seen a face which, at once, suggested such sensitivity, but, at the same time, reflected such intelligence and uncompromising will. Following the lines of his cheekbones there was a stitching of tribal tattooing. He wore a robe of green and brown, with slashes of black. Against the background of jungle growth, blending with plants and shadows, it would be difficult to detect. He also wore a low, round, flat-topped cap of similar material. On the first finger of his left hand he wore a fang ring, which, I had little doubt, would contain a poison, probably that of the deadly kanda plant.

The second letter which I had handed Msaliti lay now on the table before the man.

"That letter," I said, "is for Shaba, the geographer of Anango."

He picked up the letter. "I am Shaba," he said, "the geographer of Anango."

12

BUSINESS IS DISCUSSED IN SCHENDI; I ACQUIRE A NEW GIRL

"I have come to negotiate for the ring," I said.

"Do you have the false ring, and the notes with you?" asked Shaba.

"No," I said.

"Are they in Schendi?" asked Shaba.

"Perhaps," I said. "Do you have the ring with you?"

"Perhaps," smiled Shaba.

I did not doubt that he had the ring with him. Such an artifact would be far too valuable to leave lying about. Having the ring with him, too, of course, he was terribly dangerous.

"Do you come to us as an agent on behalf of Bejar, a captain of Port Kar?" inquired Shaba.

"Perhaps," I said.

"No," said Shaba. "You do not, for you know of the ring's value and Bejar would know nothing of it." He looked at me. "A similar argument would demonstrate," he said, "that you are not a simple speculator, interested in the resale of the notes."

I shrugged. "You could always wait, in such a case, for their cancellation and reissue," I said.

"Yes," he said, "providing they would be reissued, and we had months in which to dally."

"You have a project afoot?" I asked.

"Perhaps," said Shaba.

"And you wish to move ahead on it quickly?" I asked.

"Yes," he said.

"It is perhaps imperative for you to move quickly?" I asked.

"I think so," said Shaba. He smiled.

"What is your project?" I asked.

Msaliti was looking at him, curiously.

"It is personal business," said Shaba.

"I see," I said.

"Since," said Shaba, "you come neither from Bejar nor as a simple speculator, I think we may infer that you come to us from one of two sources. You come to us either from Kurii—or from Priest-Kings."

I glanced uneasily at the two large fellows, those with the shields and stabbing spears, who stood near us.

"Do not fear," said Msaliti, "my askaris do not speak Gorean." The word 'askari' is an inland word, which may be translated roughly as 'soldier' or 'guardsman.'

"Regardless from which camp I come," I said, "you have what we wish, the ring."

"The ring," said Msaliti, "may not be returned to Priest-Kings. It must go to Kurii."

"I will bring with me, when I return, of course," I said, "the false ring, that it may be borne to the Sardar."

"He is with us," said Msaliti. "No agent of Priest-Kings would wish the ring conveyed to the Sardar."

This confirmed in my mind the soundness of the speculation of Samos that the false ring involved some serious threat or danger.

"You will then, of course," I said, to Shaba, "as an agent of Priest-Kings, bear the ring to the Sardar."

"Do you not think it is a little late for that now?" inquired Shaba.

"We must try,"

"That is the plan," said Msaliti, earnestly.

"You must carry out your part of the bargain," said the dark-haired girl.

Shaba looked at her.

"Be silent," said Msaliti, angrily, to her.

She drew back, angry.

"You do not look like one who would serve Kurii," said Shaba to me, smiling.

"You do not look like one who would betray Priest-Kings," I said to him.

"Ah," he said, leaning back. "How difficult and subtle are the natures of men," he mused.

"How did you find us here?" asked the girl.

"He followed you, of course, you little fool," said Msaliti. "Why do you think you were kept another night at the tavern of Pembe?"

"You could have told me," she said.

Msaliti did not respond to her.

"How did you know I was on the roof?" I asked. The askaris had been waiting for me.

"It is an old Schendi trick," said Shaba. "Look, up there. Do you see those tiny strings, those little threads?"

"Yes," I said. There were several, about a foot in length, dangling from the ceiling. At the end of each there was a tiny round object.

"It is not uncommon for burglars to enter houses through these grilles," said Shaba. "Those are dried peas on threads. They are inserted under certain boards and in certain cracks in the ceiling. When the roof is stepped on the tiny movements in the ceiling boards, and the pressures, release the peas. It is then known that someone is on or has been on the roof."

"It gives a silent warning," I said.

"Yes," he said. "The house owner may then, if he wishes, warn the intruder away or, if he wishes, fall upon him when he enters the house."

"What if the dwellers in the house are asleep?" I asked.

"Small bells are attached to the grille slats," said Shaba, "which dangle down, near the ears of the sleepers. If one attempts to cut the strings or draw the bells up, of course, a noise is made, one usually sufficient to waken the occupants of the house."

"That is clever," I said.

"Actually," said Shaba, "you did extremely well. Only a few of the threads have been dislodged. Your step was light. Indeed, none were dislodged apparently until you withdrew from the roof."

I nodded. To be sure, I had withdrawn from the slatted grille with less care than I had approached it. I had feared little in my retreat. I had thought it secure. I had not known about the simple device of the threads and peas.

"Why was I not told that I was to be followed?" asked the girl.

"Be silent," said Msaliti.

She stiffened, angrily.

"You eluded me brilliantly in the tavern of Pembe, the Golden Kailiauk," I told Msaliti. "The exchanging of the girls was ingenious."

He shrugged, and smiled. "It required, of course," he said, "the aid of Shaba, and the ring."

"Of course," I said.

"I did my part well, too," said the girl.

"Yes, you did," I said.

She looked triumphantly at the men.

"You took the girl into the tavern," I said, "and covered her with your aba, that she might not move. Shaba, under the cover of the ring, drugged the paga which I drank. When my attention was distracted he, under the cover of the ring, carried away the blond girl, and this female, by prearranged plan, took her place."

"Yes," said Shaba.

"My pursuit of you was foiled," I said, "by the results of the drug you placed in my paga."

"The drug," said Shaba, "was a simple combination of sajel, a simple pustulant, and gieron, an unusual allergen.

154

Mixed they produce a facsimile of the superficial symptoms of Bazi plague."

"I could have been killed," I said, "by the mob."

"I did not think many would care to approach you," said Shaba.

"It was not your intention then that I be killed?" I asked.

"Certainly not," said Shaba. "If that was all that was desired, kanda might have been introduced into your drink as easily as sajel and gieron."

"That is true," I said.

"We only wished to make certain that you did not contact us before our own determinations were made. You see, we did not know who you were. We wished to find out first what we could from the girl. Perhaps it would not be necessary to contact you at all."

"The stupid slave," said the dark-haired girl, "knew nothing."

"Had I not found your headquarters tonight, then," I said, "you would have contacted me?"

"Of course," said Shaba, "tomorrow. But we speculated that you would find us tonight. We speculated that you would discover or reason out the girl's role in our business and try to use her as a lead to find us. This possibility was confirmed when you made inquiries of Kipofu, the beggar, in the Utukufu square."

"You were there," I said.

"Of course," he said, "under the cover of the ring, but I could not approach as closely as I desired. Kipofu has unusually keen hearing. When my presence was detected I simply withdrew."

"Why did you not just contact me directly?" I asked.

"For two reasons," said Shaba. "We wished, a second time, to interrogate the blond-haired slave, before making contact, and, also, we were curious to see if you could find us by yourself. You did so. You have our congratulations. You are obviously worthy of conducting business on behalf of the Kurii."

"How long have you known I was in Schendi?" I asked.

"Since the arrival of the *Palms of Schendi*," he said. "We could not be certain, at first, that your arrival was not a coincidence. Soon, however, it became clear that you were an object for our concern. You appeared at the market of Uchafu. You trailed Msaliti from the market. You waited in the Golden Kailiauk."

"I have been under surveillance since arriving in Schendi," I said.

"Yes," said Shaba, "from time to time."

"You know, then, doubtless, my new residence," I said, "that which I acquired following my departure from the Cove of Schendi."

I had taken a large room on the ground floor, behind a cloth-worker's shop, just off the Street of Tapestries. Wearing the aba taken from Msaliti, hooding myelf with it, that my face and eyes not be seen, Sasi on my shoulder, rolled in a blanket tied tightly closed with ropes, I had acquired the lodging. The free woman who rented me the room asked no questions. When I had given her a copper tarsk as a tip she had looked down at the tightly tied blanket, containing its helpless burden, and had looked up at me, grinning. "Enjoy yourself," she had said, slipping the tarsk into a pouch tied at her hip.

"If we knew it," said Shaba, "men, even now, would be ransacking it for the ring and notes."

"Of course," I said.

"You moved quickly," said Shaba. "By the time I had brought the blond slave here and returned to the Cove of Schendi, you had already made your departure."

"I see," I said. I was pleased that I had made the haste I had.

"But now," said Shaba, "we are all friends."

"Of course," I said.

"When will you deliver the notes?" he asked.

"And the false ring," pressed Msaliti.

"Tomorrow evening," I said.

"You choose to move under the cover of darkness?" asked Shaba.

"I think it might be wise," I said.

"Very well," said Shaba. "Tomorrow evening, at the nineteenth Ahn, meet us in this place. Bring the notes and the false ring. I will have the true ring ready then for exchange."

"I shall be here," I promised.

"Our business then," said the dark-haired girl, flushing with pleasure, "will at last be well consummated."

"Let us have a drink," said Shaba, "to celebrate this long-awaited rendezvous." Then he smiled at me. "You do not fear to drink with us, I trust," he said.

I smiled. "Of course not," I said. "Do you have the paga of Ar, of the brewery of Temus?"

"Woe," smiled Shaba. "We have here only Schendi paga, but I think it is quite good. It is, of course, a matter of taste."

"Very well," I said.

"You will find it is better without sajel and gieron in it," he said.

"That is reassuring," I said.

"The symptoms induced by the paga tendered to you at the Golden Kailiauk," he said, "should have disappeared by the following morning."

"They had," I said.

"My dear," asked Shaba, of the dark-haired girl, "would you bring us paga?"

She stiffened.

"Fetch paga, Woman," said Msaliti. "You are least among us."

"Why am I least among you?" she asked.

"Forgive us, my dear," said Shaba.

"I will bring the paga," she said.

In a few moments she returned with a bottle of Schendi paga and four cups. She filled these cups.

"Forgive me," I said to Shaba, taking the cup which she had placed before him.

He smiled and extended his hands. "Of course," he said.

Then the four of us lifted our cups, touching them, one to another.

"To victory," said Shaba.

"To victory," we said, and drank. I had little compunction about drinking this toast. Each of us may not have had in mind the same victory, of course.

"I have not been introduced to this lovely agent," I said, regarding the dark-haired girl.

"Forgive me," said Shaba. "It was careless of me. I did not wish to be rude." He looked at me. "You are going by the name of Tarl of Teletus, I believe," he said, "if my inquiries in Schendi have served me properly."

"That is correct," I said. "That name will do. It will serve to cover my true identity."

"Many agents use code names," said Shaba.

"Yes," I said.

"Tarl of Teletus," said he, "may I introduce Lady E. Ellis? Lady E. Ellis, Tarl of Teletus."

We inclined our heads to one another.

"Is 'E' an initial or a name?" I asked her.

"An initial," she said, "it stands for Evelyn. But I do not like that name. It is too feminine. Call me 'E.' "

"I will call you Evelyn," I said.

"You may do as you wish, of course," she said.

"I see that you know how to treat a woman," said Shaba. "You impose your will upon her."

"Is Evelyn Ellis your real name?" I asked, smiling.

"Yes," she said, "it is. Why do you smile?"

"It is nothing," I said.

Msaliti and Shaba, too, smiled. It amused me to see that the girl thought she had a name.

"I must admire the perception of Kur recruiters," I said. "You are obviously highly intelligent and very beautiful."

"Thank you," she said.

"She has been well trained," said Msaliti.

"I have been not only well trained," she said, "but thoroughly and intensively trained, even brilliantly trained. Nothing has been left to chance. The smallest details have been attended to. In order to play my role more effectively here I have even permitted my body to be branded."

"I recall," I said. I had seen her in the Golden Kailiauk, of course, in pleasure silk.

She looked at me, angrily.

"My awe at the cleverness and thoroughness of the practices and techniques of Kur espionage knows few limits," I said, "and I must admit that my admiration for the products of their schooling, as in the present case, exceeds almost all bounds."

She flushed with pleasure, flattered and mollified.

I threw down the last of my paga.

"I would like to see further evidence of your skills," I said. "I am out of paga," I said.

She reached to the bottle, to refill the cup.

"No," I said.

She looked at me.

"Did they not teach you how to serve paga as a paga slave?" I asked.

"Of course," she said.

"Show me," I said.

"Very well," she said. She drew back, taking the bottle and cup. In most taverns no bottle is brought to the table but the paga is brought to the table, by the paga slave, a cup at a time, the cups normally being filled from a vat behind the counter. She filled the cup there, before me, and left it be-

158

hind. She returned the bottle then to the table, and went back again for the cup.

She lifted it in both hands.

"Put it down," I said.

She did so, looking at me puzzled.

"You are garbed strangely for a paga slave," I said, indicating the clogs, the black slacks and the black, buttoned top.

"Do you wish me to put on pleasure silk?" she asked, icily.

"No," I said.

She tossed her head.

"In many Gorean taverns," I said, "the paga slaves serve naked."

"Yes," she said, slowly, "they do."

"Did they not teach you how to do that?" I asked.

"Yes," she said.

"I would see evidence of your skills," I said.

"Very well," she said, angrily, in her vanity, taunted.

She slipped from the clogs, and was barefoot. She slipped from the black slacks, and removed the black, buttoned top. She slipped from the panties and, in a moment, had discarded her brassiere. She was furious, but yet I could see, too, as doubtless could the others, that she was sexually charged. She was naked, before clothed men. This can be sexually stimulating to a woman. It is hard for her, in such circumstances, not to see them as her masters and herself, before them, as an exposed slave. Similarly she knew that, in a moment, she would be, naked, on her knees, serving them. For reasons that have to do with nature these things can be erotically momentous to a woman. The relation of master and slave, of course, in a psychophysical organism, of a high order of intelligence, such as the human being, is a beautiful and profound expression of the fundamental and central truth of animal nature, that of order and structure, and dominance and submission. It is merely the articulated, legalized expression, to be expected in rational organisms, of the biological context in which human sexuality developed, a context which can be betrayed but can never, because of the ingrained nature of genetic dispositions, be fully forgotten or, in the long run, successfully denied. In denying it we deny our own nature. In betraying it we betray no one but ourselves. The master will never be happy until he is a master. The slave will never be happy until she is a slave. It is what we are.

I looked upon the girl. She bit her lip. I saw that she was lovely.

159

"Wait," said Msaliti, "one more item is needed to complete the effect."

"Of course," said Shaba.

He left the room and, in a moment, returned with the collar. "Oh!" she said, as he, from behind, snapped it about her throat. I noted that he slipped the key into his pouch. I did not think it would be soon removed from the girl.

Msaliti joined us at the table.

The girl stood, loftily, before us. "Do I meet with the approval of Masters?" she asked.

"Serve us paga, Slave," said Msaliti.

She stiffened. Then she smiled. "Yes, Master," she said.

I, too, smiled. I saw that she thought she was playing a role. Did she not know that she had been truly branded and that, in the touch of the iron, as it marked her, she had been made truly a slave? I sensed now that her slavery, latent until now, was soon to be specifically activated. Indeed, it had now been activated, but she did not know it. She thought herself a free woman, serving as a slave. She did not know that she was truly a slave, who, amusingly, still thought herself free. It was a rich joke on the proud girl, one fitting to be played on an insolent slave.

"Paga, Master?" she asked, kneeling before me, the metal cup held before her, in her two hands.

"Yes," I said.

She proffered the cup to me. She knelt back on her heels, her knees wide, and extended her arms to me, the cup in her hands.

"Did you not neglect to kiss it?" I asked her.

She drew back the cup and, pressing her lips to it, kissed it.

"Is that how a slave kisses the cup of a master?" I asked.

She again turned her head to the side and pressed her lips softly, lingeringly, against it. Then she kissed it. I saw a tremor course through her body. I think, then, for the first time, she had begun to understand what it might be truly, to kiss the cup of a master. Then again, kneeling back on her heels, her knees wide, extending her arms to me, the cup in her hands, she proffered me the drink.

"Your head should be down, between your arms," I said. She put her head down. Again I saw a small movement in her body, a tremor, subtle. She had put her head down before a man. Another consequence of this position is that the girl's eyes, in the specific act of her serving, do not meet those of the master. They are lowered before his, as one who submits.

160

This is also reminiscent, in an experienced girl, of her training. Often, in training, a girl is not permitted to look into the eyes of the trainer, unless he should specifically extend this permission. Indeed, in some cities, the girl in training may not raise her eyes above the trainer's belt, unless, again, specifically accorded this permission.

"Speak," I said to her.

"Your paga, Master," she said.

But I did not take the paga. "Do you know other phrases?" I asked. There were many, actually, and they tended to vary from tavern to tavern, and from city to city. There was, really, no standardization in such matters.

She trembled, head down, proffering me the paga.

"Your girl brings you drink, Master," she said.

"Any others?" I asked.

"Here is your drink, Master," she said. "I beg to serve you further in any way I may."

"Another," I said.

"Do not forget I come with the price of the cup," she said. "Use me as you will, Master."

"Another," I said sharply.

"For your pleasure," she said, "I bring you paga and a slave."

"Personalized phrase," I said.

"E.," she said.

"Evelyn," I corrected her.

"Evelyn tenders drink humbly to Master," she said. "Evelyn hopes Master will later find her suitable to give him pleasure."

"Another," I said.

"I am Evelyn," she said. "I serve you, naked and collared. Take me later to the alcove. I beg to be taught my slavery."

I then took the paga. "You may now serve others," I said to her.

"You made her serve well," said Shaba.

"Thank you," I said.

The girl trembled, and then regained her composure. Then, in turn, as a naked paga slave, she served Msaliti and Shaba. I observed her technique. I thought she could probably survive in a paga tavern, under real conditions, not those artificial conditions under which she had served in the tavern of Pembe, the Golden Kailiauk, though doubtless she would be often beaten in the beginning.

When the girl had finished serving Shaba she straightened

up and came about the table, to where her cup rested on the low wood.

She reached for it, but Msaliti moved it out of her reach. She looked at him, puzzled.

"Does a paga slave drink at the table of masters?" he asked.

She laughed. "Of course not," she said.

"You could be whipped for that," he said.

"Yes," she said, "that is true." She smiled. She then went to where her clothing had been discarded, on the floor. She bent to pick it up, to reclothe herself.

"Do not dress," said Msaliti.

"Why not?" she asked.

"Kneel there," said Msaliti, indicating a place about a yard from the table.

"Why?" she asked.

"There," he said.

She knelt there, puzzled. It was about where a paga slave might kneel, close enough to be ready to serve at the merest signal, far enough away to be unobtrusive.

"You see," she said to me, "I have been well trained."

"Yes," I said.

"You were not given permission to speak," said Msaliti to the girl.

She looked at him, puzzled.

"You could be whipped also for that," he said.

"Of course," she laughed. Then she looked over to the blond-haired barbarian. The blond-haired girl, miserable, still blindfolded, knelt by the wall. Her slender ankles were shackled. Her hands were tied behind her back. A rope, looped through her collar, tied her to a slave ring behind her, about a yard off the floor. "Do you want her whipped again?" asked the dark-haired girl.

"No," said Msaliti.

"I thought you said the whip was to be used again tonight," she said.

"I did," said Msaliti.

"Are you going to beat her?" she asked.

"No," he said.

"I do not understand," she said.

Msaliti looked at her. "It is nearly time, my dear," he said, "for you to be returned to the tavern of Pembe."

"No!" she said. "You said that tonight was my last night of feigned service there."

162

"It was," said he. "But this is also the first night of your true service there."

"I do not understand," she said.

She got up, angrily, and went toward the small anteroom. But the two askaris blocked her way. She turned about, facing us. "I would like to get the key," she said, angrily, "to remove this—this collar!" she indicated the collar.

"I have the key here," said Msaliti, lifting it, he having taken it a moment ago from his pouch.

"Oh," she said. Then she walked toward us.

"Do not approach more closely without permission," said Msaliti.

She stopped, about five feet from the table.

"Kneel," he said.

"I do not understand," she said.

"Kneel," he said. I noted that he had repeated a command. Masters do not care to repeat commands.

She knelt. "I do not understand," she said.

I did not think she was unintelligent. It was only that her Earth mind was not quick to grasp that she might, almost unbelievably, almost incomprehensibly to her, be placed in certain categories.

"Give me the key," she said.

"Whose collar do you wear?" he asked.

"That of Pembe, of course," she said.

"What do you wish to do with it?" he asked.

"Remove it, of course," she said.

"But it is Pembe's collar," he said.

"Yes," she said.

"Thus," said he, "if or when it is removed is surely a determination to be made not by you but by Pembe."

"What are you saying!" she cried.

"Are all women on your former world as dull as you?" he asked.

"What do you mean 'my former world'?" she asked.

"Precisely what I said," said he, "that world which was formerly yours. Surely you must now know that your world is Gor, that it is the Gorean world, and only the Gorean world, which is now yours."

"No!" she cried.

"You are a Gorean slave girl," he said.

"No! No!" she cried. She leaped to her feet and ran toward the door, but the two askaris seized her and flung her again to her knees, before us.

163

"You're joking!" she begged.

"No," said Msaliti.

"Take it off!" she cried, yanking at the collar, suddenly. "Take it off! Take it off!"

"No," said Msaliti.

She looked at him. The steel collar remained inflexibly fastened on her throat.

Msaliti, in the speech known to the askaris, spoke briefly. They seized the girl by the arms and dragged her to the side of the room. They put her on her knees, facing the wall. They braceleted her wrists about one of the four slave rings in the wall, the one farthest from the blond-haired barbarian and closest to the door. It was, like the others, about a yard from the floor. Msaliti, standing, leaving the table, shook loose the blades of the slave whip.

"I am not a slave!" she cried, looking at him over her right shoulder.

"You were a slave," said Msaliti, "the instant you were branded, only you did not know it."

"No! No!" she cried. Then she cried, "I served you well!"

"Yes," said Msaliti, "but you are now no longer needed."

"I served you well," she wept.

"It is fitting that a slave well serves her masters," said Msaliti.

"I am your colleague!" she said.

"Never were you anything but our slave, you little white fool," said Msaliti.

"What if our superiors find out!" she cried.

Msaliti laughed. "I act in accord with their instructions," he said. "Surely you do not think women such as yourself were brought to Gor with any object in mind other than to ultimately wear the collar."

"No," she cried. "No!"

He then stepped behind and to one side of her, with the whip.

"Shaba!" she cried. "Shaba!"

"Your services are no longer required, my dear," said he.

"No!" she cried.

"Hear me, Slave," said Msaliti. "I have long been patient with you. But the time of masters being patient with you is now at an end. We shall ignore thousands of infractions and insubordinations in the past, presumptions, and speakings and actions, and consider only the past few moments. But a few Ehn earlier you dared to touch a cup on the table of masters,

164

as though it were your own, and would have, if not stopped, drunk from it. Also, you have spoken without permission. Also, once you did not respond to the first issuance of a command, but required its repetition. Also, but a moment ago, you addressed a free man not as Master, but by his name."

"Msaliti!" she begged.

"Ah," said he, "what a dull slave. You have repeated the offense."

"You would not dare to strike me!" she said.

"Earlier I told you," said he, "that the whip would be later used. You said, as I recall, that you would look forward to it."

"Do not strike me," she begged.

"Prepare to be beaten as what you are, a slave," he said.

"I do not fear the whip," she said.

"Have you ever felt it?" he asked.

"No," she said.

"You will find the experience instructive," he said.

"I am not one of those girls," she said, "who at a touch of the leather will crawl to you and kiss your feet."

"Speak bravely," said he, "after you have felt the whip."

She tensed at the ring, preparing for the stroke. Her eyes were open. She held the ring with her small, braceleted hands.

Then it fell upon her, once, the slash of the five-bladed Gorean slave whip.

I saw disbelief, startled, wild, enter her eyes. Then she shut her eyes, tightly, tears squeezed from between their lids, wetting the lashes and her cheeks. Her knuckles were now white on the ring they clutched. "No," she whispered, "it cannot be."

Msaliti did not immediately again strike her. He knew the whip. He gave her several Ihn, that she might begin to feel the pain of the first stroke.

"I will obey you," she whispered. "Do not strike me again."

Then the second stroke fell upon her and she screamed with misery, her grip lost on the ring, half thrown against the wall, scratching at it with her braceleted hands, the side of her face against the heavy boards. There were now two layers of pain in her body, overlapping, each reinforcing and intensifying the other. Her body, sensitized by the first stroke, helpless, raw, aware, expectant, exposed, felt the second, as was intended, mingling with the burning echoes, the searing,

165

throbbing wounds of the first, a thousand times more cruelly. "It is enough!" she wept, gasping, sobbing. "It is enough! I will do whatever you want!"

Msaliti then began her beating.

"No, Master!" she screamed at the ring, twisting and writhing. But Msaliti administered to her an efficient, though brief, discipline. As beatings go it was not particularly severe. On the other hand, it was genuine. Evelyn had been truly beaten. She had felt the whip.

"Have mercy, Master, on your slave!" she wept.

Msaliti then, after some ten or twelve strokes, lowered the whip. He spoke to the askaris. They unlocked the left slave bracelet of the girl, freeing her from the ring. She fell to her stomach, weeping.

"To my feet," said he.

She crawled to his feet and kissed them. "Yes, Master," she said.

Msaliti again spoke to the askaris and they pulled the girl's wrists behind her back and, refastening her left wrist in the left slave bracelet, the right still locked on her right wrist, secured them there.

Msaliti looked down at her, on her stomach at his feet.

"What a miserable, worthless thing you are," he said.

I recalled that these had been the words the dark-haired girl had used to the blond-haired barbarian, still kneeling blindfolded, but now terribly frightened, to one side. She knew little of what was going on. She did understand, of course, that some sister in bondage, near to her, had just been disciplined.

"Yes, Master," she said.

"Behold," said Msaliti, smiling, to Shaba and myself. Then, to the dark-haired girl, he said, sharply, "Nadu!"

She struggled to her knees and, as she could, her wrists braceleted behind her, assumed before him the lovely, elegant position of the pleasure slave.

"Despicable slave," smiled Msaliti to the girl.

"Yes, Master," she said, sobbing.

These words, too, I recalled, had been used by the dark-haired girl earlier to the blond-haired barbarian.

The dark-haired girl now knelt, collared, before Msaliti, herself, too, now only a girl, and slave, at the mercy of men.

Msaliti spoke again to the askaris. He gave one of them the key to the girl's collar.

"Several days ago," said he to the kneeling girl before him, "your sale to Pembe was arranged. Tonight you will be delivered to him."

"Yes, Master," she said.

"It seems he has taken a fancy to you," said Msaliti. "He thinks that you may have in you the makings of a paga girl. I do not know if it is true or not. I would, however, if I were you, attempt to do my best to justify Pembe's confidence in you. Pembe is not a patient man. He has taken the hands and feet from more than one girl."

She turned white. "Yes, Master," she said.

The askaris lifted her to her feet, one holding each arm. "Master," she asked.

"Yes," he said.

"May I have permission to speak?" she asked.

"Yes," he said.

"Do I have even a name?" she asked.

"No," he said, "unless Pembe should choose to give you one."

"Master," she said.

"Yes," he said.

"What did you get for me?" she asked.

"You have a slave girl's vanity," he said. "Do you not?"

She put down her head. "Yes, Master," she said.

"That is an excellent sign," he said. "Perhaps you will even survive."

She looked at him, piteously.

"Four copper tarsks," he said.

"So little?" she said.

"In my opinion it is more than you are worth," said Msaliti. Then he waved his hand to the askaris, and they turned the slave about and thrust her, ahead of them, from our presence, out into the anteroom. There, in the anteroom, one of them retrieved the tiny scrap of yellow pleasure silk the girl had brought with her, wadded in her hand, when she had come earlier to the building. He tied this, snugly, on her collar. She looked back at us, frightened. Then she was thrust stumbling though the outside door, and into the street.

I stood up, near the table. "I shall see you, then, tomorrow evening," I said.

"Bring with you," said Shaba, "the false ring and the notes."

"And you," I said, "do not neglect to bring the genuine ring with you."

"I shall have it with me," he averred. I did not doubt it.

Msaliti, to one side, had begun his transformation into the beggar, Kunguni. He had already slipped the padded hump beneath his tunic and adjusted the straps by which it was held in place. He was now, at a mirror, with paste and ocher, attending to the matter of the simulated scar.

"What of this slave?" I asked Msaliti, indicating the blond-haired barbarian.

Msaliti shrugged. "She is now worthless to us," he said.

"What did you pay Uchafu for her?" I asked.

"Five silver tarsks," he said.

"I will give you six," I said.

"She is hot," admitted Msaliti.

"Have you subjected her to rape test?" I asked.

"No," said he. "Only to the touch of the owner's hands."

"That is usually a reliable test," I said.

"I will take six tarsks for her," said he, "if you are serious in the matter."

I gave Msaliti six silver tarsks for the girl. She was then mine. In the situation, as I assessed it, either she should have been given to me, upon my expression of interest, or I should have paid something for her in increments of silver tarsks, something over the price Msaliti had paid. Things turned out much as I had expected. I did not think Msaliti, truly, whom I took to be a shrewd, clever fellow, and one concerned with matters of wealth and power, would wish to give a girl away. Too, since he had paid for her in silver tarsks he would wish to sell her in the same denomination and, presumably, at some profit. My offer of six seemed perfect. It permitted him to satisfy his sense of venality and yet not appear excessively mercenary. Had I tried to obtain her for less than six tarsks or he tried to obtain more for her I think the situation could have become unpleasant.

Msaliti, his scar now affixed, and his disguise intact, bent down and removed the shackles from the blond barbarian's ankles. He then removed the collar from her and, with it, the rope which had tethered her to the wall. He then jerked her to her feet and unbound her hands. He then thrust her stumbling, blindfolded and naked, but otherwise unbound, to me. She stood against me, clutching me, frightened.

"I now own you," I said.

"Yes, Master," she said.

She lifted her hands to remove the blindfold.

"Do not remove the blindfold," I told her.

168

"Yes, Master," she said, her lip trembling.

"You may have the blindfold," smiled Msaliti. "Keep her in it until she is well away from here."

"Very well," I said. He did not wish her, of course, to be able to find her way again to this place.

"You are not to touch the blindfold without permission," I told her.

"Yes, Master," she said, standing quietly beside me. So simply, she a slave had been placed in the shackles of my will.

"Until tomorrow night," said Msaliti, lifting his hand.

"Until tomorrow night," I said.

He then left.

"We are now alone," I said to Shaba. The presence of the girl, of course, did not count. She was a slave.

"Yes," said Shaba, rising from behind the table.

I measured the distance to him.

"Who are you truly?" he asked.

"I think," I said, "you have the ring upon you, and would not leave it elsewhere."

"You are a shrewd man," said Shaba. He lifted his left hand, on the first finger of which was a fang ring. He folded his left hand into a fist and, with his thumb, pressed a tiny switch on the ring. The fang, of hollow steel, springing up, was then exposed.

"It contains kanda?" I asked.

"Yes," said he.

"It will do you little good," I said, "if you cannot strike me with it."

"A scratch will be sufficient," he said.

"One must, upon occasion, take risks," I said.

"I think I may easily multiply the risks," said he. He reached into his robes with his right hand. In a moment he had seemed to swirl and then, the light-diversion field activated, had vanished from my view.

"Tomorrow," I said, "I shall bring the false ring and the notes."

"Excellent," said Shaba. "I think that we now understand one another quite well."

"Yes," I said.

"It is a pleasure to do business with such an honest fellow," he said.

"I entertain a similar sentiment toward yourself," I said.

I then turned about and, taking the slave girl by the arm, left the room.

Soon I was in the street, outside.

13

I RETURN TO
THE GOLDEN KAILIAUK

"Do not fear," I said to Pembe. "It was only a passing indisposition."

His hands shook.

"Look," I said. "See. I do not have the plague."

"Your skin," said he, "is truly clear, and, too, your eyes."

"Of course," I said.

"You are well?" he asked, uncertainly.

"Of course," I said.

"Welcome to the Golden Kailiauk," he said, relieved.

"I shall return to the counter in a moment," I said. I went to the wall against which I had placed the blond-haired barbarian. I had told her to put her belly and the palms of her hands, lifted, against the wall. She remained, of course, as I had placed her.

"Kneel here," I said to her. "Back on your heels," I said to her.

She did so, by the wall.

"Now grip your ankles in your hands," I said, "and put your head down."

"Yes, Master," she said.

"And do not break that position," I said, "until given permission."

"Yes, Master," she said. "Master!" she said.

"Yes," I said.

She spoke with her head down, her ankles gripped.

"Who are you?" she said. "Who owns me!"

"Be silent," I said.

"Yes, Master," she said.

I then returned to the counter. "Do you have a white-skinned paga slave here," I asked, "a barbarian girl?"

"Yes," he said. "I obtained one only tonight, for four tarsks. I have not yet even put her on the floor."

170

"I threw him a copper tarsk. "Paga," I said, "and the slave."

"You must know the askaris of Msaliti," he said.

"I have made their acquaintance," I said.

He turned to one of the paga attendants. "Bring the new paga slave to the floor," he said. "Excellent," he said, to himself, "already there is a call for her."

I saw the girl, naked, in her collar, even the bit of yellow slave silk which had been tied to her collar gone, thrust through the beaded curtain by the paga attendant.

"Ah," I said. She had not yet seen me. "I think," I said, "you will soon make back your four tarsks on her."

"But one must figure in, too," said he, "the cost of the paga."

"That is true," I said.

"She is a new girl," he said. "If she is not entirely satisfactory, let me know, and I will have her whipped and have your money refunded."

"Very well," I said. "I will be at that table," I said, indicating a table in the rear of the tavern, not far from a red-curtained alcove.

"Yes, Master," said Pembe.

I went and sat down, cross-legged, behind the table. I had thought it wise not to go directly back to my room. If someone were to follow me, he would have quite a wait. My stop at the paga tavern, I thought, would make it easier to elude pursuit. I had stopped at this tavern, of course, because of Pembe's new paga slave. When she thought she had been pretending to serve us in the headquarters of Shaba and Msaliti she had, of course, whether she intended it or not, much aroused me. I desired her. So I would now have her. Too, I thought that it might be to the girl's advantage to be broken in by me, one more aware than would be most Goreans of the limitations of Earth girls. Usually it is the first two or three nights which are the most difficult for a girl to survive in a Gorean paga tavern. After the first two or three nights she has usually learned, and well, what she is, a paga slave. If she has not learned it in that time it is likely that her throat will have been cut by some customer, her sales price being then paid to her owner, plus a token tarsk or two, of copper, for good will.

The girl was thrust, her arm in the grip of the paga attendant, on the far side of the room, to the counter. He released

171

her before the counter. Pembe placed a goblet of paga in her hands. He then pointed in my direction.

She turned about. She nearly spilled the paga, trembling. It was well for her that she did not spill it.

Slowly, alone, a paga slave, naked and collared, she approached my table.

She then knelt there, before me.

"Press the cup to your belly," I told her.

She did so. She then held it there, in both hands. "Paga, Master?" she whispered.

"Yes," I said.

She sobbed.

"Kiss the cup," I told her.

She lifted the metal cup from her belly and, turning her head to the side, pressed her lips against it. She then kissed it. She then, her knees wide, her arms extended to me, her head down, between her arms, proffered the paga to me. "Your paga, Master," she whispered.

I did not yet take the paga. "Has Pembe given you a name yet?" I asked.

"No, Master," she said.

"For purposes of your service to me tonight," I said, "I name you Evelyn."

"Yes, Master," she said.

"Use now to me," I said, "the second of the two formulas, personalized, which you earlier used to me, when you had so foolishly thought yourself a free woman."

"I am Evelyn," she said. "I serve you, naked and collared. Take me later to the alcove. I beg to be taught my slavery."

"Very well," I said.

She knelt back, about a yard from the table. I looked at her. I sipped the paga.

"You are a pretty slave, Evelyn," I said.

"Thank you, Master," she said.

"Are you white silk?" I asked.

"I am a virgin," she said.

"Then you are white silk," I said.

"Yes, Master," she said.

"Have you ever been curious," I asked, "about what it would be to be a slave?"

She looked at me.

"Beware," I said. "You are naked and kneeling. You wear a slave collar. It will not be easy to lie."

172

"Yes," she said, putting her head down, "I have been curious to know what it would be to be a slave."

"You will learn," I told her.

"Yes, Master," she said.

I then gave my attention to the paga, and to my thoughts. In time I sent her back for another cup. The price for the second cup, in the tavern of Pembe, was only a tarsk bit. I paid it to the paga attendant, who collected it at the table. The girls in Pembe's tavern, as in many taverns, are not permitted to touch coins. Evelyn, of course, who had come with the higher price of the first cup, was mine until I chose to leave the tavern or in some other way release her.

"May I have permission to speak?" she asked.

"Yes," I said.

"Is it Master's intention to use me?" she asked.

"Perhaps," I said, "and perhaps not. I will do what I please."

"Yes, Master," she said.

I nursed the second cup of paga. Then, after a time, I thrust it from me.

"Is Master going to leave?" she asked.

"Go to the alcove," I said.

She looked at me, agonized. She rose to her feet and, scarcely able to move, numbly, went to the alcove. She could not bring herself to enter, through the red curtains.

I took her by the left arm and thrust her within, onto the furs at my feet. I then turned about and drew shut the curtains, hooking them shut.

I then turned about, again, to face her.

She sat, numbly, on the furs, her knees drawn up. I took the ankle ring and chain which lay at the right corner of the alcove, as you enter. The chain is about a yard long and runs to a ring bolted in the floor. There are similar chains in the four corners of the room, and in the center of the wall, near the floor, opposite the red curtains. In the left-hand corner of the room, as you enter, of course, on its chain, is another ankle ring. At the far corners of the room, of course, the chains terminate with wrist rings. In the center of the wall, near the floor, opposite the curtains, the chain terminates with a collar. There are provisions for lengthening and shortening the chains. All these devices work from locks, answering to a common key, which hangs high on the wall, toward the back and left, as you enter. Needless to say that key cannot be reached by the prisoner if even one of the chains is

173

fastened upon her. Near that common key, which hangs on a peg, there is a second peg. From the second peg hangs a slave whip.

I locked the girl's left ankle in the first ankle ring. She looked, wonderingly, at the steel locked on her ankle. She lifted the chain, leading to the locked ankle ring on her left ankle. She looked at me. "You have chained me," she said. "Oh," she said. I thrust her to her back on the furs. I then fastened her left and right wrists in their respective wrist rings. I then put the alcove collar on her, shortening its chain, fitting it over Pembe's collar. She could not then rise more than a few inches from her back. I then went to her right, and shortened the chain there. I then took her right ankle. "Oh!" she said, as I pulled it far to her right. I then locked it in the ankle ring, on its shortened chain, which is at the left of the alcove entrance, as one enters.

She looked up at me, terrified. I looked down at her. "Do you now begin to understand," I said, "what it might be to be chained as a slave?"

"Yes, Master," she said.

"Look now to your right, high on the wall," I said. "What do you see?"

"A slave whip," she said.

"Do you now begin to understand what it might be to be a slave?" I asked.

"Yes, Master," she said.

"This is an alcove," I said. "But you may think of it as a very special sort of place."

"Yes, Master," she said.

"As a chamber of submission," I said.

"Yes, yes, Master," she said.

"Think of it now," I said, "think of it deeply and keenly, with every fiber and particle of your lovely body, as a chamber of submission, a chamber in which you, a slave girl, must bend in all respects, a chamber in which you, only a female slave, must submit, in every bit of you, totally, completely, to the will of men."

"Yes, Master," she said.

"I will now touch you," I said.

"I am frigid," she wept. "Do not kill me, I beg of you."

"Think deeply now, fully," I said. "You are in the chamber of submission."

"Yes, Master," she wept.

I then touched her, with exquisite gentleness.

174

Her haunches leaped, the chains shook. She looked at me, startled.

"Do you submit, fully?" I asked her.

"Yes, Master," she said. Then she lifted her body, piteously. "Please touch me again," she said.

I let her wait for a time. Then, again, I touched her, very gently.

"Aiii!" she cried out, squirming. I continued to touch her for a bit. "Oh, oh," she began to moan.

Then I stopped touching her.

She looked up at me. "What are these sensations?" she asked.

"Apparently you should be whipped," I said.

"Why?" she asked. "Why, Master?"

"Because you have lied," I said. "You told me that you were frigid."

She looked up at me, frightened.

"But you are not," I said. "You are only another hot slave."

"No, no," she said. "Not a hot slave, not I!"

"Let us see," said I.

"Oh, oh," she moaned, softly.

She looked up at me. "How can you respect me?" she asked.

"You are not to be respected," I told her. "You are only a slave."

"Yes, Master," she said.

"You no longer have any pride to guard," I said. "A slave is not permitted pride."

"Yes, Master," she wept. "Oh, oh." Then she threw her head to the side, on the furs. "I want to respect myself!" she cried.

"Your obligation is not to respect yourself," I told her, "but to be yourself."

She looked at me, tears in her eyes. "I dare not be myself," she whispered.

"Is it wrong for a woman to be a woman?" I asked.

"Yes," she said, "yes! It is wrong, and demeaning!"

"Interesting," I said. "What should a woman be?" I asked her.

"She should be a man!" she said.

"But, quite simply, you are not a man," I told her.

"I dare not be a woman," she wept.

"Why?" I asked.

"Because," she said, "I sense, in my heart, that a woman is a slave."

"Is it not permissible for a slave to be a slave?" I asked.

"No!" she said.

"Why?" I asked.

"I do not know!" she wept. "I do not know!"

"Can it be wrong to be what one truly is?" I asked.

"Yes, yes!" she said.

"It is wrong for the tree to be a tree, the rock a rock, the bird a bird?" I asked.

"No, no," she said.

"Why, then," I asked, "is it wrong for a slave to be a slave?"

"I do not know," she said.

"Perhaps it is not wrong for a slave to be a slave," I said.

"I dare not even think that," she said. Then she said, "Please do not stop touching me, Master."

"Does a slave beg?" I asked.

"Yes, Master," she said. "Evelyn begs Master not to stop touching her."

I kissed her, softly, about the breasts, but did not stop touching her.

"Thank you, Master," she breathed.

Then, suddenly, she tore at the chains, trying to free herself, but could not, of course, do so.

"What is wrong?" I asked her.

"I must resist you!" she cried. "I must not yield! I must not yield!"

"Why not?" I asked.

"I sense the thing in me," she said. "I have never felt it before, but this must be it. It is like waves, from so deep in me. It is beginning to overwhelm me. It is fantastic. It is unbelievable. No! No! You must stop touching me!"

I stopped touching her. "Why?" I asked.

"I was beginning to come to you," she said.

"So?" I asked.

"You do not understand," she said. "I was beginning to come to you—as a slave to her master!"

"But you are a slave," I told her.

"Yes, Master," she said.

"And you are in the chamber of submission," I said.

"You give me no choice," she said.

I smiled at her. "This time, and this time alone," I said, "I will give you a choice."

176

"A choice?" she said.

"A slave's choice," I told her.

"What is it?" she asked.

"You may yield—or die," I told her.

She looked at me with terror. "I choose to yield, Master," she said.

"Of course," I said, "you are a slave."

"Yes, Master," she said.

"Next time," I said, "you will not even be given that choice. It will not be necessary. Your slavery has now been confirmed. You will thenceforth be accorded no choice whatsoever, no alternative, however dire, to the enforcement of your submission upon you."

"Yes, Master," she said.

Then I began again to touch her, lifting her to the heights she had chosen, the degrading joys of bondage, the humiliating ecstasy of the chained slave girl.

"Aiii!" she cried, throwing her head back. "I yield me yours, my Master!" she cried.

I had not even, this early in the evening, elected to enter her.

"Please touch me, hold me," she wept, helplessly. I did so. How piteous were her small hands, opening and closing, in the wrist rings.

"I did not know it could be anything like that," she said.

"It was nothing," I told her.

"Nothing!" she wept. "It was the most incredible experience of my life."

"It was only a minor slave orgasm," I said.

"When I came to you," she said, "I was submitting, and owned. It is the most beautiful and glorious feeling I have ever had."

Then, after a time, I began to touch her again.

"What is Master going to do now to his girl?" she asked.

"I am going to teach her a little more of her slavery," I told her.

"Yes, Master," she said.

This time, in less than ten Ehn, she began to squirm and cry. Then, suddenly, she looked at me, frightened. "It is coming," she said. "It is greater than the first. I will not be able to stand it. It will kill me. I will die!"

"No, you will not," I told her.

"Aiii!" she cried out, head back. Then she wept, "I'm

177

chained. I'm chained. Hold me, please. Do not let me go. Stay warm, and near to me. Please, Master. Please, Master."

I held her, and kissed her. Again I had not even elected to enter her.

She looked up, tears in her eyes. "Please come in me," she begged. "I want to be fully yours, had without mercy by my master. Take me, I beg you. Have me!"

"Later," I told her. "I have not yet begun to warm you."

"Yes, Master," she whispered, frightened.

Later, toward morning, near dawn, I awakened, Evelyn's lips so intimate upon me.

During the night I had unchained her, save for the steel and chain on her left ankle.

She awakened me as I had instructed her. It is pleasant to be awakened in that fashion. I put my hands down to her hair, as she pleasured me.

During the night I had taught her some small things, some techniques, little, simple things, for her mouth and hands, and breasts, her hair, her lips, her feet, and tongue. They might help her, I thought, to survive in Pembe's tavern. Most importantly I had tried to impress upon her the fundamental importance of submission, and that she was a slave girl. All else, for most practical purposes, follows from that.

I cried out, softly, and she looked up, pleased that she had made me do that.

"Finish your work, Slave," I told her.

"Yes, Master," she said.

My hands knotted in her hair, tightly, holding her helplessly to me. Then I released her.

I pulled her up to me, and, in the dim light of the alcove, filtering through the red curtain from the slatted grilles in the roof of the main room, wiped her mouth with her hair.

"It is morning, Master," she whispered.

"Yes," I said.

I held her arms, as she looked down at me.

"Speak," I told her.

She then, whispering, said the following. I had taught it to her last night.

He is Master, and I am Slave.
He is owner, and I am owned.
He commands, and I obey.
He is to be pleased, and I am to please.

178

Why is this?

Because he is Master, and I am Slave.

I took her and put her to her back, beside me. I looked down into her eyes.

"Good morning, Slave," I said.

"Good morning, Master," she said.

"Did you sleep well?" I asked.

"In the little time you permitted me to sleep," she said, "I never slept better before in my life."

"Did you dream?" I asked.

"I dreamed I was a slave," she said. "And then I awakened, and found that it was true."

I smiled at her.

"I am a slave," she said, "you know."

"Yes," I said.

"When I awakened this morning," she said, "I knew that it was true. You taught it to me last night."

"Do you think free women could have felt what you felt?" I asked.

"Never," she said, "for they are not slaves." She looked up at me. "What I felt were the feelings of a slave in the arms of her master. Those are feelings no free woman will ever know."

"Unless she is put in bondage," I said.

"Yes, Master," she smiled. Then she said, "How I pity them, those poor free woman, such as I was. How ignorant they are. No wonder they are so hostile to men. Would not any woman hate a man who did not have the strength to put her in a collar?"

"Perhaps," I said. I thought of a girl once known, one who once had been my free companion. I thought of her cruelty to me once, in the house of Samos, when she had thought me helpless and crippled. She had once been the daughter of Marlenus of Ar, but he had disowned her, for once, when she had been the helpless slave of the forest girl, Verna, she had begged to be purchased, a slave's act. Rather than submit to this stain upon his honor he, the Ubar of glorious Ar itself, had sworn against her, upon his sword and upon the medallion of his office as well, the fierce oath of disownment. She lived now, free, but deprived of citizenship, sequestered in Ar. Her left thigh would still bear the brand of Treve, for once, long ago, she had fallen slave to Rask of Treve, a captain and tarnsman. I wondered if he had made her yield well

179

as a slave, when he had owned her. I did not doubt it. I thought the brand of Port Kar might look well upon her body, placed above that of Treve. I wondered how she might look in scarlet silk, dancing as a slave before any men.

"We belong in collars," said Evelyn.

I heard, outside the curtain, the sounds of the early morning. Tables were being moved aside, that the floor might be cleaned. This work is usually done by paga attendants. The girls, at this time, are usually asleep, chained in their kennels.

"It is morning," I said.

"You are going to go in a moment, aren't you," she asked, "leaving me behind, a chained slave?"

"Of course," I told her, "paga girl."

"Don't go yet," she said. "I beg you, Master."

'Very well," I said.

"I wear Pembe's collar," she said, touching the encircling steel on her neck. "I would wear yours."

I looked at her.

"Surely what you did to me last night," she said, "means something to you?"

"It was only a night's pleasure with a paga girl," I said.

"Oh," she said.

"Any Gorean male could do it to you," I said.

"Make me yield like that," she asked, "as such a slave?"

"Of course," I told her, "Slave Girl."

"Yes, Master," she said.

"What do you think now of your collar?" I asked.

"I hate it," she said. "And I love it!"

"You love your collar?" I asked.

"Yes," she said, "I love it." She looked up at me. "I love being a slave," she said. "I love being enslaved. I love being forced to yield, and to obey men."

"I see that it is appropriate that you wear a collar," I said.

"Yes," she said, defiantly. "It is fully appropriate."

"You know why it is fully appropriate?" I asked.

"Of course," she said, "because I am a true slave."

"Yes," I said, "Slave."

"And yet," she said, "I am an Earth girl." She put her hands at the collar. "How cruel that I should be put in a collar!" She looked up at me. "Will it never be taken off?" she asked.

"Undoubtedly," I said.

"Ah," she said.

"To be replaced with another," I said.

180

"Oh," she said. She looked up at the wall, to her right, at the slave whip hanging there, on its peg. "You did not whip me," she said.

"Do you wish to be whipped?" I said.

"No," she said, "no!" She had felt the whip. She then looked again at me. "I suppose," said she, "that I will be bought and sold many times."

"Doubtless," I told her.

"Do you think men will ever free me?" she asked.

"No," I said.

"Why?" she asked.

"The collar is right on you," I said.

She touched it. "Yes," she said, "it is right on me. And you knew it immediately, didn't you, you beast? That is why you made me, when I thought I was free, serve you as a naked paga slave."

"It seemed fitting," I said, "that your slavery be made manifest."

"Of course," she said. "You are a Gorean master."

"Any Gorean male looking upon you," I said, "whether you wore a collar or not, would see that you should be a slave."

"And now I am a slave," she said.

"Yes," I said.

"I do not object," she said.

"It does not matter whether you object or not," I said.

"True," she smiled.

I heard men moving about, outside, cleaning the floor. I sat up.

"Do not go, Master," she begged.

"I must be on my way," I told her.

"Leaving me here?" she asked.

"Yes," I said.

"Please remain but a bit longer," she begged.

"Would you detain me?" I asked.

"Yes," she said, "with the charms of a slave."

"You do not speak as an Earth girl," I said.

"I am no longer an Earth girl," she said. "I am now only a Gorean slave," she said.

"It is true," I said.

She slipped down my body and began, piteously, to kiss me.

"I do not have time," I told her.

181

"Dally, please dally," she begged, "if only for a few moments more."

I saw that she feared to be left behind. She looked up at me, miserably.

"You now begin to understand, do you not," I asked, "something of the meaning of your collar?"

"Yes, Master," she said.

"Surely now," I said, "you would choose freedom."

She looked up at me, boldly. "No," she said. "I have been a free woman, and I have been a slave. I have known both."

"Is not freedom inordinately precious?" I asked.

"Yes," she said, "but more inordinately precious to me is my slavery."

I looked at her.

"I choose the brand," she said, "the collar, and the hands of a master on my body."

I pulled her up beside me, and threw her to her back. "Use me ruthlessly, Master," she begged.

"I shall," I told her.

"Rape me as a slave," she said.

"It will be done," I told her.

In a few moments she screamed her submission and looked at me, unbelievingly.

"I did not know what it would be to be raped as a slave," she whispered.

"It was so swift, and brutal," she said. "Please hold me," she said.

I spurned her with my foot to the side of the alcove, and she lay there, trembling and weeping.

She held out her hand to me. "Please touch me," she said.

"Be silent, Slave," I said.

"Yes, Master," she whispered.

I began to dress.

She rose to her knees and knelt there, then, by the side wall, the steel ankle ring, with its chain, leading to the floor ring, still upon her ankle. "How you used me," she said. She was still trembling.

"Sandals," I said.

She crept to me and, head down, placed my sandals on my feet. She then tied them, drawing the thongs tight and then fastening them. "How you used me," she whispered. Then she held my legs and pressed her cheek against the side of my left leg, above the knee. I did not kick her from me. She

182

looked up, tears in her eyes. "If one is a true slave," she said, "it is not wrong to be a slave, is it?"

"No," I said.

She held my legs, looking up at me. "If one is a true slave," she said, "it is right that one should be a slave, is it not?"

"Yes," I said.

"I am a true slave," she said.

"Yes," I said.

"It is thus right that I should be a slave," she said.

"Yes," I said. I lifted her to her feet, holding her by the arms before me.

"It is right," she said, "that a true slave should be enslaved."

"Of course," I said.

"I am a true slave," she said.

"I know," I said.

"It is thus right," she said, "that I should be enslaved."

"Yes," I said.

"I am enslaved," she said.

"Yes," I said. I then threw her to my feet and, turning, parted the curtains of the alcove.

"Master," she wept.

I turned to look at her.

"But one more kiss, please, Master," she said.

She knelt on the furs, chained by the ankle, and I crouched before her, and took her in my arms. We kissed. Then I thrust her back, and stood up.

"You subjected me earlier to slave rape," she said, soft tears in her eyes, with tender reproach.

"Yes," I said.

"And afterwards spurned me from you."

"Yes," I said.

"Keep me, Master!" she suddenly begged. "Keep me!"

I looked down upon her. She knelt before me. She was so soft and beautiful, her eyes and lashes wet with tears, her hair dark and soft on her shoulders, her lip trembling.

"Keep me," she begged.

She had been an agent of Kurii.

"Take me with you," she begged. "Do not leave me behind in this place."

She had been an agent of Kurii.

"Speak," I said.

Tremblingly, head down, she spoke.

183

"He is Master, and I am Slave.
He is owner, and I am owned.
He commands, and I obey.
He is to be pleased, and I am to please.
Why is this?
Because he is Master, and I am Slave."

"Each night, for a month," I said, "after you are chained in your kennel, and before you fall asleep, say that."

"Yes, Master," she said.

"Similarly, for the same month," I said, "repeat it to yourself many times during the day."

"Yes, Master," she said.

"It may help you to survive," I said.

"Thank you, Master," she said.

"Remember to yield well to men," I said.

"I will not be able to help myself, Master," she smiled.

"Remember submission, and that you are a slave girl," I said.

"Yes, Master," she said.

"You may now find this difficult to believe," I said, "but the time will come when you will find that you are unable to part these curtains and enter this alcove from the floor outside without being hot and wet. Merely to cross this threshold, that of an alcove, that of a chamber of submission, will make you ready for a man's pleasure."

"I do not find it difficult to believe, Master," she whispered. "Merely to look at the curtains excites me." She touched her collar. "Merely to touch my collar excites me. To kneel on the furs, to feel them on my body, to be kneeling itself, before a man, excites me. To be naked before him, on my knees, makes me miserable with the desire for his touch."

"I think you will survive, Slave," I told her.

"May I kiss your feet but once more, Master," she said.

I permitted this.

I felt her lips, so sweet on my feet, her tears and hair. "Keep me," she begged. "Keep me, Master."

I looked down once more at the slave at my feet, who had been an agent of Kurii.

Then I turned about and left the alcove.

"Master!" she cried.

I looked back at her, once more. She was on her belly, half through the curtains, her left leg extended behind her, held

184

by the ankle ring and chain. She held out her right hand to me. "Please buy me! Don't leave me here!" she wept.

"How was she?" asked a paga attendant, pausing in his work, buffing goblets.

"I will not demand a refund," I told him.

"Do you think she will work out?" he asked. "Pembe was curious."

"Probably," I said. "It is hard to know about those things. It is my guess that she will prove satisfactory."

"Is her slavery close to the surface?" he asked.

"Yes," I said. "Doubtless it will soon become fully manifest."

"Does she have slave fire?" he asked.

I remembered her sobbing in my arms, kissing and licking, and begging for my least touch.

"Yes," I said.

"That is good," he said. "Perhaps there is hope for the wench. I grow weary of carrying bodies to the harbor."

I went to the place, near the rear wall, where I had left the blond-haired barbarian. She had fallen asleep, slumped, blindfolded, there. She had, of course, released her ankles.

I touched her gently, and she, with a little moan of anguish, awakened. She realized then, suddenly, she had dropped off to sleep. Suddenly, fearfully, she assumed the kneeling position in which I had placed her, head down, gripping her ankles.

"No," I told her, softly.

I then took her gently in my arms. How small and light she was. I do not think she weighed more than one hundred and ten pounds.

"I am leaving by the back way," I told the paga attendant.

"As you wish," he said.

Outside I waited for a few moments, to see if the door, behind me, should be moved ajar. I examined, too, the dust of the alley, to see if it moved, or otherwise stirred, as it might have, if a foot had passed. I looked about, at the roofs about. The door did not move. The dust did not stir. The tops of the buildings, as nearly as I could determine, seemed clear.

I looked at the girl in my arms. She was again asleep. For a moment I felt moved to tenderness toward her. Her life, in the past few weeks, had not been easy. She had been a pawn in the cruel games of worlds. Too, it is sometimes traumatic for a proud, free woman of Earth to discover that she has

185

suddenly become an owned slave. I would let the girl sleep. I carried her through the streets of Schendi. I did not take a direct route to my room.

14

A GIRL BECOMES MORE BEAUTIFUL; I MUST TAKE MY LEAVE OF SASI

Sasi opened the door.

"Master," she said.

"Prepare a chain for the new girl," I said.

"Yes, Master," she said.

I do not think Sasi was too pleased when I carried the blond slave over the threshold and placed her on the straw by the slave ring. Gorean slaves, incidentally, are commonly carried over the threshold when they first enter a master's house or place of residence. This is reminiscent of a bridal custom on Earth, of course. That custom, an ancient one, makes tacitly clear the bride's ownership by the male, and has clear implications of capture and bondage. It is natural that the bride desires this ceremony, and will plead for it. The oafish male, commonly, does not even understand what is going on. He should, of course, take her directly to the bed, and throw her upon it, his.

Women wish to be the slaves of their men. What woman would want a man who is not strong enough to be her master?

Not all Gorean slaves, of course, are carried over a threshold. Some are leashed and enter on their hands and knees. Some, perhaps bound and collared, are thrust through. The common denominator of these customs, of course, is that the slave must understand that force, either explicitly or implicitly, is involved, and that she will enter the stronghold of the master, and as a slave, whether she wills to do so or not.

"Is that not the girl from the *Palms of Schendi*?" asked Sasi. The blond girl, exhausted, was still asleep.

"Yes," I said.

Sasi fastened a short chain to the slave ring, locking it,

186

with its own lock, on the ring. She then, with a key, the same key which would open the chain lock, opened the chain's ankle ring.

"What do you want her for?" asked Sasi. She handed me the opened ankle ring.

"She interests me, at least for the moment," I told her. I shut the ankle ring then on the blond's left ankle. She was secured. Sasi rose and put the key on a hook to one side of the room. Near it, on another hook, there hung a slave whip. From one of the overhead beams, near the side of the room, there was a whipping ring, to which a slave could be tethered, which could be lowered. It was a furnished room. Slaves, it must be understood, are not that uncommon on Gor.

I covered the blond with one of our blankets. The poor thing was exhausted.

"You did not carry me across the threshold," said Sasi.

"You were bound in a blanket, and on my shoulder," I said, "when I entered this room."

"I mean before," she said.

"No," I said, "I did not. I did, however, if you will remember, when first I used you, order you to my blankets."

"I have never forgotten," she said. She shuddered with pleasure, remembering the moment. "I was simply ordered to your blankets," she said.

A similar sort of thing is done sometimes when a master brings home a new girl to a house which is completely empty, if necessary, by prearrangement, and new to her, and orders her to enter alone. "Warm wine," he tells her. "Light the lamp of love. Spread furs. Crawl naked into them, and await me."

"Yes, Master," she says.

She then enters the house, obeying. Not a shackle or a cord is on her body. But few women could be more slave than she, entering fearfully the strange, empty house, and preparing herself for her master's pleasure.

"It is difficult to convey to a man," she said, "the feelings of a woman at such a time."

"They are the feelings of a slave," I said.

"So simply put!" she said. "Yes," she said, "they are the feelings of a slave. But I wonder if a man, ever, will truly understand what a woman's collar can mean to her. I wonder if he, ever, truly, will be able to fathom the nature and depth of the emotions of the woman who kneels at his feet."

187

"Surely free women, too, have emotions," I said.

"I was free," she said. "I did not know what it was to feel until I became a slave. I was free. There was no need to feel, or be aware. But this has changed since I became a slave. I must now be sensitive to the feelings of others. I have never been so aware of other human beings as now. And I cannot always have my way, and I must yield to male domination. I can be commanded, and I must obey, and be pleasing. This answers to something very deep in me, Master."

"Of course," I said, "to the slave in you."

"Yes," she said, "to the woman, and slave, in me."

"They are the same," I said.

"Yes," she said.

"It is hard to be a man," I said, "until one stands in a relation to a woman. And, I suppose, it is hard to be a woman until one stands in a relation to a man."

"What relation," she asked, "Master?"

"That of the natural order of nature," I said.

"Yes, Master," she said.

I looked at her. "I cannot know well the nature of your feelings," I said, "but I know, and well, that women are deep as well as beautiful."

"We are so different from you," she said. "I fear you will never understand us."

"It is doubtless easier to put you on your knees and push the whip to your teeth than it is to understand you," I said.

"The man who truly understands us," she laughed, "is the first to put us on our knees and make us kiss the whip."

"Take off my sandals," I said.

"Yes, Master," she said. She looked up. "Never until I was a slave," she said, "did I feel so helpless, alive and vulnerable."

I said nothing.

"I must untie your sandals," she said. "I must crawl to you, if you wish. I must do anything you want. I am happy."

"Attend to your work," I told her.

"Yes, Master," she said. Then she had removed the sandals. She kissed them, and looked up at me.

"Tonight," I said, "before I leave the room, I will pierce your ears."

"Thank you, Master," she said.

"You will then be," I said, "for all practical purposes, irrevocably a slave."

"Yes, Master," she said. She looked up. "You do understand us, don't you?" she asked.

"It will improve your price," I told her.

"Yes, Master," she smiled.

"I think also," I said, "I will pierce her ears, too." I indicated the sleeping blond girl. She had been an agent of Kurii. I decided that I would guarantee, for all practical purposes, that she would remain in a collar on Gor. I would pierce her ears.

I looked over to the sleeping girl, so worn and exhausted. I went over to her and, with one hand, lifted the blanket away from her. She stirred, troubled, sensing the difference in the temperature, the air, upon her skin. "No," she whimpered, softly, in English. "I do not want to get up." How beautiful she was, lying soft and helpless in the straw. She stirred again, and lifted her knee, shifting the position of her shackled ankle. "No, I do not want to get up," she whimpered, in English. She reached down, searching for the blanket. I then held her by the upper arms. "Oh!" she said, half awakening, twisting. But I held her. "Oh," she said, "oh," suddenly, rudely, returning to a slave's reality, then understanding that she lay in straw, her back on a wooden floor, held in the arms of a man. She moved her ankle, frightened, and felt the shackle and chain.

"Who is it?" she asked.

I did not speak to her.

"Is it my Master?" she asked.

"Yes," I said.

"Who is my Master, please," she begged.

I said nothing to her.

"Who is my Master!" she cried out, miserably.

"I am," I told her.

"Who owns me?" she begged.

"I do," I told her.

She turned her head to the side, and moaned. Then she again turned her face toward me, its upper portions obscured by the black, knotted blindfold.

"Why are you holding me like this?" she asked.

I said nothing to her.

"What are you going to do to me?" she asked.

I did not speak to her.

"What do you want of me?" she asked. "Oh, no, please," she said. "I am a virgin!" Her lip trembled. "No, please!" she said. She tensed. "No," she said, "please, no, please do not

189

take my virginity like this, not like this. I am blindfolded! I cannot see you! I cannot even see you. I want to see who takes my virginity from me!" Then she cried out, softly, and wept.

"It was your Master, Slave," I told her.

"Yes, Master," she whispered.

I held her very still.

"How sweet and strong it is," she breathed. "And how helplessly I am held. I could not escape now, unless you were to release me."

I did not speak.

"Would Master deign to kiss a slave?" she asked.

I put my lips, gently, to hers, and she lifted her lips to mine, tenderly, and kissed me, and then she put her head back to the straw and the floor.

"Thank you, Master," she said.

"This first time," I said, "doubtless it is difficult and painful for you."

"It does not hurt," she said.

"Oh," I said.

"I have never been had before," she said. "I did not know what it was like, to lie like this."

"Do you like it?" I asked.

"Yes," she said, "yes, Master." She then held my arms. "Master," she whispered.

"Yes," I said.

"I begin to feel like I want to respond to you," she whispered. "May I move, Master?"

"Yes," I said.

"Oh," she said, softly, moving, "I did not know it could be like this. Never before have I been locked in a man's arms in this fashion. How sweet it is. How helpless I feel. I am beginning to become excited, Master. I am beginning to become terribly excited, Master!"

She lifted her lips, suddenly, to me, and kissed me, and then she put her head back, and turned it from side to side, lost in her pleasure and in the darkness of the blindfold.

Suddenly she clutched my arms. "Master!" she said.

"Yes," I said.

"We are completely alone, are we not?" she asked.

"No," I said.

"Oh!" she cried out in misery. "Oh, no!" Then she asked, "who else is present?"

"Another woman," I told her.

190

"Oh, no, no, no, no!" she wept. "No, no!"

"Do not fear," I said. "It is only another slave."

"Behold how the brute abuses me!" she called out. "What we women suffer at the hands of such beasts!"

I was startled. Sasi looked at me, puzzled.

"Rape me as a slave," she called out. "You will get no pleasure from me!"

That seemed to me highly unlikely.

Then the chained girl lay back, pressing her hands against me, her head turned to the side.

"Have your will with me," she said. "I am inert. I can endure. It means nothing to me."

"Are you being troublesome?" I asked her.

"No, Master," she said.

"Have you felt the whip?" I asked.

"Yes, Master," she said.

"Do you wish to feel it again?" I asked.

"No, Master," she said.

"You, then," I said, "have my permission to again respond."

"Surely," she said, "you did not think I was earlier responsive to you?"

"You now have my permission to again respond," I said.

"I cannot possibly respond with another woman in the room," she whispered to me. "Surely you must understand that, Master."

"Respond," I told her.

"I am commanded?" she asked, disbelievingly.

"Yes," I said.

"How can you command such a thing?" she asked.

"As I have done," I said.

"Yes, Master," she said.

"And, further," I said, "you will respond as a slave."

"Yes, Master," she said, miserably. She began to move, timidly, slightly, about me.

"I will try to forget that there is another woman in the room," she said.

"No," I said, "keep it clearly in mind."

"Master?" she said.

"Show her your slave heat," I said.

"But should one not be ashamed of one's passion?" she asked.

"Why?" I asked.

"I do not know," she said.

191

"Is there any rational reason?" I asked. "I do not doubt there may be many irrational reasons, or causes."

"Perhaps because, in a man's arms, it makes a woman a slave," she said.

"That," I said, "is doubtless true, but it is a reservation which, if pertinent at all, is pertinent only, surely, to free women."

"Yes," she said, uncertainly.

"You are already a slave," I said.

"Yes," she said.

"It is permissible, I suppose," she said, "for a slave to be passionate."

"It is not only permissible for a slave to be passionate," I said.

"Master?" she asked.

I held her very tightly.

"Yes Master," she whispered.

"A slave," I said, "must be passionate."

"Master?" she asked.

"Yes," I said, 'the slave girl has no choice. She must be passionate."

'Yes, Master," she whispered.

"Moreover," I said, "she is to be proud of her passion. It is one of the most splendid, and beautiful and joyful things about her."

"Yes, Master," she whispered.

"Begin," I told her.

"Yes, Master," she said.

She began to move, and try to kiss me.

"Oh, no," she said. "I am too miserable. It is too embarrassing."

"Continue," I told her.

"But if I continue I may become excited," she said.

"You will become excited," I told her.

"But there is another woman present," she said.

"Move," I told her.

"Yes, Master," she sobbed.

"Be proud of your slave heat," I told her.

"Yes, Master," she said.

"Show her your slave heat," I said.

"Yes, Master," she sobbed. Then, in a few moments, despite her intent, I heard a moan of pleasure escape her. "Oh, no," she added.

"It is not wrong to experience sexual pleasure," I told her.

"But there is another woman present," she said.

"Show her your slave heat," I said.

"Forgive me," she cried out, calling to whoever might be in the room, "I cannot help myself. The Master is exciting me!"

"Master," said Sasi, unable to restrain herself. "Withdraw from her! Let me serve your pleasure!"

"No, no!" said the blond-haired barbarian, clutching me. "He is with me now!" Her lip trembled. "Do not withdraw from me," she begged.

"Why not?" I asked.

"I want to serve your pleasure," she whispered.

"What do you know of serving a man's pleasure," said Sasi. "Beg his forgiveness for disappointing him, and let him seize me in his arms."

"No!" said the blond-haired barbarian. Then she said to me, "I am sorry if I disappoint you, Master."

"You have not yet disappointed me," I said.

"I will try not to disappoint you, Master," she said.

"Let me serve your pleasure, Master," begged Sasi.

"It is now I who am serving his pleasure!" said the blond girl.

"If you call that serving his pleasure," said Sasi.

"Help me," begged the blond girl.

"Lift your body against his," said Sasi, "squirm, kiss!"

The blond moaned with misery. "That is like a slave," she whispered.

"Obey!" said Sasi.

"Is she first girl?" asked the blond.

"Yes," I said.

"Yes, Mistress," said the blond, miserably. Then she obeyed, for she was a slave. From time to time Sasi and I made simple suggestions to the blond who, for the first time, was being ravished. We forced her to cooperate in her rape. I began to grit my teeth.

"Stop moving," I told her.

She stopped moving. But she did not want to stop moving. She clutched my arms.

"My passion is making me a slave," she whispered.

"You are already a slave," I told her.

"Yes, Master," she said.

"Passion, technically," I said, "has nothing to do with the imposition of the yoke of slavery. It is, of course, afterwards required of the enslaved woman. Passion is commanded of her."

"Yes, Master," she said.

"The sense in which passion makes you a slave," I said, "is that it puts you in what is in effect a slave's position, helpless, yielding, submitting to the master."

"Yes, Master," she whispered.

"But you will not even begin to know what true passion is, ignorant girl," I said, "until you have been longer a slave."

"Yes, Master," she whispered.

"You may begin again to respond now, Slave," I told her.

"Yes, Master," she said. Then she began again to move and, soon, was crying out, softly.

"I think she will be a hot slave," I said to Sasi.

"Yes," said Sasi, "I think so, Master."

"Please do not use those words of me," she begged.

"Say," I told her, " 'I am proud to be a hot slave.' "

"I am proud to be a hot slave," she cried out, miserably.

"And you are proud of it, you know," I told her.

She clutched me, startled. Her lip trembled. "Yes," she said, suddenly, "it is true. How incredible! I am proud! I am proud to be a hot slave!"

"Of course," I told her, "Slave."

"No, no!" she said. "I am ashamed to be a hot slave!"

"Whether you are proud or ashamed," I told her, "in any event, you are a hot slave."

"Yes, Master," she said. That could not be denied.

"I come from a far world," she said. "The girl from that world is ashamed. The girl on this world, the slave, is not ashamed. She is proud." She put her head to the side. "How shamelessly proud she is," she said.

"The girl from the far world," I told her, "no longer exists. What exists now, in her place, is herself transformed, herself become a beautiful slave at the mercy of a master."

"Yes, Master," she said.

"What is the name of your former world?" I asked.

"It is called Earth," she said. "Have you heard of it, Master?" she asked.

"Yes," I said. "Her women are not unknown in our markets."

"Oh," she said.

"They make excellent slaves," I said.

She said nothing.

"Do you find that hard to believe?" I asked.

"No, Master," she said. Then she lifted her lips, and kissed me. "Master," she said.

"Yes," I said.

"You took my virginity," she said. "Now, I beg you, consummate your will upon me."

"Do you beg as a slave?" I asked.

"Yes, Master," she said. "I beg as a slave."

"Beg," I told her.

"Take me," she begged. "Make me yours. Have me, as your slave."

"Do you yield," I asked her, "fully and completely, and as a slave?"

"Yes, Master," she whispered. "I yield, fully and completely, and as a slave."

I then took her.

"I thought it might be you, Master," she said, lifting her lips from my feet.

I had removed her blindfold.

It was now the sixteenth Ahn, several Ahn after I had taken the slave's virginity.

"From the first instant I saw you," she said, "I dreamed of being your slave. Now it is true."

"Help Sasi clean the dishes," I told her.

"Yes, Master," she said.

She put her fingers to her ears, and turned her head, from side to side, looking at the rings in her ears.

"They are very beautiful," she said, regarding herself in the mirror.

They were of gold, about an inch in diameter. I had pierced her ears, and put her in them.

"How glorious it is to again see," she said. The blindfold lay discarded, to one side. She was no longer shackled to the slave ring.

Seeing my eyes upon her, she knelt. "Am I beautiful, Master?" she asked.

"Almost," I told her.

She looked, kneeling, in the mirror. "I do not wish to sound vain," she said, "but I think that I must be as beautiful as almost any woman upon Earth."

"You doubtless are," I said. "But are you as beautiful as a Gorean slave girl?"

"Surely, Master," she said, "that would depend on the Gorean slave girl."

"Do you think you are as beautiful as the general run of Gorean slave girls?" I asked.

She put down her head. "No, Master," she said, "I do not. I did not know such women could exist, until I saw several in Cos, when I was free, and some on the wharves of Port Kar and Schendi, after I myself, sold in a market, became a slave." She looked at me. "Sometimes," she said, "it seems almost wrong that a woman should be so beautiful and desirable."

"Why?" I asked.

"I do not know," she smiled. "Perhaps it is because I am not so beautiful and desirable. Perhaps it is because men are so fond of them. Perhaps I am jealous of their beauty and desirability, and am envious because they, and not I, are found so attractive by men."

"It is natural for the ugly to find an error in beauty," I said.

"I am not ugly, am I?" she asked.

"No," I said, "you are not. Indeed, you are almost beautiful."

"I wonder if Gorean men, such as yourself," she said, "understand how fortunate they are, that there should be such women on their world."

"Are their not plenitudes of such women on your world," I asked, "beautiful and desirable who, loving and helpless, beg to serve and please?"

"How you Gorean beasts," she said, "take naively for granted the glorious riches at your disposal."

I shrugged.

She looked at me. "How is it," she asked, "that on your world things are not as on my world?"

"Gorean men are not weaklings and fools," I said.

She looked at me.

"They have not chosen to surrender the dominance which is the blood and backbone of their nature."

She swallowed hard.

"They keep it," I told her.

"Yes," she said.

"Yes, what?" I asked.

"Yes, Master," she said.

"What of me?" asked Sasi. "Am I not beautiful? Are not my earrings lovely?"

"Yes," I said, "you are beautiful, and your earrings, you little she-sleen, are marvelous upon you." Sasi's earrings, too, of gold, were the same as those of the blond-haired barbarian.

"Thank you, Master," she said. Sasi was in a good mood. After I had had the blond this morning, early, upon returning from the tavern of Pembe, I had slept for several hours. But when I had awakened I had contented her slave appetites. We had then eaten, from foods which she had, during my rest, I having given her a few coins, purchased in Schendi. Some of this food I gave to the blond who, at that time, was still blindfolded. I thrust it, some bread and fruit, in her mouth, while she had knelt in the position of the pleasure slave. This is something done with a girl in her first feeding, or feedings, and may, upon occasion, be repeated. She is fed as an animal, and from the hand of the master, and while in the position of the pleasure slave. This helps to reinforce the centrality of her condition upon her. This helps her to understand what she is.

"At least," smiled the blond, "I am almost beautiful."

"Perhaps," I said, "You will someday become beautiful."

She looked at me.

"Women grow in beauty, and slavery," I told her.

She looked in the mirror. "Beautiful even for a Gorean slave girl?" she asked.

"Yes," I said, "I think that someday you may find that you have become beautiful even for a Gorean slave girl."

Her eyes were startled.

"Yes," I said, "I think that possibly one day you will find that you have become exquisitely beautiful and desirable, and that your least movement, that of even a wrist or hand, or smallest expression, will be tormentingly attractive to a man. You may then tremble in terror, for you will have become a beautiful Gorean slave girl."

"I am afraid," she said.

"Of course," I said.

"I am afraid to be beautiful," she said.

"Naturally," I said. "But I am afraid you will not be able to help yourself."

"But as I become more beautiful, and desirable," she said, "I would become more helpless, more a slave, more than ever at the mercy of these mighty men of Gor."

"Yes," I said, "of course. You would be then only their helpless, beautiful slave."

"How fearful," she said.

I said nothing.

"Do you truly think I might become beautiful?" she asked. She lifted her hair over her head, straightening her body, and regarded herself in the mirror.

"Yes," I said.

She then removed her hands from her hair. Behind her, her hair came, falling, to the sweetness of her shoulder blades. This was a bit short for the hair of a Gorean slave girl. Their hair, as is required by most masters, is usually somewhat long. There is more that can be done with long hair, both with respect to adding variety to the girl's appearance and in the furs, than with short hair. Sometimes the girl is even tied in her own hair. Most importantly, perhaps, long hair is beautiful on a girl, or surely, at least, on many girls. Too, many masters enjoy unbinding it, before ordering a girl to the furs. Unbinding a girl's hair, on Gor, incidentally, is culturally understood as being the act of one who owns her. A free woman, captured, whose hair her captor unbinds, usually the first time by the stroke of a knife, a precaution against poison pins and other devices, knows full well by this act that she will soon be made his slave. Many Gorean masters, incidentally, shape and trim the hair of their own girls. This is less expensive than having it done in a pen. Too, it is pleasant to cut the hair of a girl one owns. She generally kneels, a wrap of rep-cloth about her shoulders, while this is done. Beneath the wrap of rep-cloth, of course, she is naked and in the position of the pleasure slave. When one is through with the cutting it is then convenient to have her.

She looked at herself, kneeling, in the mirror.

"The earrings are beautiful," I said.

"Yes, Master," she said. She brushed her hair back with her two hands and, turning her head from side to side, her finger tips at her ears, again regarded herself.

She had the vanity of a lovely slave.

"What do you see in the mirror?" I asked.

"A slave girl," she said.

"Yes," I said.

"A girl to be bought and sold, and abused for a master's pleasure."

"Of course," I said.

"I may not be beautiful," she said, "but I am delicate and lovely, am I not?"

"Yes," I said, "you are."

"Could you truly bring yourself to put me beneath your heavy and uncompromising will?" she asked.

"Certainly," I said.

"You could, and you will, won't you?" she said.

"Yes," I said.

"Could you whip me?" she asked.

"Yes," I said.

"It is a strange feeling, being a slave," she said.

"You will grow used to it, Slave Girl," I said.

"Yes, Master," she said.

I went to her, behind her, standing there, before the mirror.

"What do you see?" I asked.

"A slave girl," she said, "at the feet of her master."

I put my hand in her hair, and turned her head, from side to side. Then I stopped.

"What do you see?" I asked.

"A slave girl, at the feet of her master," she said, "his hand in her hair, commanding her, making her do what he wishes."

I then, with my hand in her hair, turned her to the side and bent back her body, exposing, as she knelt there, helpless, the lovely slave bow of her beauty.

"What do you see?" I asked.

"A displayed slave," she said. I did not release her. Suddenly she said, "No! Oh, no!"

I waited for a full moment, holding her helplessly there, letting her see well whatever it might be that she saw. And then I released her. She knelt there, terrified, shuddering, before the mirror.

"What did you see?" I asked.

"It is hard to explain," she said, shuddering. "Suddenly, for a fearful moment, I saw myself as incredibly beautiful, as beautiful as I might someday be, but the beauty was not the cool and formal beauty of a free woman, something I can understand, but the hot, sensuous, helpless beauty of an owned slave, and I was the slave! And, too, for a moment I thought I understood how such a woman might look to a man. It was so frightening! How we must fear that they might simply seize us and tear us to pieces in their lust! Then suddenly I understood the brand and collar, the whip, the chain! Of course they would brand us, marking us as their own. Of course they would put us in steel collars, which we could not remove! Of course they could chain us to their walls and slave rings! Of course they would use the whip unhesitantly upon us if we were in the least displeasing!"

She knelt before the mirror, shuddering. "Perhaps now," I said, "you understand, in some small particular, what it is for a woman to be attractive to a man."

"They want us," she whispered, frightened, "literally."

"Yes," I said.

"They want to own us," she said, "own us!"

"Of course," I said.

'I did not know such desire, such lust, could exist," she said.

"Yes," I said.

"And I could be owned by such a man," she said. Then she looked up at me, and then, suddenly, put down her head. "And I am owned by such a man," she said, trembling.

"And what do you feel of this?" I asked.

"Nothing on my own world has prepared me for this, Master," she said.

"There is a stain of blood on your thigh," I said.

"My Master took my virginity," she said.

"You are now a red-silk girl," I said.

"Yes, Master." she said, "I am now a red-silk girl."

"Whose red-silk girl?" I asked.

"Your red-silk girl, Master." she said.

I walked back to the center of the room and turned, facing her. She knelt before the mirror.

"Stand up," I told her.

She did so.

"Turn and approach me." I said.

"But I am naked," she said.

"Do you wish for me to repeat a command?" I asked.

She turned white. "No, Master," she said. She then approached me, and stood quite closely before me. She had not been taught to stand this closely before me. She knew, instinctively, in the circumstances, where she would stand. This pleased me for it indicated, whether she knew it or not, that she was a natural slave. This distance, of course, was not cultural for her. She came from a culture which requires a significant distance, usually a yard or more, between male speakers and as much, or more, between speakers of the opposite sex. Yet she knew readily, or instinctively, or intuitively, or naturally, or somehow, that she should be, in these circumstances, standing as she was before me, at a distance

200

where I might, if I wished, without inconvenience, simply take her in my arms.

She looked up at me. "Master?" she asked.

The Gorean slave girl, incidentally, will space herself from her master quite differently in different situations. For example, if she is somewhat farther away, it is easier for her to display herself in all her beauty; if she wishes to wheedle for his caress she may approach quite closely; if she is receiving instructions she may kneel a few feet away; if she is begging to serve his pleasure she may kneel at his feet, perhaps kissing them, and holding his ankles; obviously, too, a girl who fears she is to be disciplined will commonly hang back; sometimes, too, a girl will fear to approach too closely until the master, by an expression or small sign, indicates that she is not in obvious disfavor and may do so.

I took the head of the blond-haired barbarian in my hands and looked at her. She lowered her eyes. How magnificent it is to own a woman! What can compare with it?

I turned her head, from side to side. How exciting were the earrings, penetrating the soft flesh of her ear lobes. I looked at the tiny wires vanishing in the minute punctures and then emerging, looping her ears, as though in a slave bond, making them the mounting places from which, thus fastened upon her, by my will, dangled two golden rings, barbaric ornaments enhancing the beauty of a slave. I smiled to myself. On Earth I had thought little of earrings. Yet now, in the Gorean setting, how exquisite and exciting they suddenly seemed. Perhaps then, for the first time, I truly began to sense how the Gorean views such things. Surely these things are symbolic as well as beautiful. The girl's lovely ears have been literally pierced; the penetrability of her sweet flesh is thus brazenly advertised upon her very body, a proclamation of her ready vulnerability, in incitement to male rapine. And when she wears the earrings, he can see the metal disappearing in the softness of her ear, literally fixed within it. Her flesh is doubly penetrated, her softness about the intruding metal, before his very eyes. The wire loop, too, or rod, when it emerges from the ear and, by one device or another, fastens the ring upon her, may suggest her bondage. Too, if the ring itself is closed, perhaps it suggests her susceptibility to the locked shackle, say, a wrist ring or slave bracelet; would there not, in the two rings, be one, so to speak, for each wrist? It is little wonder that Gorean free women never pierce their ears; it is little wonder that, in the beginning, it was only the lowest and most exciting of pleasure slaves who had their ears pierced; now, however, it is not uncommon on Gor for almost any pleasure slave to have her ears pierced; the custom of piercing the ears of a slave has now become relatively widespread: it has been done in Turia, of course, for generations. Too, of course, the ring is an obvious ornament. The girl placed in it has thus been ornamented. Ornamentation is not inappropriate in a slave. Lastly, the ring is beautiful. Thus it makes the slave more beautiful.

I held her head still, and lifted it, that it might face me. She opened her eyes, looking up at me. "Master?" she asked.

I looked down at her.

"You are a legal slave," I told her.

"Yes, Master," she said.

"But what you do not yet know," I said, "is that you are also a true slave, a natural slave."

"I come from a world," she said, "where women are not slaves."

"Is that the world called 'Earth'?" I asked.

"Yes," she said.

"I have heard," I said, "that on that world women are piteous slaves, only they lack masters."

"That lack," she said, "in my case, on this world, will surely be made up."

"Yes," I said.

I released her head and held her, then, by the upper arms.

"I will obey you," she said, softly. "I will do anything, and everything, that you might want."

"That is known to me," I said.

"Yes, Master," she said, tossing her head, a bit irritably.

"Would you like to be made more beautiful?" I asked.

"Of course," she said, lightly, "if it is my master's wish."

I then released her, and she stood there.

I went to the side of the room and picked up my sea bag. I threw it to the center of the room. She looked down at it, puzzled. It was of heavy blue material, canvas, and tied with a white rope.

"Lie down upon it," I told her, "on your back, your head to the floor."

She did so.

"No, please," she said, "not like this." It is a common position for a disciplinary slave rape. In it the woman feels very vulnerable, very helpless.

I then took her.

"No," she wept, in English, "have you no respect for my feelings? Am I nothing to you?"

I stood up. I had, by intent, given her no time to respond, other than as a brutalized slave, no time to feel, other than as a girl unilaterally subjected to her master's pleasure. She looked up at me, miserably.

"Crawl now to the mirror," I told her, "on your hands and knees, and regard yourself."

Miserable, she did so, her hair falling before her face, trembling, her sweet breasts pendant. She lifted her head, and gasped, looking in the mirror.

"Do you see?" I asked.

"Yes," she said, and then wept, her head down.

"Lift your head again," I said, "and again look."

She did so.

"Do you see?" I asked.

"Yes," she said, weeping, "the slave is more beautiful than before." She then put down her head again, crying.

"Crawl now to the straw, by the slave ring," I told her. "Lie down there, drawing your legs up."

"Yes, Master," she said.

I then went to her, with a blanket, and threw it over her, but not yet covering her head.

She looked up at me, so vulnerable and delicate, so helpless and frightened. "I am more beautiful now," she said. "But how? How could it be?"

"It is the result of an inward change in you," I said, "outwardly manifested in expression and bodily mien."

"But what?" she asked.

"Speak your feelings," I told her.

"Never before," she said, "did I feel so helplessly owned."

"That has something to do with it," I told her.

"You subjected me so casually, so forcibly, to your will," she said.

"That, too, has something to do with it," I told her.

"You are my Master, aren't you?" she asked.

"Yes," I said.

"You can do with me whatever you want, can't you?" she asked.

"Yes," I said.

"And you will, won't you?" she asked.

"Yes," I said.

"I love being owned," she said, suddenly.

"Of course," I said, "you are a woman."

"If a woman loves being owned," she said, "must she not be a natural slave?"

"Answer your own question," I told her. "You are the woman."

"I dare not answer it," she whispered.

"Do so," I told her.

"Yes," she whispered, frightened, "she must be a natural slave."

"And you are a woman," I said.

"Yes, Master," she said.

"Draw your conclusion," I told her, "out loud."

"I am a natural slave, Master," she said.

"Yes," I said.

She looked up at me. "Never, never did I think I would admit that in my life," she said.

"It takes great courage," I told her.

There were tears in her eyes.

"But, as yet," I said, "it is largely only an intellectual recognition on your part. It is not yet internalized, not yet a part of the totality of your being and responses."

"Yes, Master," she said.

"Nonetheless, the intellectual recognition, abstract and superficial as it is, is a useful first step in the transformation of your consciousness, and the freeing of your deepest self, with her profundities of emotions and needs."

"My deepest self is feminine," she said.

"Yes," I said, "it is only your present consciousness which has been to some extent masculinized and, to a larger extent, neuterized. Beneath the patterns, the trainings, the roles, lies the woman. It is she whom we must seek. It is she whom we must free."

"I am afraid to be feminine," she said.

"You will be punished for femininity on this world," I told her, "only by free women."

"Free!" she laughed, miserably.

"They think themselves free," I said

"Could I dare to be a woman on this world?" she asked.

"Yes," I told her.

"But what if I wish to crawl to a handsome man, and beg to obey him?" she asked.

"On this world," I told her, "you may do so."

"But would he not then, as a gentleman, scandalized, lift me hastily to my feet, embarrassed, implicitly belittling me, and encouraging me to the pursuit of masculine virtues?"

"Would you fear that?" I asked.

"Yes," she said.

"Is that why you would hesitate to crawl to a man?" I asked.

"Of course," she said.

"On this world, as a slave," I said, "you need have no fear."

"What would he do on this world?" she asked.

"Perhaps instruct you in the proper way to crawl to his feet," I said.

"Oh," she said.

"If you did not do so beautifully enough," I said, "he might whip you."

"Whip me?" she asked.

"Yes," I said.

She looked at me.

"Gorean men are not easy to please, Slave," I said.

"Yes, Master," she said.

"Masculinity and femininity are complementary properties," I told her. "If a man wishes a woman to be more feminine, he must be more masculine. If a woman wishes a man to be more masculine, she must be more feminine."

"I am thinking of the far world from which I came, Master," she said. "I think there may be a fearful corollary to what you have said. Perhaps if a man fears a woman he will want her to be more like a man, and if a woman fears a man she will want him to be more like a woman."

"Perhaps," I said. "It may depend on the individuals. I would not know."

"I am more beautiful now," she said. "I saw it in the mirror."

"Yes," I said.

"I still do not understand, clearly," she said, "how it could be."

"You were taught," I said, "that you were owned, and that you were subject, totally, to the male will."

"Yes, Master," she whispered.

"You had begun to learn just a little then, you see," I said, "that you, a lovely woman, were truly under male domination."

"And that made me more beautiful?" she asked.

"Yes," I said.

"How?" she asked.

"By releasing, in response, more of your femininity," I said.

She looked up at me, frightened.

"It is a natural thing," I said. "As a woman becomes more feminine, she becomes more beautiful."

"I am afraid to be feminine, and beautiful," she said.

"As well you might be, on this world, as a slave," I said, "knowing what it will mean for you, how it will excite the lust of masters and make men mad to own you."

"No," she said. "That is not it. It is rather that I fear that self. I fear it might be truly me."

"Have you never wondered," I asked, "what it might be like, men with whips standing near you, to dance naked in the firelight, your feet striking in the sand, before warriors?"

"Yes," she said. "I have wondered about that."

"You see," I said, "that self you fear is truly you."

"Give me a choice," she begged.

"You will be given no choice," I told her. "Your femininity will be forced to grow, nurtured, if necessary, by the whip."

"Yes," she whispered.

"Yes, what?" I said.

"Yes, Master," she said. "Master!" she protested, but I lifted the dark blanket and threw it over her head, so that she was completely covered. She could not then speak, or rise up, for the blanket was over her.

I got to my feet. From the sea bag I drew forth the notes for fortunes, made out to Shaba, to be drawn on various of the banks of Schendi, and the false ring, that which he was supposed to carry to the Sardar in place of the true ring. For the notes I, as a putative agent of Kurii, was to receive the true ring, the Tahari ring, which I would then return to Port Kar, that Samos might arrange for its delivery to the Sardar. I did not think I would kill Shaba. If he should actually dare to deliver the false ring to the Sardar he would doubtless there fall into the power of the Priest-Kings. They would then deal with him as they saw fit. If he did not choose to deliver the false ring to the Sardar I might then, at a later date, hunt him down, to kill him. My first priority was surely to return the Tahari ring to Samos as swiftly and safely as possible.

It was now near the eighteenth Ahn.

"Master," said Sasi. "I fear your eyes."

"I must leave now," I told her.

"I fear your eyes," she said, "how you look at me. Will you return to us?"

206

"I will try," I told her.

"I see by your eyes," she said, "that you fear you will not return to us."

"It is a hard business on which I embark," I told her. "In the sea bag," I said, "are various things. The key to your collar is there, for example. Too, there are coins. They should, in the event that I do not return, or do not soon return, keep you and the barbarian alive for a long time."

"Yes, Master," she said. Then she looked at me, wonderingly. "You would let me put my hand on the key to my own collar?" she asked.

"Schendi may not be an easy place in which to survive," I told her. "You may find it convenient, in some circumstances, to remove your collar."

"Are you freeing me?" she asked. It did not even occur to Sasi that anyone might consider freeing the blond-haired barbarian. She, so luscious, and becoming so beautiful, could obviously, on a world such as Gor, be only slave meat.

I looked at Sasi. Swiftly she knelt. "Forgive me, my Master," she said. "Please do not slay me."

"No," I said. "But Schendi may not be an easy place in which to survive. You may find it convenient, in some circumstances, to remove your collar."

"I am branded," she said. "I would fear to masquerade as a free woman."

"I would not advise that," I said. "You might be fed to tharlarion. But, still, it might be better for you not to be recognized as the girl of Tarl of Teletus."

"Who are you, truly, Master?" she asked.

"Look to the beam above your head, and behind you," I said. "What dangles there, which might be conveniently lowered?"

"A whipping ring," she said.

"What hangs on the wall behind you, to your left?" I asked.

"A slave whip," she said.

"Do you again request to know my true identity?" I asked.

"No, Master," she said.

"You are an agile, clever slave, Sasi," I said, "as quick-witted as you are curvacious. You have lived as a she-urt on the wharves of Port Kar. I have little fear for you." I glanced at the barbarian, beneath the blanket.

"Do not fear, Master," said Sasi. "I will teach her to hide, and eat garbage and be pleasing to paga attendants."

"I must go now," I said.

"Yes, Master," she said.

"In time," I said, "if I do not return, you will both presumably be caught and put up for public auction."

"Yes, Master," she said.

I turned to leave.

"Must you leave this moment?" she asked.

I turned about, and looked at her.

"I may never see you again," she said.

I shrugged.

"I do not want to be free," she said.

"Do not fear," I told her, "you will not be."

"Please, my Master," she said. "Make now to me a gentle love."

I went to Sasi, and crouched down, and took her in my arms.

15

MSALITI AND I ARE TRICKED BY SHABA; WHAT OCCURRED OUTSIDE THE HEADQUARTERS OF MSALITI AND SHABA

"You are late," said Msaliti.

"I have brought the notes," I told him.

"It is past the nineteenth Ahn," he said.

"I was detained," I said.

"Have you brought the notes," he asked.

"Yes," I said, "I have brought them." He was clearly nervous.

He admitted me, from the street to the small, dingy anteroom, that leading to the larger room in which we had, the preceding day, discussed our business.

"Is Shaba here?" I asked.

"No," he said.

"Then what is so important about me being late?" I asked

"Give me the notes," he said. "Give me the ring."

"No," I said. I entered the larger room, that in which we had conferred on matters of importance yesterday.

"Where are the askaris?" I asked. They were not in the room.

"They are elsewhere," said he.

"The room was more attractive yesterday," I said, "when it contained the two female slaves."

Msaliti and I sat down, cross-legged, near the low table.

"Yesterday evening," I said, "after we parted, I paid a visit to the tavern of Pembe. I made use there of the slave who had once been Evelyn Ellis. She is not bad in a collar."

"She is frigid," said Msaliti.

"Nonsense," I said. "The poor girl is paga hot."

"I find that surprising," said he.

"She cannot now help herself," I said.

"Pathetic thing," he said.

"It required only a bit of chaining and teaching her, so to speak, to kiss the whip."

"Excellent," said Msaliti.

"You seem distracted," I said.

"It is nothing," he said.

My thoughts strayed to the blond-haired barbarian and Sasi.

"Keep her under the blanket for an Ahn after I have left," I had told Sasi. "You may then release her, if you wish. If you do not wish to do so, of course, then leave her there as long as you please."

"Yes, Master," said Sasi.

"She is an ignorant girl, and a natural slave," I said, "so keep her under strict discipline."

"Yes, Master," said Sasi.

"Do not hesitate to use the whip on her," I said.

"No, Master," said Sasi.

"Remember that she is a natural slave," I told Sasi.

"We are all natural slaves, Master," she said. "But have no fear. I will keep her under a very strict discipline."

"As is fitting for any slave," I said.

"Yes, Master," smiled Sasi.

I had then kissed her and left.

"Why do you not give me the notes and the ring?" asked Msaliti.

"My orders," I said, "are to exchange them with Shaba for the authentic shield ring."

"To whom will you return the ring?" he asked.

"To Belisarius, in Cos," I said.

"Do you know his house?" asked Msaliti.

"Certainly not," I said. "I will be contacted."

"Where will the contact be made?" asked Msaliti, regarding me narrowly.

"At the Chatka and Curla," I said, "in Cos."

"Who is Master of the Chatka and Curla?" asked Msaliti.

"Aurelion of Cos," I said. "Of course."

"Yes," said Msaliti.

"Have no fear," I said, "I will do my best to see that the ring reaches the proper authorities."

Msaliti nodded. I smiled.

"Why would you wish the ring?" I asked.

"To assure that it reaches the beasts," he said. "They would not be pleased, should it be again lost."

"Your concern for their cause is commendable," I said.

"I have no wish to be torn to pieces," he said.

"That is understandable," I said. "Neither would I cheerfully look forward to such a termination."

"You seem in a good mood," he said.

"Surely you, too, should be in a pleasant frame of mind," I said. "Is our business not nearly completed?"

"That is my hope," said Msaliti.

"Do you truly fear the beasts so?" I asked.

"Our business has been delayed," he said. "It is my fear that the beasts themselves will come for the ring."

"But I am to pick up the ring," I said.

"I do not even know you," said Msaliti.

"I do not know you either, really," I said.

"We were looking for the blond girl," he said.

"She was delayed," I said. "She was enslaved," I pointed out, cheerfully.

"A pity," he said.

"Nonsense," I said. "Slavery is good for a woman."

"I do not trust Shaba," he said.

"I am sure he does not trust us either," I said. "At least we trust each other."

Msaliti drummed his fingers on the low table.

"Are you sure we are alone?" I asked.

"Of course," said Msaliti. "None have entered. Before I came the askaris, in the anteroom, guarded the door."

"They neglected, I see," I said, "to replace the peas on

their threads in this room, those dislodged by my peregrination of yesterday evening on the roof."

"Of course they replaced them," said Msaliti.

"I would not be too sure then," I said, "that we are alone."

Msaliti looked quickly upward. Several of the strings, with the tiny peas attached, dangled downward.

"The grille, too, I note," I said, "has been removed."

"You are observant," said Shaba.

Msaliti staggered to his feet, stumbling backward.

Across the table from us, in his customary place, sat Shaba. There had been a momentary blurring in the area, a sort of twisting swirl of light, something like a whirlpool of light, and then, calmly, he had sat before us.

"I did not think you would be late," I said. "You seemed a punctual fellow."

"It is you who were late," he said.

"Yes," I said, "I am sorry about that. I was detained."

"Was she pretty?" asked Shaba.

I nodded. "Yes," I said.

"Matters of great moment are afoot here," said Msaliti. "With your permission, that of both of you, if you please, I would like to attend to them."

"It is my understanding," said Shaba to me, "that you have brought the notes and the false ring."

"Yes," I said. I put the notes on the table.

"Where is the false ring?" asked Msaliti.

"I have it," I told him.

Shaba looked at the notes, carefully. He did not hurry. "These notes seem to be in order," he said.

"May I see them?" asked Msaliti.

Shaba handed him the notes. "You do not trust our broad-shouldered courier?" he asked.

"I trust as few people as possible," said Msaliti. He looked at the notes, very closely. Then he handed them back to Shaba. "I know the seals and signatures," he said. "They may truly be drawn on the banks indicated."

"There are twenty thousand tarns of gold there," I said.

"Cash them before you carry the false ring to the Sardar," said Msaliti. "It is in our interest, in these circumstances, to bargain in good faith."

"But what if I do not carry the false ring to the Sardar?" asked Shaba.

"I would do so if I were you," said Msaliti.

"I see," said Shaba.

211

"The beasts," he said, "do not deal lightly with traitors."

"That is understandable," said Shaba.

"This business could be conducted in the morning," I said, "at the banks in question. You might then verify the notes and withdraw or redeposit the gold as you please."

"Kunguni the beggar," said Msaliti, "cannot well enter the edifices on Schendi's Street of Coins."

"Then enter as Msaliti," I said.

Msaliti laughed. "Do not speak foolishly," he said.

I did not understand his answer.

"I am satisfied to do the business tonight," said Shaba. "If the notes are not genuine, obviously I would not carry the ring to the Sardar."

"Remember," said Msaliti, "do not depress the switch on the false ring. It must be depressed only in the Sardar."

The hair on the back of my neck rose. I then realized that what I had suspected must be true, that the false ring was of great danger.

Shaba put the notes within his robes. He then, from about his neck, removed a long, light chain. It had hung hitherto within the robes, concealed. He opened the chain.

I saw the ring on the chain.

My heart was pounding.

He extended his hand. "May I have the false ring?" he asked.

"I think there is little point in carrying the false ring to the Sardar," I said. "The delay has surely been such as to provoke suspicion." This was true. Actually I was not eager, for a personal reason, for Shaba to deliver the ring. I respected what he had done in the exploration of Gor. I knew him to be a man of intelligence and courage. He was a traitor, yes, but there was something about him, indefinable, which I found to my liking. I did not particularly wish to see him subjected to whatever Priest-Kings, or their human allies, might deem fit as the fate of a traitor. I did not think that if they set their minds to it they would be less ingenious than Kurii. Perhaps it would be better if I slew him. I would do so swiftly, mercifully.

"The ring, please," said Shaba.

"Give him the ring," said Msaliti.

I handed Shaba the false ring and he slipped it on the chain.

"Were there not eleven strings dangling from the ceiling?" he asked.

212

Msaliti quickly turned and looked. "I do not know," he said. "Are there more now?"

I had not taken my eyes from Shaba. "There were twelve," I said.

"There are twelve now," said Msaliti, counting.

"Then there are the same number now as before," said Shaba.

"Yes," I said, regarding him evenly.

"I must commend you," said Shaba. "You have powers of observation worthy of a scribe—or of a warrior."

He turned the chain and slipped a ring from it, handing it to me.

Geographers and cartographers, of course, are members of the Scribes.

I allowed for the turning of the chain. I received in my hand the ring which had originally hung on the chain.

Shaba, the false ring on the chain, again fastened the chain behind his neck.

He stood up, and so, too, did Msaliti and myself. "I am leaving Schendi tonight," said Shaba.

"I, too," said Msaliti. "I have lingered too long here."

"It would not be well for you to be too much missed," smiled Shaba.

"No," said Msaliti. I did not understand their exchange.

"I wish you well, my colleagues in treachery," said Shaba.

"Farewell," said we to him. He then, bowing, took his leave.

"Give me now the ring," said Msaliti.

"I will keep it," I said.

"Give it to me," said Msaliti, not pleasantly.

"No," I said. I then looked at the ring. I turned it in my hand. I wished to see the minute scratch which would, for me, identify the Tahari ring. I turned the ring feverishly. My hand shook. "Stop Shaba!" I said. "This is not the ring!"

"He is gone," said Msaliti. "That is the ring from the chain on his neck, where he carried the shield ring."

"It is not the shield ring," I said, miserably.

I had been outwitted. Shaba was a brilliant man. He had established for us, earlier, yesterday evening, that the ring on the chain had been the shield ring. Tonight, however, he had substituted a new ring. I might have discerned this had he not appeared to be intent on misdirecting our attention, calling it to the simple warning system, that of the threads and peas, in the ceiling, presumably to effect a switch of the rings while

213

our attention was diverted. I had not permitted my attention, however, to be diverted. Too, when he had turned the chain, I had made certain that the ring which he had surrendered to me had been the ring originally on the chain. The exchange of rings, of course, had actually taken place earlier, in privacy. The ring he had apparently intended to exchange for the true ring would have been the false ring, returning it to us as the true ring. I had not permitted this. My smugness at preventing this exchange had blinded me, foolishly, to the possibility that the ring on the chain this evening might not have been the true ring to begin with.

Msaliti looked sick. I gave him the ring.

Shaba now had both the true ring, the Tahari ring, and the false ring, that which Kurii had intended to be delivered to the Sardar in lieu of the true ring.

"How do you know it is not the true ring?" asked Msaliti.

"Surely you have been taught to identify the true ring?" I asked.

I thought swiftly.

"No," said Msaliti.

The copy of the true ring was well done. At the edge of the silver plate, that held in the ring's bezel, there was indeed a minute scratch. It was similar to, but it was not the identical marring which I recalled from the Tahari. The jeweler who had duplicated the ring for Shaba had failed slightly in that particular. There was a slight difference in the depth of the scratches, and one small difference in the angulation.

"This resembles the true ring closely," I told Msaliti. "It is large, and of gold, and, in its bezel, has a rectangular silver plate. On the back of the ring, when you turn it, there is a circular, depressible switch."

"Yes, yes," said Msaliti.

"But look here," I said. "See this scratch?"

"Yes," he said.

"The true ring, according to my information, possesses no such identifying marks," I said. "It is supposedly perfect in its appearance. Had it been thusly marred I would have been informed of this. Such a sign would make identification simple."

"You are a fool," said Msaliti. "Doubtless Shaba scratched it."

"Would you yourself treat so valuable an object with harshness?" I asked.

Msaliti turned the ring about. He looked at me. Then he

depressed the switch. Nothing happened. He howled with rage, the ring clutched in his fist.

"You were tricked!" he cried.

"We have been tricked," I corrected him.

"Shaba then has the perfect ring," he said.

"True," I said. Shaba had the perfect ring, which was the false ring. He also had the true Tahari ring, which the ring in Msaliti's hand so ingeniously resembled.

"You must put men upon Schendi's Street of Coins," I said. "Shaba must not be permitted to cash the notes he carries."

"Surely he must realize that could be done," said Msaliti. "He is not mad. How does he expect to get his gold?"

"He is quite intelligent, even brilliant," I mused. "Doubtless he has anticipated such a move. Yet it must be made."

"It will be made," said Msaliti, angrily.

"How then, I wonder," said I, "does he intend to obtain the gold?"

Msaliti looked at me, in fury.

"He must have a plan," I said.

"I am leaving," said Msaliti.

"Surely you will wish to don your disguise," I said.

"I do not need it longer," he said.

"What are you going to do?" I asked.

"I must move swiftly," he said. "There are many instructions to be issued. There must be an apprehension of Shaba."

"How may I be of assistance?" I asked.

"I will handle matters from here on out," he said. "Do not trouble yourself about them."

He threw a brocaded aba about his shoulders and, angrily, strode from the room.

"Wait!" I called.

He had left the room.

Angrily I followed him. As soon as I had passed through the anteroom and stepped across the threshold, to the street outside, I felt my arms pinioned behind me. A dozen or more men were there waiting, beside the building, on either side of the door. Some seven or eight were askaris, including the two huge fellows whom I had seen yesterday, black giants in skins and feathers, with golden armlets. Another five or six were guardsmen of Schendi. There was also an officer there of the merchant council of Schendi.

"Is this he?" asked the officer of the merchant council.

"That is he," said Msaliti, turning about. "He claims to be Tarl of Teletus but he will be unable to substantiate that identity."

"What is going on here?" I shouted. I struggled, trying to free myself of the four men who held me. Then I felt two daggers pressed through the fabric of my tunic.

I ceased struggling, feeling the points in my flesh. Both could be driven home before I could hurl my captors from me.

My hands were taken behind me and tied.

"These men were waiting for me," I said to Msaliti.

"Of course," said he.

"I see that you were determined, in any event," I said, "to be the one who would return the ring to our superiors."

"Of course," said Msaliti. "I will then stand higher in their favor."

"But what of me?" I asked.

He shrugged. "Who can tell what may have happened to you?" he asked.

"You are an officer of Schendi," I said to the man in charge of the guardsmen. "I demand to be released."

"Here is the paper," said Msaliti to the officer.

The officer took the paper and looked it over. Then he looked at me. "You are the one who calls himself Tarl of Teletus?" he asked.

"Yes," I said.

The officer placed the paper inside his robes.

"There is no place in Schendi," he said, "for criminal vagabonds."

"Look in my wallet," I said. "You will see that I am not a vagabond."

The wallet was cut from my belt. The officer shook out gold pieces and silver tarsks into his hand.

"You see?" I asked.

"He arrived in Schendi," said Msaliti, "in the garb of a metal worker. You see him now in the garb of a leather worker." Msaliti smiled. "What metal worker or leather worker," he asked, "carries such funds?"

"He is obviously a thief, doubtless a fugitive," said the officer.

"The work levy imposed on Schendi is due to leave in the morning," said Msaliti. "Perhaps this fellow could take the place of a good citizen of Schendi in that levy?"

"Would you find that acceptable?" asked the officer.

Msaliti looked at me. "Yes," he said.

"Splendid," said the officer. "Put ropes on the sleen's neck."

Two leash ropes were knotted on my neck.

"This is not justice," I said.

"These are hard times," said the officer. "And Schendi fights for her life."

He then lifted his hand to Msaliti and withdrew, taking his guardsmen with him.

"Where am I to be taken?" I asked Msaliti.

"To the interior," he said.

"You had the cooperation of the council of Schendi," I said. "Someone in a high place must have ordered this."

"Yes," said Msaliti.

"Who?" I asked.

"I," said Msaliti.

I looked at him, puzzled.

"Surely you know who I am?" he asked.

"No," I said.

"I am Msaliti," he said.

"And he?" I asked. "Who might he be?"

"Why, I," smiled Msaliti.

"And you?" I asked.

"I thought it was known to all," he said. "I am the high wazir of Bila Huruma."

16

KISU

"Get back!" I shouted, striking at it with the shovel. The edge of the shovel struck, cutting, at the side of its snout. It hissed. The noise is incredibly loud, or seems so, when one is close to it. I saw the pointed tongue. The jaws distended, more than a yard in height, with the rows of backward-leaning fangs.

I had managed to get my foot on the lower jaw and, with the shovel, pry up the jaw, releasing the hold on the lacerated leg of Ayari, who, bleeding, scrambled back. I had felt the draw of his chain against my own collar.

I thrust the shovel out again, against the upper teeth, thrusting back, shouting.

Other men, too, to the right of Ayari and to my left, screamed, and struck at it with their shovels.

Eyes blazing it backed away, twisting, small legs, with the stubby, clawed feet, stabbing at the water. Its gigantic tail thrashed, striking a man, hurling him back a dozen feet. The water was to my thighs. I pushed back again, with the shovel. The transparent eyelids on the beast, under the scaly eyelids, closed and opened. It hissed more, its tongue sopping at the blood of Ayari in its mouth.

"Back!" cried the askari, in the inland language, with his torch, thrusting it into the beast's mouth.

It roared with pain. Then, thrashing, squirming, hissing, it backed off in the shallow water. I saw its eyes and snout, nostrils open, almost level with the water.

"Away! Away!" shouted the askari, in the inland speech, brandishing his torch. Another askari, at his side, armed with a lance, gripping it with two hands, shouted, too, ready to support his fellow.

Interestingly the incident did not much affect the work in the area. From where I stood I could see hundreds of men, workmen and askaris, and many rafts, some weighted with supplies, others with logs and tools, some with mud and earth we had dug out of the swampy terrain, mud and earth which would be used to bank the flanking barricades, that the area in which we worked might be drained, that a proper channel might later be excavated.

"Are you all right?" I asked Ayari.

He wiped the flies away from his head. "I think I am sick," he said.

There was blood in the water about his leg.

"Return to work," said the askari with the torch, wading near us.

"You have had a narrow escape," I told Ayari.

He threw up into the water.

"Can you work?" asked the askari.

Ayari's leg seemed to buckle under him. He half fell in the water. "I cannot stand," he said.

I supported him.

"It is well that I am on the rogues' chain," grinned Ayari. "Never before have I been so pleased with my profession," said he. "Had I not been chained, doubtless I would have been pulled away."

"That is quite possible," I told him.

Ayari was of Schendi, a thief. He had been put on the work levy for the canal of Bila Huruma. Schendi was using the misfortune of the levies in order, as much as possible, to rid itself of its less desirable citizens. I supposed she could scarcely be blamed. Ayari, of Schendi, of course, spoke Gorean. Happily, for me, he could also speak the tongue of the court of Bila Huruma. His father had, many years ago, fled from an inland village, that of Nyuki, noted for its honey, on the northern shore of lake Ushindi. The incident had had to do with the theft of several melons from the chief's patch. His father had returned some five years later to purchase his mother. They had then lived in Schendi. The inland speech had been spoken in the home. It is estimated that some five to eight percent of the people of Schendi are familiar with the inland speech.

"Can you work?" asked the askari of Ayari.

Such simple phrases I could now make out, thanks to Ayari's tutoring.

More impressive to me was Ayari's capacity to read the drums, though, I am told, this is not difficult for anyone who can speak the inland speech fluently. Analogues to the major vowel sounds of the inland speech are found in certain of the drum notes, which differ, depending on where the hollowed, grooved log is struck. The rhythm of the drum message, of course, is the rhythm of the inland speech. Thus, on the drum it is possible to duplicate, in effect, the vowels and intonation contours of inland sentences. When one adds to this certain additional drum signals corresponding, in effect, to keys to the message or to certain consonantal ciphers, one has, in effect, a direct, effective, ingenious device at one's disposal, given the drum relays, for long-distance communication. A message may be conveyed by means of drum stations for hundreds of pasangs in less than an Ahn. Needless to say Bila Huruma had adopted and improved this device and it had played, and continued to play, its role in the effectiveness of his military machine and in the efficiency of the administration of his ubarate. As a communication device it was clearly superior to the smoke and beacon ciphers of the north. There was, as far as I knew, nothing on Gor to compare with it except, of course, the advanced technological equipment at the disposal of the Priest-Kings and Kurii, equipment of a sort generally forbidden, in the weapons and communication laws, to most Gorean humans. I found it astonishing, and I think most Goreans would have, even those of Schendi, that a ubarate of the size and sophistication of that of Bali Huruma could exist in the equatorial interior. One of the most amazing evidences of its scope and ambition was the very project in which I was now unwillingly engaged, the visionary attempt to join Lakes Ushindi and Ngao, separated by more than four hundred pasangs, by a great canal, a canal that would, via Lake Ushindi and the Nyoka and Kamba rivers, then link the mysterious Ua river, it flowing into Lake Ngao, to gleaming Thassa, the sea, a linkage that would, given the Ua, open up to the civilized world the riches of the interior, riches that must then pass through the ubarate of Bila Huruma.

"Can you work?" repeated the askari to Ayari.

"No," said Ayari.

"Then I must have you killed," said the askari.

"I have made a speedy recovery," said Ayari.

"Good," said the askari and waded away, holding his torch above the water. The other askari, he with the tharlarion lance, accompanied him.

In a few moments the mud raft, of logs bound together with lianas, to be loaded with excavated mud, was again poled to our vicinity.

"Can you dig?" I asked Ayari.

"No," he said.

"I will dig for you," I said.

"You would, wouldn't you?" he asked.

"Yes," I said.

"I will dig for myself," he said.

"How is your leg?" I asked.

"It is still there," he said.

Most of the workers on the canal were not chained. Most were impressed free men.

Waters from the overflow of Lake Ngao entered the great marsh between Ngao and Ushindi, and, thence, made their ways to Ushindi, which, by means of the Kamba and Nyoka, drained to gleaming Thassa, the sea. The intent of the engineers of Bila Huruma was to set in place two parallel walls, low walls, some five or six feet high, placed about two hundred yards apart. The area between these walls, the marsh waters diverted on either side, was then to be drained and readied for the digging of the main channel. In this work draft tharlarion and great scoops, brought from the north, as well as gigantic work crews, would be used. In the event that the central channel, when completed, would not prove sufficient to handle the overflow of Ngao, as seemed likely, conducting it geometrically to Ushindi, side channels were contemplated. The eventual intent of Bila Huruma was not only to open the rain forests of the deep interior, and whatever might lie within the system of the Ua and her tributaries, to commercial exploitation and military expansion, but to drain the marshes between the two mighty lakes, Ushindi and Ngao, that that land, then reclaimed, thousands of square pasangs, might eventually be made available for agriculture. It was the intent of Bila Huruma not only to consolidate a ubarate but found a civilization.

I slapped at insects.

"Work," said an askari, wading by.

I shoveled another load of mud from the marsh and flung it on the mud raft.

"Work, work," said the askari, encouraging others along the chain.

I looked about myself, at the hundreds of men I could see from where I stood. "This is an impressive project," I said to Ayari.

"Doubtless we can be pleased that we are a humble part of so mighty an undertaking," he mused.

"I suppose so," I said.

"On the other hand," said Ayari, "I would be content to surrender my part in this noble endeavor to others more worthy than myself."

"I, too," I admitted.

"Dig," said an askari.

We continued to shovel mud onto the mud raft.

"Our only hope," said a man to my left, also, like Ayari, from Schendi, "are the hostile tribes."

"That is some hope," said Ayari. "If it were not for the askaris they would fall upon us with their slaughtering knives."

"Surely there is resistance to the canal," I said.

"There are the villages of the Ngao region, on the northern shore," said Ayari. "There is trouble there."

"That is the most organized resistance," said the man on my left.

"The canal is expensive," I said. "It must constitute a financial strain on the coffers of the ubarate of Bila Huruma. This must generate discontent in his court. The work levies, too, must be resented by the villages."

"Those of Schendi, too," said Ayari, "are not too pleased with the project."

"They fear Bila Huruma," I said.

"Yes," said Ayari.

"There are mixed feelings in Schendi," said the man to my left. "She would stand to profit if the canal were completed."

"That is true," said Ayari.

There was shouting from ahead.

Askaris rushed forward.

"Lift me up," said Ayari. He was not large.

I lifted him to my shoulders.

"What is it?" asked the man to my left.

"It is nothing," said Ayari. "It is only a raiding party of three or four men. They threw their spears and then fled. The askaris are pursuing them."

I lowered Ayari again to the water.

"Was anyone killed?" asked the man to my left.

"No," said Ayari. "The workers saw them and withdrew."

"Last night," said the man, "ten men were killed." He looked at us. "And none were chained," he said.

"It is true," said Ayari, "that we would be much at the mercy of such raiders."

"It is unlikely that such, however," I said, "could truly do more than delay the progress of the canal."

"Yes," said Ayari.

"Could they not free and arm the work crews?" asked the man to my left.

"The men of the work crews are not of their tribes," said Ayari. "You think like one of Schendi, not one of the interior." Ayari waved at the lines of men behind us. "Besides," said he, "most of these men are, in their way, loyal subjects of Bila Huruma. When their work tours are finished they return to their villages. Most of them would not be again impressed for labor for two or three years."

"Ah," said the man to my left, disgustedly.

"There are two obvious ways in which Bila Huruma might be stopped," said Ayari. "First, he must be defeated. Second, he might be killed."

"The first," I said, "is unlikely, considering his army and its training. There is nothing in these terrains which is likely to be able to meet it in open battle."

"There are the rebels of the northern shore of Ngao," said the man.

"How can they be rebels?" I asked.

222

"Bila Huruma, in virtue of the discoveries of Shaba," said Ayari, "has claimed all lands in the Lake Ngao region. Those who oppose him are thus rebels."

"I see now," I said. "To be sure, the distinctions of statecraft sometimes elude me."

"It is basically simple," said Ayari. "One determines what one wishes to prove and then arranges one's principles in such a way that the desired conclusion follows as a demonstrable consequence."

"I see," I said.

"Logic is as neutral as a knife," he said.

"But what of truth?" I asked.

"Truth is more troublesome," he admitted.

"I think you would make an excellent diplomat," I said.

"I have been a fraud and charlatan all my life," said Ayari. "There would thus be no transition to make."

"Five days ago," said the man to my left, "hundreds of askaris, in canoes, went past us, east, before you were entered upon our chain."

"Their objective?" I asked.

"To meet and defeat in battle the rebel forces of Kisu, former Mfalme of the Ukungu villages."

"If they are successful," said Ayari, "that will finish organized resistance to Bila Huruma."

"They will be successful," said the man.

"Why did you say 'former Mfalme'?" I asked.

"Bila Huruma," he said, "it is well known, has bought off the chieftains of the Ukungu region. In council they have deposed Kisu and placed their leader, Aibu, in power. Kisu then withdrew with some two hundred warriors, loyal to him, to continue the fight against Bila Huruma."

"In the arts of politics," said Ayari, complacently, "gold is more insidious than steel."

"He should withdraw to the forests, to continue the fight from there," I said.

"War from the forests," said Ayari, "is effective only against an enemy which is weak or humane. The weak enemy lacks the power to exterminate the population of the forest. The humane enemy will not do so. Bila Huruma, unfortunately, I fear, is neither weak nor humane."

"Surely he must be stopped," I said.

"Perhaps he could be killed," said Ayari.

"He is well guarded, surely," said the man to my left.

"Surely," said Ayari.

"Our only hope," said the man to my left, "is a victory by the forces of Kisu."

"Five days ago," said Ayari, "the askaris went east to engage him in battle."

"Perhaps, by now," said the man to my left, "the battle has taken place."

"No," I said. "It is surely too soon."

"Why?" asked Ayari.

"Kisu is severely outnumbered," I said. "He would maneuver for position. He would choose his time of battle with great care."

"Unless it were forced upon him," said Ayari.

"How could that be?" I asked.

"Do not underestimate the efficiency of the askaris of Bila Huruma," said Ayari.

"You speak," I said, "as though they were professional warriors, under astute generalship, skilled in scouting, in flanking and cutting off retreats."

"Listen!" said Ayari. He held up his hand.

"I hear it," I said. "Can you make it out?"

"Quiet!" said Ayari. "I am listening."

It was only some two pasangs away, ahead of us, and nearing us. But, in a moment its message was taken up from behind us, some four pasangs down the workway, west, leading toward Ushindi. It would then, swiftly, station to station, be transmitted back to the grass palace of Bila Huruma.

"The forces of Kisu have been met in battle and defeated," said Ayari. "That is the message of the drum."

Askaris about us were lifting their weapons over their heads and shouting with pleasure.

Behind us, further down the workway, too, men were shouting with pride, many lifting their shovels.

"Look!" said Ayari.

I could see the craft now. It was a shallow-drafted, dismasted dhow. It was being drawn by dozens of men, wading in the marsh, pulling on ropes. They wore slave collars. They were chained together, in groups of eight or ten, by the neck. Askaris, some wading, some in canoes, flanked them. The askaris were jubilant, resplendent in their skins and feathers, with their golden necklaces and armlets, their narrow, tufted shields and short-handled stabbing spears. On the foredeck of the dhow there was mounted a log drum. On this, methodically, an askari drummer, with two long sticks, was beating out, again and again, the message of victory. Many askaris, too, rode the dhow, mostly officers, judging from the arrangements of their gold and feathers, for it is by these things, serving as insignia, that their rankings to those who could read them, as I could not, were made clear. Behind the dhow, some wading and others in canoes, came more than a thousand askaris. In place of the mast on the dhow, mounted in the mast socket, was a "T" frame with a small crossbar mounted on the vertical beam. On this "T" frame a man was chained. His arms were placed over and behind the horizontal bar of the frame, his hands chained together, the chain running before his body, holding him to the frame. His feet had been positioned on the small crossbar. His ankles were also chained, a loop of chain holding them close to the vertical beam. He was a large man, with tattooing. He had apparently been wounded and, surely, had been much beaten. I thought that he might be dead but, as the dhow came closer, I saw him, possibly revived by the shouting and noise, raise his head. He then straightened his body and, as he could, stood proudly, head high, surveying us, on the frame.

The askaris pointed their spears at him, and turned to us, and shouted.

There was no mistaking the name they cried.

"Kisu!" they cried. "Kisu! Kisu!"

"It is Kisu," said Ayari.

17

MSALITI HAS FORMED A PLAN

The white slave girls, nude, toweled my body.

"Away," said Msaliti, sharply. They fled away, their bare feet pattering on the woven mats of my quarters, within that gigantic compound that constituted the palace of Bila Huruma.

"These robes," said Msaliti, indicating robes spread upon the couch, "will be found suitable for an ambassador of Teletus." He then indicated a small chest at the couch's foot. "Those gifts, too," he said, "will appear seemly from one interested in negotiating a commercial treaty with one of the stature of Bila Huruma."

I slipped on a tunic.

"Why could you not apprehend Shaba at the banks?" I asked.

"He never cashed the notes," said Msaliti.

I looked at him.

"He feared to do so?" I asked.

"We were tricked," said Msaliti. "He signed the notes over to Bila Huruma, and it was agents of the Ubar himself, who cashed them."

"Twenty thousand tarns of gold," I said.

"The money," said Msaliti, in fury, "is being invested in the formation of a fleet of a hundred ships, fully fitted and supplied, and crewed by fifty men each. These ships are being specifically built to be sectioned and rejoinable, to make possible their portage about difficult areas. Our money, that which we paid for the ring, is being used to outfit an expedition for the exploration of the Ua!"

"That is a venture," I said, "surely of interest to both a geographer, such as Shaba, and a Ubar, such as Bila Huruma."

"I thought he wanted the gold for himself!" said Msaliti.

"Gold is perhaps of less interest to him than glory," I said.

"He will not get away with it," said Msaliti. "We will recover the ring."

"It will take time to prepare such ships," I said.

"The work commenced, months ago," said Msaliti.

"Surely this could not have been unknown to you," I said.

"The work was done in the shipyards of Ianda," he said. "I had heard rumors of such a project but did not understand the nature of the ships or that this ubarate was involved. But now the ships are already moving upstream on the Nyoka."

"It seems," I said, "that Bila Huruma does not take you into his full confidence."

"He is a secretive man," said Msaliti.

"Perhaps it is fortunate for him that he does not fully trust you."

"Surely the hand of Shaba may be seen in this," said Msaliti.

"Doubtless," I said.

"Of those in these lands," said Msaliti, "only you and I, and Shaba, know of the ring."

"I gather that you now know the whereabouts of Shaba," I said.

"He is here, the bold rascal," said Msaliti, "in this very palace, living openly, protected by Bila Huruma."

"He is a courageous fellow," I said.

226

"He thinks he has little to fear," said Msaliti.

"What is your plan?" I asked.

"Bila Huruma, this very morning," said he, "holds court. You, in the guise of an ambassador of Teletus, will bring forward gifts for his viewing. I will do the speaking. You need do little or nothing. Almost no one present will be able to understand Gorean. I will explain that the details of your proposal for a commercial treaty will be discussed with the appropriate wazir, and presented later for approval."

"In short," I said, "it will appear little more than an official greetings exchanged between governments."

"That would be appropriate at this stage of negotiation," said Msaliti.

"Very well," I said. "But what do you have further in mind?"

"Shaba, as one close to Bila Huruma, will be present in the court," he said. "You will attack Shaba and slay him. I will then have you placed under arrest by askaris. I will obtain the ring from the body of Shaba, and you, later, by arrangement, will be permitted to escape. I will pay you a hundred tarns of gold and I myself will then return the ring to the beasts."

"Bila Huruma will not connect my attack with you in any way?" I asked.

"Presumably not," said Msaliti. "I must remain in the clear, you understand."

"Of course," I said. "Why do you not hire just any assassin to do this thing?" I asked.

"You are a fellow agent of Kurii," he said. "You seem an ideal choice."

"Of course," I said.

"I think I may trust you," he said.

"Why is that?" I asked.

"You have had a taste of the canal," he said.

"If I am not fully cooperative," I said, "you will return me to the rogues' chain?"

"I have that power," he said.

"Permit me to don the robes of an ambassador of Teletus," I said.

"Certainly," said he.

18

WHAT OCCURRED WHEN COURT WAS HELD IN THE PALACE OF GRASS; I MEET BILA HURUMA; A NEW PLAN MUST BE FORMED

"Do you have the dagger?" whispered Msaliti to me.

"Surely," I said, "in the sleeve sheath."

He then left my side. There were more than two hundred individuals in the great court, both men and women, of high station, and certain commoners with causes to plead. Too, there were guards, and chieftains, and envoys. The robes were generally of animal skin, some marvelously marked. There was much gold and silver jewelry. Anklets and wristlets of feathers were common. The hair of the men and women was worn in a variety of fashions. Too, there were ornate headdresses in evidence, usually of skins and feathers. In the lips of some of the men were brass plugs. Facial tattooing, in various designs, was common. The opulence and color of the court of Bila Huruma was quite impressive. I was sure that it would have shamed the display and pageantry of many Ubars in the north. There were various racial types represented in the court, almost all black. I was the only white present. There were some brown fellows from Bazi, though, and one of the attending physicians was oriental. Even among very similar black types there was variety in hair style and tattooing, and dress, which I took as evidence of cultural or tribal difference. One of the difficulties in the ubarate of Bila Huruma was this sort of racial and tribal heterogeneity. Fortunately most of these people, generally all from the Ushindi region, spoke closely related dialects. This heterogeneity was surely a challenge to the ubarate of Bila Huruma and that his government was as stable as it was said as much, I think, for the intelligence of his governance as for the ruthlessness of his policies and the indomitability of his will.

When I entered the court Bila Huruma had just finished accepting the reports of his officers on the battle with the forces of Kisu. This battle, interestingly, had occurred in the marshes well west of Ngao, indeed, only a few pasangs from the work lines. Kisu, with his small handful of men, as it turned out, incredibly enough, had been marching on Bila Huruma. So bravely and pathetically might an ant have attacked a giant. I had no doubt as to the courage of Kisu; I was less confident, however, that he had the common sense and wisdom expected of a Mfalme.

Some of these officers presented men before him who were then commended for their deeds in the recent action.

Rings of gold and now insignia of rank, feathers and necklaces, were distributed.

Once Bila Huruma lifted his hand and said, "Good." The soldier then commended would then, I think, rather have died than betray Bila Huruma. Such small things, I think, may be scorned by those who do not understand the nature of war or men, and be seen as manipulative and laughable, and yet such a small commendation, when warranted and sincere, is worth more to some men than the material treasures that might move those who hold themselves their superiors. Let each man choose his own treasures. The cynical, mercantile mind will never understand the mind of the soldier. The soldier has stood with comrades in arms, and held. I do not think he would exchange that for the contemptuous pretense to wisdom of those whom he protects, who would scorn him. He has maintained his post. But perhaps some, even those who have never marched in the mud, with comrades, singing, on a clear and windy morning, a spear upon their shoulder, can understand this. Why does the nibbling urt chatter and laugh at the larl? Is it because he himself is not a larl, or is it because he fears its paw?

I looked up at the high, conical ceiling, of interwoven branches and grass, of the court of Bila Huruma. It was some seventy feet over my head. The room itself, a great round room, was a hundred feet in width.

Msaliti again slipped to my side. "Are you ready?" he asked.

"Yes," I said.

Bila Huruma was then hearing cases at law, selected for his attention.

Perhaps one day the warrior in man would die, and, with him, the fighter, the wanderer, the wonderer, the explorer, the adventurer, the rover, the doer and hoper. The days of the lonely ones, the walkers, and seekers, would then be at an end. Men might then become, as many wished, as cattle and flowers, and be free to spend their days in placid grazing, until they died beneath the distant, burning, unsought suns.

But it was difficult to know what the mists of the morning would bring.

I contented myself with the thought that deeds had been done, which now, whether recollected or not, or however viewed, were irrevocably fixed in their fullness and truth in the fabric of eternity. They had been. Nothing, nothing ever, could change that. The meaning of history lies not in the future but in the moment. It is never anywhere but within our grasp. And if the history of man, terminated, should turn out to have been but a brief flicker in the midst of unnoticing oblivions let it at least have been worthy of the moment in which it burned. But perhaps it would prove to be a spark which would, in time, illuminate a universe.

It is difficult to know what the mists of the morning may bring.

Much depends upon what man is.

Much depends upon what he shall decide himself to be.

"Are you ready?" pressed Msaliti.

"Yes, yes," I said. "I am quite ready for what I intend to do."

He then again left my side. I could see Shaba in the group of people near Bila Huruma.

His first case dealt with a widow who had been defrauded by a creditor. The fellow was dragged screaming from the court. His hands would be cut off, as those of a common thief. His properties were to be confiscated and divided, half to the widow and half, predictably, to the state.

The next fellow was an actual thief, a mere boy, who had stolen vegetables. It turned out that he had been hungry and had actually begged work in the gardens of his victim. "No one who wants to work in my ubarate," said Bila Huruma, "will go hungry." He then directed that the boy be given work, if he wished, in his own gardens, which were considerable. I supposed that if one did not wish to work, one might well expect to starve. Bila Huruma, I conjectured, was not one to be patient with laggards. Fairness is a central thesis of sound governance.

Two murderers were next brought to him for sentencing. The first, a commoner, had slain a boatsman from Schendi. The second, an askari, had killed another askari. The commoner was ordered to have his fingers cut off and then be put upon a tharlarion pole in Lake Ushindi. That his fingers be removed was accounted mercy on the part of Bila Huruma, that he be able to cling less long to the pole and his miseries be the sooner terminated. He had slain not one of the domain of Bila Huruma but one of Schendi. His crime, thus, was regarded as the less heinous. The askari was ordered to be speared to death by one of his own kin. In this fashion his honor would be protected and there would be no beginning of a possible blood feud between families. The askari petitioned, however, to be permitted to die instead fighting the enemies of the ubarate. This petition was denied on the grounds that he had, by slaying his comrade, not permitted this same privilege to him. This judgment was accepted unquestioningly by the askari. "But am I not of my own kin, my Ubar?" he asked. "Yes," had said Bila Huruma. He was taken outside. He would be given a short-handled stabbing spear and would be permitted to throw himself upon it.

The next fellow had lied about his taxes. He would be hung, a hook through his tongue, in a market. His properties were to be confiscated and distributed, half to be given to members of his village and half to the state. It was conjectured that, when he was removed from the pole, if he were still alive, he would be more careful in his accounts.

From outside I heard the cry of the askari. He had performed upon himself the justice of Bila Huruma.

The next to appear before Bila Huruma were two members of the nobility, a man and his companion. He complained of her that she had been unwilling to please him. By one word and a stroke of his hand between them Bila Huruma dissolved their companionship. He then ordered that the man be put in the dress of a woman and beaten from the court with sticks. This was done. He then ordered that the woman be stripped and a vine leash be put on her neck. She was then sentenced to a barrack of askaris for a year, that she might learn how to please men.

Kisu, the rebel, in chains, was then dragged before Bila Huruma. He was thrown upon his knees. He was sentenced to the canal, to be put upon the rogues' chain, that he might now, at last, well serve his sovereign, Bila Huruma. Kisu, kept on his knees, was then dragged to one side. Next to approach Bila Huruma was Mwoga, ambassador of the villages of Ukungu, representative of the high chief, Aibu, who had organized the chiefs of Ukungu against Kisu, and deposed him. He presented gifts, skins and feathers, and brass rings

231

and the teeth of tharlarion, to Bila Huruma, and swore to him the fealty of the Ukungu villages. Too, to seal the bonds of these political bargains, he, on behalf of Aibu, offered to Bila Huruma the very daughter of the high chief, Aibu, himself, a girl named Tende, as one of his companions.

"Is she beautiful?" asked Bila Huruma.

"Yes," responded Mwoga.

Bila Huruma shrugged. "It does not matter," he said. I supposed it did not matter. There were doubtless many womens' courts in his house. He had, I had heard, already more than two hundred companions, not to mention perhaps twice the number of slave girls, captures, purchases and gifts. If the body of Tende appealed to him he could get heirs upon it. If it did not, he could forget her, leaving her neglected, a sequestered souvenir of state, another girl lost in one of the womens' courts in the palace.

"May I address our prisoner?" inquired Mwoga.

"Yes," said Bila Huruma.

"Is Tende not beautiful?" he asked.

"Yes," said Kisu, "and she is as proud and cold as she is beautiful."

"Too bad she is not a slave," said Bila Huruma. "She might then be made to crawl and cry out in passion."

"She is worthy to be a slave," said Kisu. "She is the daughter of the traitor, Aibu!"

Bila Huruma lifted his hand. "Take him away," he said. Kisu was dragged, struggling, from the court.

Mwoga shortly thereafter, bowing and stepping backwards, took his leave.

Msaliti then appeared by my side, and thrust me gently, through the crowd, forward. "Be ready," he said.

Bila Huruma and those about him, including Shaba, regarded me. Shaba gave no sign that he recognized me. If he revealed that I was not what I seemed, it might seem reasonable to inquire into the sources of his knowledge. It would then be a short step to making clear his involvement with the ring. Such a trinket, doubtless, would be of great interest to the Ubar, Bila Huruma. It was not in the best interest of Shaba, or myself, or Msaliti, for the power of the ring to come to the attention of the sovereign of this vast equatorial ubarate.

When I was near Bila Huruma I was to draw the dagger, slay Shaba and then, by prearranged plan, be immediately apprehended by askari guardsmen, to be placed under arrest.

232

Msaliti was supposed to obtain the ring from the body of Shaba. I was later supposed to receive a hundred tarns of gold and my freedom. I smiled to myself.

"Are you armed?" asked Msaliti, both in the inland speech, some of which I had learned from Ayari, and in Gorean.

"Why, yes," I said pleasantly, revealing the sleeve sheath, and handing him the dagger.

For an instant, just an instant, I saw in the eyes of Msaliti a flash of incredible fury. Then he nodded, and accepted the dagger, which he handed to an askari.

I showed the sleeve sheath to Bila Huruma, who was interested in it. Such sheaths are common in the Tahari but, in the equatorial interior, where men are commonly bare-armed, I gathered they were an interesting novelty.

Bila Huruma said something to an aide. It had to do with seeing that a robe was made for him which contained such a device.

"Greetings, Great Ubar," said I, "and noble gentlemen, all." I smiled at Shaba. "I bring you greetings from the merchant council of Teletus, that council sovereign in that free island. Aware of the wealth and mighty projects of the ubarate we desire to arrange the apparatus for commercial interaction with your state. Should the great canal be completed we are well aware that this ubarate will become a crucial link between the equatorial east and west. We now wish, as doubtless will other merchant holdings, such as our sisters, Schendi and Bazi, to accord you our best wishes and to sue for your favor, that our shipping and merchants may be permitted to prove themselves of service in your future ventures."

Msaliti did his best, not happily, to translate this for Bila Huruma.

I wished to make such declarations for various reasons. First I thought it possible that some of the blacks in the room, besides Shaba and Msaliti, perhaps close counselors of Bila Huruma, might know Gorean. It was important to me to seem to be truly an envoy from Teletus. Secondly, I thought it might be amusing to try my hand at diplomatic bombast. I seldom received such an opportunity, and I have always been impressed by that sort of thing. I gathered, from the looks of those about, that the sort of things I said were the usual sorts of things, mostly vacuous, which are said upon such occasions. This pleased me. Thirdly, I think I might have enjoyed

233

discomfiting Msaliti, hoisting him, so to speak, by his own pe-
tard.

Msaliti then signaled to a man who brought forward the
gifts for Bila Huruma, in the small coffer.

He acknowledged them, and then they were put to the
side. I was informed, through Msaliti, the Ubar speaking, that
the greetings of Teletus were accepted, that his ubarate
expressed similar greetings to those of the island, that his
ubarate appreciated our interest in its future and that his
wazir of trade would speak to me within the next ten days. I
then, as I had seen others do, smiled and bowed, and, walking backward, withdrew from his presence.

The next envoy was from Bazi. He presented to Bila
Huruma four chests of gold, and ten black slave girls, nude,
in golden chains.

This did not much please me. I thought that Msaliti might
have done better on behalf of Teletus. The envoy from Bazi,
I noted, would receive an audience with the wazir of trade
within five days.

Shortly after the business with the envoy of Bazi the court
of Bila Huruma was adjourned. I think that one of the slave
girls had struck his fancy. I hoped that she was well trained.
He was a Ubar. He would not be easy to please.

Msaliti and I were then alone in the great, conical-roofed
court.

I sheathed the sleeve dagger which, after the adjournment
of the court, the askari had returned to me.

He was beside himself with rage. "Why did you not kill
Shaba!" he demanded. "That was the plan."

"It was not my plan," I said. "It was your plan. I have a
different plan."

"I will have you immediately returned to the canal," he
said, in rage.

"That will be difficult to do," I said. "You have already established, and I am grateful, that I am an ambassador or envoy from Teletus."

He cried out with rage.

"Surely," I said, "you did not think I would be fool enough
to do what you wanted. As soon as Shaba was slain you
would have had the askaris, at a word, in the heat of the
thing, slay me. You would then have me out of the way, who
knows about the ring, and free access to the ring itself."

"You thought I would betray you?" he asked.

"Certainly," I said. "You would have, wouldn't you?"

234

"Yes," he said.

"I thought so," I said. "You see," I said, "you do have the makings of an honest, truthful fellow in you."

I slipped the sleeve dagger loose.

"It will do you no good to kill me," he said.

"I am just testing the sheath," I said. I replaced the blade.

"It appears we must work together," he said.

I again slipped loose the blade. "Yes," I said.

He watched the steel. "What is your plan?" he asked.

"We must act quickly," I said. "We do not know how much time we have. Bila Huruma's wazir of trade will doubtless soon detect that I know little of the merchants or affairs of Teletus. We must act quickly."

"What do you wish to do?" he asked.

"It is simple," I said. "Shaba has the ring. Show me his chambers and I will fetch it this very night."

"Shaba knows you are in the palace," he said. "He will surely be on his guard."

"Then send another," I said.

"Only we, and Shaba," said he, "know of the ring."

"Precisely," I said.

"I will show you his quarters tonight," said he.

"Good," I said.

"How do I know you will treat me fairly?" he asked. "How do I know you will not simply vanish the ring?"

"You do not know," I said.

"Oh, that is a splendid aspect of your plan," said he, irritably.

"I find it attractive," I admitted. "If you wish to essay the quest in the chambers of Shaba yourself feel free to do so," I said.

"If I should fail," said he, "it would mean the end of my position at the court."

"Doubtless," I granted him. "Also, if you should be so unfortunate as to run afoul of Shaba's fang ring it would mean the end of more than your position. It contains kanda, as I understand it."

"It appears there are few sensible alternatives to your plan," he said.

"I am the one who is supposed to recover the ring, you know," I said.

"I know," he said. "I know."

"Surely you trust me," I said, as though hurt.

"I trust you as my own brother," he said.

235

"I did not know you had a brother," I said.

"He once betrayed me," said Msaliti. "I arranged that he appear guilty of a violation of state trust, and had him slain for treason against the ubarate."

"It was a mistake to trust such a fellow," I said.

"Precisely," he said.

"Until tonight," I said.

"Bila Huruma," he said, "is the one who truly stands in the way of obtaining the ring. He is the patron of Shaba, his protector. If Bila Huruma were gone, it would be easy to arrest Shaba and secure the ring."

"That may or may not be," I said, "but obviously Shaba is the fellow with the ring. It is he from whom we must seek that elusive artifact."

"Shaba may not be willing to surrender the ring," said Msaliti.

"It is my hope to be able to persuade him to do so," I said.

"Will you please replace that dagger in the sheath," said Msaliti. "It is making me nervous."

"Very well," I said. I slipped the steel back in the sheath.

"What did you think of our Ubar?" asked Msaliti.

"He is surely a big fellow," I said, "but I scarcely noticed him." Bila Huruma, indeed, had been an extremely large man, and long armed. He had sat upon a royal stool, of black, lacquered wood, mounted on the crossed, tied, horns of kailiauk. His arms and legs had been bare, and they had glistened from oil. He had worn armlets and bracelets, and anklets, of gold. He had worn at his loins the pelts of the yellow panther. He wore, too, the teeth of his beast as a necklace. Behind and about him had swirled a gigantic cloak of yellow and red feathers, from the crested lit and the fruit tindel, brightly plumaged birds of the rain forest. In making such a cloak only two feathers are taken from the breast of each bird. It takes sometimes a hundred years to fashion such a cloak. Naturally it is to be worn only by a Ubar. His head was surmounted by an elaborate headdress, formed largely from the long, white, curling feathers of the Ushindi fisher, a long-legged, wading bird. It was not unlike the common headdress of the askari. Indeed, save for the length of the feathers and the intricate leather and beading, in which the feathers were mounted, it might have been such a headdress. It made clear that he, the Ubar, Bila Huruma himself, was one of them, himself an askari. His face had been broad, and the eyes widely spaced. On his cheeks and across the bridge

236

of his nose there had been a swirling stitching of tattoo marks, the record of his transition, long years ago, into manhood.

"Surely you must have seen him well," said Msaliti, "for you were presented before him."

"I noticed externals," I said, "and I remember the things you told me of his signs of office, but my mind was more on Shaba, and yourself, than the Ubar. I saw him, but I did not truly see him."

"Your mind was distracted," said Msaliti.

"Yes," I said.

"Perhaps it is just as well that you did not look deeply into him," said Msaliti.

"To truly see a Ubar," I said, "to look into his heart can be a fearful thing."

"Only one can sit upon the throne," said Msaliti.

"That is a saying in the north," I said.

"I know," said Msaliti. "But it is a saying that is also known east of Schendi."

"Even east of Schendi," I smiled, "the throne is a lonely country."

"He who sits upon the throne, it is said," said Msaliti, "is the most alone of men."

I nodded. Perhaps it was just as well not to have looked too deeply into the eyes of Bila Huruma. It is not always desirable to look deeply into the eyes of a Ubar.

"Until tonight," said Msaliti, withdrawing.

"Until tonight," I said.

19

A BASKET OF OSTS;
A CHAIN OF GOLD;
THE EYES OF THE UBAR

"Why is there no guard?" I asked.

"He has been disposed of," said Msaliti. "Have no fear." He gestured to the portal. "Enter," he said.

"Surely Shaba will have others of his caste with him, geographers of the scribes," I said.

"Enter," said Msaliti.

"Lend me your lamp," I said. He carried a small lamp, with a shallow bowl, which burned tharlarion oil.

"Askaris might see the flame through the walls of the room," he said. "There are many about. Hurry."

I slipped into the room. It was totally dark within. I stood with my back to the grass wall, to the left of the door, as I had entered.

The sleeping platform, I was told, was near the center of the room. Shaba, I suspected, would have the ring about his neck. Very slowly, inch by inch, every sense alert, I began to move toward the center of the room. Msaliti had brought me himself to the room. He had not been accompanied by askaris. I found this strange.

"As few as possible must know of our deed," he had said.

"Yes," I had said.

But surely he would not trust me to return the ring to him. I had expected that he would be accompanied by askaris, whom he would set upon me, to slay me, once I had either killed Shaba or obtained the ring. But I saw none. It had been my hope, of course, and a risk which Msaliti, for his part, would have had to accept, that I might, with the ring, elude his askaris, even if the room were surrounded. The odds, had I the ring, would, I think, have been in my favor. They were odds, of course, which Msaliti had been given no chance but to accept. I could always leave the room, of course, by kicking and tearing through the grass wall at any point of my choosing.

Looking behind me I saw, outside the room, the lamp of Msaliti lift and lower twice.

I smiled to myself. That, I took it, was his sign to his askaris that I was within the room, his sign to them that they were then to surround it.

But then I was troubled. I saw no askaris appearing from the darkness outside.

Suddenly I heard a rush of feet. Instantly I crouched, dagger drawn, blade up, my left hand, too, ready, in the on-guard position for knife combat. But the feet had not approached me. I was startled. I thought I heard climbing. Then, suddenly, from in front of me, in the darkness, I heard a hideous cry of pain. Then I heard a wild, piteous shriek which terminated in spasmodic coughing and gasping. I heard fingernails scratching at a wooden surface and the turning and thrashing of a body.

I turned to leave the room, but, at the door, I was met

with the leveled stabbing spears of several askaris. I saw no sign of Msaliti. I lifted my hands, dropping the knife. Men entered with lamps.

I saw then that I was not in the room of Shaba.

In the center of the room, on a high platform, some nine feet high, supported by eight poles, sitting, cross-legged, naked, save for the panther teeth about his neck, was not Shaba, but the ubar, Bila Huruma.

Men seized my arms then, pinioning them behind me. I felt my wrists being tied.

The room was now well lit from the several lamps. Other lamps, too, at a sign from the ubar, were lit.

I looked to the round, shallow, circular pit in the center of the room. It was about a foot deep. The poles supporting the sleeping platform were set within it. In the pit, his hands still clutching, fingernails bloody, at one of the round poles supporting the platform, lay an askari. His body was twisted horribly, and contorted. The flesh had turned a blackish orange and, in places, had broken open, the skin peeling back like burned paper. A knife, fallen, lay near him in the pit. About his body, small, nervous, sinuous, crawled tiny snakes, osts. Each of these, startlingly, had tied to it a thin string. There were eight such diminutive reptiles. The strings, fastened behind their heads, led up to a pole at the head of the sleeping platform, where they were tied. A woven basket hung, too, near the foot of the sleeping platform. The ost is usually an orange snake, but these were Ushindi osts, which are red with black stripes. Anatomically, and with respect to toxin, I am told they are almost identical to the common ost.

"What is going on, my Ubar?" cried Msaliti, entering. He was in disarray as though he might have been aroused by the screaming. He did not have the lamp with him. In his hurry, of course, he would not have had time to light a lamp. I admired him. He was a shrewd fellow.

Suddenly Msaliti stopped, startled. He seemed astonished, but only for an instant. "My Ubar!" he cried. "Are you all right?"

"Yes," said Bila Huruma.

Upon entering Msaliti had called out to the Ubar, but when he actually saw him he had reacted briefly, stunned. I realized he had called out to make it clear to all that he had expected the Ubar to be alive when he entered, but, when he saw that the Ubar, truly, was alive, he had been for the moment startled. He had recovered himself almost instantaneously. But surely he would not have expected me to have killed the Ubar. I sought the ring. If I had not found it on Shaba's person I surely would not have killed him, perhaps losing it forever.

Msaliti looked into the shallow pit below the high poles of the sleeping platform of Bila Huruma. He looked sick.

"What happened?" he asked. He looked closely at the contorted figure, its discolored hands still clutching at the pole of the sleeping platform. "It is Jambia," he said. "Your guard."

"He tried to kill me," said Bila Huruma. "He was doubtless highly paid. He did not know of the osts. That man is doubtless his accomplice."

I then understood the brilliance of Msaliti. But Msaliti had underestimated the genius of his Ubar.

I had been told that the guard had been disposed of. Actually he had been within, in the hire of Msaliti, awaiting his signal with the lamp. I recalled then that Msaliti, in the morning, had told me that Bila Huruma was he who stood in the way of obtaining the ring, and that if he were gone it would be easy to arrest Shaba and secure the ring. His plan then had been simple. Bila Huruma was to be slain by Jambia, who would then escape, presumably by cutting through the grass wall. It would be I who would be found in the Ubar's chamber. Perhaps Jambia himself was to make the discovery. The rent in the grass wall would be taken, of course, the grass pressed inward, to have been my entrance into the Ubar's chamber, rather than the exit of Jambia. If the plan had been successful Bila Huruma would have been dead and Shaba, without his protector, would be much at the mercy of Msaliti who, as high wazir, would immediately assume, at least temporarily, the reins of government. My false identity, that which Msaliti had constructed for me, as an envoy of Teletus would not then, in the circumstances, any longer protect me. Any diplomatic immunity, so to speak, which I might have possessed would, in the circumstances, have been stripped away from me. I might then be dealt with as Msaliti pleased. His plan, if successful, then, would permit him not only to secure the ring but rid himself of me as well, one who shared with him the secret knowledge of the ring and one who might desire to be himself the agent by which the ring was to be transmitted to Belisarius in Cox, for subsequent return to the Kurii. I had been troublesome to Msaliti. I might prove troublesome to him in the future. He had thus found a useful place for me in his plans. Too, of course, if it were thought I were the assassin, investigative scrutiny would then be directed away from the court rather than within it.

But Msaliti's plan had not succeeded.

"Kill him," said Msaliti, pointing to me.

Two askaris drew back the short stabbing spears to drive them into my chest.

"No," said Bila Huruma.

They lowered the stabbing spears.

"Do you speak the Ushindi speech?" asked Bila Huruma of me.

"Only a little," I said. Ayari, with whom I had shared the rogues' chain in the canal, had been generous in his help. We both knew Gorean and so I had made rapid progress with the lexicon. The grammar, of course, was much more difficult. I spoke the inland speech very poorly, but, as would be expected, thanks to Ayari, I could follow a reasonable amount of what was going on.

"Who hired you?" asked Bila Huruma.

"No one hired me," I said. "I did not know this was your chamber."

One by one, slowly, almost tenderly, on their strings, Bila Huruma lifted the tiny osts from the floor of the pit and placed them, one by one, in the basket near the foot of the sleeping platform.

"Are you of that caste called assassins?" he asked.

"No," I said.

He held the last of the osts on its string, suspended, about five feet from the floor of the pit.

"Bring him near," he said.

I was dragged to the edge of the pit. Bila Huruma extended his arm. I saw the small ost, red with its black stripes, on its string, near my face. Its tiny forked tongue slipped rapidly back and forth between the tiny jaws.

"Do you like my pet?" he asked.

"No," I said. "I do not."

The snake twisted on the string.

"Who hired you?" he asked.

"No one hired me," I said. "I did not know this was your chamber."

"You do not know, probably, who it was who truly hired you," he said. "Doubtless they would not do so, openly."

"He is white," said a man nearby. "Only those in Schendi might hire such a killer. They are familiar with the sleen of the north."

241

"Perhaps," said Bila Huruma.

I now saw the snake lifted until it was level with my eyes.

"Is Jambia, who was my guard, known to you?" asked Bila Huruma.

"No," I said.

"Why did you wish to kill me?" asked Bila Huruma.

"I had no wish to kill you," I said.

"Why were you here?" he asked.

"I came to find something of value," I said.

"Ah," said Bila Huruma. Then he spoke rapidly to an askari. I could not follow what he said then.

Bila Huruma took the tiny snake and then, carefully, placed it in the hanging basket. He then placed the lid on the basket. I breathed more easily.

Suddenly a necklace of gold, heavy, with solid links, was looped about my neck. It had been taken from a coffer to one side.

"You were a guest in my house," he said. "If you wished something of value you should have asked for it. I would then have given it to you."

"My thanks, Ubar," I said.

"Then, if I thought you should not have asked for it," he said, "I would have had you killed."

"I see," I said.

"But I give you this freely," he said. "It is yours. If you are an assassin, take it in lieu of the pay which you would not otherwise receive. If you are, as I suspect, a simple thief, take it as a token of my admiration of your boldness, for it must have taken courage to enter the chamber of a Ubar."

"I did not even know this was your chamber," I said.

"Keep it then as a memento of our meeting," he said.

"My thanks, Ubar," I said.

"Wear it in the canal," he said. "Take him away."

Two askaris turned me about and thrust me toward the door. At the door I stopped, startling the askaris. I turned about, dragging them with me, to again face Bila Huruma.

Our eyes met.

I then, truly, for the first time looked into the eyes of Bila Huruma.

He sat upon the high platform, above the others, solitary and isolated, the necklace of panther teeth about his neck, the lamps below him.

I sensed then, for a moment, what it must be to be a Ubar. It was then, in that instant, that I first truly saw him, as he was, and as he must be. I looked then on loneliness and decision, and power. The Ubar must contain within himself dark strengths. He must be capable of doing, as many men are not, what is necessary.

Only one can sit upon the throne, as it is said. And, as it is said, he who sits upon the throne is the most alone of men.

It is he who must be a stranger to all men, and to whom all men must be strangers.

The throne indeed is a lonely country.

Many men desire to live there but few, I think, could bear its burdens.

Let us continue to think of our Ubars as men much like ourselves, only perhaps a bit wiser, or stronger, or more fortunate. That way we may continue to be comfortable with them, and, to some extent, feel ourselves their superior. But let us not look into their eyes too closely, for we might see there that which sets them apart from us.

It is not always desirable to look deeply into the eyes of a Ubar.

The askaris again turned me about. I saw, briefly, the face of Msaliti.

Then I was conducted from the chamber of Bila Huruma, his gift, a necklace of gold, about my neck. I remembered him behind me, sitting on the high platform, a sleeping platform from which hung a basket of osts.

20

I DO NOT KILL KISU

"That is pretty," said the askari.

"Yes," I said.

He reached for it and I thrust back his hands.

"I want it," he said.

"It was a gift from Bila Huruma," I said.

He backed away from me. I thought he would trouble me no more.

"It is pretty," said Ayari.

"At least it will not rust in the rain," I smiled. I looked at the heavy linkage of the gold chain, slung over the iron collar and work chain I wore.

"Now there is something really pretty," said Ayari.

We stood near the mud raft, that raft of logs and liana vines on which we placed our shovelfuls of mud. In this place, in this great irregular marsh, the water was only to our knees. In some places there were risings above the marsh and hills of relatively dry land. In some places, in pockets, the water was so high as our chests, in others, shallow places, as low as our ankles.

I looked in the direction which Ayari, with his head, had indicated.

I gripped the shovel, startled.

"I heard yesterday, from an askari," he said, "that they would pass here today. They are gifts from Bila Huruma to Tende, daughter of the high chieftain, Aibu, of the Ukungu villages, serving slaves. It is his intention to take Tende into companionship."

"The companionship," said one of the men, "will consolidate the relation of the Ukungu villages with the ubarate."

"I would not mind receiving such lovely gifts," said another man.

"Too bad Tende is a woman," said another.

The two girls were on a raft, being drawn through the marsh by five chained slaves. Four askaris waded beside the raft. The girls were standing. A pole, mounted on two tripods, had been fastened some six feet above the surface of the raft, and parallel to its long axis. The girls stood beneath this pole, their small wrists locked in slave bracelets, fastened above their head and about the pole. Both were barefoot. About their left ankles and throats were wound several strings of white shells. Each, about her hips, wore a brief, wrap-around skirt, held in place by tucking at the left hip, of red-and-black-printed rep-cloth.

"Ho!" I cried, striding toward the raft, as far as the chain on my neck would permit me.

"Master!" cried the blond-haired barbarian.

Both girls were blond, blue-eyed, white, bare-breasted slaves. They were a matched set, selected to set off the dark beauty of Tende, daughter of Aibu, high chieftain of the Ukungu villages.

"Sasi and I were taken almost immediately," cried the blond-haired barbarian. "We were put up for sale!"

"Where is Sasi?" I called.

"Silence!" said one of the askaris near me, lifting his stabbing spear in my direction.

244

"She was sold to a tavern keeper in Schendi," called the girl, "one called Filimbi."

One of the askaris wading beside the raft climbed angrily to its surface. The girl then stood very straight, frightened, looking straight ahead. But he, holding his shield and stabbing spear with his left hand, struck her twice, snapping her head back and forth, with his right hand. Blood was at her mouth. She had spoken without permission. The askari near to me, one supervising the chain, thrust me back with his shield and I fell in the water, and he hit me four times with the handle of the stabbing spear. I then regained my feet, angrily. He threatened me with the blade of the spear. I twisted my head, angrily, in my collar. Other askaris, too, stood about. I stood still in the water. On the surface of the raft the askari who had administered slave discipline to the blond-haired barbarian for her outburst thrust a slave whip, crosswise, in her mouth, thrusting it back between her teeth. This would keep her quiet. If she dropped it, of course, she would be beaten with it.

I saw the raft, slowly, being pulled beyond our chain. The blond-haired barbarian did not now dare look back. She looked straight ahead, the whip between her teeth. The other girl, also blond-haired and blue-eyed, did look back, once. I think she was puzzled to see one on the rogues' chain who wore a necklace of gold. I supposed she, too, was a barbarian, for they were a matched set, possibly also from Earth, though doubtless brought to the shores of Gor, like most, as a simple girl for the markets.

"Dig," said the askari who had struck me.

I would have thought that Sasi might have been able to elude capture longer than she had, but I had been mistaken. Apparently both girls had been taken again almost immediately as slaves. Soon thereafter, apparently, they had been put up for sale. They had been good merchandise, it seemed. Certainly both had been promptly vended, Sasi to Filimbi, whom I had heard of, the owner of a paga tavern, and the blond-haired barbarian directly or indirectly to an agent of Bila Huruma, quite possibly with the immediate object in mind of being used as a component in a matched set of girls, white, serving slaves, gifts for Tende, another projected political companion for the inland Ubar.

"Dig," said the askari, menacingly.

Naturally there had been on the raft, besides the girls, a chest of riches for Tende, riches which, according to the askaris, with whom Ayari took pains to be on good terms, would include such things as bolts of cloth, jewelries, cosmetics, coins and perfumes. This made good sense, of course, and made clear the generosity of the Ubar, Bila Huruma. His gifts to her would surely have been demeaning had they been limited to the presentation of two half-naked, white slaves.

The handle of the short stabbing spear struck down, viciously, across my shoulder.

"Dig!" said the askari.

"Very well," I said, and thrust the shovel again into the mud at my feet.

"You, too!" cried the askari to a man further down the line. "Dig! Dig!"

The fellow on the chain, tall, regal, regarded him contemptuously. Then he turned again, to look after the raft, bearing the gifts for Tende. The askari struck him about the shoulders and chest, repeatedly. Then, without deigning to look upon the askari, he began again to dig.

That man was Kisu, who had been the leader of the Ukungu rebels.

After a time, when the askaris had withdrawn a few yards, I said to Ayari, "Convey my greetings to Kisu." I had seen him look after the raft, and had read the cold rage, the fury like iron, in his body.

We waded, dragging the chain on our necks, toward Kisu. The men behind us, at our sign, moved with us.

Ayari spoke to Kisu, and he lifted his head, regarding me disdainfully.

"I have conveyed your greetings to Kisu," said Ayari, speaking to me in Gorean.

"He did not respond," I said.

"Of course not," said Ayari. "He is Mfalme of Ukungu. He does not speak to commoners."

"Tell him he is no longer the Mfalme of Ukungu," I said. "Tell him he was deposed. If there is any longer a Mfalme of Ukungu it is Aibu, the wise and noble."

Actually Aibu would become a district administrator, as high chieftain of Ukungu, under the sovereignty of Bila Huruma.

"Have your shovel ready," said Ayari to me, in Gorean.

"I will," I said.

But Kisu did not, upon receipt of my message, attack. He stiffened, and regarded me with fury, but he did not move to strike me with the shovel. For a proud man, and one both high-strung and powerful, he restrained himself creditably.

"Tell him I wish to talk with him," I said. "If necessary, he may, as Mfalme of Ukungu, elevate me to the nobility."

Ayari conveyed this cheerfully to Kisu.

Again Kisu restrained himself. Then he turned away. He began to dig.

"Tell him," said I, "that Bila Huruma, his own Ubar, speaks to commoners. Tell him that a true Mfalme listens to, and speaks with, all men."

Kisu straightened up, and turned to face me. His knuckles were white on the shovel.

"I have told him what you said," said Ayari. The speech of Kisu was closely related to the inland speech, and Ayari had no difficulty in communicating with him. It was harder for me, of course, for I was not that familiar with the inland speech. The inland and Ukungu speech, I suppose, would have been regarded linguistically as two dialects of the same mother tongue. The distinction between a dialect and a language is, at times, a conceptual one. In a series of villages, each village may be able to understand those proximate to it, but perhaps those in the first village cannot understand at all the speech of the tenth village. Thus one would think that the first village and the tenth speak different languages. Yet where shall the lines be drawn between them?

"Tell him," I said, "that he would do well to take lessons in leadership from a truly great leader, Bila Huruma."

This was conveyed to Kisu.

With a cry of rage Kisu leaped toward me, the shovel swinging toward my head. I blocked the blow and, bringing about the long handle of my own shovel, struck him a heavy blow alongside of the face. It would have staggered a kailiauk. To my amazement he did not go down. I then, smartly, began to deflect and parry blows. One slash or blow of the shovel would have finished me. I thrust him back twice with the handle of the shovel, the second time plunging the handle into his solar plexus. He stopped, paralyzed by the latter blow. But he did not fall. He could not then defend himself. I was breathing heavily. I did not, of course, strike him. That precise point of the body is one of the target areas taught to warriors. Such a blow is usually given with a thrust of the butt of a spear, generally in the crowding of close combat when you cannot bring the weapon about.

Kisu was, I had little doubt, quite similar in strength to

247

myself. He was not, however, a trained warrior. It was little wonder that he and his forces had been defeated by the askaris of Bila Huruma.

He lifted his head, looking at me in amazement. He did not understand how such a blow could have stopped one of his strength. Then he threw up in the marsh.

The askaris waded to us, shouting angrily. They struck both of us with the handles of their stabbing spears.

We were separated and each thrust back to our own places, the chain line being then again strung out.

After a time Kisu turned about and called to Ayari. Ayari then spoke to me. "He wants to know why you did not kill him," he asked.

"I did not want to kill him," I said. "I only wanted to talk with him."

This was conveyed to Kisu. He then, again, said something.

"He is Mfalme of Ukungu," said Ayari to me. "He cannot speak to commoners."

"Very well," I said. This assent was conveyed then to Kisu.

"Dig!" called the nearest askari.

We returned then to our digging.

21

WHAT I SAW ONE NIGHT IN THE MARSH, WHILE I WAS CHAINED IN THE ROGUES' CAGE

"Awaken," said Ayari, nudging me.

I rolled over in the chain, on the raft.

"Something is coming," he said.

"Raiders?" I asked.

"I do not think so," he said.

I struggled to a crouching position, the iron ring, with its chain, heavy on my neck. The raft on which the rogues' chain was kept was a long one, covered by a barred cage, locked.

I peered into the darkness.

"I do not see anything," I said.

"I saw the brief glint of a dark lantern, momentarily unshuttered," said Ayari.

"Whoever it is, then, moves in stealth," I said. Raiders, of course, would not possess such lanterns.

"Listen," said Ayari.

Suddenly the snout of a tharlarion, half lying on the edge of the raft, thrust against the bars. I drew back. It grunted. It kept its snout for a time on the edge of the raft. Then, with a soft splash, it slipped back in the dark, shallow water.

"Listen," said Ayari.

"I hear it now," I said. "Oars, muffled, several of them."

"How many vessels?" asked Ayari.

"Two, at least," I said, "and moving in tandem order." I could hear, slightly out of time, the softer entry into the water of a second set of oars.

"They could not be askaris," said Ayari.

"No," I said. Askaris used not oars but paddles, and used canoes. Moreover, when moving at night, each canoe's paddles kept the exact rhythm of that of the lead canoe. This makes it difficult to count their number. It is common, of course, to use a tandem order in night rowing, the first vessel's untroubled passage marking the safe channel, its impeded passage marking the location of an obstacle.

"How do you judge the draw?" asked Ayari.

"The craft are light," I said, "and, being rowed in this water, must be shallow-drafted."

"The number of oars suggests length," said Ayari. "They must be light galleys."

"No," I said. "I know the draw of a light galley. These vessels are too light for even such a galley. Furthermore, any light galley with which I am familiar, though comparatively shallow-drafted, would be too deeply keeled to traverse this marsh."

"What manner of vessels can they be?" asked Ayari. "And where would they come from?"

"They can be but one thing," I said, "and yet that they should be here, now, at night, is madness."

We then heard a thrash in the water, as a tharlarion, perhaps the same one which had thrust its snout against the bars of our cage, struck against wood in the darkness, some twenty yards from us.

We heard a cry of anger and, for an instant, a dark lantern was unshuttered. We saw two men, in the prow of a low, medium-beamed, bargelike vessel. One pushed down with a

249

spear, forcing the broad head of the tharlarion away from the vessel.

I clutched the bars of the cage in which, on the raft, I was confined.

Then the dark lantern was again shuttered. The vessels slipped past us. There were three of them. The shafts of the oars, where they rested in the open, fixed-position, U-shaped oarlocks, had been wrapped in fur, that they might make no sound as they moved against these fulcrums. The oars themselves had barely lifted from the water and had then entered and drawn again, almost splashlessly. The oarlocks, too, had been lined with fur.

"What is wrong?" asked Ayari.

"Nothing," I said.

In the light of the dark lantern, when it had been briefly unshuttered, I had seen the faces of three or four men, the faces of those in the prow and two others, who had stood near to them. One of the faces I knew. It had been that of Shaba, the geographer.

I clenched the bars. I was helpless. For a moment I shook them with futile rage. Then I was quiet.

"What is wrong?" asked Ayari.

"Nothing," I told him.

22

I CONTINUE TO DIG
IN THE CANAL

I hurled mud from my shovel to the mud raft.

I had heard no drums coming from the west, nothing to suggest that there was a pursuit of Shaba.

Yet I was certain that it had been he who had passed us in stealth in the night. There had been three vessels, of the sort which had been prepared in Ianda and brought to Schendi, and then to Lake Ushindi by way of the Nyoka, part of the fleet which Bila Huruma was organizing to support the explorations of Shaba, navigating the Ua, into the far interior. But there had been only three of the vessels, out of some one hundred. And Shaba had moved in secrecy. There had been, as far as I could tell, no convoy of askari canoes with him, nor askaris, as far as I saw, in the vessel I had seen. The men with him, I suspected, or most of them, were members of his own caste, geographers of the scribes, perhaps, but men inured to hardships, perhaps men who had been with him in his explorations of Ushindi and Ngao, men he trusted and upon whom he could count in desperate situations, caste brothers.

I brushed insects away from my face.

It seemed clear to me that Shaba must be in flight, and I had little doubt that he must have the ring with him, to obtain which had been the object of my journey to Schendi. He had now passed us, moving silently, secretly, to the east.

I thrust the shovel again down, hard, into the mud at my feet.

I dug, and Shaba, my quarry, moved further away from me with each thrust of the shovel, each bite and sting of each tiny insect.

I hurled another shovelful of mud onto the mud raft.

"There is no escape," said Ayari. "Do not think foolish thoughts."

"How do you know I think of escape?" I asked.

"See how white are your knuckles on the shovel," he said. "If the marsh were an enemy you would have cut it to pieces by now." He looked up at me. "Beware, my friend," he said, "the askaris, too, have noted you."

I looked about. One of the askaris, it was true, was looking in my direction.

"They might have killed you by now," said Ayari, "but you are strong. You are a good worker."

"I could kill him," I said.

"He carries no key," said Ayari. "The metal on your neck is hammered shut. Dig now, or we will be beaten with the handles of spears."

"Tell Kisu," I said, "that I would speak with him, that I would escape."

"Do not be foolish," said Ayari.

"Tell him," I said.

Once again, as before, yesterday, my words were tendered to Kisu. He looked about. He responded.

"He does not speak to commoners," said Ayari to me.

I slashed down at the marsh with my shovel, gouged out a weight of mud and flung it to the mud raft.

Had it been Kisu he would have been destroyed.

23

ESCAPE; KISU PAYS A CALL ON TENDE

"Is she not beautiful?" whispered Ayari.

"Yes," I said.

"Be quiet," said an askari.

"Stand straight," said another askari. "Hold your heads up. Keep the line straight."

"Which is the one called Kisu?" asked an askari, wading up to us.

"I do not know," I said.

"That is he," said Ayari, indicating tall Kisu a few places from us.

Slowly the state platform was drawn toward us. It, fastened planks, extending across the thwarts of four long canoes, like pontoons, moved slowly toward us, drawn by chained slaves. On the platform, shaded by a silk canopy, was a low dais, covered with silken cushions.

"Why did you tell him which one of us was Kisu?" I asked.

"She would know him, would she not?" he asked.

"That is true," I said.

On the cushions, reclining, on one elbow, in yellow robes, embroidered with gold, in many necklaces and jewels, lay a lovely, imperious-seeming girl.

"It is Tende," whispered one of the men, "the daughter of Aibu, high chief of the Ukungu district."

We had known this, for the message of the drums, coming from the east, had preceded her.

On either side of Tende knelt a lovely white slave girl, strings of white shells about her throat and left ankle, a brief, tucked, wrap-around skirt of red-and-black-printed rep-cloth, her only garment, low on her belly, high and tight on her thighs. Both slaves were sweetly bodied. Each had marvelously flared hips. I found it hard to take my eyes from them. They were among the gifts which Bila Huruma had sent ahead to his projected companion, Tende. I smiled and licked my lips. Though they had been bought to be the serving slaves of a woman I had little doubt that their purchase had been effected by a male agent. In the hands of each of the slaves was a long-handled fan, terminating in a semicircle of colorful feathers. Gently, cooling her, they fanned their mistress.

I looked at the blond-haired barbarian, she who had been Janice Prentiss, who knelt now to my right, at Tende's left. She did not meet my eyes. Her lower lip trembled. She did not dare to give any sign that she recognized me.

About Tende's right wrist, I noted, fastened to it by a loop, was a whip.

"Stand straighter," said an askari.

We stood straighter.

On the raft, near Tende and her two lovely, bare-breasted white slaves, stood four askaris, men of Bila Huruma, in their skins and feathers, with golden armlets. Like most askaris they carried long, tufted shields and short stabbing spears. The daughter of Aibu, I gathered, was well guarded. Other askaris, too, waded in the water near the platform.

One other man, too, other than the askaris, stood upon the platform. It was Mwoga, wazir to Aibu, who was now conducting Tende to her companionship. I recognized him, having seen him earlier in the palace of Bila Huruma. He, like many in the interior, and on the surrounding plains and savannahs, north and south of the equatorial zone, was long-boned and tall, a physical configuration which tends to dissipate body heat. His face, like that of many in the interior, was tattooed. His tattooing, and that of Kisu, were quite similar. One can recognize tribes, of course, and, often, villages and districts by those tattoo patterns. He wore a long black robe, embroidered with golden thread, and a flat, soft cap, not unlike a common garb of Schendi, hundreds of pasangs distant. I had little doubt but what these garments had been gifts to him from the court of Bila Huruma. Bila Huruma himself, of course, in spite of the cosmopolitan nature of his court, usually wore the skins, and the gold and feathers, of the askari. It was not merely that they constituted his power base, and that he wished to flatter them. It was rather that he himself was an askari, and regarded himself as an askari. In virtue of his strength, skill and intelligence, he was rightfully first among them. He was an askari among askaris.

"Behold, Lady," said Mwoga, indicating Kisu, "the enemy of your father, and your enemy, helpless and chained before

253

you. Look upon him and inspect him. He opposed your father. Now, on a rogues' chain, he digs in the mud for your future companion, the great Bila Huruma."

The Ukungu dialect is closely related to the Ushindi dialect. Ayari, softly, translated the conversation for me. Yet, had he not done so, I could have, by now, followed its drift.

Kisu looked boldly into the eyes of the reclining Tende.

"You are the daughter of the traitor, Aibu," he said.

Tende did not change her expression.

"How bravely the rebel speaks," mocked Mwoga.

"I see, Mwoga," said Kisu, "that now you are wazir, that you have risen high from your position of a minor chief's lackey. Such, I gather, are the happy fortunes of politics."

"Happier for some than others," said Mwoga. "You, Kisu, were too dull to understand politics. You are headstrong and foolish. You could understand only the spear and the drums of war. You charge like the kailiauk. I, wiser, bided my time, like the ost. The kailiauk is contained by the stockade. The ost slips between its palings."

"You betrayed Ukungu to the empire," said Kisu.

"Ukungu is a district within the empire," said Mwoga. "Your insurrection was unlawful."

"You twist words!" said Kisu.

"The spear, as in all such matters," smiled Mwoga, "has decided wherein lies the right."

"What will the stories say of this?" demanded Kisu.

"It is we who will survive to tell the stories," said Mwoga.

Kisu stepped toward him but the askari at his side forced him back.

"No people can be betrayed," said Mwoga, "who are not willing to be betrayed."

"I do not understand," said Kisu.

"The empire means security and civilization," said Mwoga. "The people tire of tribal warfare. Men wish to look forward in contentment to their harvests. How can men call themselves free when, each night, they must fear the coming of dusk?"

"I do not understand," said Kisu.

"That is because you yourself are a hunter and a killer," said Mwoga. "You know the spear, the raid, the retaliation, the seeking of vengeance, the shadows of the forest. Steel is your tool, darkness your ally. But this is not the case with most men. Most men desire peace."

"All men desire peace," said Kisu.

"If this were true, there would be no war," said Mwoga.

Kisu regarded him, angrily. "Bila Huruma is a tyrant," he said.

"Of course," said Mwoga.

"He must be resisted," said Kisu.

"Then resist him," said Mwoga.

"He must be stopped," said Kisu.

"Then stop him," said Mwoga.

"You style yourself a hero, who would lead my people into the light of civilization?" asked Kisu.

"No," said Mwoga, "I am an opportunist. I serve myself, and my superiors."

"Now you speak honestly," said Kisu.

"Politics, and needs and times, calls forth men such as myself," said Mwoga. "Without men such as myself there could be no change."

"The tharlarion and the ost have their place in the palace of nature," said Kisu.

"And I will have mine at the courts of Ubars," said Mwoga.

"Meet me with spears," said Kisu.

"How little you understand," said Mwoga. "How naively you see things. How your heart craves simplicities."

"I would have your blood on my spear," said Kisu.

"And the empire would endure," said Mwoga.

"The empire is evil," said Kisu.

"How simple," marveled Mwoga. "How dazed and confused you must be when, upon occasion, you encounter reality."

"The empire must be destroyed," said Kisu.

"Then destroy it," said Mwoga.

"Go, serve your master, Bila Huruma," said Kisu. "I dismiss you."

"We are grateful for your indulgence," smiled Mwoga.

"And take these slave girls with you, gifts for his highness, Bila Huruma," said Kisu, gesturing to Tende and her two servitors.

"Lady Tende, daughter of Aibu, high chief of Ukungu," said Mwoga, "is being conveyed in honor to the ceremony of companionship, to be mated to his majesty, Bila Huruma."

"She is being sold to seal a bargain," said Kisu. "How could she be more a slave?"

Tende's face remained expressionless.

255

"Of her own free will," said Mwoga, "the Lady Tende hastens to become Ubara to Bila Huruma."

"One of more than two hundred Ubaras!" scoffed Kisu.

"She acts of her own free will," averred Mwoga.

"Excellent," said Kisu. "She sells herself!" he said. "Well done, Slave Girl!" he commended.

"She is to be honored in companionship," said Mwoga.

"I have seen Bila Huruma," said Kisu. "No woman could be other than a slave to him. And I have seen luscious slaves, black, and white, and oriental, in his palace, girls who know truly how to please a man, and desire to do so. Bila Huruma has his pick of hot-blooded, trained, enslaved beauties. If you do not wish to remain barren and lonely in your court you will learn to compete with them. You will learn to crawl to his feet and beg to serve him with the unqualified and delicious abandon of a trained slave."

Still Tende's face did not change expression.

"And you will do so, Tende," said Kisu, "for you are in your heart, as I can see in your eyes, a true slave."

Tende lifted her hand, her right hand, with the whip, on its loop, fastened to her wrist. She moved her hand indolently. Her two slaves, tense, frightened, desisted from fanning her.

Tende rose gracefully to her feet and descended from the cushions and dais, to stand at the edge of the platform, over Kisu.

"Have you nothing to say, my dear Tende, beautiful daughter of the traitor, Aibu?" inquired Kisu.

She struck him once with the whip, across the face. He had shut his eyes that he not be blinded.

"I do not speak to commoners," she said. She then returned to her position, her face again expressionless, and looking straight ahead.

She lifted her hand, indolently, and again her two slaves began, gently, to fan her.

Kisu opened his eyes, a diagonal streak of blood across his face. His fists were clenched.

"Continue on," said Mwoga to one of the askaris on the platform.

The fellow called out sharply to the chained slaves drawing the platform, pointing ahead with his spear. They then began to wade forward, drawing the canoes, with the platform of state affixed athwart them.

We watched the platform, with its passengers, and canopy, moving west.

I looked at Kisu. I did not think, now, I would have long to wait.

"Dig," said a nearby askari.

With a feeling of satisfaction, and pleasure, I then thrust the shovel deep into the mud at my feet.

We sat in the long cage, bolted on the extended raft. I ran my finger under the collar, to move it a bit from my neck. I could smell the marshes about.

With a movement of chain, he crawled toward me in the darkness. With my fingernail I scratched a bit of rust from the chain on my collar. Far off, across the marsh, we could hear the noises of jungle birds, the howling of tiny, long-limbed primates. It was about an Ahn after the late evening rain, somewhere about the twentieth Ahn. The sky was still overcast, providing a suitable darkness for the work which must soon be at hand.

"I must speak with you," he said, in halting Gorean.

"I did not know you could speak Gorean," I said, looking ahead in the darkness.

"When a child," he said, "I once ran away. I lived for two years in Schendi, then returned to Ukungu."

"I did not think a mere village would content you," I said. "It was a long and dangerous journey for a child."

"I returned to Ukungu," he said.

"Perhaps that is why you are such a patriot of Ukungu," I said, "because once you fled from it."

"I must speak with you," he said.

"Perhaps I do not speak with members of the nobility," I said.

"Forgive me," he said. "I was a fool."

"You have learned, then," I said, "from Bila Huruma, who will speak to all men."

"How else can one listen?" he asked. "How else can one understand others?"

"Beggers speak to beggers, and to Ubars," I said.

"It is a saying of Schendi," he said.

"Yes," I said.

"Do you speak Ushindi?" he asked.

"A little," I said.

"Can you understand me?" he asked, speaking in the dialect of the court of Bila Huruma.

"Yes," I said. Gorean was not easy for him. Ushindi, I was sure, was no easier for me. Ayari, to my right, knew Ushindi well enough to transpose easily into the related Ngao dialect spoken in the Ukungu district, but I did not. "If I cannot understand you, I will tell you," I said. I had little doubt but what, between his Gorean and my understanding of the Ushindi dialect spoken at the court of Bila Huruma, we could communicate.

"I will try to speak Gorean," he said. "That, at least, is not the language of Bila Huruma."

"There are other things in its favor as well," I said. "It is a complex, efficient language with a large vocabulary."

"Ukungu," he said, "is the most beautiful language in all the world."

"That may well be," I said, "but I cannot speak it." I, personally, would have thought that English or Gorean would have been the most beautiful language in all the world. I had met individuals, however, who thought the same of French and German, and Spanish, and Chinese and Japanese. The only common denominator in these discussions seemed to be that each of the informants was a native speaker of the language in question. How chauvinistic we are with respect to our languages. This chauvinism can sometimes be so serious as to blind certain individuals to the natural superiority of English, or, perhaps, Gorean. Or perhaps French, or German, or Spanish, or Chinese, or Japanese, or, say, Bassa or Hindi.

"I will try to speak Gorean," he said.

"Very well," I said, generously. I breathed more easily.

"I want to escape," he said. "I must escape."

"Very well," I said. "Let us do so."

"But how?" he asked.

"The means," I said, "have long lain at our disposal. It is only that I have lacked the cooperation necessary to capitalize on them."

I turned to Ayari. "Pass the word down the chain," I said, "in both directions, in various languages, that we shall escape tonight."

"How do you propose to do this?" asked Ayari.

"Discharge your duties, my friendly interpreter," I said. "You will see shortly."

"What if some fear to escape?" asked Ayari.

"They will then be torn alive out of the chain," I told him.

"I am not sure I am in favor of this," said Ayari.

"Do you wish to be the first?" I asked him.

"Not me," said Ayari. "I am busy. I have things to do. I am passing the word down the chain."

"How can we escape?" asked Kisu.

I reached out and measured the chain at his collar, and slipped my hands down the chain until, about five feet later, it lifted to the collar of the next man. I pushed them closely together, to drop the chain, in a loop, to the log floor of the extended raft. By feeling I dropped the loop between the ends of two logs and drew it back, about two feet in from the end of the log it was now looped beneath. The bottom of the loop was then under water and about one log. I put one end of the chain in the hands of the powerful Kisu and took the other end in my own hands.

"I see," said Kisu, "but this is an inefficient tool."

"You could ask the askaris for a better," I suggested.

We then began, smoothly and firmly, exerting heavy, even pressures, to draw the chain back and forth under the log. In moments, using this crude saw, or cutting tool, we had cut through the bark of the log and had begun, rhythmically, to gash and splinter the harder wood beneath. The spacing and twisting of the links, in the motion of the metal, served well in lieu of teeth. There was an occasional squeak of the metal on the wet wood but the work, for the most part, was accomplished silently, the sound being concealed under the surface of the water. It was a mistake on the part of the askaris to have left us in neck chains in a cage mounted on a log platform. We ceased work, once, when a canoe of askaris, on watch, paddled by.

My hands began to bleed on the chain. Doubtless Kisu's hands, too, were bloodied.

One man crept close to us. "This is madness," he said. "I am not with you."

"You must then be killed," I told him.

"I have changed my mind," he said. "I am now with you, fully."

"Good," I said.

"The sound will carry under the water," said another man. Sound does carry better under water than above it, indeed, some five times as well. The sound, of course, does not well break the surface of the water. Thus the sound, though propagated efficiently either beneath or above the surface, is not well propagated, because of the barrier of the surface, either from beneath the surface to above the surface, or from above the surface to beneath the surface.

"It will attract tharlarion, or fish, and then tharlarion," he said.

259

"We will wait for them to investigate and disperse," I said.

Ayari was near to me. "It is dark," he said. "It is a good night for raiders."

A bit of wood, moved by the chain, splintered up by my feet.

I slid the loop of chain down toward the end of the log, near the end of the other log, to which it was adjacent.

The chain, thus positioned, might exert more leverage.

"Pull," I said. Kisu and I, drawing heavily on the chain, splintered the log upward, breaking off some inches of it. With my foot and hands I snapped off some sharp splinters.

"We will now wait for a time," I said.

We heard a tharlarion, a large one, rub up against the bottom of the raft.

I looped the chain in my bloody hands, to strike at it if it should try to thrust its snout through the hole.

"Cover the log. Seem asleep," whispered a man.

We sat about the piece of log, our heads down, some of us lying on the floor of the log raft. I saw the light, a small torch, in the bow of another canoe pass us, one containing ten armed askaris.

They did not pay us much attention.

"They fear raiders," said Ayari.

After a time, when it seemed quiet, I said, "Bring the first man on the chain forward."

He, not happy, was thrust toward me. "I will go first," I said, "but I cannot, as I am toward the center of the chain."

"What about the fellow at the end of the chain?" he inquired.

"An excellent idea," I said, "but he, like you, might be reluctant, and it is you, not he, whose neck is now within my reach."

"What if there are tharlarion?" he asked.

"Are you afraid?" I asked.

"Yes," he said.

"You should be," I said. "There might be tharlarion."

"I am not going," he said.

"Take a deep breath," I told him, "and keep moving, for others must follow. Make for the mud raft. There are shovels there."

"I am not going," he said.

I seized him and thrust him headfirst downward through the hole. The next man slid feet first through the hole. The next, heavy, squeezed with difficulty through the aperture between the logs. Another man slipped through. The first man's head broke the surface sputtering. He started toward the mud aft. One after another, I and Kisu, and Ayari, toward the center of the chain, the same forty-six prisoners of the cage slipped free.

"Take shovels and bring the raft," I said.

"Which way shall we go?" asked Ayari.

"Follow me," I said.

"You are going west!" said Ayari.

"We must free ourselves," I said. "In the chain we cannot long escape. If we go west we may deceive inquiring askaris. And west, only a pasang away, lies the smiths' island, where men are added to the chain."

"There will be tools there," said Ayari.

"Precisely," I said.

"Let us go east, or toward the jungles north or south," said a man.

Kisu struck him on the side of the head, knocking him sideways.

I looked at Kisu. "Does it not seem wise to you, Mfalme," I asked him, "to proceed westward?"

He straightened himself. "Yes," he said. "We will go westward."

His agreement pleased me. Without his cooperation, and the significance of his prestige and status, it would be difficult, if not impossible, to enforce my will on the chain. Without his aid and influence I do not think it would have been possible to have escaped the cage. I had seen, from his striking the fellow in the chain, that he had been in agreement with me as to the advisability of proceeding westward. I had then, using the title of Mfalme, asked him to make this concurrence explicit. His declaration had helped to reassure the men. In asking him I had also, of course, indicated my respect for his opinion, which, incidentally, I did respect, and, in using the title of Mfalme, I had acknowledged that I, for one, would continue to recognize his lofty status in Ukungu. Had I not anticipated his agreement I do not know what I would have done. I suppose then one or the other of us would have had to beat or kill the other.

Soon, leading the chain from the center, its ends behind and on either side of us, I, and Kisu, and some others between us, were wading westward, shovels in hand. Some men behind, on either side, thrust the mud raft along with us.

"You are a clever fellow," said Kisu to me.

"Surely you do agree that our best direction at the moment is west?" I asked.

"Yes," he said.

"They will not expect us to head west, and there are tools there."

"There is something else there, too," he said, "which I want."

"What is that?" I asked.

"You will see," he said.

"Askaris!" said Ayari. "Ahead!"

"We have been released by other askaris, and sent westward for safety," I told him. "We were even given our tools. There were raiders."

"Who is there? Stop!" called an askari.

We stopped, obediently. Nervously I saw that there were several askaris, about, more than I had originally realized, some twenty of them, with their shields and stabbing spears. The white feathers of the headdresses marked their positions. In raids askaris sometimes remove these headdresses. When actually engaged in combat in darkness, of course, it helps them keep their formations and tell friend from foe. Although doubtless there are advantages and disadvantages to the headdress it is, tactically, in my opinion, a liability. Like the shako of the hussar, it makes too good a target.

"Raiders!" called out, Ayari, pointing backward. "We were released by askaris and commanded to march west for protection."

"Raiders!" cried one of the askaris.

"It is a good night for them," said another.

"You will protect us, will you not?" begged Ayari.

"Where are the askaris who released you?" demanded one askari.

"Fighting!" said Ayari.

"Sound the drums," said the man. An askari rushed away. "Prepare to relieve the beleaguered section," said the man.

"Column of twos!" called another.

The askaris formed themselves into a double column.

"Who will stay to protect us?" inquired Ayari.

"March to the rear," said the officer. "You will be safe there."

"There is a relief," said Ayari.

"Hurry!" said the officer.

We immediately began to wade westward again. The askaris hurriedly began to wade east. Soon we could hear a drum. Its sound would marshal new askaris.

"Hurry," said Ayari.

Twice in our march west we were passed by columns of askaris, and then by two canoes filled with such troops.

"They will soon discover it is a false alarm," said Kisu.

"Hurry," I said.

In a few moments we clambered onto the smiths' island. Askaris moved past us.

"What is going on?" asked one of the smiths, holding a torch, standing outside his sleeping shelter.

He, and his fellows, in the shelter, were then ringed with desperate men.

"Remove our chains," I told him.

"Never," said one.

"We can do it ourselves," said Ayari. Shovels were lifted. The smiths, threatened, hurried, escorted by chained men, to their anvils.

The collars, swiftly, were opened and the heavy bands, struck with sharp, expert blows, were bent wide. We thrust the smiths back into their sleeping shed and threw them to their bellies. We tied them hand and foot, gagging them with choking wads of marsh grass, forced into their mouths and fastened in place with wide strips of leather. I tied shut the door of the wooden shelter, to keep it from being pushed inward by tharlarion which might crawl to the surface of the small island.

"Disperse," I said to the men. "It is now each man for himself."

They disappeared into the darkness, making their way in various directions.

Kisu, I, and Ayari, remained on the island.

"Where are you going?" asked Kisu.

"I must go east," I said. "I follow one called Shaba. I seek the Ua River."

"That will suit my purposes well," he said, grimly.

"I do not understand," I said.

"You will, in time," he said.

"Do you menace me?" I asked.

He put his hands on my shoulders. "By the crops of Ukungu, no," he said.

"Then I do not understand you," I said.

"You will," he said.

"I must be on my way," I said. "Time is short."

"You are not facing east," he said.

"I have a stop to make first," I said.

"I, too, have some business to attend to," he said.

"That is in accord with some plan of yours?" I asked.

"Exactly," he said.

"It is my intention to recover a lost slave," I said. I recalled the lovely blond-haired barbarian, Janice Prentiss. I wanted her at my own feet.

"That is why you brought along the mud raft," smiled Kisu.

"Of course," I said.

"I think I, too, will take a slave," he said.

"I thought you might," I said.

"I do not understand why the askaris have not yet returned," said Ayari. "By now they must understand it to be a false alarm."

"I would think so," I said.

"Let us hurry," said Kisu.

We set off through the darkness, westward, pushing the mud raft with us, our shovels placed upon it.

"Why are you not with the other askaris, fighting in the east?" asked Ayari.

"I am guarding the Lady Tende," he said. "Who are you? What is that?"

"Where is the rogues' chain?" asked Ayari.

"I do not know," he said. "Who are you? What is that raft?"

"I am Ayari," said Ayari. "This is the mud raft used by the rogues' chain."

"The rogues' chain is to the east," said the man. "We passed it earlier today."

"What is going on here?" asked Mwoga, returning from the eastern edge of the platform of planks fixed over the four canoes.

"It is a worker, looking for the rogues' chain," said the askari.

Mwoga peered into the darkness. He could not see Ayari well. Obviously the man was a worker, for he was not chained. Probably the mud raft had broken loose and the worker was intent upon returning it, if unwisely in the darkness.

"One askari," called Ayari, "is not enough to guard so great a personage as the Lady Tende."

264

"Have no fear, fellow," said Mwoga. "There is another about."

"That is all I wanted to know," said Ayari.

Kisu and I had located one guard apiece. The others had apparently joined in the investigation to the east.

"I do not understand," said Mwoga.

With the flats of our shovels Kisu and I struck the two guards senseless.

Mwoga had informed us that there were only two to concern ourselves with, and that we might proceed with dispatch. He had been quite helpful.

Mwoga looked from his left to his right. Without speaking further, or attempting to draw his dagger, he leaped from the planks into the water, falling, scrambling up, and plunging away into the darkness.

The chained slaves who drew the platform and were sitting and crouching forward, on its surface, had, cautioned by Ayari, remained silent.

The darkness was loud with the drums.

"I cannot sleep," said the Lady Tende, emerging from the small, silken shelter, one of two, one for her and her slaves, and one for Mwoga, pitched aft on the platform.

Then she saw Kisu.

24

WE OBTAIN A CANOE;
KISU MAKES TENDE A SLAVE

It was getting light.

We thrust the mud raft ahead of us.

Some askaris straggled past, some wounded. A canoe, with bleeding askaris, half drifted, half paddled, passed us, a hundred yards away, on our right.

More than an Ahn ago we had passed the point at which the prison raft, from which we had escaped, had been anchored.

"There were raiders," said Kisu.

"It was a good night for them," said Ayari.

We continued to push the mud raft ahead of us. The dawn,

a rim of luminescent gray, lay before us. On Gor, as on Earth, the sun rises in the east.

An askari limped past, moving painfully through the thigh-high water. "Do not proceed further," he said. "There is action in the east."

"My thanks for your advice, my friend," called out Ayari. "Prepare to turn about," he said, loudly, to us. We, pushing from the sides, turned the heavy raft, heaped with piled mud, slowly about. When the askari was some seventy-five yards away we turned about again and continued eastward. He was not, I am sure, aware that we were not following him. If he was, he was in no condition to pursue us.

Concealed by a thin layer of mud on the raft were two shields and two stabbing spears, which Kisu and I had taken from the two askaris we had subdued on the platform of Tende. Our shovels lay in plain sight on the mud heaped on the raft.

We continued to push the raft toward the east.

Ayari looked up at the sky. "It must be about the eighth Ahn," he said.

"How far ahead is Ngao?" I asked Kisu.

"Days," said Kisu.

"It is hopeless," said Ayari. "Let us make for shore."

"They will expect us to do that," I said. "And if we are seen we may fall to hostile natives or, if they be allies of Bila Huruma, be taken, or our position indicated by the drums."

"Listen," said Kisu, suddenly.

"I hear it," I said.

"What?" asked Ayari.

"War cries, ahead and to the right," I said, "men fighting." I climbed to the surface of the raft. Kisu followed me.

"What do you see?" asked Ayari.

"There is an engagement there," I said, "in canoes and in the water, some hundred askaris, some forty or fifty raiders."

"There may be numerous such engagements," said Ayari. "Let us avoid them."

"To be sure," I said.

Kisu and I clambered down, splashing into the water, and again thrust the raft eastward.

Twice more, before noon, we scouted such engagements. It had rained heavily about the ninth Ahn, but we, drenched, had not ceased to push the raft toward the western shore of Ngao, somewhere ahead of us.

"Down!" said Ayari.

We crouched down in the water, our heads scarcely above the surface, shielded by the raft. On the other side of the raft passed two canoes of askaris returning to the marsh camps of the west. They had seen, from their point of view, only a mud raft, loosed and drifted from the work area.

"Askaris are returning," said Ayari. "The raiders have been driven away."

Kisu lifted the headdress of an askari from the water, and threw it from him. "Not without cost," he said.

"We are safe now," said Ayari.

"Keep a watch for tharlarion," said Kisu. He reached under the water and pulled a fat, glistening leach, some two inches long, from his leg.

"Destroy it," said Ayari.

Kisu dropped it back in the water. "I do not want my blood, pinched from it, released in the water," he said.

Ayari nodded, shuddering. Such blood might attract the bint, a fanged, carnivorous marsh eel, or the predatory, voracious blue grunt, a small, fresh-water variety of the much larger and familiar salt-water grunt of Thassa. The blue grunt is particularly dangerous during the daylight hours preceding its mating periods, when it schools. Its mating periods are synchronized with the phases of Gor's major moon, the full moon reflecting on the surface of the water somehow triggering the mating instinct. During the daylight hours preceding such a moon, as the restless grunts school, they will tear anything edible to pieces which crosses their path. During the hours of mating, however, interestingly, one can move and swim among them untouched. The danger, currently, of the bint and blue grunt, however, was not primarily due to any peril they themselves might represent, particularly as the grunt would not now be schooling, but due to the fact that they, drawn by shed blood, might be followed by tharlarion.

The spear, slender, some seven feet in length, bit into the mud near my hand.

"Raiders!" cried Ayari.

We heard screaming.

Kisu tore at the mud, scratching for one of the shields and stabbing spears.

A fellow leaped to the surface of the raft. I slipped under the water.

I thrust my way through submerged marsh grass. A spear struck down at me. Then I managed to get beneath the canoe and stood up, suddenly, screaming, tipping its occupants into

267

the water. There, suddenly, over the waters of the marsh, roared the war cry of Ko-ro-ba. I dropped one man lifeless, his throat wrenched open, into the water. One man thrust at me with his spear and the others, startled, stood back. I tore the spear from him and kicked him from it. He slipped and I thrust the iron blade into him and thrust him down, pinning him, blood and bubbles bursting up, to the bottom of the marsh. I regarded the other four men, standing back, who faced me. I saw they did not move to attack. I pressed the body of the man under the surface from the spear blade with my foot and drew the weapon up. The body, twisting, now head down, emerged in the grass.

I stepped to one side. The men facing me were standing still.

Kisu stood on the raft, like a black god, the shield on his arm, a bloodied stabbing spear in his right hand. In the water, to his left, struck from the raft, lifeless, inert, buoyant, rolled two bodies.

I waved my hand. "Begone!" I cried. "Begone!"

I do not think they understood my words but my meaning was clear. The four men backed away and then turned and fled.

I righted the canoe. Kisu, leaving the raft, fetched two sealed calabashes of meal from where they floated in the marsh. Tied in the canoe itself was a long, cylindrical basket of strips of salted, dried fish.

Ayari waded out to the canoe. "Do you think they have gone?" he asked.

"Yes," I said.

"Perhaps there are others," he said. He was retrieving paddles from the water.

"I think it is late now for raiders," I said. "Perhaps they will come again in a few days, to again attack the workers at the canal. I think there is little to fear from them at the moment."

"Bila Huruma will burn their villages," said Kisu.

"He must be careful," I said. "He would not wish to alienate the friendly shore communities, either of the marsh or of Ngao."

"He will do what he thinks is necessary to achieve his ends," said Kisu.

"Doubtless you are right," I said. Indeed, I had no doubt but what Bila Huruma would design a sober and judicious course, gentle, if necessary, harsh, if necessary, to bring about those ends which he might seek. He, a Ubar by nature, would not be an easy man to deal with, or to stop.

Ayari placed the paddles he had found, some six of them, in the canoe. This gave us, altogether, a total of eight paddles, not counting two which were lost, floated away, for there were two paddles, extra paddles, tied in the canoe. It is quite common, of course, for a war canoe or raiders' canoe to carry extra paddles, a sensible precaution against the loss of one or more of these essential levers. Indeed, even a canoe which is not one of war or raiding may carry extra paddles, particularly if it is to be propelled through turbulent waters.

I moved the canoe to the side of the raft. From the heaped mud on the raft, unobtrusively, protruded three hollow stems, of broken marsh reed. Kisu, with his hands, dug in the mud. He reached under the mud and seized the blond hair of a slave girl, cords of pierced shells looped about her neck. He pulled her free, by the hair, from the mud. The reed, through which she had breathed, fell from her teeth. Her eyes were frightened, and wide. Her wrists were tied behind her and her ankles, too, were crossed and bound. Kisu submerged her, shaking her, rinsing mud from her body. Then he handed her to me.

"Master," said the blond-haired barbarian.

"Be silent, Slave," I said.

"Yes, Master," she said.

I carried her to the canoe. I placed her in the canoe, on her belly, as a slave.

Kisu had then freed the second blond-haired slave from the mud and, submerging her, she also bound hand and foot, rinsed her clean. He then handed her to me and I placed her, as I had the first, she who had once been Janice Prentiss, in the canoe. I placed the second girl forward in the canoe, so that her feet were at the head of the first girl, the blond-haired barbarian. This would make communication between them difficult. Such small touches aid in the control and management of girls.

"Beast!" screamed Tende to Kisu, sputtering and coughing as she was pulled up from the water. "Free me! Free me!"

"I did not think you spoke to commoners," he said. Ayari grinned, affording me the translation of their remarks. If I had spoken Ushindi more fluently I could probably have made out their discourse, as Ayari did, for the Ukungu speech is a closely related language. My Ushindi, of course, was poor. In the next few days I would learn to make

269

transpositions between Ushindi and Ukungu. The vocabularies are extremely similar, except for pronunciation. The grammars, in their basic structures, are almost identical. I have little doubt that most of the black equatorial stock on Gor, descendants of individuals brought to this world by Priest-Kings on Voyages of Acquisition, perhaps hundreds of years ago, derive from one of the Earth's major linguistic families, perhaps the Bantu group. Gorean itself shows innumerable evidences of being derived largely from languages of the Indo-European group.

Tende stifled an angry cry.

Kisu threw her, in her soiled robes, to the surface of the raft. He untied her hands from behind her back and, turning her roughly, almost as though she might have been a slave, retied them before her body, leaving a long loose end which might serve as a tether. She gasped with indignation and, lying on her side, looked at him with anger. He then untied her ankles and threw her from the raft. He led her by the bound wrists, she stumbling in her robes, about the raft and tied the tether on her hands to the sternpost of the canoe. The tether was some seven feet in length. She stood in the water, in the muddied robes. The water was to her hips. She was slender and about five and a half feet tall.

"Let us untie the two slaves," said Kisu. "They may aid us in paddling."

I unbound the two white girls and knelt them, frightened, in the canoe. They were bare-breasted. About their throats and left ankles were coils of white, pierced shells. About their thighs, now muddied, were brief, wrap-around skirts of red-and-black-printed rep-cloth, suitable garments for slaves. I thrust a paddle into the hands of each.

"We must make haste," said Ayari, taking a position forward in the canoe.

The two girls, one behind the other, knelt behind him. I knelt, paddle in hand, behind the second slave, she who had once been Janice Prentiss. She was attractive. I was pleased that I had taken her.

Behind me, also with a paddle, was Kisu. We had placed weapons in the canoe, the shields and stabbing spears from the two askaris, and some spears and another shield, from the raiders.

Tende screamed, and we turned about. We saw the body of one of the raiders, seized in the jaws of a tharlarion, pulled beneath the surface. It had been drawn to the area

270

probably by the smell of blood in the water, or by following other forms of marine life, most likely the bint or blue grunt, who would have been attracted by the same stimulus. It is not unusual for tharlarion to follow bint and grunt. They form a portion of its diet. Also they lead it sometimes to larger feedings.

Kisu and I, the girls following, lowered our paddles into the water, and moved the canoe eastward.

Tende, tethered to the sternpost, stumbled after us. Looking back I saw two more tharlarion nearby.

I then again lowered the paddle into the marsh.

Some forty yards behind I could now hear the water churning. The tharlarion, when it takes large prey, such as tabuk or tarsk, or men, commonly drags the victim beneath the surface, where it drowns. It then tears it to pieces in the bottom mud, engorging it, limb by limb.

"Please, Kisu," begged Tende, "let me enter the canoe."

But he did not respond to her. He did not even look at her.

"I cannot wade in these robes!" she wept. "Please, Kisu!"

She stumbled and fell, and was, for a moment, under the surface, but the tether on her wrists pulled her again to the surface and, moaning, she regained her feet and staggered to again follow us.

I looked back again to the vicinity of the mud raft. I saw one body move as though leaping out of the water and then saw that it was caught in the jaws of two rearing tharlarion, who fought for it. Each would keep part of it.

I saw four more tharlarion, low on the surface, eyes and nostrils above the surface, knifing toward the feast.

"Kisu!" wept Tende. "Please, Kisu!"

But he did not look at her.

We continued with our paddling.

"It will be only a matter of time, Kisu," I said, in Gorean, "until the tharlarion have fed and there is no more there. Some may then follow a scent in the water, that of sweat and fear."

"Of course," said Kisu, not looking back.

I glanced back once at Tende. She was looking back over her shoulder.

I then continued with my paddling. We did not set a harsh pace. The girl must be able to keep up. And we must not move so swiftly that the tharlarion might become confused or lose the scent.

"Kisu," cried the girl. "Take me into the canoe!"

But, again, he did not speak to her.

"Kisu!" she cried. "I cannot wade in these robes!"

"Do you wish me to remove them from you?" asked Kisu.

"Were you not once fond of me, Kisu?" she called.

"You are the daughter of my hated enemy, Aibu," said Kisu, coldly.

"Why will you not take me into the canoe?" she asked.

"You are where the tharlarion can take you, within my sight," he said.

"No!" she screamed. "No! No!"

"Ah, but, yes, my dear Tende," he said.

"Please, Kisu!" she begged. "Please!"

"I hear but the voice of the proud free woman, Tende, daughter of my hated enemy, Aibu," said Kisu.

She began to weep. She tried to approach the canoe more closely but Kisu, as she would approach, would, with a powerful stroke, move the canoe more swiftly forward, keeping her at the length of the tether. Once he let her approach the stern but, as she reached out with her bound hands, he, with the paddle, thrust her back. She stood there in the water. He then again moved the canoe forward. Again she followed at the length of her tether.

"Please, Kisu," she begged.

But, again, he did not respond to her.

We paddled on, not speaking, for a quarter of an Ahn.

"Look," said Ayari, after a time, looking back.

"Are they there now?" asked Kisu.

"Yes," said Ayari, "four of them, tharlarion."

Tende looked back over her shoulder.

At first I could not discern them. Then, because of the subtle movement of the water, I saw them. Their bodies, except for their eyes and nostrils, and some ridges on their backs, as they swam, were submerged.

They were about eighty yards away. They did not hurry, but moved with the fluid menace of their kind.

We stopped the canoe.

Tende, lower in the water than we, then saw them.

"Kisu!" she screamed. "Take me into the canoe!"

"You are where I want you," he said, "where the tharlarion may take you, within my sight."

"No!" she screamed. "No! No, please! No, please!"

"I hear the voice of the proud free woman, Tende," said Kisu, "who is the daughter of my hated enemy, Aibu."

"No," she wept, "no!"

"Then what voice is it that I hear?" inquired Kisu.

"The voice of a helpless female slave," cried Tende, "who begs her master to spare her life!"

"You are pretending to be a slave," said Kisu.

"No," she cried, "no! I am a true slave!"

The four tharlarion were now some twenty yards away. They, sensing the static position of their prey, slowed their approach.

"In your heart?" asked Kisu.

"Yes, yes, Master!" she cried.

"A natural and rightful slave?" he asked.

"Yes, I am a natural and rightful slave!" she cried.

The tharlarion stopped swimming now; they drifted toward her. This has the effect of minimizing the pressure waves projected before their bodies, an effect that might otherwise alert a wary, but unsuspecting prey. With tiny backward movements of their short legs they then became motionless, watching her.

"What is your name?" asked Kisu.

"Whatever Master pleases," she wept. The answer was suitable.

"Do you beg slavery?" he asked.

"Yes, yes, Master!" she cried.

"Perhaps I shall consider it, Girl," said he.

"Please, Master!" she cried.

With a tiny, almost imperceptible movement, the tiniest motion of their short legs, the four tharlarion, almost ringing the girl, seemed to drift again toward her, like half-submerged, meaningless logs, save for the methodicality of their convergence. There would then be a sudden lunge, and the snapping of the great jaws, the fighting for the prey.

"Master!" cried Tende.

Kisu, suddenly, reached out and, seizing the girl by the bound wrists, she screaming, wrenched her bodily in a shower of water across the thwart of the canoe.

At the same time, sensing the sudden movement of the prey, the four tharlarion, lashing the water with their tails, cut toward her. Two of them struck toward the stern of the canoe. Another uttered an explosive cry, half grunt, half bellow, which, in rage and frustration, sounded across the marsh. The fourth, jaws distended, more than a yard in width, attacked the side of the canoe. I beat it back with the paddle.

The canoe began to tip backward as another tharlarion

clambered, half out of the water, onto its stern. Kisu thrust at it with his paddle. It bit the paddle in two. The girls, clinging to the thwarts, screamed. Ayari moved toward the bow of the canoe, half standing, to try to balance the weight. With the splintered handle of the paddle Kisu jabbed at the tharlarion. It slipped back off the stern. The canoe struck with a crash in the water, nearly capsizing. Another tharlarion struck at the side of the canoe with its snout. I heard wood crack, but not break. It turned, to use its tail. Another tharlarion slipped beneath the canoe.

"Move the canoe!" cried Kisu. "Do not let them under it!"

I thrust at the water with the paddle, and then, as the tharlarion began to surface under the slender vessel, pushed down at it. The canoe slipped off its back, and righted itself. Ayari, seizing one of the paddles, and I, then moved the canoe forward.

The tharlarion were quick to follow, snapping and bellowing. Kisu, with the splintered paddle handle, thrust back one of them.

Then I saw a handful of dried fish fly into the maw of one of the beasts. Ayari, his paddle discarded, was reaching into the cylindrical basket of dried fish, torn open, which had been among the supplies of the canoe. He hurled more fish to another tharlarion, which, with a snapping, popping noise, clamped shut its jaws on the salty provender. He similarly threw fish to the other two beasts.

"Hand me another paddle," I said to the first girl in the canoe. She was crouching, trembling, head down, in the bottom of the canoe.

"Perform, Slave," I said.

"Yes, Master," she whispered. She handed the paddle back to the blond-haired barbarian who, half in shock, numb, handed it back to me. She looked at me, frightened, and then looked away. I think she knew that she again belonged to me. I pulled the paddle from her fingers and passed it back to Kisu, who took it calmly. Kisu and I then began to propel the canoe eastward. Tende, wrists bound beneath her body, lay shuddering between Kisu and myself, in the bottom of the canoe. Ayari then threw bits of fish into the water, where the tharlarion must swim to them, to obtain them. He threw successive tidbits further and further away, behind the canoe. Then he scattered several scraps of fish at one time, in an arc behind the tharlarion. Kisu and I continued to propel the canoe from the vicinity. The tharlarion, distracted and feeding, did not follow.

After a quarter of an Ahn Kisu laid aside his paddle. He put Tende to her back, crouching beside her. He untied her hands.

She looked up at him.

"It is right, is it not," he asked, "to enslave a rightful and natural slave?"

"Yes, Master," she said.

He then, gently, removed her clothing.

"You are beautiful," he said.

"A girl is pleased, if Master is pleased," she said.

"It is too bad you are only a slave," he said.

"Yes, Master," she said.

I then removed the white shells and cord from the throat and left ankle of the blond-haired barbarian, and snapped the two cords in half. I then retied shells on her throat and left ankle. The two remaining pieces of cord, with their shells, I gave to Kisu. He then tied them on the throat and left ankle of Tende.

"You have ornamented me as a slave, Master," said Tende.

"It is fitting, Slave," said Kisu.

"Yes, Master," she said.

She then saw her clothing, with the exception of a silken strip, a foot in width and some five feet in length, ripped from an undergarment, dropped overboard into the marsh. Kisu carefully folded the silken strip into small squares and slipped it between his waist and his loincloth's twisted-cloth belt. It could serve her as a brief, wrap-around skirt, similar to those of the other girls, if he later saw fit to clothe her.

"Your slave lies naked before you, Master," said Tende.

"I have always desired you, Tende," he said.

She lifted her arms to him.

"You are a slave, aren't you, Tende?" he asked.

"Yes, Master," she said. She put her arms down. She looked up at him.

"Since I was a little girl," she said, "I wanted to be your slave. But I never thought you would be strong enough to make me your slave."

"In Ukungu," he said, "it was not possible." He looked down at her, his hands hard on her arms. "Here," he said, "it is possible."

"Here," she said, "it is reality." Then she winced, for his

275

hands, in his desire, tightened more upon her arms. "Oh," she said, "you're hurting me."

"Be silent, Slave," he said.

"Yes, Master," she said.

He looked at her, fiercely. She could not meet his eyes. I think she had not known before that a man could so desire her. She had not before been a slave.

"I name you 'Tende'," he said.

"Yes, Master," she said, now wearing that name like a collar, it having been put upon her as a slave name.

"To whom do you belong?" he asked.

"You, Master," she said.

"Do you think you will have an easy slavery with me?" he asked.

"No, Master," she said.

"You are right," he said. "Your slavery will be a full slavery."

"I desire no other," she said, turning her head to face him. I could smell the heat of her. "Are you now going to claim me, as your slave?" she asked. They seemed oblivious of the others in the canoe. Yet had they not been, it would have made no difference, for the girl was only a slave.

"I claim you, Tende," said he, "as my slave."

"Are you going to take the rights of the Master?" she asked.

"When, and as I please," he said.

"Yes, Master," she said. "Oh!" she said, forced down, roughly, in the canoe.

"I claim you, Tende, daughter of my hated enemy, Aibu," he said, "as my slave, and now, for the first time, I assert over you the full and uncompromising rights of my mastery."

"Yes, Master," she said. "Yes, Master."

Ayari and I, and the two bare-breasted, lovely white slaves, property girls, each of us now with a paddle, not speaking, propelled the long canoe quietly eastward.

25

WE REACH THE SILL;
I AM NOT PLEASED WITH
A SLAVE

"Look," said Ayari, in the bow of the long canoe, pointing forward.

"At last," said Kisu, in the stern, resting his paddle.

The two white slaves, kneeling one behind the other, before me, lifted their paddles from the water, laying them across the sides of our narrow vessel.

Behind me, directly, before Kisu, Tende withdrew her paddle, too, from the water. Kisu kept her in the canoe immediately before him. He wanted her within his reach. She knew herself constantly under his scrutiny. She dared not shirk, no more than the other slaves, in the heavy work set her. More than once Kisu had struck her across the shoulders with his broad-bladed, ornately carved paddle when she, weary, arms aching, had faltered in the rhythm of the stroke.

We had come to the sill, that place where the marsh gives way to the waters of Ngao.

Kisu and I slipped into the water and, wading, slipping in the mud, thrust and hauled the canoe forward.

Then the marsh reeds parted and I saw, before us, sparkling in the sun, broad and shining, the waters of Lake Ngao.

"How beautiful it is," breathed the blond-haired barbarian, in English.

It had taken us fifteen days to reach the sill.

We had lived by spear fishing, and drinking the fresh water of the marsh.

The sun shone on the wide, placid waters.

Shaba, I recalled, had been the first of civilized men, or outlanders, to have seen this sight.

"It is beautiful," I thought to myself. Unfortunate, I thought, that the first civilized person to have seen this sight had been the treacherous Shaba.

"Ukungu," said Kisu, "lies to the northeast, on the coast."
Ukungu was a country of coast villages, speaking the same or

277

similar dialects. It was now claimed as a part of the expanding empire of Bila Huruma.

"You are no longer welcome there," I said to Kisu.

"True," said he.

"Is it your intention to return," I asked, "in an attempt to foment rebellion?"

"That is not a portion of my current plan," he said.

"What is your current plan?" I asked.

"I shall speak to you of it later," he said.

"I am seeking one called Shaba," I said, "one with whom I have business to conclude. My task takes me to the Ua."

"I, too," smiled Kisu, "am on my way to the Ua River."

"That is a part of your plan?" I asked.

"Yes," he said, "it is a part of my plan."

"I myself," I said, "may perhaps find it necessary to enter upon the Ua River itself."

"I, too, may find that necessary," he said.

"The country of the Ua, I suspect," I said, "is a perilous country."

"I am counting on that," said Kisu.

"Is that, too," I asked, "in accord with the plan you guard so secretively?"

"It is," grinned Kisu.

"Are you familiar with the Ua?" I asked.

"No," said Kisu. "I have never seen it."

I steadied the canoe. It floated free now, fully, at the outer edge of the Ngao waters.

"Let us be on our way," I said.

Kisu, the water now again to his thighs, reached into the canoe. He took a narrow, short length of leather and bound Tende's wrists, tightly, behind her body. He then, similarly, crossing them and lashing them together, secured the girl's ankles.

"Why does my Master bind me?" she asked, kneeling helplessly in the canoe.

"I do not expect to see canoes of Ukungu," said Kisu, "but if we do, you will, thus bound, perhaps not be tempted to leap into the water and swim to safety."

"Yes, Master," she said, putting her head down.

"These other slaves, too," I said, "might be tempted to seek an easier slavery within the collar of the empire."

"Let us then discourage them, too, from foolish thoughts of escape," said Kisu.

278

I then bound the other two girls as Kisu had bound Tende. We then, with two long lengths of leather, fastened them, all three, together, one strap putting them in throat coffle, the other in left-ankle coffle.

"Do not tie me with white slaves, Master," begged Tende, but Kisu laughed at her, and it was done to her.

Kisu and I re-entered the canoe and took up our paddles. We then set forth, paddling calmly, on the broad, shining waters of Ngao.

We paid no attention to Tende, who was weeping with the degradation which had been inflicted upon her.

The proud daughter of Aibu, high chief of the Ukungu district, was now well learning that she was only a slave.

"You there," I said, "crawl to my arms."

I lay in the canoe, on one elbow, under the moons of Gor, the canoe like a tiny bit of wood in the vastness of the shimmering lake.

"Yes, Master," she said.

The blond-haired barbarian, her body pale in the light of the moons, carefully, moved toward me. I heard the shells about her neck click softly together.

"Nestle," I told her.

"Yes, Master," she said. She nestled obediently in the crook of my left arm.

We had kept the girls in high-security ties only for the first two days upon Ngao. Then we had been far out on the lake, much farther away from the shores than any canoe would be likely to travel. After the first two days we had, for another two days, kept them merely in left-ankle and throat coffle. On the fifth day they were merely in throat coffle. On the sixth day we had relieved them of even that bond.

"Kiss me," I said.

She did so. And then she lay with her head on my left shoulder.

"You are frightened," I said. She had lost much ground since Schendi. "Do you not remember the beautiful girl you saw in the mirror, in Schendi?" I asked.

"She was a slave," whispered the girl.

"Of course," I said.

"I fear her," she said.

"She is the slave beauty within you," I said. "Indeed, she is the true you, glimpsed but for an instant, your true self, seen but for a moment, begging to be freed."

279

"I dare not free her," she said. "She is too beautiful, and sensuous."

"You do not dare to be what you are?" I asked.

"No," she said. "If that is what I am, I dare not be it."

"Why?" I asked.

"It is too beautiful, and sensuous, and helpless and yielding."

"And yet, in your heart," I said, "you ache to be it."

"No," she said, "no."

I said nothing.

"I am in conflict," she said, miserably.

"Resolve the conflict," I told her. "Free the slave within you, she who is suppressed, your true self."

"No, no," she said, pressing her cheek against my shoulder. I felt tears.

"You will never achieve happiness," I told her, "until you have acknowledged her."

"No," she whispered.

"She must be freed," I said, "that lovely girl, the slave, yearning for a collar within you, your truest and deepest self."

"I dare not free her," she said.

"Is honesty so terrible?" I asked.

"A woman must have dignity," she said.

"Are self-deceit, and lies and hypocrisy, so noble?" I inquired.

"I dare not free the slave," she said.

"Why not?" I asked.

"I fear that I may be she," she whispered.

"You are she," I said.

"No, no," she whispered.

"Yes," I said.

"I am not a Gorean girl," she said.

"The women of Earth, collared and broken to the whip," I said, "make superb slaves."

"Oh," she said, as I touched her.

"You are dry and tight," I told her.

"Forgive me, Master," she said, bitterly.

"You are not now on Earth," I told her. "Here no one will chide you for being lovely and sensuous. Here you need not feel guilty for being loving and feminine."

"I am not a Gorean slut," she said.

"Do you think that I am patient?" I asked.

"If Master wishes to use his girl, please do so," she said, "and then let me crawl back to my place."

I took her head between my hands.

"Please, you're hurting me," she said.

"Do you think that I am patient?" I asked.

"I am ready to obey, Master," she said, tensely, frightened.

"Do you think that I am patient?" I asked holding her.

"I do not know, Master," she whispered, strained.

"There is a time to be patient, and a time not to be patient," I said.

"Yes, Master," she said.

"Beware," I said, "of the time when I decide not to be patient."

"Yes, Master," she said.

I released her.

She lay on her side in the canoe, her body tense, beside me. "Do you want me now, Master?" she asked, frightened.

"No," I told her. "Return to your place."

"Yes, Master," she said. She crawled back to her place.

I lay on my back, looking up at the stars, and the moons.

I heard her fingernails dig at the wood of the canoe. She had been a rejected slave.

26

WE ENTER UPON THE UA; WE HEAR DRUMS

The blond-haired barbarian dipped her paddle into the water, and drew it backwards.

"Is the lake endless?" she asked.

"No," I said.

We had been twenty days upon the lake, living by fishing, drinking its water.

I could see brownish stains in the lake. I could smell flowers. Somehow, the mouth of the Ua must lie ahead.

"Do you carry slaves into danger?" asked the blond-haired barbarian.

"Yes," I told her.

She trembled, but did not lose the stroke of the paddle. She had tried to speak to me at various times during the past few days, but I had responded little to her, usually confining my responses to curt utterances. Once I had gagged her, with her own hair, and leather.

She continued to paddle, miserably, knowing herself to be in disfavor with her master.

"Surely, by now," said Ayari, speaking from the bow, "we must be near the Ua."

"Observe the water," said Kisu. "Smell the flowers and the forest. I think that already we may be within its mouth."

I was startled. Could its mouth be so wide? Already we were perhaps within the Ua.

Kisu pointed overhead. "See the mindar," he said.

We looked up and saw a brightly plumaged, short-winged, sharp-billed bird. It was yellow and red.

"That is a forest bird," said Kisu.

The mindar is adapted for short, rapid flights, almost spurts, its wings beating in sudden flurries, hurrying it from branch to branch, for camouflage in flower trees, and for drilling the bark of such trees for larvae and grubs.

"Look!" said Ayari, pointing off to the left.

There we saw a tharlarion, sunning itself on a bar. As we neared it it slipped into the water and swam away.

"We are within the river," said Kisu. "I am sure of it."

"The lake is dividing," said Ayari.

"No," laughed Kisu, pleased. "That is an island in the river. There will doubtless be many of them."

"Which way shall we go?" I asked.

"Go to the right," said Kisu.

"Why?" I asked. I am English. It seemed to me more natural to pass on the left. That way, of course, one's sword arm faces the fellow on the other side of the road who might be passing you. Surely it is safer to keep a stranger on your right. Goreans generally, incidentally, like the English, I am pleased to say, keep to the left of a road. They, too, you see, are a sensible folk. They do this, explicitly, for reasons quite similar to those which long ago presumably prompted the English custom, namely, provision for defense, and the facilitation, if it seems desirable, of aggression. Most Goreans, like most men of Earth, are right-handed. This is natural, as almost all Goreans seem to be derived from human stock. In Gorean, as in certain Earth languages, the same word is used for both stranger and enemy.

"In entering a village on the Ngao coast," said Kisu, "one always enters on the right."

282

"Why is that?" I asked.

"One thus exposes one's side to the blade of the other," said Kisu.

"Is that wise?" I asked.

"How better," asked Kisu, "to show that one comes in peace?"

"Interesting," I said. But, for my part, I would have felt easier in passing to the left. What if the other fellow does not desire peace? As a warrior I knew the value of an eighth of an Ihn saved in turning the body.

"Thus," said Kisu, "if there are men in these countries, and their customs resemble those of the Ngao villages, and Ukungu, we shall make clear to them our peaceful intentions. This may save us much trouble."

"That sounds intelligent to me," I said. "If there are men in these countries, they may then be encouraged to leave us alone."

"Precisely," said Kisu.

"And we might, of course, if need be," I said, "bring the canoe about."

"Yes," said Kisu.

We then took the canoe to the right. In half of an Ahn the island was on our left. It was pasangs in length.

"I do not even think there are men in these countries," said Ayari. "We are too far to the east."

"You are probably right," said Kisu.

It was then that we heard the drums.

"Can you read the drums?" I asked.

"No," said Ayari.

"Kisu?" I asked.

"No," he said, "but doubtless they are announcing our arrival."

27

THE FISHING VILLAGE;
A SLAVE BEGS TO BE TOUCHED;
AYARI ACQUIRES INFORMATION

They were scampering about on the scaffolding, it extending far out into the river. We could understand little of what they said. From the scaffolding, a double row of peeled logs, about ten feet apart, with numerous connecting bars and crossbars, fastened together with vines, more than a hundred yards in length, extending out into the flowing waters, hung numerous vine ropes, attached to which were long, conical, woven baskets, fish traps.

"Away! Away!" screamed one of the men, first in Ushindi and then in Ukungu. He, and others, waved their arms aversively. There were only men and male children on the scaffolding. Back on the shore, almost invisible in the jungle, were the huts of the village. On the palm-thatched roofs of these huts, in rows, exposed to the sun, were drying fish. We could see women on the shore, some with bowls, come out to the edge of the river to see what was occurring.

"Go away!" cried the fellow in Ukungu and Ushindi.

"We are friends!" called Ayari, speaking in Ushindi.

"Go away!" screamed the fellow again, this time in Ushindi. He was, we gathered, the village linguist. Other men, too, some eight or nine of them, and some seven or eight boys, of various ages, came out farther on the platform, balancing themselves expertly over the flowing waters, to bid us be on our way.

"I would know," I said, "if Shaba came this way, and how long ago."

More than one of the men now drew forth knives and threatened us.

"They are not overly friendly," observed Ayari.

"This is not good," said Kisu. "We could use supplies, bush knives and trade goods."

"With what will you purchase them?" I asked.

"You have the golden chain, given to you by Bila Huruma," he said.

I touched the chain. "Yes," I said, "that is true."

I lifted the chain from my neck and displayed it to the men on the long scaffolding.

They continued to encourage us to be on our way.

"It is no use," said Ayari.

Even the children were screaming at us, imitating their elders. To them, of course, objectively, I supposed it made no difference whether we came ashore or not. This was the first settlement we had come to on the river. It lay only an Ahn beyond the first island, one of several, we had encountered.

"Let us continue on our way," said Kisu.

I heard a sudden scream, that of a boy, and, looking about, saw one of the lads, some eight years in age, tumble from the scaffolding. He began almost immediately to be washed downstream. Without thinking I dove into the water. When I surfaced I heard Kisu calling out to turn the canoe. I stroked quickly after the boy, moving swiftly in the current. Then I was to where I thought, given my speed, he should be, or to where I thought I might be able to see him. He was not there. A few moments later the canoe glided beside me.

"Do you see him?" I called out to Ayari.

"He is safe," said Ayari. "Come into the canoe."

"Where is he?" I asked, crawling dripping over the bulwark of the light vessel.

"Look," said Kisu.

I looked back, and, to my surprise, saw the lad half shinnied up one of the poles of the scaffolding. He was grinning.

"He swims like a fish," said Ayari. "He was never in danger."

None of the men, I noted, had leapt from the platform. Yet the boy had screamed. Yet he had seemed to be washed downstream, apparently in jeopardy of being carried away by the current.

One of the men on the platform gestured for us to come closer. He had sheathed his jagged-edged knife, a fisherman's knife. We paddled closer. As we did so he helped the lad climb up to the surface of the scaffolding. I saw that both the men and boys stood upon it, and moved upon it, with a nimble, sure footing. They were less likely to fall from it, I realized, than an Earthling to tumble from one of his sidewalks. They knew it intimately and conducted the business of their livelihood upon it for hours a day.

285

The lad, and others, were grinning at us. One of the men, perhaps his father, patted him on the head, congratulating him. He had played his part well.

"Come ashore," said one of the men in Ushindi, he who had earlier used this language, and Ukungu as well. "You would have saved the boy," he said. "It is thus clear that you are our friends. Be welcome here. Come ashore, our friends, to our village."

"It was a trick," said Kisu.

"Yes," I said.

"But a nice trick," said Ayari.

"I do not like to be tricked," said Kisu.

"Perhaps, on the river," I said, "one cannot be too careful."

"Perhaps," said Kisu.

We then guided the canoe about the platform and made for shore.

We tied the hands of the three girls behind them, and sat them in the dirt.

We were within a stick-sided, palm-thatched hut in the fishing village. A small fire in a clay bowl dimly illuminated the interior of the hut. There were shelves in the hut, of sticks, on which were vessels and masks.

Individual tethers ran from the bound wrists of each girl to a low, stout, sunken slave post at one side of the hut.

There had been much singing and dancing. It was now late. Kisu and I sat opposite one another, across the clay bowl with its small fire.

"Where is Ayari?" I asked Kisu.

"He remains with the chief," said Kisu. "He is not yet satisfied."

"What more does he wish to learn?" I asked.

"I am not sure," said Kisu.

We had learned that three boats, with more than one hundred and twenty men, several in blue tunics, had passed this village several days ago. They had not stopped.

We were far behind Shaba and his men.

"Master," said Tende.

"Yes," said Kisu.

"We are naked," she said.

"Yes," said Kisu.

"You traded the bit of silk you had permitted me to wear

286

about my hips," she said. "You traded the shells about my throat. You traded even the shells about my ankle."

"Yes," said Kisu. The shells and silk, interestingly, had been of considerable value to these fishermen. The shells were from Thassa islands and their types were unknown in the interior. Similarly silk was unknown in the interior. The shells from about the throats and ankles of all the girls, of course, had been traded. We had also traded, of course, the strips of red-and-black-printed rep-cloth from about the hips of the two blond slaves. We had retained the golden chain which I wore, which had been a gift of Bila Huruma. It might be useful, we speculated, at a later date. In civilization, of course, it had considerable value. Here we did not know if it would have more value than metal knives or coils of copper wire. The results of our trading had been two baskets of dried fish, a sack of meal and vegetables, a length of bark cloth, plaited and pounded, from the pod tree, dyed red, a handful of colored, wooden beads, and, most importantly, two pangas, two-foot-long, heavy, curve-bladed bush knives. It was the latter two implements in which Kisu had been most interested. I did not doubt but what they might prove useful.

"I am not pleased, Kisu," said Tende.

He leaped across the fire bowl toward her and savagely struck her head to the left with a fierce blow of the flat of his hand.

"Did you dare to speak my name, Slave?" he asked.

She lay at his feet, on her side, terrified, blood at her mouth, her wrists bound behind her, the line on them taut to the slave post. "Forgive me, Master," she cried. "Forgive me, Master!"

"I see it was a mistake to have permitted you any decoration or clothing whatsoever, proud slave," he said.

"Forgive me, Master," she begged. It was true that a slave may wear in the way of cosmetics, clothing or ornament only what the master sees fit to permit her. Sometimes, of course, this is nothing.

"I see another item," said Kisu, angrily, "which might perhaps be traded in the morning, before we leave the village."

"What?" she asked.

"It lies at my feet," he said.

"No, Master!" she cried.

"I wonder what you would bring in trade," he mused.

"Do not trade me, Master," she begged. She might, of

287

course, be traded as easily as a sack of meal or a knife, or a bit of cloth, or a tarsk or vulo. She was a slave.

"You are not much good as a slave," he said.

"I will try to be better," she said, struggling to her knees. "Let me please you tonight. I will give you pleasures you did not know exist. I will so please you that in the morning you will not wish to trade me."

"It will not be easy," said he, "—with your hands tied behind you."

She looked at him, frightened.

He loosened her tether from the slave post and carried her, wrists still bound behind her back, to the side of the hut. He put her on her knees there and then, indolently, lay down, on one elbow, between her and the stick wall of the hut. He looked at her.

"Yes, Master," she said, and then, piteously, as a slave, addressed herself to his pleasure.

I sat beside the clay bowl with its small, glowing fire, thinking. In the morning, early, we must be again on our way. With a tiny stick I prodded the fire. Shaba was far ahead of us. Why, I wondered, had he fled to the Ua. With the ring he might have slipped to a thousand more secure safeties on the broad surface of Gor. Yet he had chosen the dangerous, unknown route of the Ua. Did he think men would fear to pursue him upon its lonely waters, penetrating such a lush, perilous, mysterious region? Surely he must know that I, and others, to seek the ring, would follow him even into the steaming, flower-strewn wilderness of the Ua. He had, I conjectured, made a serious mistake, a misjudgment surprising in one of so subtle a mind.

"Master," I heard, softly.

I turned.

The first blond-haired girl, not she who had been Janice Prentiss, whom I have referred to as the blond-haired barbarian, knelt at the end of her tether, her wrists extended behind her, bound, their line taut to the slave post. This was she who had, with the blond-haired barbarian, been purchased as one of the matched set of serving slaves which Bila Huruma had given to Tende, among her other companionship gifts. This girl was also blond and barbarian, also clearly, given her accent, her teeth, which contained two fillings, and a vaccination mark, of Earth origin. She, too, like the blond-haired barbarian, bore on her left thigh the common Kajira mark of Gor.

"Master," said the first girl. The blond-haired barbarian, her wrists tied behind her, tethered to the same post, sat nearby, angrily, in the dirt.

"Yes?" I said.

"I crawl to the end of my tether, where I kneel before you," she said.

"Yes?" I said.

She put down her head. "I beg your touch," she said.

I heard the blond-haired barbarian, near her, gasp in indignation.

I could hear the sounds of pleasure, from Kisu and Tende, at the side of the hut.

The kneeling girl lifted her head, regarding me. "I beg your touch," she said. "My need is much on me."

Again I heard the blond-haired barbarian gasp, but this time in amazement. She could not believe that she had heard a woman admit to sexual desire. Did the other slut not know that this was something that no woman must do! Was it not sufficiently horrifying even to experience sexual desire, without admitting the fact?

"Slave!" chided the blond-haired barbarian. "Slave! Slave!"

"Yes, slave," said the first girl to her. "Please, Master," she said to me.

I went near to her, but not so near that she could touch me. "Please," she begged.

"You are a barbarian," I said to her.

"I am now a Gorean slave girl," she said.

"Are you not from a world called Earth?" I asked.

"Yes, Master," she said.

"How long have you been on Gor?" I asked.

"More than five years," she said.

"How did you come to Gor?" I asked.

"I do not know," she said. "I went to sleep one night in my own room on my own world. I awakened, perhaps days later, chained in a Gorean market."

I nodded. Gorean slavers usually keep their lovely prizes drugged enroute between worlds.

"What is your name?" I asked.

"Whatever Master wishes," she said.

"It is true," I said.

She smiled at me. "I have been owned by many men," she said. "I have had many names."

"What was your barbarian name?" I inquired.

"Alice," she said. "Alice Barnes."

"That is two names, is it not?" I asked.

"Yes, Master," she said. "'Alice' was my first name. 'Barnes' was my second name."

"'Alice'," I said, "is a slave name."

'So I have learned on this world," she said. "On my old world, however, it may also function as the name of a free woman."

"Interesting," I said.

She smiled. Feminine first names of Earth are often used on Gor as slave names. Sometimes they are even given to slave girls of Gorean origin. They tend to excite masters, and often improve a girl's price. The origin of the custom is probably a simple one. Most girls brought to Gor are brought as slaves. It is thus natural that their original names be regarded as the names of slaves. Many Goreans, even those educated to the second knowledge, that afforded the higher castes, find it hard to believe that the delicious Earth women who show up in their markets could possibly have been free on their native world. They are just too obviously marvelous slave meat. "If they were free, they should not have been," say many Goreans. "At any rate," they add, "they are now in the collar where they belong, and they will stay there!" It is true, incidentally, that a girl of Earth origin is almost never freed on Gor. They are on the whole just too wonderful, too desirable, to free. Perhaps one would have to be insane to free such a woman. Would it not be madness to let such beauties, kneeling before you, out of your collar? A Gorean saying, of the second knowledge, has it that a steel collar locked on the throat of an Earth woman is perfect. If you should be a female, and are reading this, and should be so unfortunate as to be taken to Gor as a slave, do not hope for freedom; rather learn your lessons swiftly and well, and resign yourself to the service of masters; fight your collar, if you wish, but in the end it will do you no good; you are slave.

"I name you 'Alice'," I said.

"Thank you, Master," she said.

"You wear the name now as a slave name," I said.

"I know," she said.

"Do you like it," I asked, "now wearing your old name, but now afresh, put upon you as a degraded slave name?"

"I love it," she said. "It is delicious. It makes me quiver with desire."

She strained at the tether, trying to reach me.

290

"It is said," I said, "that the women of Earth are natural slaves."

"It is true," she whispered.

"It is also said they are the lowest and most miserable of slaves, and are to be used as such."

"It is true, Master," she said. She looked down. "That has been well taught to me on Gor," she said. She looked up. "Please take me in your arms," she said. "I am an Earth woman who has been made a Gorean slave girl. You need not respect me as you might a Gorean woman and I am further only a slave. Do not respect me!"

"I do not," I told her.

"Thank you, Master," she said.

"I am an imbonded Earth woman," she said. "I am among the lowest and most miserable of slaves. Take me in your arms, I beg you, and treat me as such."

I took her in my arms.

"So use me that I fear that I may die, Master," she begged.

I thrust my lips to her throat, and she put her head back.

"Slave! Slave!" chided the blond-haired barbarian.

"Yes, slave!" wept the girl in my arms. I lowered her to the dirt. I stayed with her a long time. I did not, however, bother to untie her hands. I would only have had to retie them later.

The blond-haired barbarian turned away, bitterly. She lay on her side in the dirt. I heard her cry. Her small fists, behind her, were clenched in frustration.

I thought that, in a few days, it might well be she who would crawl kneeling to the end of her tether, her bound wrists extended behind her, the line taut to some slave post, and beg, perhaps weeping, the touch of a master.

It was late when Ayari returned to the hut.

The girls were asleep. Tende, when Kisu had finished with her, had been returned to her place. She now, too, like the other girls, lay sleeping in the dirt, her wrists tied behind her, tethered to the slave post.

"Did you learn more?" I asked.

"Others," said he, "than your Shaba and his followers have passed here. I learned this, finally, from the chief, and two of his men, with whom I spoke."

"They were reluctant to speak?" asked Kisu.

"Quite so," said Ayari. "They were frightened, even to speak of what they saw."

"What was it?" I asked.

"Things," said he.

"What sort of things?" I asked.

"They would not say," said Ayari. "They were too frightened." He looked at me. "But I fear that it is not we alone who seek your Shaba."

"Others pursue as well?" asked Kisu.

"I think so," said Ayari.

"Interesting," I said. I lay down beside the fire. "Let us get rest now," I said. "We must be on our way early in the morning."

28

THE BOX IN THE RIVER

"There!" said Ayari. "Bring the canoe to the right."

We turned the light vessel a quarter to starboard. "I see it," I said.

We were four days from the fishermen's village where we had been cordially received. In these four days we had passed two other villages, where farming was done in small clearings, but we had not stopped at either.

The river was generally two to four hundred yards wide at these points. At night we would pull the canoe ashore, camouflage it, and make our camp about a half pasang inland, to minimize any danger from possible tharlarion, which tend to remain near the water.

The box, about a foot wide and deep, and two feet long, floating, heavy, almost entirely submerged, with an ornate ring lock, rubbed against the side of the canoe. By its metal handles I drew it into the canoe. With the back of one of the heavy pangas I struck loose the ring lock. There were varieties of ring locks. This one was a combination padlock, in which numbers, inscribed on rotating metal disks, fitted together, are to be properly aligned, this permitting the free extraction of the bolt. This, as is the case with most single-alignment ring locks, was not a high-security lock. The materials in the box, I was confident, would not be of great value. The numbers on the lock were in Gorean. I thrust up the lid.

"Ah," said Kisu.

In the box, jumbled, were rolls of wire, mirrors, pins and knives, beads, shells and bits of colored glass.

"Trade goods," said Kisu.

"Doubtless from one of the vessels of Shaba," said Ayari.

"Doubtless," I agreed.

We put the goods in one of the sacks we had had and saved from the fishermen's village, and threw the broken lock and opened box again into the river.

"Let us proceed with caution," said Kisu.

"That seems to me wise," I said.

29

BARK CLOTH AND BEADS

We sat about the small fire, some half pasang inland from the river, in the rain forest.

A great spined anteater, more than twenty feet in length, shuffled about the edges of the camp. We saw its long, thin tongue dart in and out of its mouth.

The blond-haired barbarian crept closer to me.

"It is harmless," I said, "unless you cross its path or disturb it."

It lived on the white ants, or termites, of the vicinity, breaking apart their high, towering nests of toughened clay, some of them thirty-five feet in height, with its mighty claws, then darting its four-foot-long tongue, coated with adhesive saliva, among the nest's startled occupants, drawing thousands in a matter of moments into its narrow, tubelike mouth.

She drew a bit further away, trembling. She was a naked woman, and a slave, on the barbaric planet of Gor. Perhaps she did not relish being dependent on men, and their protection, for her very life, but she was, and she knew it.

We had brought certain goods with us from the canoe to our camp.

"Oh!" cried the girl, startled. A grasshopper, red, the size of a horned gim, a small, owllike bird, some four ounces in weight, common in the northern latitudes, had leaped near the fire, and disappeared into the brush.

293

She restrained herself from approaching me more closely. She put her head down, embarrassed.

Kisu, with a knife, was cutting a length from the rough, red-dyed cloth, plaited and pounded, derived from the inner bark of the pod tree, which we had obtained in trade some days ago at the fishermen's village. It has a cordage of bark strips resembling a closely woven burlap, but it is much softer, a result in part perhaps due to the fact that the dye in which it is prepared is mixed with palm oil. Tende was watching him closely.

I chuckled to myself.

"Do I amuse Master?" asked the blond-haired barbarian, irritably.

"I was thinking about this afternoon," I said.

"Oh," she said.

This afternoon, late, when we had come inland, almost in the dusk, she had become entangled in the web of a rock spider, a large one. They are called rock spiders because of their habit of holding their legs folded beneath them. This habit, and their size and coloration, usually brown and black, suggests a rock, and hence the name. It is a very nice piece of natural camouflage. A thin line runs from the web to the spider. When something strikes the web the tremor is transmitted by means of this line to the spider. Interestingly the movement of the web in the air, as it is stirred by wind, does not activate the spider; similarly if the prey which strikes the web is too small, and thus not worth showing itself for, or too large, and thus beyond its prey range, and perhaps dangerous, it does not reveal itself. On the other hand, should a bird, such as a mindar or parrot, or a small animal, such as a leaf urt or tiny tarsk, become entangled in the net the spider swiftly emerges. It is fully capable of taking such prey. When the blond-haired barbarian stumbled into the web, screaming, trying to tear it away from her face and hair, the spider did not even reveal itself. I pulled her away from the net and slapped her to silence. Curious, as she, sobbing, cleaned herself with leaves and saliva, I located the gentle, swaying strand which marked the location of the spider. It, immobile on the ground, was about a foot in diameter. It did not move until I nudged it with a stick, and it then backed rapidly away.

"You need not have struck me," she said reproachfully.

"Be silent, Slave," I said.

"Yes, Master," she said. That a slave has irritated one in

the least particular is, of course, more than enough reason for striking her. Indeed, one does not need a reason for striking a slave. One may do so at one's purest caprice. The girls know this. This helps in their discipline. In this particular instance, of course, aside from my irritation at her outburst, I did not want her cries to mark our position in the forest. We did not know who, or what, besides ourselves, might trek, perhaps at our side, in that lush habitat.

"Master," said the girl.

"Yes," I said.

"You need not have struck me, earlier this afternoon," she said. "But I suppose that you are the judge of that, for you are the Master," she added, airily.

I looked at her.

"Surely one needs a reason for striking a slave," she said.

"No," I said.

"I see," she said, putting her head down. She trembled.

"Come here," I said. "Kneel before me, back on your heels."

She did so, looking at me. "Master?" she asked.

Suddenly I struck her, a fierce blow which flung her, mouth bloodied, to her side in the dirt.

I stood up. "Do you see?" I asked.

"Yes, Master," she whispered, looking up at me, horrified.

"Now kneel before me and kiss my feet," I said, "and thank me for having struck you."

Tremblingly, she crawled to me, and knelt before me. She put her head down. I felt her lips on my feet. "Thank you for having struck me, Master," she whispered. She looked up at me.

"Do you now understand that you are a slave?" I asked.

"Yes, Master," she said.

"Do you still think that a master requires a reason to strike you?" I asked.

"No, Master," she said.

"And why is that?" I asked.

"Because I am a slave," she said.

"It is true," I said.

"Yes, Master," she said.

I then sat down again, cross-legged, and turned my attention to Kisu. He was displaying the strip of cloth, about a foot wide and five feet in length, to Tende.

I hoped that the blond-haired barbarian had learned her

lesson. It might help her to survive on Gor. A girl does not question what her master does to her. She is slave.

Tende knelt before Kisu and put her head to the dirt. "I beg clothing, Master," she said.

"Earn it," said he to her.

"Yes, Master," she said, eagerly, and then well did she earn it. When she was finished Kisu threw her the strip of cloth which she then, delightedly, wrapped about her hips, tucking it closed. He then, from a sack brought from the canoe, threw her two strings of colored wooden beads, blue, and red and yellow, which we had obtained in trade from the fishing village earlier.

"Thank you, my master," breathed Tende, and she then displayed herself before him, the brief bark cloth, scarlet, snug about her hips and the beads about her lovely throat.

"It is now time to tie you for the night," said Kisu.

"Yes, Master," she said.

The first blond, Alice, gazed enviously upon Tende. She then crept to me, head down. "I beg clothing, Master," she whispered.

I looked upon her.

"I am a humbled, naked slave," she said. "I beg clothing of my master."

"Are you prepared to earn it?" I asked her.

"Yes, Master," she said, smiling.

"Whore!" cried the blond-haired barbarian.

I took Alice in my arms, kissing her, and she put her head back, with her eyes closed.

"Whore! Whore!" cried the blond-haired barbarian.

"What do you think slave girls are for," laughed Alice, her eyes still closed, delightedly, "you silly girl?"

"Whore! Whore!" cried the blond-haired barbarian.

I kissed Alice. "Gather some wood for the fire. Build it up a little," I said to the blond-haired barbarian.

"Yes, Master," she said.

Alice looked up at me. "Your touch is masterful," she said. She smiled up at me. "The Earth woman yields to her Gorean master," she said.

The fire had now burned low.

It was some two Ahn before dawn.

Alice, her wrists bound now behind her, tethered by them to a tree, to which Tende lay similarly secured, lay asleep. About her hips was the wrap-around skirt, tucked shut, of scarlet bark cloth, which she had well earned. I had cut the skirt for her following her performance. I had also given her, as Kisu had Tende, two strings of wooden beads. They were attractive on her. She, too, now, like Tende, was a clothed, ornamented slave. Tende was asleep. So, too, were Ayari and Kisu.

I looked over to the blond-haired barbarian who sat by the fire. She poked at the fire with a green stick.

"Go sit by the slave post," I said to her, referring to that slim tree to which the other girls were secured, which served us as slave post, "and cross your wrists behind you."

She did so.

"Oh," she said, as I, with the end of a long, narrow strip of leather, fastened her wrists, tightly, together. I then tied the free end of the tether about the slave post, or tree, fastening her to it.

"Master," she said.

"Yes," I said.

"Am I not to be given clothing?" she asked.

"Are you ready to earn it?" I asked.

"If you command me," she said, "I must obey. I am slave."

"And if I do not command you?" I asked.

"Master?" she asked.

"Would you beg for the opportunity to earn clothing?" I asked.

"Never!" she said. "Never!"

"It is time now to go to sleep," I said.

"I want clothing," she said. "Please, Master!"

"Lie down," I said. "It is time to sleep."

She lay down on her side. "I cannot beg clothing," she sobbed. "I am an Earth woman."

"So, too, is Alice," I said.

"She is a slave," said the blond-haired barbarian.

"And you?" I asked.

"Yes," said the blond-haired barbarian, sobbing. "I, too, am a slave."

"Beg, if you wish," I said.

"I cannot," she wept.

"Go to sleep now," I said. "The day will be long and hard tomorrow."

"Master," she whispered.

"Yes," I said.

"You taught me a lesson this evening, did you not?"

"Perhaps," I said.

"That a master requires no reason, to put me under even the harshest of disciplines."

"That is true," I said.

"In your cruel way, are you not kind," she asked, "to a girl who is a slave?"

"Do you wish to be whipped?" I asked.

"No, Master," she said.

"Your slavery will be of little use to men," I said, "if you, through your ignorance, must be soon thrown alive to sleen or tharlarion."

"I see," she said, bitterly. "You are not kind."

"No," I said.

"You are merely training an animal to know her station in life."

"Yes," I said. I smiled. I resisted an impulse to tenderness. I resisted, too, an impulse to seize her fair ankles, turn her to her back by means of them, throw them apart, and then rape her in the dirt.

She struggled up to one elbow. She looked at me. "What do men want of a slave girl?" she asked.

"Everything," I told her.

She lay back in the dirt, miserably.

"Master," she said.

"Yes," I said.

"A man may do to me whatever he wants, at any time, may he not?" she asked.

"Yes," I said.

"He needs no reason," she said.

"No," I said.

"But a man, commonly," she asked, "would not hurt me or abuse me without a reason, would he?"

"He may do so, if he wishes," I said, "particularly in your training, but, of course, normally he would not do so. There would simply be no point to it. There are better things to do to a woman, once she is trained, than hurt her."

"If I please my master, he will not hurt me, will he?" she asked.

"He will, if it pleases him," I said.

"But if I am totally pleasing to him, fully, and as an abject slave girl," she pressed, "he will not be likely to be pleased to hurt me, will he?"

"No," I said, "of course not. You must understand, of course, that if you are displeasing in the least particular that

298

will be a sufficient reason for him to put you under whatever discipline he desires."

"I understand that, clearly," she said. "But I will try to be pleasing to my master."

"Totally pleasing, and fully, and as an abject slave girl?" I asked.

"Yes," she said, "I shall strive with all my might to be pleasing in that way to my master."

"Masters," I said.

She swallowed hard. "Yes, Masters," she said. She knew she might have many masters on Gor.

I saw that the slave girl in her was near the surface.

"Are you now ready," I asked, "to beg to earn your clothing?"

"I cannot do that," she said, horrified. I saw that the slave girl in her was again thrust back. Again the iron door of her prison, like a heavy hatch, was flung shut over her and the bolt thrust shut. The slave, lying on the narrow stairs, leading from her dungeon, wept. She pressed her small fingers against the damp wall to her left, and against the heavy iron door, bolted shut, obdurate above her, which confined her. The lovely slave lying on the narrow, damp steps, hidden beneath the iron door, shut out again from the sun, cried in the lonely, quiet darkness, her existence once again denied.

"Very well," I said. "Remain naked."

"Very well," she said. "I shall."

"You have had the opportunity to beg to earn clothing," I told her. "You refused it. It is possible that that opportunity may not be again offered."

She looked at me, frightened.

"Sleep now," I said.

"Yes, Master," she said.

I then went to sit by the small fire. I would watch for a time, and then awaken Kisu. In this fashion, he then taking the watch, I would have some sleep before dawn.

I was interested in the fauna of the river and the rain forest. I recalled, sunning themselves on exposed roots near the river, tiny fish. They were bulbous eyed and about six inches long, with tiny flipperlike lateral fins. They had both lungs and gills. Their capacity to leave the water, in certain small streams, during dry seasons, enables them to seek other streams, still flowing, or pools. This property also, of course, makes it possible for them to elude marine predators and, on the land, to return to the water in case of danger. Normally they remain quite close to the water. Sometimes they even sun themselves on the backs of resting or napping tharlarion. Should the tharlarion submerge the tiny fish often submerges with it, staying close to it, but away from its jaws. Its proximity to the tharlarion affords it, interestingly, an effective protection against most of its natural predators, in particular the black eel, which will not approach the sinuous reptiles. Similarly the tiny fish can thrive on the scraps from the ravaging jaws of the feeding tharlarion. They will even drive one another away from their local tharlarion, fighting in contests of intraspecific aggression, over the plated territory of the monster's back. The remora fish and the shark have what seem to be, in some respects, a similar relationship. These tiny fish, incidentally, are called gints.

I poked the fire.

I wondered if I should give the blond-haired barbarian an opportunity again to beg to perform, that she might earn a bit of cloth and a handful of beads. I would make that decision later.

"Kisu," I said. "Wake up. Take the watch."

He stirred himself and I lay down. I thought about the river, and was soon asleep.

30

WE MAKE FURTHER PROGRESS UPON THE RIVER

"Do not permit the canoe to be swept away!" screamed Kisu, straining to be heard over the rushing water.

We had been two weeks upon the Ua. We had come to another of its cataracts.

It is impossible to paddle against these currents as the river, descending rapidly, plunges in torrents among a jungle of rocks.

I and Kisu, and the blond-haired barbarian and Tende, waded beside the canoe, thrusting it ahead of us. On the shore, each with a rope, one extending from the bow, one from the stern, stumbled Ayari and Alice. Ayari held the bow rope and Alice the rope extending from the stern. We could port the canoe but only with great difficulty. It was an eight-man raiders' canoe.

"Do not lose your footing, Naked Slave!" cried Tende to the blond-haired barbarian.

"Yes, Mistress," she cried, over the water, struggling to remain upright.

We had made Tende first girl. She had been, after all, the former mistress of the two white slaves.

They would obey her with perfection. If they did not we would beat them. If Tende, for her part, did not do well as first girl Kisu and I had agreed that Alice should have the opportunity. Tende, we were sure, fearing to be at the mercy of one of her former slaves, would strive to be a good first girl.

Tende and Alice had taken to calling the blond-haired barbarian 'Naked Slave'. She had, among us, no other name. We had not given her one. Calling the blond-haired barbarian by that descriptive and accurate appellation made clear the distinction between her and the others. She was low girl. We all used her to fetch and carry, and perform the most servile of our tasks. The blond-haired barbarian would weep at night, but we paid her no attention, unless it be to order her to silence.

"Hold the lines!" called Kisu.

Ayari and Alice kept the lines taut.

"Push!" called Kisu.

We, wading, half blinded with water, thrust the canoe forward.

31

WE STOP TO TRADE; THE ADMISSIONS OF A SLAVE

"Trade! Trade! Friends! Friends!" they called.

"Do not take me in there, unclothed, Master," begged the blond-haired barbarian.

We had pulled the canoe up on the shore. I tied the blond-haired barbarian's hands behind her and put a rope on her neck, the loose end of which I threw to Alice. It would be more seemly, we had conjectured, if she, as she was not clothed as the other girls, was led in, like a stripped, recently

301

captured slave. It might tend to allay suspicion that she was not in favor. If that were known the bidding might be fierce upon her, the villagers being eager to capitalize on her dissatisfaction with her and acquire her as a cheap piece of trade goods, perhaps for transmittal into the interior. As it was, if she had been newly roped, we might not be willing to sell her, not yet having had an opportunity to truly determine whether or not she might have promise.

"How is it that you are coming from the west on the river with her?" asked a man who knew snatches of Ushindi.

I did not understand his question.

The blond-haired barbarian shuddered with misery, seeing the honesty of the men's eyes upon her.

"Is she a taluna?" asked a man.

I did not understand his question.

The blond-haired barbarian moaned in misery as the men's hands were upon her, some of them intimately. "Look," said a man crouching beside her, holding her leg, indicating her brand. This excited interest. They had never seen a brand on a woman before. Alice's brand was covered by her brief skirt of red bark cloth. Unnoticed she drew the skirt down an inch or so on her thigh, to better conceal her own slave mark. The blond-haired barbarian twisted in the grasp of the men. Her small hands pulled at the tightly looped, knotted strap that bound them behind her back. It was just as well, I realized, that we had tied her as we had. If she had tried to push away the villagers, or prevent them from touching her, they might have wanted her hands cut off. She cried out with anguish. I made a sign and we advanced, Alice pulling the blond-haired barbarian forward, away from the men.

We entered the gate of the village.

"Trade," I called. "Friends! Friends!"

Ayari was a remarkable man.

I doubt that anyone in the village knew more than a few dozen words of Ushindi, but Ayari, with his Ushindi, his gestures, his quick wit and a stick, with which he drew in the dust of the village, not only conducted his trading in a brisk and genial fashion but managed to gather valuable information as well.

"Shaba was here," said Ayari.

"When?" I asked.

"The chief says only 'long ago'," said Ayari. "Some of his men were ill. He stayed here a week."

"That explains," I said, "how it is that some here know some words of Ushindi."

"Of course," said Ayari, "and doubtless Shaba and his men set themselves to learn something of the speech of this village."

I nodded.

We had obtained in the trading, for some knives and colored glass, several sacks of meal, fruit and vegetables.

"Is there anything else?" I asked.

"Yes," grinned Ayari. "We are supposed to turn back."

"Why?" I asked.

"The chief says the river is dangerous beyond this point. He says there are hostile tribes, dangerous waters, great animals, monsters and talunas, white-skinned jungle girls." He indicated the blond-haired barbarian, kneeling, her hands tied behind her back, her neck-rope in the hands of Alice, who, in lovely repose, stood beside her. "He thought she might be one," he said. "I told him she was only an ordinary slave."

I looked at the blond-haired barbarian. "That is true," I said.

She put her head down.

"Shaba, did he not," I asked, "go upriver?"

"Yes," said Ayari.

"I, too, then," I said, "am going upriver."

"We all are," said Kisu.

I looked at him.

"It is part of my plan," he said.

"Your mysterious plan?" I asked.

"Yes," he smiled.

"Did the chief, or the others," I asked Ayari, "say anything about the 'things,' or whatever they were, which were mentioned at the fishing village, about which the fishermen were reluctant to speak."

"I asked them," said Ayari. "They have seen nothing out of the ordinary."

"Then we have lost them," said Kisu.

"Perhaps," I said.

"Shall we be on our way?" I asked.

"Of course not," said Ayari. "There is to be a feast tonight, and singing and dancing."

"Of course," I said.

That night, late, we slept in a hut in the village, within its

303

palisade. It was the first village we had come to on the river which was surrounded by a palisade.

I pondered on this. The river, eastward from this point, was said to become more dangerous.

I heard the blond-haired barbarian stirring. She, like the others, had her small hands tied behind her. A five-foot line, lying loosely behind her, ran from her bound wrists to the slave post, to which it tethered her. Through half-closed eyes, in the half-darkness, as moonlight filtered through the thatched roof and sides of the hut, I watched her struggle to her knees. She moaned, softly. On her knees, inch by inch, she moved toward me, until her wrists were extended behind her and she could approach no more closely. "I know that men are my masters," she whispered, so softly that I knew she did not speak to awaken me. Too, she spoke in English, which language, native to her, she did not believe any in the hut could understand. "I have learned that, incontrovertibly, on this natural world, though I think always, in my heart, I knew it to be true. I am yours, sweet master. Why do you not take me and use me, as the slave I am? You made me yield as a slave so absolutely in Schendi. Do you think I could have forgotten those sensations which you induced in me? Do you think a girl could ever forget those feelings, so rapturously, so helplessly overwhelming, those feelings which made me, a proud Earth woman, a helplessly submitting slave girl? I, a slave, long to lie again in the arms of my master. Why have you not again taken me in your arms? I long to serve you, Master. Am I not pleasing? What is it that you would have me do? Must I crawl to you, as the slave I am, and beg your touch? Do you not understand that I cannot admit men are my masters, for I am a woman of Earth? Do you not understand that I cannot crawl to you, as the slave I am, and beg your touch, for I am a woman of Earth?" She sobbed, softly, the tortured prisoner of her conditioning. "Why have the men of Gor not surrendered their natural dominance?" she asked. "Why have they remained strong and proud, joyful and mighty, and free, so unlike the men of my world? Have they not been taught that it is wrong for them to be true men, that it is wrong for them to fulfill themselves and be happy? Have they not been taught that frustration, and conflict and misery, is the proper condition of the human male, that he is to be approved only in so far as he subjects himself to external standards, foreign to his own nature, that he is to be praised only in so far as he denies himself to himself, that he must avoid at all costs satisfying genetic realities locked in every cell in his body? Is it truly better for a man to torture his system, inflicting guilt and fear upon it, inducing irregularities within it, and to die prematurely of a variety of loathsome diseases than to be happy? I do not know. I am only a woman. Why are the men of Gor different from those of Earth? Is it because poisoned minds were not brought to Gor? Is it that it is only a matter of chance, that on Earth and not Gor due to a chance dynamic or a particular situation, the consequences of which were not understood, civilization developed not as the expression, celebration and enhancement of nature, constituting a palace within which nature might thrive, but as its nemesis, its stunting foe? I do not know. Perhaps those they call Priest-Kings, if they exist, have been thoughtful in this respect. Or perhaps it is simply that the men of Gor, unlike the men of Earth, do not choose to unman themselves. Why should we do so, they might ask. And there is, I think, no answer to that question. The men of Gor, like beasts and loving gods, subject the women they own to their total mastery. It pleases them to do so. They are men. Should I be distressed, or displeased? Not truly, for I am a woman. I admire their honesty, that they scorn to conceal the sovereignty which is theirs by nature. They do not play games. They put me to their feet, where I belong. Should I be displeased? No, for I am a woman. Only where there are true men can there be true women. Whatever be the reasons, whether genetic or cultural, or both, the men of Gor are different from those of Earth. They have remained men, perhaps simply because it has pleased them to do so. This also pleases me because only where there are true men can there be true women." She put down her head.

I did not stir, but continued, through half-shut eyes, to regard her. In the filtered moonlight, in the hut, tethered to the slave post, she again lifted her head. "I did not know such men could exist," she whispered again, again in English, which language she used to express her most intimate thoughts, again so softly that she might not awaken me. She pulled toward me, on her knees, her wrists extended behind her, tethered to the slave post. "Even to look upon them," she whispered, "makes the slave in me scream for fulfillment." She sobbed, and half choked. Then she said, "How terrible I am. It is fortunate that my tether is so short. I want to crawl to you and please you with my tongue and mouth. I hope that you would not beat me, if I so disturbed your rest." She was silent for a moment and then she said, so softly that I could scarcely hear it, and again in English, "I, though a woman of Earth, admit that men are my masters. I, though a woman of Earth, admit that I am a slave. I, though a woman of Earth, beg my master for his touch."

I did not move.

Slowly, softly, she crept back to the vicinity of the slave post, and lay down. I heard her sob, softly. I smiled to myself. She had come far this night on the road to slavery. She had uttered slave admissions, though so softly that she thought I could not hear, though in a language she thought I could not understand.

32

FEMALE DISPLAY BEHAVIORS; A SLAVE GIRL'S DREAM; BARK CLOTH AND BEADS

"Do not drop it," said Kisu, strained, sweating.

The girls cried out in anguish, slipping, trying to keep the canoe from falling. Ayari struggled with the bow. Behind him were the three girls, then Kisu, amidships, and myself, at the stern. We could hear the cataract some two hundred yards away. The canoe, on our shoulders, tilted upward at a twenty-degree angle. Rocks slipped behind us, rolling down the grade.

"This is impossible," said Ayari.

"Keep moving forward," said Kisu.

"I am tired," said Ayari.

"Upward, upward!" said Kisu.

"Very well," said Ayari. "I never argue with big fellows."

The portage was not easy, and it was not our first. This was the eleventh cataract of the Ua.

Sometimes we used rollers beneath the canoe, and hauled with ropes.

The boats of Shaba had been sectioned, to facilitate such portages. He had had numerous strong men to carry the burdens. We had only ourselves, and three slight-bodied female slaves.

"I can go no further," said Ayari. This was the fourth portage of the day.

"Let us rest," I said.

Gently we lowered the canoe. While the others held it I, with rocks, braced it that it might not slip backwards down the grade.

Trees surrounded us. Overhead bright jungle birds flew. We could hear the chattering of guernon monkeys about.

"Bring up the supplies," said Kisu.

"Yes, Master," said the girls, sweating. They went back down the grade some hundred yards to gather up the paddles and sacks, and roped bundles, which contained our various goods. We moved these things separately, usually a hundred or two hundred yards at a time. Kisu and I took turns at the stern. It requires great strength to brace and support the canoe at that point.

"Shaba passed here," said Kisu, sitting down, wiping the sweat, like river water, from his head.

"Our portages," I said, "would be much more difficult if he had not preceded us."

"That is true," grinned Kisu. We generally followed the portage routes determined by Shaba and his scouts. They had located sensible geodesic contours and, in traversing the area, had, because of their larger vessels, cut away various trees, vines and obstacles.

I smiled to myself. I had little doubt that we, now, were moving much more swiftly than Shaba. Too, he had lost a week, with the illness of several of his men, a dozen or so, as we had learned, at the village at which we had recently traded.

I was pleased with the situation. I suspected, from the degree of recovery of the jungle following the passage of Shaba and his men, that he was not more than fifteen or twenty days ahead of us on the river.

I looked down the grade. Approaching us, in single file, led by Tende, came the slaves, carrying supplies. Last in the line, naked, came the blond-haired barbarian, erect and lovely, balancing on her head, steadying it with her hands, one of the bundles of our supplies. She looked at me. I saw that she looked at me as a slave girl at her master. It pleased me. She put down the bundle. She then, like the other girls, who had also discarded their burdens, returned down the grade. These transports of goods took them two trips.

Ayari was lying on his back, looking up at the sky. Kisu,

sitting, was looking down through the trees at the swift, churning water of the river.

In a few minutes the girls, again, made their way upward. Again they came in a single file. Again the blond-haired barbarian was the last in the line, again, lovely and erect, balancing on her head a bundle, one roped heavily and wrapped in bark cloth.

"Do not put down your burden," I said to her. I then rose to my feet and went to where she stood, beautiful and obedient. She straightened herself even more, steadying the bundle on her head. I walked slowly about her, inspecting the slave beauty of her.

"You make a lovely beast of burden," I told her.

"I am a beast of burden, Master," she said. "I am a slave."

I looked at her, and our eyes met, and she lowered her eyes, frightened. Could I know the truth of her? Could I know how she had confessed herself slave and needful of my touch? Of course not, for I had been asleep, and I could not understand her English. Yet, from the very morning following that night of her secret acknowledgments, five days ago, our relationship had been subtly, deliciously, different. She had begun, from that time, timidly, to look upon me with the vulnerable need of a slave girl. She had, secretly, acknowledged herself slave and mine. It was now merely up to me to do what I wished with her. She lifted her eyes again to mine. For an instant they were frightened. Could I know her secret? Of course not. How could I? Swiftly she again lowered her eyes.

"You may put down your burden," I said.

"Thank you, Master," she said.

"Rest now," I told her. "Lie on your stomach, head to the left, with your legs spread, and your hands at your sides, backs of your wrists to the ground, palms facing upwards."

"Yes, Master," she said.

The day had been long and hard.

We had now made camp. A small stream was nearby, which led into the Ua.

She stood before me and then, without asking, gently, delicately, untied, and opened and took from me the shreds of the soiled tunic which I wore. It was muddied and caked with dirt, from the days in the jungle, from the muddy banks of the Ua. As she removed it from me she kissed me softly, tenderly, about the chest and left hip.

308

"Are you a trained slave?" I asked her.

"No, Master," she said.

She then knelt before me, holding the tattered, muddied garment against her. "Master's garment is muddied," she said.

I said nothing.

Then she leaned forward and kissed me, softly.

"Does the Earth woman kiss her Master?" I asked.

"Yes, Master," she said.

Then she leaned forward and again kissed me, softly.

"Surely you are a trained slave," I said.

"No, Master," she said, looking up at me. And then she rose to her feet.

I crouched by the stream and watched her, on her knees, in the fashion of the primitive, owned female, clean and rinse the garment of her master. The proud Earth woman, unbidden, served as my laundress.

When she had finished with the garment and wrung it much dry, I had her replace it on my body. I would let it finish its drying on my body. Before she tied shut the tunic she kissed me again, softly, this time on the chest and belly, and then again knelt before me, her head down.

"Gather wood for the fire," I told her.

"Yes, Master," she said.

It was now late, and the others were asleep.

Tende and Alice were already, hands tied behind them, wrist-tethered to the small tree which served us as slave post.

The blond-haired barbarian regarded me, and then lowered her eyes, and put a bit more wood on the fire.

It is not always easy to make a fire in the forest. There are commonly two large rains during the day, one in the late afternoon and the other late in the evening, usually an Ahn or so before midnight, or the twentieth hour. These rains are often accompanied by violent winds, sometimes, I conjecture, ranging between one hundred and ten and one hundred and twenty pasangs an Ahn. The forest is drenched. One searches for wood beneath rock overhangs or under fallen trees. One may also, with pangas, hack away the wet wood of fallen trees, until one can obtain the dry wood beneath. Even during the heat of the day it is hard to find suitable fuel. The jungle, from the heat and rain, steams with humidity. Too, like the roof of a greenhouse, the lush green canopies of the rain forest tend to hold this moisture within. It is the fantastic oxygenation produced by the vegetation, conjoined with the humidity and heat, and the smell of plant life, and rotting vegetable matter and wood, that gives the diurnial jungle its peculiar and unmistakable atmosphere, an encompassing, looming, green, warm ambience which is both beautiful and awesome. The nocturnal jungle is cooler, sometimes even chilly, and the air, a little thinner, a shade less rich, is different, the sun's energy no longer powering the complex reaction chains of photosynthesis. Yet, at night, perhaps one is even more aware of the presence and vastness of the jungle than during the day. In the daylight hours one's horizons are limited by the encircling greenery. In the night, in the darkness, one senses the almost indefinite extension of the jungle, thousands of pasangs in width and depth, about one.

The blond-haired barbarian stirred the fire with a stick. I watched her.

One does not make one's camp in the jungle near tall trees. Because of the abundant amount of moisture the trees do not send down deep tap roots, but their root systems spread more horizontally. In the fierce winds which often lash the jungle it is not unusual for these shallowly rooted trees, uprooted and overturned, to come crashing down.

It seemed she wished to speak, but then she did not speak.

There is an incredible variety of trees in the rain forest, how many I cannot conjecture. There are, however, more than fifteen hundred varieties and types of palm alone. Some of these palms have leaves which are twenty feet in length. One type of palm, the fan palm, more than twenty feet high, which spreads its leaves in the form of an opened fan, is an excellent source of pure water, as much as a liter of such water being found, almost as though cupped, at the base of each leaf's stem. Another useful source of water is the liana vine. One makes the first cut high, over one's head, to keep the water from being withdrawn by contraction and surface adhesion up the vine. The second cut, made a foot or so from the ground, gives a vine tube which, drained, yields in the neighborhood of a liter of water. In the rain forest some trees grow and lose leaves all year long, remaining always in foliage. Others, though not at the same time, even in the same species, will lose their foliage for a few weeks and then again produce buds and a new set of leaves. They have maintained their cycles of regeneration but these cycles, interestingly, are often no longer synchronized with either the northern or southern winters and springs.

"Master," said the girl.

"Yes," I said.

"It is nothing," she said, looking down.

In the rain forest we may distinguish three separate ecological zones, or tiers or levels. Each of these tiers, or levels or layers, is characterized by its own special forms of plant and animal life. These layers are marked off by divergent tree heights. The highest level or zone is that of the "emergents," that of those trees which have thrust themselves up above the dense canopies below them. This level is roughly from a hundred and twenty-five feet Gorean to two hundred feet Gorean. The second level is often spoken of as the canopy, or as that of the canopies. This is the fantastic green cover which constitutes the main ceiling of the jungle. It is what would dominate one's vision if one were passing over the jungle in tarn flight or viewing it from the height of a tall mountain. The canopy, or zone of the canopies, ranges from about sixty to one hundred and twenty-five feet high, Gorean measure. The first zone extends from the ground to the beginning of the canopies above, some sixty feet in height, Gorean measure. We may perhaps, somewhat loosely, speak of this first zone as the "floor," or, better, "ground zone," of the rain forest. In the level of the emergents there live primarily birds, in particular parrots, long-billed fleers, and needle-tailed lits. Monkeys and tree urts, and snakes and insects, however, can also be found in this highest level. In the second level, that of the canopies, is found an incredible variety of birds, warblers, finches, mindars, the crested lit and the common lit, the fruit tindel, the yellow gim, tanagers, some varieties of parrot, and many more. Here, too, may be found snakes and monkeys, gliding urts, leaf urts, squirrels, climbing, long-tailed porcupines, lizards, sloths, and the usual varieties of insects, ants, centipedes, scorpions, beetles and flies, and so on. In the lower portion of the canopies, too, can be found heavier birds, such as the ivory-billed woodpecker and the umbrella bird. Guernon monkeys, too, usually inhabit this level. In the ground zone, and on the ground itself, are certain birds, some flighted, like the hook-billed gort, which preys largely on rodents, such as ground urts, and the insectivorous whistling finch, and some unflighted, like the grub borer and lang gim. Along the river, of course, many other species of birds may be found, such as jungle gants, tufted fishers and ring-necked and yellow-legged waders. Also in the ground zone are varieties of snake, such as the ost and hith, and numerous species of insects. The rock spider has been mentioned, and termites,

311

also. Termites, incidentally, are extremely important to the ecology of the forest. In their feeding they break down and destroy the branches and trunks of fallen trees. The termite "dust," thereafter, by the action of bacteria, is reduced to humus, and the humus to nitrogen and mineral materials. In the lower branches of the "ground zone" may be found, also, small animals, such as tarsiers, nocturnal jit monkeys, black squirrels, four-toed leaf urts, jungle varts and the prowling, solitary giani, tiny, cat-sized panthers, not dangerous to man. On the floor itself are also found several varieties of animal life, in particular marsupials, such as the armored gatch, and rodents, such as slees and ground urts. Several varieties of tarsk, large and small, also inhabit this zone. More than six varieties of anteater are also found here, and more than twenty kinds of small, fleet, single-horned tabuk. On the jungle floor, as well, are found jungle larls and jungle panthers, of diverse kinds, and many smaller catlike predators. These, on the whole, however, avoid men. They are less dangerous in the rain forest, generally, than in the northern latitudes. I do not know why this should be the case. Perhaps it is because in the rain forest food is usually plentiful for them, and, thus, there is little temptation for them to transgress the boundaries of their customary prey categories. They will, however, upon occasion, particularly if provoked or challenged, attack with dispatch. Conspicuously absent in the rain forests of the Ua were sleen. This is just as well for the sleen, commonly, hunts on the first scent it takes upon emerging from its burrow after dark. Moreover it hunts single-mindedly and tenaciously. It can be extremely dangerous to men, even more so, I think, than the Voltai, or northern, larl. I think the sleen, which is widespread on Gor, is not found, or not frequently found, in the jungles because of the enormous rains, and the incredible dampness and humidity. Perhaps the sleen, a burrowing, furred animal, finds itself uncomfortable in such a habitat. There is, however, a sleenlike animal, though much smaller, about two feet in length and some eight to ten pounds in weight, the zeder, which frequents the Ua and her tributaries. It knifes through the water by day and, at night, returns to its nest, built from sticks and mud in the branches of a tree overlooking the water.

I listened to the noises of the jungle night, the chattering, and the hootings, and the clickings and cries, of nocturnal animals, and birds and insects.

I glanced to the blond-haired barbarian. It was nearly time to secure her for the night.

Contrary to popular belief the floor of the jungle is not a maze of impenetrable growth, which must be hacked through with machete or panga. Quite the contrary, it is usually rather open. This is the result of the denseness of the overhead canopies, because of which the ground is much shaded, the factor which tends to inhibit and limit ground growth. Looking about among the slender, scattered colonnades of trees, exploding far overhead in the lush capitals of the green canopy, one is often exposed to vistas of one to two hundred feet, or more. It is hard not to be reminded of the columns in one of the great, shaded temples of Initiates, as in Turia or Ar. And yet here, in the rain forest, the natural architecture of sun, and shade, and growth, seems a vital celebration of life and its glory, not a consequence of aberrations and the madness of abnegations, not an invention of dismal men who have foresworn women, even slaves, and certain vegetables, and live by parasitically feeding and exploiting the superstitions of the lower castes. There are, of course, impenetrable, or almost impenetrable, areas in the jungle. These are generally "second-growth" patches. Through them one can make one's way only tortuously, cutting with the machete or panga, stroke by stroke. They normally occur only where men have cleared land, and then, later, abandoned it. That is why they are called "second-growth" patches; they normally occur along rivers and are not characteristic of the botanical structure of the virgin rain forest itself.

The blond-haired barbarian dropped some turgs on the fire.

"Why are you feeding the fire now?" I asked.

"Forgive me, Master," she said.

I smiled. She did not wish to retire so soon. But surely she knew it was nearly time for me to tie her at the slave post.

"It is time to secure you," I said.

"Must I be secured tonight?" she asked. Then she looked frightened. "Forgive me, Master," she said. "Please do not whip me."

"Go sit with your back to the slave post, in binding position," I said.

"Yes, Master," she said.

I let her sit there for a few minutes. She did not dare to look back at me over her shoulder.

"Come here," I then said, "and kneel before me."

313

She did so. "Please do not strike me, Master," she begged.

"What is on your mind tonight?" I asked.

"Nothing, Master," she stammered, her head down.

"You may speak," I said.

"I dare not," she whispered.

"Speak," I said.

"Tende and Alice are clothed," she said.

"They are scarcely clothed," I said, "and the bit of rag they wear may be stripped away from them in an instant on the least whim of a master."

"Yes, Master," she said.

She looked at me, agonized, tears in her eyes.

"Do you, an Earth woman," I asked, "desire again that opportunity, once afforded to you, but rejected by you, to beg to earn clothing?"

"Yes, Master," she said. "I beg that opportunity."

"Though you are an Earth woman?"

"Yes, though I am an Earth woman, Master," she said.

"It is yours, Earth woman," I said.

She put down her head. "I beg clothing, Master," she sobbed.

"Do you beg to earn it?" I asked.

"Yes, Master," she said.

"In any way that I see fit?" I asked.

"Yes, Master," she sobbed.

"In such a situation as this, formerly," I said, "you spoke of Alice, your sister in bondage, as a whore."

"Yes, Master," she said.

"It now seems that it is you," I said, "who are the whore."

"Yes, Master," she said. "It is now I who am the whore."

"But you are mistaken," I said, "in your own case, as you were in the case of Alice."

She lifted her head. "Master?" she asked.

"In your vanity," I said, "you dignify yourself."

"Master?"

"Do you think you are free?" I asked.

"No," she said.

"The whore," I said, "is a free woman. Do not presume, in your insolence, lest you be cut to pieces, to compare yourself with her. She is a thousand times higher than you. You are a thousand times lower than she. She is free. You are slave."

"Yes, Master," she said, sobbing, head down. "Please forgive me, Master." She shook with emotion.

I regarded her.

314

"I beg to earn clothing, in any way my master may see fit," she said, "and I, humbly, beg this as what I am, only a slave."

She lifted her head. Our eyes met.

"Engage in female display behaviors," I said.

"Master?" she asked.

"Female display behaviors," I said. "Surely you are familiar with the biological concept, and the sorts of behavioral patterns which are subsumed beneath it."

She looked at me.

"They are quite common," I said, "in the animal kingdom."

"I am not an animal," she said.

"The human being," I said, "is not alien to nature, nor disjointed from it. He is, in some respects, one of its most interesting and sophisticated products. He is not something out of nature nor apart from nature but one of its complex fulfillments. It is not that he is less an animal than, say, the zeder or sleen, but rather that he is a more complicated animal than they. In a sense, given the rigors of evolution and selection, the human contains in itself not less animality than his brethren whom we choose to place lower on the phylogenetic scale than ourselves but more. The human is not less of an animal than they, but more. In him there is, in a sense, that of complexity and sophistication, a greater animality than theirs."

"I am aware, as any educated person," she said, "of our animal heritage."

"It is not only your heritage," I said. "It is, now, and recognize it, if you dare, your reality."

She looked down.

"Perhaps, someday," I said, "sleen will become sufficiently intellectual to make mistakes in reasoning. When they do, their first fallacy will doubtless be to decide that they are not really sleen."

"That is silly," she said. She smiled.

"Is it less silly," I asked, "if it is done by human beings?"

"Perhaps not," she said.

"To be sure," I said, "if I have a problem in algebra I will give it to a mathematician before I will turn it over to a sleen. The reason for that, however, is not that the sleen is an animal and the mathematician is not, but rather that the mathematician is better at algebra than a sleen. The word 'animal' may be used in various senses, not all of them complimentary to animals. In the literal sense of 'animal' the human being is an animal. In a rather different sense of 'animal', we sometimes draw a distinction between human beings and animals, that is, we take the category of animals and divide it in two, calling one sort of animals, ourselves, human beings, and letting what is left over, the other sorts of animals, count as the animals. Do not ask me to explain the logic of that distinction. There are also senses of 'animal' which are complimentary and derogatory, for example, 'He has an animal charm' or 'He acts like an animal when he is drunk'."

I looked at her.

"Also," I said, "if you are interested in these matters, you are not simply an animal in the literal sense, in the biological sense of 'animal', but in the sense that persons, individuals with rights before the law, are distinguished from animals."

She regarded me, frightened.

"In that sense, my dear," I said, "I am not an animal, and you are an animal. Yes, my dear, you are legally an animal. In the eyes of Gorean law you are an animal. You have no name in your own right. You may be collared and leashed. You may be bought and sold, whipped, treated as the master pleases, disposed of as he sees fit. You have no rights whatsoever. Legally you have no more status than a tarsk or vulo. Legally, literally, you are an animal."

"Yes, Master," she whispered.

"You may now engage in female display behaviors," I said.

"I do not know any," she said.

I laughed.

"I am not a lewd girl," she said.

"Does the slave have pride?" I asked.

"No, Master," she said.

"Perform," I said.

"I do not know how," she wept. "I do not know how!"

"Peel away the hideous encrustations of your antibiological conditioning," I told her. "Hidden in every cell in your body, in the genetic codes of each minute cell, the product of a long, complex evolution, lie the marvels of which I speak. In the deepest part of your brain lies the provocation to these truths. You are the result of thousands upon thousands of women who have pleased men. Evolution has selected for such women. Do not tell me that you do not know these behaviors. Deny them, if you will, but they have been bred into

316

you. They are a part of your very being. They are, my sweet slave, in your very blood."

"No," she wept.

"Perform," I said.

She threw back her head with misery, and clutched at her hair and then, suddenly, startled, her hands at her hair, looked at me, her eyes wide. The line of her breasts had been lifted nicely.

"Yes," I said, "consult the animal in you."

"What am I doing?" she wept.

She now sat, and extended her leg, and took her right ankle in her hands, and moved her hands slowly from her ankle to her calf. Her toes were pointed, emphasizing the sweet curve of her calf.

"Is it not now coming back to you?" I asked. "Is it not almost like a memory, a kinesthetic and intellectual recollection? Are you not now getting in touch with certain feared basic and rudimentary feelings and reactions? Can you not, now, begin to sense the ancient truths, those of the female before the male?"

"I am frightened," she whispered.

"Build up the fire," I said.

"Master?" she asked.

"That I may better see my female perform."

"Yes, Master," she said.

I watched her gather twigs, how she walked, how she held them, how she returned to the fire and, kneeling, sometimes glancing at me, placed them on the fire. As I had thought she was even then engaging in female display behavior. I had thought she would. I wondered if she were fully conscious of what she did. I suspect she was only partly aware of it. And yet, clearly, I saw that she was excited. How subtly and marvelously she manifested her beauty. In so small a thing as the way in which a woman places a plate on the table before a man, or a twig upon a small fire, she may invite him to her rape. I do not think she was fully conscious of how provocative she was. Yet, doubtless, she was intensely aware of my eyes upon her. I wondered if women knew how beautiful they were. I supposed not. Otherwise why would any of them be puzzled when they were enslaved. I observed her movements. She had begun to recognize her bondage, to understand, in her heart, that she was truly a slave girl.

"You move as a slave girl before her master," I said.

"I am a slave girl before my master," she said.

317

The slave girl moves, and carries herself, differently from a free woman. This is evident in such small things as fetching a cup for her master or in pouring his wine. These movements, and bodily attitudes and postures, subtle and beautiful, difficult to fully disguise, have betrayed more than one slave beauty who, disguised as a free woman, has sought to flee a city. The spears of guards, lowered, to her dismay, suddenly block her way. "Where are you going, Slave?" they ask. She is then knelt and stripped, her collar and brand revealed. Returned to her master, she may be confident that her punishment will not be light.

I looked at the slave.

An Earth woman who exhibits sensuous movement is commonly ostracized or in some other way socially punished. The contempt in which the exotic dancer on Earth is held, despite the richness of her music and beauty, is a symptom of this pathology. The freedoms of the Earth woman do not extend to the point where she is permitted to move as a woman. That she is not supposed to be free to do. The freedoms of the Earth woman, in effect, are freedoms to conform, within reasonably narrow limits, to certain socially approved stereotypes. Females of Earth, not permitted to move as women, are expected to perform what are, in effect, male-imitation movements. It is little wonder that they occasionally, crying out with frustration, dance naked before a mirror. It is little wonder that in their dreams they are roped and thrown to warriors. On Gor, of course, the woman, if she be slave, is no longer prohibited, because of cultural requirements, from expressing the kinesthetic realities of her womanhood. The slave girl learns to think of herself as deeply and radically feminine, as uncompromisingly feminine. She thus, soon unconsciously, thinks and moves as what she is, a female. Moreover there is a special modality to the movements of the slave girl. She knows not only that she is a female, but a female in the most radical and profound sense, an owned female, one at the bidding of masters. This excites her, and cannot help but be reflected in her movements. She is the most natural, biological and profound of women, the woman at the mercy of men, who must obey and serve them, the slave girl.

The blond-haired barbarian put a bit more wood on the fire. I smiled. The men of Earth think often of sex as a simple matter of explicit congress. This is, however, much too limited. The perimeters of sex are not limited to those of physiological union. Any woman, I suppose, knows this; it is

318

unfortunate that it is not recognized by more men. The blond-haired barbarian and I, she beneath my will, were now surely intensely engaged in sex; yet she was feet from me, and I was not touching her.

"The fire is high enough," I said. "Now kneel before me, Slave."

"Yes, Master," she said.

"Stretch like the sleek little animal you are," I said.

"Yes, Master," she said.

"Now rise gracefully," I said, "and walk back and forth before me."

"Yes, Master," she said.

I watched her. "You are a pretty slave," I said.

"Thank you, Master," she said.

"Now stand before me, and lower your head."

"Yes, Master," she said.

"Lift your head again, and lower it again," I said, "this time more deferentially."

"I obey, Master," she said. She again lifted her head and, this time, slowly, gracefully, deferentially, inclined it to me.

"Excellent," I said.

"Thank you, Master," she said.

"You now stand before your master," I said, "your neck bent in submission."

"Yes, my Master," she said.

"Lift your head now," I said, "and look at me."

"Yes, Master," she said. She did so.

"You are an Earth woman," I said. "On Earth, as I understand it," I said, "your delicious and vulnerable animality, your feminine animality, the most basic and deepest female of you, helpless and needful, was, as a matter of cultural policy, consistently suppressed and frustrated."

"Yes, Master," she whispered.

"Did you daydream?" I asked.

"I fought them," she said.

"Foolish," I said.

"But they kept recurring," she said.

"Of course," I said.

She looked at me.

"Was there a common theme?" I asked.

"Yes," she said, "myself in a position of submission before men."

"That is natural," I said.

"Yes, Master," she said.

"And at night," I said, "occasionally erupting from the depths of your mind, indicative of your cruelly frustrated needs and desires, were certain sorts of dreams."

"Yes, Master," she whispered.

"Describe to me now one of them."

"There was one of them which more than once I dreamed," she said, "which returned to me, again and again."

"Describe it to me," I said.

"But such things are so private to a girl," she said.

"Speak, Slave," I said.

"Yes, Master," she said. "It seems I was in the jungles of South America, a continent on my native world, Earth, or perhaps it was some other world. I do not know. I was a traveler, or tourist. There was some group involved. The details are unclear. We were examining the ruins of an ancient civilization, great blocks of stone, huge, frightening carvings."

"Yes?" I said.

"I wore boots, and a skirt and short-sleeved blouse," she said, "and a helmet, of lightweight material, to protect me from the sun. Too, I wore sunglasses, pieces of colored glass sometimes worn by those of Earth before their eyes, sometimes to guard their expressions and features, but usually to reduce the glare of a bright sun."

"I understand," I said.

" 'What is that carving?' I asked our native guide. He was a tall, red man, handsome and strong. He wore an open-throated blue shirt, with the sleeves rolled up. It is like a half-tunic for the torso, with sleeves. Too, he wore blue trousers. Such a garment covers the lower body, and fits about the legs."

"I am familiar with such garments for the upper and lower body," I said. "They are worn in Torvaldsland and in other areas, generally in the northern latitudes."

" 'Is it not obvious?' he asked. 'It is the carving of a naked slave girl kneeling before her master.' I was so embarrassed. 'Perhaps she is only a captive,' I said, angrily. 'Look,' he said, pointing. 'She wears a neck belt.' 'Oh,' I said. 'See its knot and disk,' he asked, 'the distinctive slave knot, and the disk, that identifying the master?' 'Yes,' I said. 'It is the neck belt of a slave,' he said. 'I see,' I said. 'She is a slave,' he said. 'Then,' I said, 'she would have to do what her master tells her.' He then, with two hands, removed my sunglasses. He looked directly into my eyes. 'Yes,' he said. I trembled, for, in that instant, he had looked upon me as a woman, one perhaps containing within herself a slave. He then turned me so that I must look again upon the carving of the subservient girl, the kneeling slave at the feet of her master. I then saw it in the bright and direct light of the sun. It was clear that she was lovely, even in the rudeness of the carving. On her throat was the neck belt of bondage, doubtless tied shut with a slave knot, and, fastened to it, identifying her, the disk of the master. How horrifying it is to look upon such a reality so directly. How much better it is to deny it, or to see it only, as through colored glass, through the softened, tinted lies of civilization. He then handed me back the sunglasses. 'Do not put them back on,' he said. How angry I was! Immediately, angrily, I put them back on."

"Continue," I said. "What occurred next in this dream?"

"That night, of course," she said, "I was captured, ruthlessly gagged and bound with black straps. For days I was carried into the jungle. I began to stink. My clothing, rotting from my sweat, and the heat and humidity, began to disintegrate on my body. Too, it was half torn away from snagging on thorns, and from the lashings of branches. In the beginning I was tied on a pole, carried on the shoulders of men. Then a sack was put over my head and I was thrown on my belly in a canoe. Then, later, at some point I did not recognize, after I had again been carried into the jungle, the sack was removed. I was then, hands tied behind me, marched before my captors. I stumbled before them for days. When I dallied I was beaten with sticks. At last we came to a clearing in the jungle. There was a city in this clearing. The architecture of the city was identical to that of the ruins we had earlier visited, but this city was not in ruins. It was a living city, populated, thriving, hidden in the jungle. It was not known what had become of the population of the city which had been permitted to fall into ruins. No marks of war or fire, or other forms of sudden destruction, had been discernible. Meals had apparently been left uneaten, and fires untended. At a given point, perhaps determined by their priests or chiefs, for no reason that is clear to us, the population, it seemed, had abandoned the city, marching away into the jungles. The fate of the population was one of anthropology's mysteries. I was thrust toward the city. I, perhaps alone of all white people, now understood, or thought I understood, what had become of the population of the city which, over centuries, had fallen into ruins. They had come here, it seemed, to this point in the jungle, and, here, had rebuilt their city. The numerous individuals, red men and women, in their colorful feathers and robes, on the walks and terraces of this city, maintaining their old way of life, it seemed, were their living descendants. Sticks, pushed against my back, guided me to a narrow doorway, leading into a room, carved out of living rock, in the base of what I took to be a temple. There four red girls, who were beautiful, were awaiting me. I was unbound and turned over to the four red girls, who treated me with great deference. They fed me and, gently removing my clothing, bathed me. They combed my hair and perfumed me. I was given golden sandals to wear and a single robe, high-collared, ornate, of brocaded gold. My old clothing, and my boots, which the girls, laughing, cut to pieces with small knives, were burned. Outside the doorway, with large, curved knives, stood two huge men, warriors, on guard."

The blond-haired barbarian looked at me.

"Continue," I told her.

"That night they came for me," she said. "My hands were tied behind my back. Then two straps were put on my neck and, by two men, the girls following, I was led forth. I was conducted down a long street, between mighty buildings. Men and women followed me, with long-handled, feathered fans. There was much singing. There were numerous torches, and drums. At the end of the street, before a group of men standing on the wide steps and the surface of a broad, stone platform, some ten feet in height, we stopped. The drums and singing, too, suddenly stopped. A sign was given, by one of the men on the height of the platform. The straps were removed from my neck. My hands were freed. I looked up at them. Another sign was given. The girls removed my sandals and then, gracefully, drew away my robe. I looked up again at the men. I was now stark naked. The man on the height of the platform, red, in his robes and feathers, regarded me for some time. Then, by nodding his head, and a simple gesture, he indicated his approval. There was a shout of pleasure from the crowd which made me shudder. My wrists were seized and a long thong was tied on each wrist. Men then began, by these wrist leashes, to drag me up the steps. The singing and drums had then again commenced. 'No!' I screamed, when I reached the top of the platform, for I then saw, before me, a large, oblong piece of stone, a massive, primitive stone altar, discolored with huge stains of dried blood, with iron rings. 'No! No!' I screamed. But I was lifted from my

322

feet and, my back to the ground, screaming, carried by many men, was helplessly hurried to its surface. I was thrown on my back on the altar and my hands, by the wrist leashes, were fastened apart and over my head to iron rings. At the same time my legs, by the ankles, were jerked apart, painfully so. I felt thongs tied on my ankles. I cried out. My legs were pulled even more widely apart. Men strung the thongs on my ankles through the iron rings at the foot of the altar. I screamed. By the thongs my legs were drawn apart even more. I was then, as I wept and begged for mercy, fastened in that cruel position. The ceremony began. The priest, from a golden dish, lifted up a knife. It was long and translucent, eighteen inches in length, of slender, bluish stone. I twisted on the altar, under the torches. All about me were the robes and feathers, the savage red faces; the thongs bit deeply into the flesh of my wrists and ankles; the singing, the drums, began to intensify in crescendo; they became deafening; the priest lifted the knife. It was then that I saw him, sitting on an oblong pillar of stone, some eight feet in height, some forty feet from the altar. He was sitting cross-legged, watching, impassively. Though he now wore the robes and feathers of this savage people, I recognized him instantly. It was he who had been the guide of the tour in which I had been a member, that tour with which I had been visiting the ruins of the mysteriously abandoned city. It was he who had explained to me the meaning of the carving of the kneeling girl, who had told me not to replace my sunglasses, he whom I had disobeyed. 'Master!' I screamed to him. 'Master!' "

" 'Master'?" I asked.

"Yes," she said, "I called him 'Master'."

"Why?" I asked.

"I do not know," she said. "It startled me, that I should have called him that. Yet the utterance came naturally, helplessly, from deep within me, an irrepressible, incontrovertible acknowledgment."

"You called him 'Master'," I said, "because, in your heart, you knew that he was your Master."

"Yes, Master," she said. "That is it. I suppose I had known from the first instant I had seen him that he was my Master, and I was his Slave, but how could I, an Earth woman, have admitted that, even to myself, let alone to the superb, red brute."

"What occurred then in the dream?" I asked.

"He lifted his hand and spoke out to the priest and the men about the altar.

"I lay there, helpless. He pointed to me and said something in his own tongue. I could tell that it was scornful.

"The priest, angrily, returned the knife of blue stone to the golden dish. Others, too, were angry. The thongs at my ankles were cut free. My wrist leashes were untied from the iron rings. The crowd began to become ugly. By a hand on my arm I was thrust from the altar. It seemed now they did not want me on the altar. I was struck by a man. I cowered. My wrist leashes were seized by two men and I was dragged before the pillar of oblong stone on which sat he to whom I had called out 'Master'. The anger of the men, and the crowd, I suddenly realized, was not directed at the red brute sitting upon the stone, but, startlingly, frighteningly, at me. They were not angry with him for interfering with their ceremony but somehow, for no reason I understood, with me. I shuddered, held naked by the wrist leashes before the stone, the object of the contempt and wrath, the scorn and fury, of the multitude. I, terrified, felt their hatred directed upon me, almost as though it came in waves. 'Why did you not tell us you were a slave?' he asked of me. He spoke in English. 'Forgive me, Master,' I begged. 'To our gods,' he said, 'the offer of a contemptible slave would be an insulting sacrifice.' 'Yes, Master,' I said. 'The first time I saw you,' he said, 'I thought you were a slave. Yet when I ordered you not to replace your sunglasses, you did so.' 'Forgive me, Master,' I said. 'Surely you know that any free man has authority over a slave girl?' he asked. 'Yes, Master,' I said. 'When you did not obey,' he said, 'I then thought perhaps that I had been mistaken about you, that perhaps you were not a slave, but a free woman, and thus might serve as a suitable sacrifice to our gods.' 'Yes, Master,' I said, my head lowered. 'But, as I had originally thought,' he said, 'you were only a slave.' 'Yes, Master,' I said. I did not raise my head. 'When I ordered you not to replace your sunglasses, you did so,' he said. 'Yes, Master,' I said. 'Why?' he asked. 'Forgive me, Master,' I said. 'You were disobedient,' he said. 'Yes, Master,' I said. 'Whip her,' he said."

The blond-haired barbarian looked at me.

"Continue," I said.

"There were two rings before the stone, about five feet apart," she said. "They knelt me down."

"Kneel down," I said, "precisely as in your dream."

"Yes, Master," she said. She knelt down. "My wrist leashes," she said, "were then slipped through the rings, the free ends of each in the hands of a standing man."

"It is interesting that that should be in your dream," I said. "It is a device for maintaining a differential tension in the body of a beaten girl."

"It seemed natural," she said.

"It is natural," I said. "Now place your wrists exactly as they were at the beginning of your beating."

"Yes, Master," she said. She extended her wrists downward and to the sides.

"What then occurred?" I asked.

"I was beaten," she said.

"How many strokes?" I asked.

"Eleven," she said. "Ten for disobedience, and one to remind me that I was a slave."

"Interesting," I said. "That, too, is sometimes done."

"Yes, Master," she said.

"You will now," I said, "count the strokes, and, after each count, react as you did in your dream."

"Yes, Master," she said.

I observed her. The beating, in her dream, had apparently been quite efficient. I studied her facial expressions, the movements of her body. Sometimes under the blows or in fearful anticipation of them she twisted or changed position, once sitting, sometimes crouching, once on her stomach; most of the blows were across her back, but two had been delivered frontally, and two to her left side, and one to her right side. In all this I was conscious, in her movements, of how the two men with the wrist leashes, tightening or slackening them, toyed and played with her, as one sometimes does with a slave, skillfully managing her in her beating.

"The beating was then finished?" I said.

"Yes, Master," she said.

"Apparently you were well beaten," I said.

"Yes, Master," she said, "I was well beaten."

"At the end of the beating you well knew that you were a slave," I said.

"Yes, Master," she said, "I well knew then that I was a slave."

"What occurred then?" I asked.

"I cowered kneeling, sobbing, before my master," she said. "The men then thrust my wrist leashes back through the rings and, by means of them, dragged me to my feet. I looked up

325

at my master, piteously, searching his face for the least sign of kindness. But there was none. I was a woman of a foreign and hated race, and a slave. 'You are a worthless slave,' he said. 'Yes, Master,' I wept. He gestured to his right. I was dragged to the side by the wrist leashes. Stumbling I saw before me a circular opening in the stone, like a sunken, sheer-sided pool some eight feet in diameter. The men went to either side of the pool, dragging me by the wrist leashes toward it. I heard grunting and movement, and stirred water, in the pool. In the light of lifted torches I saw its contents. I screamed. In the pool, clambering over one another, lifting their jaws upward were crocodiles, beasts like river tharlarion but differently hided and plated."

I nodded. The marsh tharlarion, and river tharlarion, of Gor are, I suspect, genetically different from the alligators, caymens and crocodiles of Earth. I suspect this to be the case because these Earth reptiles are so well adapted to their environments that they have changed very little in tens of millions of years. The marsh and river tharlarion, accordingly, if descended from such beasts, brought long ago to Gor on Voyages of Acquisition by Priest-Kings, would presumably resemble them more closely. On the other hand, of course, I may be mistaken in this matter. It remains my speculation, however, that the resemblance between these forms of beasts, which are considerable, particularly in bodily configuration and disposition, may be accounted for by convergent evolution; this process, alert to the exigencies of survival, has, I suspect, in the context of similar environments, similarly shaped these oviparous predators of two worlds. Certain other forms of Gorean beast, however, I suspect do have an Earth origin. This seems to be the case with certain birds and rodents and, possibly, even with an animal as important to the Gorean economy as the bosk.

"Struggling, trying to pull back, fighting the wrist leashes, screaming, inch by inch," she said, "I was drawn toward the pool. 'Master! Master!' I screamed. Then I was drawn to the very edge of the pool. I looked back wildly over my shoulder, sobbing. 'Please, Master!' I wept. 'Have mercy on me, Master! Mercy, Master, mercy! Take pity on a worthless slave!' The wrist leashes then tightened, to plunge me forward into the lifted, waiting, lunging jaws. I threw my head back. I do not know from where within me came then that piteous wild cry that I then uttered. 'Let me please you!' I cried. He must have given a sign, perhaps raising his hand, for the wrist leashes, tight on my small wrists, no longer pulled me forward, but neither did they let me move an inch back. 'Let your girl try to please you, Master!' I cried. 'The girl begs to please her master!' I could scarcely believe that I had uttered those words. I was horrified that I had said them. They were the words, surely, of a slave. Yet how naturally and spontaneously they had come from me! What could it mean? I was dragged back before the oblong stone. There my wrist leashes were removed. I ran, terrified, to the stone, and pressed myself against it. I scratched at it with my fingernails, and looked up at him. 'Do you desire to please your master?' he asked. 'Yes, Master,' I said. 'As a slave?' he asked. 'Yes, Master,' I said, 'as a slave.' I looked at him. I now knew what the words I had uttered had meant, those words which had so horrified me, and which, yet, had come so naturally and spontaneously from me. They had meant that I was truly a slave, and truly desired to please my master. Then, in my own heart, my slavery was well confirmed in me. 'Do so,' he said. 'Yes, Master,' I said, and stepped back from the stone."

I listened to the noises of the jungle night. I threw some more twigs on the fire.

" 'You understand clearly, do you not,' he asked, 'that if you are not sufficiently pleasing, you will be thrown to the crocodiles?' 'Yes, Master,' I said."

"Continue," I told her.

"I was terrified," she said. "I looked up at the brute. I knew that, if I were to live, I must please him, and please him well, and as a slave."

"What did you do?" I asked.

"I moved before him," she said, "as a slave."

"Do so now," I said, "precisely, in every detail, as you did in your dream."

"Ah!" she said. "How clever you are, Master. How cleverly you have tricked me!"

I regarded her, not speaking.

"It is again a matter of female display behaviors, is it not?" she asked.

"Of course," I said.

"But these behaviors," she said, "would now be extracted from my most intimate and secret dreams."

I did not speak.

"You are a bold, demanding master," she said.

I did not speak.

"Do not make a girl so expose her needs," she begged.

327

"The slave girl must honestly expose her needs," I said. "The hypocrisy of the free woman, her concealment, her subterfuges, her lies, are not permitted to the female slave."

"Oh, Master," she wept, miserably.

"Are you prepared to perform?" I asked.

"Do not so violate the privacy of a girl's dreams!" she begged.

"You have no privacy," I said. "You belong to me."

"Am I not to be permitted the least vestige of my pride?" she asked.

"No," I told her.

"I am a slave," she said.

"Yes," I said.

"I shall now perform for my master," she said.

"Do so," I said, "and precisely, in each and every detail, as in your dream."

"Yes, my master," she said. She looked at me. "Remember," she said, "that I was forced to do this, that I not be hurled to the waiting jaws of crocodiles, beasts much like river tharlarion. That I not suffer so horrible a fate I knew that I must please him well, and as the slave which I had now been proven to be."

"For your very life you performed," I said.

"Yes, Master," she said, "as a terrified slave."

"Perform," I commanded.

Almost instantaneously she seemed transformed. I was startled. I found myself, for the first time, partner to a woman's dream. How vividly she was re-enacting the experience. Nay, how intensely was she reliving it. I could sense almost the high, oblong stone, that rude, barbaric eminence, on which, cross-legged, sat her master. I could almost sense the torches, the pool of reptiles to one side, the rude altar, with its rings, in the background. I could almost feel and see the savages, those red men and women, in their ornate robes and feathers, in the midst of whom a white beauty, freshly enslaved, piteously strove to save her life by pleasing her stern red master.

I watched her perform. I marveled. I think that no one will ever again be able to lie to me about women. How incredibly exciting and marvelous they are! What a fool a man is who does not seek, and release, the deepest slave in them!

Then she was on her belly, whimpering, scratching at the turf, her face pressed against it. Delicately she extended her tongue and licked a stone. Then, moaning, she rolled onto her back and twisted, moving her head from side to side, in the dirt before me. The firelight was beautiful on her body. I think there was no aspect or attitude of her beauty which she had not, pleadingly, presented before me for my inspection and appraisal. Then she lay on her back, her knees drawn up, before me. She arched her back. Her breasts were lifted beautifully. I observed their lovely rise and fall, correlated with the respiratory cycle of her small lungs. Then she lay back, her shoulders in the dirt, and pressing against the earth with her small feet, piteously lifted before me, for my examination, and seizure, if I pleased, the deep belly of her, the sweet cradle of her slave's heat. How vulnerable are female slaves! I rose to my feet, my fists clenched. She lay back, before me, at my feet. "It was thus," she said, "that I tried to please him." I scrutinized, from head to toe, the naked slave who lay at my feet. I could feel my fingernails in the palms of my hand. I gritted my teeth. I must not now take her. She was not yet fully ready. One must sometimes be patient with slaves. The next time I took her, I resolved, she would be a well-prepared feast. On the occasion of that feast it was my intention to teach the girl who she was, truly, to free at long last the hidden slave which was her secret self, her true self, that girl which, hitherto, had been permitted to emerge only in the disguise of clandestine dreams, that piteous girl, denied and suppressed, who had been for so long so cruelly imprisoned in the dungeon of her mind. I would free the secret slave from her dungeon; then I would make her mine. I would call her 'Janice'.

The girl sat up. I sat down, cross-legged. The fire was now low.

"What then occurred in your dream?" I asked.

"My master descended then from the height of the great stone," she said, "and, with his hand, indicated a direction in which I must precede him. He followed me, with a torch. I walked through the city and then, coming to a great temple, or building, with stone steps, stopped. He indicated I must climb upwards. The edifice was constructed of mighty blocks of stone. Its construction paid tribute to the engineering skills of his people. There were mighty carvings on many of the stones. I found the building, somehow, familiar. He then directed me to walk to my left, and I walked upon one of the broad terraces, many feet from the ground, which, like tiers, were integral to the structure of the edifice. I had the feeling I had been here before. In the light of his torch I could see

329

that many of the carvings were colored, the natural hues and pigments not worn away by wind or rain. In the daylight the building, or temple, must be incredibly barbaric and colorful. 'Stop,' he told me. I stopped. 'Turn and kneel,' he said. I turned about, facing him, and knelt down, on the hard, broad stone of the terrace. He then lifted the torch to the wall of stone which was at my left. I gasped. Kneeling beside me, carved in relief on the great stone, was a naked girl. 'It is a likeness of myself,' I whispered. 'Yes,' he said. I could see, from the carving, and the pigments, that the girl was figured like myself, and was light-skinned, and had yellow hair and blue eyes. But she wore a yellow neck belt and I did not. I knew then why the building seemed so familiar. It was identical to that which, in ruins, had been visited by our tour. And I now knelt, as the girl in the carving I had earlier seen had knelt. 'I had this carving prepared,' he said. 'I ordered it made, sending a runner ahead, almost the first moment I saw you.' 'You had determined then,' I said, 'that you would have me as your slave.' 'Of course,' he said. He then placed his torch in an iron rack, projecting from the wall. On an iron table, to the right of the rack, there was a flat box. 'Lie on your right side, exposing your left thigh,' he said. 'Yes, Master,' I said. From the box he then took a small, curved knife and a tiny, cylindrical leather flask. I gritted my teeth, but made no sound. With the small knife he gashed my left thigh, making upon it a small, strange design. He then took a powder, orange in color, from the flask and rubbed it into the wound. 'Kneel,' he said. I did so. From the flat box he then took a yellow neck belt, two inches in height, and beaded. It is fastened with a thong, which ties before the throat. 'Say "I am a slave. I am your slave, Master," ' he said. 'I am a slave,' I said. 'I am your slave, Master.' He then put the neck belt on me, tying it shut with the thong, with what I knew must be a slave knot. From the box then he took a yellow leather disk, which had a small hole, possibly drilled with a tiny stone implement, near its top. There was writing in some barbaric script upon it. He threaded an end of the thong through the hole and then, using the other end of the thong, too, knotted the disk snugly at the very base of the collar, in the front, below my throat. He looked down at me. 'You have been knife branded,' he said. 'The orange mark upon your thigh will be recognized in the jungle for hundreds of miles around. If you should be so foolish as to attempt to escape any who apprehend you, seeing the mark, will return you to

330

the city as a runaway slave.' 'Yes, Master,' I said. 'Master,' I asked, 'did the girl in the carving, in the ruined city, have such a mark on her thigh?' It could not have been seen, of course, for, as she knelt, it was only her right side which was revealed to the viewer. 'Yes,' he said. 'It has been put upon her.' 'I do not understand, Master,' I said. 'This is a slave's neck belt,' he said, jerking at the snug collar on my throat. I felt it pull against the back of my neck. 'It, too,' he said, 'marks you as a slave. You are not permitted to remove it.' 'Yes, Master,' I said. 'The disk, of course,' he said, 'is a personal identificatory device. It marks you as an article of my individual property.' 'Yes, Master,' I said. 'Master,' I asked, 'how could you know that the other girl, she in the other carving, wore upon her thigh a knife brand?' 'I put it there,' he said. 'Master?' I asked. 'Recollect clearly the carving,' said he. 'Can you not now recognize the girl in it, in spite of the weathering which defaced it, in spite of the lengthy ravages of time inflicted upon it?' 'Master?' I asked. 'Think hard,' said he. 'Consider the matter deeply.' 'It was I,' I whispered. 'And the master?' he asked, standing before me, his arms folded. 'You,' I whispered. I felt faint. 'The jungle,' said he, 'is a strange place. Even we, its people, do not fully understand it.' 'But the people left the city, mysteriously,' I said. 'Perhaps we never left it,' he said. 'Look about you.' I looked about, from the high tier on the temple, or building, on which I knelt. 'It is the same city,' I whispered. I shuddered. I was terrified. 'Do you not feel that it is right and fitting that you should be kneeling at my feet?' he asked. 'Yes,' I whispered, 'Master.' It was a strange feeling. 'The interstices, and cycles, of time,' said he, 'are interesting.' He looked down at me. 'Have we not been here before?' he asked. 'Do you not recognize me, my fair slave?' he inquired. 'You are my master,' I whispered. 'And I have caught you again,' he said, 'and again put you to my feet.' I looked up at him, trembling. 'Then I am an eternal slave,' I said, 'and you are my eternal master.' 'You are an eternal slave,' he said, 'but you have had many masters, as I have had many slaves.' I looked up at him, terrified. 'But you, my pretty white woman, are one of my favorites. You will serve me well, and I will get incredible pleasure from you.' 'Yes, Master,' I whispered. I knew then that I was an eternal slave, and that he was one of my eternal masters. He then withdrew from the flat box the last of the objects which it contained, a slave whip. He thrust it to my mouth and I kissed it. 'Stand,' said he. I stood. Then he looped the whip

331

about me, behind me, high on my thighs, and, drew me toward him. I felt the stiff gold of his brocaded robes against my breasts. He held me so that I could not move. I lifted my lips to his."

The blond-haired barbarian then put down her head, and did not speak.

"What happened then?" I asked.

She lifted her head, and smiled. "I do not know," she said. "I awakened."

"An interesting dream," I said. "Strange," I mused, "that in the dream of a naive Earth woman such details should occur, details such as the differential tension of the wrist straps in a beating and the extra stroke, given sometimes to remind a girl that she is a slave. Too, the kissing of the whip is a quite accurate detail, one practiced in many cities, but surely a surprising detail to occur in the dream of a girl ignorant of bondage. Knife branding, too, practiced by some primitive peoples, is quite rare. It is strange that you should have heard of it. It is a practice of which even many of those involved in cultural studies are ignorant." I looked at her. "You are quite inventive," I said.

"Perhaps I am an eternal slave," she smiled.

"Perhaps," I said.

"Do you believe," she asked, "that there can be warps in time?"

"It does not seem likely to me," I said, "but I would not know about such things. I am not a physicist."

"Do you think," she asked, "that people may have lived before, that they may have had many lives and have met one another perhaps time and time again?"

"I would not wish to rule out such possibilities," I said, "but such a thing seems to me very unlikely."

"It was an interesting dream," she said.

"I conjecture, though I do not know," I said, "that the dream was speaking to you not of truths of other worlds and other times, but of this world and this time. I suspect that the dream, in the beautiful allegory of its symbolism, was conveying to you not mysterious truths of other realities but concealed truths of your own reality, truths which your conscious mind, because of its training, could not bring itself to recognize with candor."

"What truths?" she asked.

"That woman, in her nature," I said, "is the eternal slave, that man, in his nature, is the eternal master."

"The men of my world," she said, "are not masters."

"They have been crippled," I said, "and, it seems, are being slowly destroyed."

"Not all of them," she said.

"Perhaps not," I said. "Yet if one of them should so much as question the renunciatory and negativistic values with which his brain has been imprinted he will be immediately assailed by the marshaled forces of an establishment jealously presiding over the dissolution of its own culture. Is it so difficult to detect the failure of public philosophies? Are unhappiness, frustration, misery, scarcity, pollution, disease and crime of no interest to those in power? I fear the reflex spasm. 'But we were not to blame,' they will say, as they wade in poisoned ashes."

"Is there no hope for my world?" she asked.

"Very little," I said. "Perhaps, here and there, men will form themselves into small communities, where the names of such things as courage, discipline and responsibility may be occasionally recollected, communities which, in their small way, might be worthy of Home Stones. Such communities, emerging upon the ruins, might provide a nucleus for regeneration, a sounder, more biological regeneration of a social structure, one not antithetical to the nature of human beings."

"Must my civilization be destroyed?" she asked.

"Nothing need be done," I said. "It is now in the process of destroying itself. Do you think it will last another thousand years?"

"I do not know," she said.

"I fear only," I said, "that it will be replaced by a totalitarian superstition uglier than its foolish and ineffectual predecessor."

She looked down.

"Men would rather die than think," I said.

"Not all men," she said.

"That is true," I mused. "In all cultures there are the lonely ones, the solitary walkers, those who climb the mountain, and look upon the world, and wonder."

"Why is it," she asked, "that the men of Gor do not think and move in herds, like those of Earth?"

"I do not know," I said. "Perhaps they are different. Perhaps the culture is different. Perhaps it has something to do with the decentralization of city states, the multiplicity of traditions, the diversity of the caste codes."

"I think the men of Gor are different," she said.

"They are, presumably, or surely most of them, of Earth stock," I said.

"I think, then," she said, "that, on the whole, it must have been only a certain sort of Earth man who was brought to this world."

"What sort?" I asked.

"Those capable of the mastery," she said.

"Surely there are those of Earth," I said, "who are capable of the mastery."

"Perhaps," she said. "I do not know."

"Stand, Slave," I said.

"Yes, Master," she said.

"You have moved well this night, Slave," I said. "You have well earned a brief rag for your thighs."

"Thank you, Master," she said. I do not think she could have been more pleased if I had considered allowing her a sheath gown of white satin, with gloves and pearls.

I cut a length from the red bark cloth, about five feet in length and a foot in width. I wrapped it about the sweetness of her slave hips and tucked it in. I pushed it down so that her navel might be well revealed. It is called the "slave belly" on Gor. Only slave girls, on Gor, reveal their navels.

"You make me show the 'slave belly,' Master," she said.

"Is it not appropriate?" I asked.

"Yes, Master," she said, "it is."

"Do you like it?" I asked.

"Yes, Master," she said.

"You are a slave, aren't you?" I asked.

"Yes, Master," she said. I liked it, too. It reveals, well, the roundness of her belly and, low at the hips, the beginning of subtle love curves.

"Do you understand the meaning of the tuck closing on the skirt?" I asked.

"Master?" she asked.

I then, rudely, tore away the garment, spinning her, stumbling, from me. She gasped, brutally and suddenly stripped. She looked at me, frightened, again naked before her master.

"Do you now understand?" I asked.

"Yes, Master," she said.

I threw her the garment again.

Hastily she put it on again, not neglecting to thrust it well down on her hips, that the slave belly would be well revealed.

"Excellent, Slave," I said.

334

"Thank you, Master," she said.

I then reached into a sack, near the fire. I drew forth from it a handful of strings of beads. I threw her a necklace of red and black beads, which I thought was nice.

"Master," she asked, pointing, "may I also have that string of beads."

Tende and Alice each had two strings of beads. I saw no reason why the blond-haired barbarian might not be similarly ornamented.

I handed her the second string of beads and put the others back in the sack. She had already put the first string, that of red and black beads, about her throat. She looped them twice and still they fell between her lovely breasts, one loop longer than the other. The second string of beads was blue and yellow. Both strings were of small, simple wooden beads, suitable for slave girls. "Master," she asked, holding out to me the blue and yellow beads, "would you not, please, put this string upon me?"

"Very well," I said, standing behind her, looping them twice, one loop smaller than the other, about her throat. Each loop, as with the red and black beads, fell between her sweet breasts.

"Why did you want this string?" I asked.

"Are blue and yellow not the colors of the slavers?" she asked.

"Yes," I said. Blue and yellow are often used for the tenting of slave pavilions, and in the décor of auction houses. The wagons of slavers often have blue and yellow canvas. Sometimes they bind their girls with blue and yellow ropes. Sometimes their girls wear yellow-enameled collars, and yellow-enameled wrist rings and ankle rings, with chains with blue links. In his best, a slaver will usually wear blue and yellow robes, or robes in which these colors are prominent. He will, normally, in his day-to-day business, wear at least chevrons, or slashes, of blue and yellow on his lower left sleeve.

"Are blue and yellow beads then," she asked, "not appropriate for me, for I am a slave?"

"They are very nice," I said, "but any simple, cheap beads, say, of wood or glass, will do as well for a slave."

"I see, Master," she said. "But may I keep them?"

"Until I, or any free man," I said, "sees fit to take them from you." I held her by the upper arms, from behind. "You do not own them," I said. "You only wear them, and on the sufferance of free men."

"Yes, Master," she said. "I own nothing. It is, rather, I who am owned."

"Yes," I said. I turned her about, to face me. "You are beginning to feel and understand your slavery, aren't you?" I asked.

"Yes, Master," she said. "Tonight you taught me much. For the first time in my life, tonight, I moved totally as a woman. I do not think I could go back, Master, to moving as a man."

I held her, tightly, and looked sternly into her eyes. "You are not a man," I told her. "You are a woman. That is what you are. Try to understand that. You are a woman, not a man."

"Yes, Master," she sobbed.

"It is thus permissible for you, truly, to move as a woman, and to feel and think and behave like a woman."

"I am a slave," she said, "and yet, strangely, I am beginning to feel so free."

"You are breaking through the constrictions of a pathological conditioning program," I told her.

I looked at her.

She trembled.

"Go to the slave post," I said. "Sit there, with your back to the post, your hands crossed behind your back."

"Yes, Master," she said.

I took a piece of improvised binding fiber, a narrow strip of leather some five feet long, and crouched down behind her.

"You freed me of many inhibitions tonight, Master," she said. "Was that your intention?"

"Perhaps," I said.

"I am grateful," she said.

"Oh!" she winced, as I knotted her hands behind her back.

"I am a woman," she said. "I want to be a woman, truly."

"Have no fear," I said. "You will be."

She looked at me.

"Gorean men," I said, "do not accept the conceit and pretense of pseudo-masculinity in female slaves."

"They would enforce my womanhood upon me?" she asked.

"You are a slave," I said. "You will be given no choice but to manfest your total womanhood to your master, in all its full vulnerability and beauty."

"But then I would have to obey, and please them," she said.

"Yes," I said.

"Surely they would show me some compromise," she said.

"The Gorean man," I said, "does not compromise with a female slave. If necessary, you will learn your womanhood under the whip."

"But what if, even then," she asked, "I am not sufficiently pleasing?"

"You will then perhaps be fed to sleen," I said.

"Yes, Master," she said.

I fastened the free end of the binding fiber to the slave post, and stood up.

"I am a secured slave," she said.

"Yes," I said.

"Master," she said.

"Yes," I said.

"There was one thing I did not tell you about my dream."

"What was that?" I asked.

"It is something that you will not understand," she said, "for you are a man."

"What is that?" I asked.

"It was when I must needs please my master well, and as a slave," she said.

"Yes," I said.

"I wanted to please him," she whispered.

"Of course," I said. "You were desperate to please him, for you knew that if you were not pleasing to him, you would be cruelly and horribly destroyed."

"But I wanted to please him, too, for another reason," she said.

"What was that?" I asked.

"You will not understand," she said. "A man could never understand."

"What?" I asked.

"I wanted to please him," she said, "—because he was my master." She looked at me. "A girl can want to please her master," she said, "because he is her master."

I did not speak.

"Can you understand that?" she asked.

I shrugged.

"Do you think that we would make you such superb slaves if we did not want to be your slaves?"

"Perhaps not," I said.

337

"A girl desires to please her master," she said. "Can you understand that, Master?"

"I think so," I said.

"I desire to please you," she whispered.

"I see," I said.

"Master," she said.

"Yes," I said.

"Why did you not rape me tonight, Master?" she asked. "Am I not pleasing to you?"

"Later, perhaps," I said.

"You're training me, aren't you, Master?" she asked.

"Yes," I said.

33

WHAT WE SAW FROM THE HEIGHT OF THE FALLS; TENDE DANCES; WE ENTER AGAIN UPON THE RIVER; I ANTICIPATE THE SURRENDER OF THE BLOND-HAIRED BARBARIAN

We thrust the canoe upward, Kisu and I at the stern, Ayari and the girls hauling on ropes at the forequarter. It tipped up and then settled downward, and we thrust and hauled it, laden, to the level.

The sound of the falls, to our left, plunging some four hundred feet to the waters below, was deafening.

It is difficult to convey the splendor of the Ua's scenery to those who have not seen it. There is the mightiness of the river, like a great road, twisting and turning, occasionally broken with green islands, sometimes sluggish, sometimes shattered by rapids and cataracts, sometimes interrupted by flooding cascades of water, sometimes a few feet in height and sometimes towering upwards hundreds of feet, and then there is the jungle, its immensity and wildlife, and the vast sky above it.

"I am pleased," said Kisu, happily, wiping the sweat from his brow.

"Why?" I asked.

"Come here," he said.

"Be careful!" I said to him. He was wading out into the water.

"Come here!" he called.

I waded after him, some forty or fifty feet out into the current. It was only to our knees there.

"Look!" he said, pointing.

From the height of the falls we could see for pasangs behind us downriver. It was not only a spectacular but also a marvelous coign of vantage.

"I knew it would be so!" he cried, slapping his thigh in pleasure.

I looked, the hair on the back of my neck rising.

"Tende! Tende!" called Kisu. "Come here, now!"

The girl, moving carefully, waded to where we stood. Kisu seized her by the back of the neck and faced her downriver. "See, my pretty slave?" he asked.

"Yes, my master," she said, frightened.

"It is he," said Kisu. "He is coming for you!"

"Yes, Master," she said.

"Hurry now to the shore," he said. "Build a fire, prepare food, Slave."

"Yes, Master," she said, commanded, hurrying from us to address herself to her tasks.

I looked into the distance, downriver, half shutting my eyes against the glare from the water.

Downriver, several pasangs away, small but unmistakable, moving in our direction, was a fleet of canoes and river vessels. There must have been in the neighborhood of a hundred, oared river galleys, the balance of the fleet which had been prepared for Shaba's originally projected penetration of the Ua, and perhaps again as many canoes. If there were crews of fifty on the galleys and from five to ten men in a canoe, the force behind us must have ranged somewhere between five and six thousand men.

"It is Bila Huruma!" shouted Kisu in triumph.

"So this is why you accompanied me on the Ua?" I asked.

"I would have come with you anyway, to help you, for you are my friend," said Kisu. "But our ways, happily, led us in the same direction. Is that not a splendid coincidence?"

"Yes, splendid," I smiled.

"You see now what was my plan?" he asked.

"Your mysterious plan?" I grinned.

"Yes," he said, happily.

"I thought this might be it," I said. "But I think you may have miscalculated."

"I could not in battle beat Bila Huruma," said Kisu. "His askaris were superior to my villagers. But now, as I have stolen Tende, his projected companion, I have lured him into the jungle. I need now only lead him on and on, until he is slain in the jungle, or until, bereft of men and supplies, I need only turn back and meet him, as man to man, as warrior to warrior."

I looked at him.

"Thus," said Kisu, "in destroying Bila Huruma, I will destroy the empire."

"It is an intelligent and bold plan," I said, "but I think you may have miscalculated."

"How is that?" asked Kisu.

"Do you truly think that Bila Huruma," I asked, "who owns or is companion to perhaps hundreds of women would pursue you into the jungle at great risk to himself and his empire to get back one girl, a girl whom he doubtless realizes has by now been reduced to slavery, and has thus been rendered politically worthless, and a girl who was never more to him to begin with than a convenience in a minor political situation on the Ngao coast?"

"Yes," said Kisu. "It will be a matter of principle for him."

"It might be a matter of principle for you," I said, "but I doubt that it would be a matter of principle for Bila Huruma. There are principles and there are principles. For a man such as Bila Huruma I conjecture that the principle of preserving his empire would take precedence over matters of minor personal concern."

"But Bila Huruma is on the river," said Kisu.

"Probably," I said.

"Thus," said Kisu, "you are wrong."

"Perhaps," I said.

"Do you think he follows you?" asked Kisu.

"No," I said, "I am unimportant to him."

"Thus," said Kisu, "it is I whom he follows."

"Perhaps," I said. "Perhaps you are right."

Kisu then turned and, happily, waded back to the shore.

"Remove your garment," said Kisu to Tende.

"Yes, Master," she said.

"Follow me," he said.

"Yes, Master," she said.

"You others may come, too," he said.

Wading, we followed Kisu and Tende out toward the center of the river. There was there, overlooking the falls, a large, flat rock. We climbed onto the rock. From its surface we could see downriver, and, pasangs back, the flotilla of canoes and galleys of the Ubar, Bila Huruma.

"What are you going to do with me, Master?" asked Tende.

"I am going to dance you naked," he said. He thrust her forward on the rock, facing downriver.

Tende stood there, trembling, dressed only in her slave beads.

"Bila Huruma!" called Kisu. "I am Kisu!" He pointed at the girl. "This is the woman, Tende, who was to have been your companion! I took her from you! I made her my slave!"

Bila Huruma, of course, if he were with the flotilla, as we conjectured, could not have heard Kisu. The distance was too great. Too, had he been within fifty yards he probably could not have heard him, because of the roar of the falls. Moreover, so far away was the flotilla, I had little doubt but what we could not be seen from its position. We could see the flotilla largely because of the size of its galleys and the number of its vessels, both canoes and galleys. The canoes were almost invisible from where we stood. Had there been but a single canoe it would have been extremely difficult to detect. Similarly, from the position of the flotilla we would be, of course, specks upon a larger speck, for most practical purposes invisible. I had never seen glasses of the builders in the palace of Bila Huruma. Shaba, however, I was sure, from Anango, would possess such an instrument. It would make him difficult to approach.

"This is the woman, Tende," called Kisu, facing his distant enemy, shouting against the roar of the falls, pointing to Tende. "She was to have been your companion! I took her away from you! I made her mine! I now exhibit her naked before you as my slave!"

"He cannot see you or hear you!" shouted Ayari.

"That does not matter," laughed Kisu. He gave Tende a happy slap below the small of the back.

"Oh!" she cried.

"Dance, Tende!" said he. He began to sing and clap, looking downriver.

"That is a slave song!" she cried.

He stopped clapping and singing, and regarded her.

"There are white slaves present, Master!" she cried.

He looked upon her sternly.

"I dance, my master," she cried, frightened. She flexed her legs, freeing her body to move, and extended her arms gracefully to the right, the right arm further advanced than the left.

"Is she free?" asked Ayari.

"No," said Kisu.

"Have her put her arms over her head, wrists back to back," said Ayari.

"Do so," said Kisu.

Tende complied. "How lovely that is," said Kisu.

"I have seen it done in Schendi," said Ayari. "It is one of the ways in which a slave may begin a dance."

I smiled to myself. That was true. The lovely posture which Tende had just assumed was undeniably one of the initial postures of certain slave dances. It is widely known on Gor, of course, not just in Schendi. It is, for example, quite familiar in Port Kar and, far to the southeast of that port, and somewhere far to the north and east of our present position, in the Tahari. Slave dances, of course, may begin in dozens of ways, sometimes even with the girl roped or chained at a man's feet. I looked at Tende. To be sure, only a slave dance could begin from such a posture. No free woman, for example, would dare to place herself in such a position before Gorean free men, unless perhaps, weary of her misery and frustration, she was begging them, almost explicitly, to put her in a collar. There are many stories of Gorean free women, sometimes of high caste, who, as a lark or in a spirit of bold play, dared to dance in a paga tavern. Often, perhaps to their horror, they found themselves that very night hooded and gagged, locked in close chains, lying on their back, their legs drawn up, fastened in a wagon, chained by the neck and ankles, their small bodies bruised on its rough boards as they, helpless beneath a rough tarn blanket, are carried through the gates of their city.

"Are you ready, Slave?" asked Kisu.

"Yes, Master," said Tende.

I am fond of slave dances. It is hard for a woman to be more beautiful than when she dances her beauty as a slave

342

before masters. But then a woman can be incredibly beautiful in almost all attitudes and postures. It is strange that the men of Earth are so seldom aware of the subtler beauties of women, but then they have not seen them in their full femininity, as slaves. A woman can be very beautiful simply greeting her master, head down, at the door to his chambers. She can be very beautiful in doing so small a thing as pouring his wine, eyes downcast, gracefully, as his slave. Perhaps she is a bit more beautiful, however, when she kneels helplessly before you, or lies piteously at your feet supplicating you to satisfy her slave needs. Perhaps she is most beautiful when she, collared in your arms, cries out in orgasm, acknowledging you as her master.

"Dance, Slave," said Kisu.

"Yes, Master," said Tende.

Tende then, obedient to her master's command, as Kisu clapped his hands and sang, danced on a flat rock in the Ua river, danced before Bila Huruma, so far away, her master's enemy, from whom she had been stolen.

She danced well.

I observed the eyes of the blond-haired barbarian who, with Alice, knelt on the rock. The eyes of the blond-haired barbarian, gazing on the exhibited slave, shone with excitement. How beautiful Tende was. And how stimulating it was to the blond-haired barbarian to realize that a man could force a woman to do this sort of thing.

Kisu continued to clap his hands. He continued to sing, the strains of a melodic slave song.

Dancers bring high prices on Gor. Some slavers specialize in dancers, renting them, and buying and selling them. Two such houses in Ar are those of Kelsius and Aurelius. Some say that the finest dancers on Gor are found in Ar; others say that they are found in Port Kar, and others that they are in the Tahari, or in Turia. These controversies, I think, are fruitless. I have been in many cities and in each I have found marvelous dancers. The matter is further complicated by the buying and selling of girls and their shipment, as merchandise, among cities. A dancer has usually had many masters; her fair throat has been graced by many collars. In some cities if a dancer is not thought to have been sufficiently pleasing she is thrown to the patrons of the tavern to be torn to pieces or beaten. If she is thought to have been sufficiently pleasing she may be auctioned, for the period of an Ahn, to the highest bidder.

"Enough!" called Kisu, happily. Tende stopped dancing. He then, to her surprise, with a leather strap, as she stood on the rock overlooking the falls, tied her hands behind her back. He then took her by the hair, bent her over, and waded her back to the shore. We followed him, I stopping to look once more downriver, at the tiny objects so far away, yet objects I knew to be filled with men.

Kisu and I thrust the canoe into the shallow water. As I held it he placed Tende on her knees in the canoe. He then crossed and tied her ankles. He then took two lengths of rope. He tied them both on her neck and then took the free end of one and tied it to a thwart forward of her position and the free end of the other and tied it to the thwart aft of her position, thus fastening her between these two thwarts.

"Master?" she asked.

"That should hold you," he said.

That was an understatement. Kisu tied well.

"Why are you placing me under such great security, Master?" she asked.

"Bila Huruma is now behind us," he said. "You will not, now, go running back to him."

She put back her head and laughed. "Oh, Master!" she protested.

"What is wrong?" he asked.

"I do not wish to run away from you," she said.

"Oh?" he asked.

She looked at him. "Do you not know, by now, my Master," she asked, "that Tende is your conquered slave?"

"No chances will be taken with you, Slave," he said.

"As my master wishes," she said, putting her head down.

I saw then, as I think that Kisu did not, that the proud Tende, who had been so haughty and cold, was now naught but a surrendered love slave. I smiled to myself. She was now, indeed, politically worthless.

"What of the remains of the fire?" asked Ayari. "Should we not dispose of such evidence of this brief encampment?"

"No," said Kisu. "Leave it."

"But it will mark our trail," said Ayari.

"Of course," said Kisu. "It is my intention that it do so."

We then moved the canoe, wading beside it, with the exception of Tende, fastened within it, out into the river.

Kisu, waist deep in the water, turned to look back, over the falls. He lifted his fist and shook it. "Follow me, Bila Huruma!" he cried. "Follow me, Bila Huruma, if you dare!"

His voice was almost indistinguishable against the roar of the waters. He then lowered his fist and slipped into the canoe, taking his place at the stern. Ayari and Alice entered the canoe. I then slipped into the canoe and, taking the blond-haired barbarian under the arms, drew her into the canoe. I did not immediately release her. She turned her head back, over her left shoulder. "Did you see it," she asked, "on the rock, he danced her naked!" "Of course," I said. "She is only a slave." "Yes, Master," said the blond-haired barbarian. "Like yourself," I said. "Yes, Master," she said. I then thrust her ahead of me, to her place. "Take your place, Slave Girl," I said. "Yes, Master," she said. We then lifted our paddles and lent our strengths to the task at hand.

Once she looked back at me. But my stern gaze warned her to direct her attention again to her work and the river.

I smiled to myself. I saw that the slave girl in her was now well ready to be released. This very night, I thought, she would beg explicitly for her master's touch.

34

THE BLOND-HAIRED BARBARIAN DANCES; WHAT OCCURRED IN THE RAIN FOREST BETWEEN A MASTER AND HIS SLAVE

"Watch out!" I said.

The tarsk, a small one, no more than forty pounds, tusked, snorting, bits of leaf scattering behind it, charged.

It swerved, slashing with its curved tusks, and I only managed to turn it aside with the point of the raider's spear I carried, one of four such weapons we had had since our brief skirmish with raiders, that in which we had obtained our canoe, that which had occurred in the marsh east of Ushindi. It had twisted back on me with incredible swiftness.

The blond-haired barbarian screamed.

I thrust at it again. Again it spun and charged. Again I thrust it back. There was blood on the blade of the spear and the animal's coat was glistening with it. Such animals are best hunted from the back of kaiila with lances, in the open. They are cunning, persistent and swift. The giant tarsk, which can stand ten hands at the shoulder, is even hunted with lances from tarnback.

It snuffled and snorted, and again charged. Again I diverted its slashing weight. One does not follow such an animal into the bush. It is not simply a matter of reduced visibility but it is also a matter of obtaining free play for one's weapons. Even in the open, as I was, in a clearing among trees, it is hard to use one's spear to its best advantage, the animal stays so close to you and moves so quickly.

Suddenly it turned its short wide head, with that bristling mane running down its back to its tail. "Get behind me!" I called to the girl. It put down its head, mounted on that short, thick neck, and, scrambling, charged at the blond-haired barbarian. She stumbled back, screaming, and, the animal at her legs, fell. But in that moment, from the side, I thrust the animal from her. It, immediately, turned again. I thrust it again to the side. This time, suddenly, before it could turn again, I, with a clear stroke, thrust the spear through its thick-set body, behind the right foreleg.

I put my head back, breathing heavily.

Pressing against the animal with my foot I freed the spear.

I turned to the blond-haired barbarian. "Are you all right?" I asked.

"Yes," she said. There was blood on her left leg, on the outside of the leg, about six inches up from the ankle.

I crouched down beside her. "Give me your leg," I said.

I looked at the leg. She sat on the floor of the rain forest. Her leg felt good in my hands.

"Is it serious, Master?" she asked.

"No," I said. "It is nothing. It is only a scratch." She had been fortunate.

"It will not leave a scar, will it?" she asked.

"No," I said.

"That is good," she said. She leaned back in relief, bracing her body on the palms of her hands. "I want to be pretty," she said, "both for myself, and for my master, or masters."

"You are pretty," I said. "Indeed, in the past few weeks, you have become even beautiful."

"Thank you, Master," she said. She looked at me. "I'm yours, you know," she said.

"Of course," I said.

"Yet you have not taken me since Schendi," she said.

"That is true," I said.

"You made me yield well to you there, and as a full slave," she said.

I did not speak.

"And when you threw me on my back, head down, over your sea bag, and raped me with such brutal dispatch I well learned that I was no longer a free woman."

"It is a useful lesson for a slave girl to learn quickly," I said.

"And I remember the girl I saw there, briefly, in the mirror. She was so beautiful."

"Yes," I said.

"But she was so beautiful she could be only a slave."

"Yes," I said.

"But I am an Earth woman," she said. "I could not dare to be that girl."

I smiled. Did she not realize that she had seen in Schendi, in those brief moments, the slave she had for so long concealed within herself, that she had seen then, frightened, scarcely daring to recognize her, her own self? What cruelties could men inflict upon women, I wondered, which could half compare with those they inflict upon themselves.

She leaned forward, and examined the wound on her leg.

"It is superficial," I said. "It will not scar."

"I have a slave's vanity, don't I?" she asked.

"Yes," I said.

"Is it permissible?" she asked.

"Yes," I said.

"Good," she said.

She continued to look at the wound on her leg.

"I do not think I could stand to bring a lower price than Tende or Alice," she said.

"What a slave you are," I said.

"Yes, Master," she said.

"Have no fear," I said. "Your value on the sales block has not been reduced."

"Thank you, Master," she said.

I then rose to my feet and walked a few yards away, to a fan palm. From the base of one of its broad leaves I gathered a double handful of fresh water. I returned to the girl and, carefully, washed out the wound. She winced. I then cut some leaves and wrapped them about it. I tied shut this simple bandage with the tendrils of a carpet plant.

"Thank you, Master," she said. She reached up and put her

arms about my neck. I took her hands and, slowly, pulled them from my neck. I put them to her sides. She looked at me. I cuffed her, snapping her head to the right. "Master?" she asked.

"Next time," I said, "stay behind me."

"Yes, Master," she said.

"Stand, Slave," I said.

"Yes, Master," she said.

It had been this morning, shortly before noon, that we had surmounted the height of the falls, that almost on the summit of which Kisu, in the face of the distant, oncoming forces of Bila Huruma, had danced a naked slave called Tende.

I went over to the slain tarsk.

We had then continued on, up the river, for several hours. In the late afternoon we had brought the canoe to shore, concealed it, and then went inland to make our camp.

"I feel the desire for meat," had said Kisu. "I, too," I said. "I will hunt." Kisu and I, warriors, wanted meat. Too, ahead of us we suspected that the river, as we had been warned at the last village, would become ever more dangerous and treacherous. We felt the long-term strength of meat protein would be a useful addition to our diets.

"I will need a beast of burden," I had said.

The blond-haired barbarian, immediately, had sprung to her feet. She had stood before me, her head down. "I am a beast of burden," she had said.

"Follow me," I had said.

"Yes, Master," she had said.

I lifted up the wild tarsk.

We had proceeded into the rain forest for better than two Ahn before we had come upon the tarsk. It had charged. I had killed it.

"Bend down," I told the girl.

I threw the tarsk across her shoulders. She staggered under its weight.

I then turned from her and left the clearing. My hands were free for the use of the spear. Gasping, behind me, stumbling, staggering under the weight of the tarsk I had killed, came my slave.

I looked upward, through the trees. "It is growing dark," I said. "We will not have time to reach the encampment before nightfall. We will make a small camp in the forest, and proceed in the morning."

"Yes, Master," she said.

As the girl, on her knees, tended the roasting tarsk, I cut a long stake, some four and one half feet in length and some four inches in width. About its top, about two inches from the end, I cut a groove, about an inch deep.

"What is that for?" she asked.

"It is a slave stake," I said, "for securing you for the night."

"I see," she said. She turned the tarsk on its spit. It glistened. From its sides droplets of fat and blood, popping and sizzling, dropped into the fire.

With a large rock, blow by blow, heavily, inch by inch, I drove the long, thick stake into the ground. I left about four inches of it exposed.

"The tarsk is ready," she said.

I took one end of the spit in two hands and lifted the tarsk from the fire, putting it down on leaves. I then crouched beside it, and began to cut into it, to the spit. I looked up. The girl, kneeling by the fire, watched me. I rose to my feet. I tied a long leather strap on her neck and led her to the slave stake. I tied the free end of the strap about the slave stake, using the prepared groove in the stake which I had earlier cut. "Kneel," I told her. "Yes, Master," she said. She then knelt there, tethered to the stake by the neck. I had left her about seven feet of slack in the strap. I then returned to the meat, and began to cut slices from it, and feed. After I had begun to feel full I looked at the girl. I threw her a piece of meat, which struck against her body. It fell to the ground. She picked it up in two hands and, watching me, began to eat it.

After a time I wiped my face with my forearm. I was finished eating. I again looked at the girl. "Do you want more?" I asked. "No, Master," she said.

We had drunk earlier, from the water cupped at the base of the leaves of fan palms.

I then lay on one elbow, near the fire. I regarded the beautiful slave. It is pleasant to own women.

"Are you going to tie my hands behind my back before you retire?" she asked.

"Yes," I told her.

"That is common in slave security, isn't it?" she asked.

"It is common in the open," I said, "when one does not have cages, or chains and slave bracelets, at one's disposal. A girl's hands, of course, need not be tied behind her back. They might be tied over her head or before her body, usually about a small tree."

"Are girls secured at night, in the cities?" she asked.

"Sometimes," I said, "sometimes not. They are collared. The cities are walled. Where would they run to?"

"But not all girls wish to escape, do they?" she asked.

"No," I said. "All the evidence supports the thesis that very few girls desire to escape their masters. Slavery apparently agrees with them. But all girls, whether they wish to escape or not, know that escape is almost impossible. Besides, if they should escape, they would doubtless soon fall to another master, perhaps worse than the first."

"Yes, Master," she said.

"Too," I said, "I am not certain that it is altogether wise for a girl to attempt to escape. For example, if she is caught, her feet may be cut off."

"I would be afraid to try to escape, Master," she said.

"You tried to escape in Port Kar," I said. I had caught her, and tied her and returned her to Ulafi, who had been at that time her master. I had wanted her shipped to Schendi that I might, by means of her, following her sales and exchanges, be led to the lair of the treacherous Shaba, traitor to Priest-Kings.

"I did not even begin to understand at that time," she said, "what might be involved, the almost total impossibility of escape and the drastic nature of the penalties which Gorean men might, without a second thought, so casually inflict upon me. I did not even begin to understand at that time what it might mean to be a slave girl on Gor."

"But you understand a little of what it might mean now, don't you?" I asked.

"Yes, Master," she said, kneeling there by the slave stake, the tether tied on her throat. She fingered the tether. "If I had known then what I now know," she said, "I would not have dared to move."

I nodded.

"I would have been afraid," she smiled, wryly, "to have moved even so much as a muscle, for fear one of Ulafi's men would have put me under the lash."

"Of course," I said.

Intelligent women learned swiftly the realities of Gor.

"Master," she said.

"Yes," I said.

"Not all masters would secure their slaves at night, would they, even in the open?"

"No," I said. "Much depends on the girl and the area."

"A master would not be likely to secure a conquered love slave, would he?" she asked.

"He might," I said, "if only to remind her that she is a slave."

"I see," she said.

"There is another reason, too, for securing a slave at night," I said, "for example, for locking her in her kennel or, if she is to be kept out-of-doors, chaining her to a ring in your courtyard."

"What is that?" she asked.

"To keep her from being stolen," I said.

"We could be stolen, couldn't we?" she said. She trembled.

"Of course," I said. "Slave theft is not unknown on Gor."

"I have heard," she said, "that girls are often chained at night to slave rings at the foot of their masters' couches."

"That is true," I said.

"But surely there is little danger," she said, "of a girl being stolen from her master's compartments."

"Not while he is there," I admitted.

"Then why are they chained like that?" she asked.

"Because they are slaves," I said.

"Yes, Master," she said, putting her head down.

"It is nearly time to tie you for the night," I said.

"Oh, please, Master," she said, lifting her head, "let me speak but a moment more with you. Do not tie your slave just now."

"Very well," I said.

She knelt back, happily, on her heels. She put her hands on the tether at her throat.

"Wasn't it horrifying," she asked, "what Kisu did to Tende today?"

"What?" I asked.

"Making her dance naked," she said.

"No," I said.

"Oh," she said.

"She is a slave," I reminded her.

"Yes, Master," she said. She looked at me. "It is permissible for a slave to dance naked?" she asked.

"Yes," I said.

She looked down. "Master," she said.

"Yes," I said.

"Am I a slave object?" she asked.

"Of course," I said. "And a very delicious one," I added.

"Thank you, Master," she said.

"Does it trouble you to be an object?" I asked.

"I do not feel like an object," she said.

"Technically," I said, "in the eyes of Gorean law you are not an object but an animal."

"I see," she said.

"In one sense," I said, "no living human being, nor bird nor squirrel, can be an object. They are not, for example, tables or rocks. In another sense all living creatures are objects. For example, they occupy space and obey the laws of physics and chemistry."

"You know what I mean," she said.

"No," I said, "I do not. Speak more clearly."

"A woman is treated like an object," she said, "when men do not listen to her or care for her feelings."

"Surely women, in the single-minded pursuit of certain goals, can treat other women, and men, in that way?" I asked. "And men could treat men in that way, and so on? Is not the problem you have in mind a rather general one?"

"Perhaps," she said.

"Similarly," I said, "do not confuse being treated as an object with being an object. Similarly, do not confuse being treated as an object with being regarded as an object. For example, individuals who treat human beings as objects very seldom think that they are really objects. That would suggest insanity."

"You do not respond properly," she smiled.

"Is your criterion for being treated as an object that men do not agree with you?" I asked. "If so, that is somewhat obtuse."

"I suppose perhaps it is," she said. "If men do not do what we want, then they, so to speak, have not listened to us or paid attention to our feelings."

"That is a very interesting way of thinking," I admitted. "By the same token, if women did not pay close attention to the wishes of men and comply with their desires, then men might be entitled to regard themselves as being treated as objects."

"How silly," she said.

"Yes," I said.

"It is hard to talk with you about these things," she said.

"I think so," I said.

"You are not familiar with the slogans," she said.

"That is perhaps it," I admitted.

"I shall try again," she said.

"Do so," I encouraged her.

"Men," she said, "are only interested in women's bodies."

"I have never known a man who was only interested in a woman's body," I said. "This is not to deny that some such unusual person might somewhere exist."

She looked at me.

"If what you say is true," I said, "it would be the case that it would make no difference to a man whether the woman with whom he was relating was conscious or not. Indeed, if what you say is true, it should not even make a difference to him whether he held a sentient woman in his arms or an unconscious mechanism designed to resemble such a woman. I submit, with all due respect, that that is not only libelous, but preposterous. Surely no rational person, male or female, if they took a moment to reflect, could entertain so peculiar a hypothesis. No man with whom I am familiar would be content with a woman who lacked consciousness. That sort of thing is simply stupid. It seems to me it would even have limited propaganda value."

"The men of Earth can be confused and terrorized by such assertions," she said.

"Some, perhaps," I said, "idiots."

"Perhaps," she said. "But such assertions can be politically effective."

"Yes," I agreed. "The trick is to make a charge so obviously false or hopelessly vague that your interlocutor, who is usually concerned to be polite and congenial, makes a fool of himself trying to treat it seriously. It is a little like the fellow who tries to respond to the charge that he is a mad sleen by discussing the results of his blood tests."

"Perhaps what is meant," she said, "is that men do not pay sufficient attention to the thinking and feelings of women."

"That is a totally different charge," I said, "and one that may well be true."

She looked at me.

"It is a common property of human beings," I said, "that they, for better or for worse, do not pay much attention to the thoughts and feelings of others. Thus, it would not be surprising if most men did not pay much attention to the thoughts and feelings of women. If it is any consolation, they do not pay much attention to the thoughts and feelings of

353

other men either. Similar remarks, of course, hold for women. Many women, for example, are excellent in not listening to others. No one sex has a monopoly on dogmatism." I looked at her. "If you are interested in this sort of thing from the Gorean viewpoint," I said, "free men and women are usually attentive to the thoughts and feelings of one another. Not only are they free, but they may even share a Home Stone. Free women, in being free, command attention when they speak. It is their due. The case with slaves, such as you, my dear, is of course much different. The difference, however, is that respect and attention is not due to you, that it need not be accorded to you. You are slave. In actual practice, of course, masters tend to pay a great deal of attention to the thoughts and feelings of their lovely slaves. It is rewarding and delicious to do so. How wonderful it is to know another human being so intimately, especially one one owns. There are no secrets between masters and slaves. Her deepest thoughts and desires, as well as her most trivial fancies and observations, are open to him and, because he owns her, of great interest to him. A man is much more likely to be intensely fond of a girl he owns than of a free individual toward whom he stands in a mere contractual relationship. The latter he does not own; the former he does. The owned girl is a valuable; she is precious; this makes her much different from a business partner. For what it is worth, the most intimate and deepest loves I have know have been between masters and their slaves, that between the love master and his love slave."

"But the woman is still a slave," she said.

"Yes," I said, "totally and categorically. She may even be sold, if he wills."

"The attention and love such a girl obtains," she said, "need not be accorded to her."

"No," I said. "It is a gift of the master."

"He could, at any point," she said, "simply order her to silence and put her to his feet."

"Of course," I said, "and sometimes he will, if only to remind her that she is a slave."

"She is, then, for all her freedom, yet absolutely under his will."

"Yes," I said. "She is his slave."

"I love you, Master," she whispered.

I listened to the crackling of the fire, and the sounds of the jungle night.

"As an Earth woman," I said, "you are doubtless not accustomed to thinking of yourself as an article of property."

"No, Master," she smiled.

"But I think, now," I said, "that you may be ready to understand the sense in which you are a slave object."

"Yes, Master," she said, tears in her eyes.

"You are a beautiful woman, who is owned," I said. "You may be bought and sold."

"Yes, Master," she said.

"Too," I said, "not the least attention need be paid to your desires, your thoughts or feelings."

"Yes, Master," she said.

"That is mainly what it is to be a slave object," I said.

"I understand, my master," she said.

"You see," I said, "it has nothing to do with consciousness or feelings."

"I acknowledge the justice of the expression," she said, "but somehow it seems quite inapt."

"Perhaps you will not think so," I said, "when you are put in chains and sold to a master who terrifies you."

"No, Master," she smiled.

"Why do you feel the expression is inapt?" I asked.

"Because I do not feel like an 'Object'," she said. "Never have I been so alive, so excited, and so vital, or have I felt so significant and real, as when I have been a slave. Never in the constrictions of my freedom could I have understood such experiences to exist as I have felt on this world as a lowly slave. I had not dreamed such happiness could exist. I did not know I could experience such joy."

"Perhaps I should whip you," I said.

"Please, no, Master," she said. "Be merciful to your girl."

I shrugged. I determined that I would not whip her, at least at the moment.

"So you see, Master," she said, "though in some respects I am a slave object, an article of property that may be bought and sold, a thing whose desires, whose thoughts and feelings, need not be in the least respected, in another sense, that of feeling and emotion, I am so far removed from the notion of an object that the use of such an expression is totally inadequate to convey the least understanding of my felt realities. I was far more of an "object," a thing manipulated by the internalized demands of others, a thing not daring to feel, a thing not daring to be true to itself, when I was free than I

355

am now, a slave girl in the uncompromising shackles of your bondage."

"I concede," I smiled. "For most practical purposes the expression 'slave object' is not well chosen to express the realities involved. Indeed, for most practical purposes, the expression is not only misleading and infelicitous but, as you have pointed out, inapt."

"You see," she said, "in some respects I am an object, and in other respects I am not an object."

"Yes," I said, "and in the deepest respects you are not an object."

"Yes, Master," she smiled.

I looked at her, kneeling there before me, the bit of bark cloth at her hips, the two necklaces, one red and black, one blue and yellow, about her throat, my tether knotted on her throat, fastening her to the slave stake. "But you are a slave animal," I said.

"Yes, Master," she smiled. "I am a slave animal."

"It is time to tie you for the night, my pretty slave animal," I said.

"The animal begs that you not tie her just now," she said.

"Very well," I said. I looked at her. I reclined on my elbow. She knelt.

"Most slave girls, you have told me," she said, "do not desire to escape."

"That is apparently true," I said. "That is strange, isn't it?" I asked.

"I do not find it strange," she said.

"Oh?" I asked.

"I do not want to escape," she said.

"You will be tied anyway," I told her.

"Of course, Master," she smiled.

"Master," she said.

"Yes," I said.

"Animals have needs," she said.

"What sorts of needs?" I asked.

"Many sorts," she said.

"Sexual?" I asked.

"Yes," she said. She put her head down. Her lip trembled.

"Look at me, Slave," I told her.

She looked at me. There were tears in her eyes. "Do you admit that you have sexual needs?" I asked.

"Yes, Master," she sobbed.

"Is your admission merely intellectual?" I asked.

356

"No, Master," she said. "It is deeper than that." The intellectual admission that one possesses sexual needs is cheap. It is well within the range of even the clever bigot. That sort of admission, automatic, expected and innocuous, serves often not only in lieu of an authentic emotional admission but serves often, too, as a psychological device whereby just such an honest concession to the needs of one's deeper nature may be avoided.

"Do you have sexual needs, truly?" I asked.

"Yes," she said.

"And do you wish them satisfied?" I asked.

"Yes," she said.

"Say then, aloud," I said, " 'I have sexual needs, truly.' "

"I am a woman of Earth!" she protested. "Please do not make me say that."

"Say it," I said.

"I have sexual needs," she said, "—truly."

"Say now," I said, " 'I want them satisfied.' "

"I want them satisfied," she said.

"Say," I said, " 'I will never again deny my sexual needs.' "

"I will never again deny my sexual needs," she said.

"Say," I said, " 'I will be such and behave in such a way as to attempt to secure the satisfaction of my deepest and most honest sexual needs.' "

"I will be such and behave in such a way," she said, "as to attempt to secure the satisfaction of my deepest and most honest sexual needs." She looked at me. "Even though they might be those of a slave?" she asked.

"Even though they might be those of a slave," I said.

"Even though they might be those of a slave," she said.

"Even though they are those of a slave," I said.

"Even though they are those of a slave," she repeated.

"Say now," I said, " 'I am a slave. I am your slave, Master.' "

"I am a slave. I am your slave, Master," she said. She looked at me. "I cannot believe how I feel," she said. "I am so incredibly happy, Master."

I nodded. I sensed then that the locks on the dungeon door had been opened, that the bolts had been slid back.

Then she put down her head. "I am a girl in need," she said. "I beg the touch of my master."

"Look at me," I said. "And speak clearly."

She lifted her head. "I am a girl in need," she said, boldly. "I beg the touch of my master."

I smiled, and she reddened. She had now, at last, explicitly begged for my touch.

The hands of the small, naked slave girl hidden in the dungeon, crouching on the damp, narrow, stone stairs, pressed upward against the iron door which had been bolted shut above her. It moved a quarter of an inch upward, and did not strike against its familiar bolts. The bolts had been withdrawn. She trembled and sobbed, fearing to be the victim of some cruel trick. She thrust harder against the iron door above her. An inch of light, narrow and straight, almost blinded her. She put down her head. Then again she thrust upward against the weight. She sobbed in misery. Her small strength might not be sufficient to lift the door, to thrust it back. She struggled. Then, slowly, inch by inch, she pressing upward, the door began to open; she could feel the stone of the stairs hard under her bare feet; her muscles ached; there was a heavy sound from the protesting, thick hinges; she cried out, thrusting upward; the door then, suddenly, opened, suddenly swinging back, falling away from her; there was a clang of iron on stone. Fearing to move, blinded by the sunlight, she knelt trembling on the stairs. She did not lift her head above the level of the opened door. Perhaps she feared that her mistress, Janice Prentiss, would come and whip her and put her back in the dungeon. But did not her mistress know that it was she herself who was the lovely, frightened slave? Did she not know that it would be only she herself who would feel the blows of such a whip, or she herself who would see again the iron door of the dungeon close above her head?

The blond-haired barbarian, my tethered slave, looked at me, and smiled. "I am ready to please you, in any way that you might see fit, Master," she said.

I reclined on one elbow, watching her.

"Command me," she said.

"I do not," I said.

"Master?" she asked.

"If you desire to please me," I said, "you may do so. I accord you my permission."

"But I am an Earth woman," she said. "Are you not going to order me?"

"No," I said.

"Surely you do not expect me, an Earth woman, to please a man, I mean really please him, of my own free will?" she asked.

I smiled. "It is a startling thought," I admitted.

She smiled.

"Do you want to please me?" I asked.

"Yes, Master," she said.

"You may then do so, if you wish," I said.

"But I am a slave," she said.

"Yes," I said.

"But are slaves not commanded?" she asked.

"Not always," I said.

"It is strange," she said. "I never thought that in all my life I would kneel before a man and tell him that I was ready to please him in any way he saw fit. Now I have done so, and he does not command me."

"Perhaps, if you wish," I said, "you might please me in some way that you see fit."

"But I am a slave," she said.

"Precisely," I said.

"You know, don't you," she asked, "that I want to please you as a slave?"

"Of course," I said. "That is natural. You are a slave."

"Command me," she begged.

"No," I said.

"But I am an Earth woman," she said.

"Not really any longer," I said. "You are now a Gorean slave girl."

"Yes, Master," she said. She rose lightly to her feet. She lifted the tether away from the slave stake. The tether, knotted on her throat, fastened at the other end to the slave stake, was about seven feet in length.

I watched her.

"I have sexual needs," she said. "And I want to please my master."

I shrugged.

She looked down at the slave stake. "I note that this night," she said, "you did not fasten me to a small tree, as to a slave post, but that you prepared a slave stake." She then lifted the tether. "I note, too, Master," she said, "that this tether is somewhat longer than would be needful to secure a miserable slave."

"You are a highly intelligent woman," I said. "That makes it all the more pleasant to own you."

"You knew what I would want to do, didn't you?" she asked.

"Of course," I said.

Suddenly she put her head in her hands, sobbing. "I dare not," she wept. "I dare not! Command me! Command me!"

"No," I said. I did not hurry her.

In time she took her hands from her face, and wiped away her tears. "Tie me for the night," she begged.

"Very well," I said.

"No," she said. "No!"

"Very well," I said.

She straightened herself. She smiled. Her eyes were moist. "What I am now going to do," she said, "I do fully and completely of my own free will. I have sexual needs. I shall exhibit the desperation of these needs before my master, in the hope that he will take pity on me and satisfy them. It is also a girl's hope that in what she does her master will not find her fully displeasing."

She then, gently, removed the bark skirt from her hips and dropped it to the side.

She then flexed her knees and lifted her hands, the backs of the wrists facing one another, gracefully over her head.

"Wait," I said.

"Master?" she asked.

"Have you begged to perform?" I asked.

"No, Master," she said.

"You may now do so," I said.

"I beg to perform before my master," she said.

"Very well," I said. "You may do so."

"Thank you, Master," she said.

She then danced before me, of her own free will, a girl in need, and one desiring to please her master.

Her dance grew ever more desperate and, at times, I had to throw her from me.

Then she lay at the slave stake. She held out a hand to me.

I went to her and seized her by the upper arms and threw her to her feet. She looked at me, frightened.

"You did not do badly, Slave Girl," I said. "But now it is time for you to learn how to truly dance before a man."

"Master!" she cried in misery.

"Be as you were," I told her.

Immediately, frightened, she stood again before me, knees flexed, hands raised above her head, gracefully, the backs of her wrists facing one another, in one of the attitudes of the slave dancer.

I jerked the tether on her throat. "This is a tether," I said. "It is to be well incorporated in your dance. You are a teth-

360

ered slave. Do not forget it. You may fight the tether, you may love it. It may confine your body, you may use it to caress your body, an invitation to your master, a surrogate symbol of his domination of you. You need not dance always on your feet. A woman can dance beautifully on her knees, moving as little as a hand, or on her back, or belly or side. In all things do not forget that you are a slave."

"Are you now commanding me to dance before you?" she asked.

"Yes," I said, "you dance now as a commanded slave. And if I am not well pleased have no fear but what you will be well beaten, if not slain."

"Yes, Master," she said.

I then stepped back from her. "When I clap my hands," I said, "you will dance, Slave."

"Yes, Master," she said.

I then struck my hands together, and, terrified, the girl danced.

She had not been taught the tether dance, one of the most beautiful of the slave dances of Gor, but she improvised well. Indeed, it was hard to believe that she had not had training. I am inclined to believe that the need dances and display dances of the human female may be, at least in their rudiments, instinctual. I suspect there is a genetic disposition in the woman toward this type of behavior and that certain of the movements, closely associated with luring behavior and love movements, may also be genetically based. One reason for supposing this to be the case is that a girl's growth in certain forms of dance skills does not follow a normal learning curve. It is rather like the human being's ability to acquire speech, which also does not follow a normal learning curve. It seems reasonably likely that facility in acquiring speech, which would have enormous survival value, has been selected for. Similarly, a woman's marvelous adaptability to erotic dance may possibly have been selected for. At any rate, whatever the truth may be in these matters, feminine women, perhaps to the horror of their more masculine sisters, seem to take naturally to the beauties of erotic dance. At the very least, perhaps inexplicably, they are marvelously good at it. These genetic dispositions, of course, if they exist, can be culturally suppressed.

I watched the girl dance. She was quite good.

The needs of human beings are a matter of biology. The values in a culture are the values of certain men. Many

361

people take the values of their culture for granted, as though they were somehow a part of the furniture of the universe. They should realize that the values they are taught are the values of particular men, and often, unfortunately, of men who, long ago, were short-lived, ignorant, uninformed, unhealthy and quite possibly of unsound mind. Perhaps human beings should, from the viewpoints of contemporary information and modern medicine, re-evaluate these perhaps anachronistic value structures. Values need not be something one somehow mysteriously "knows," a result of having forgotten the conditioning process by means of which they were instilled, but could be something chosen, something selected as instruments by means of which to improve human life. It is not wrong for human beings to be happy.

"Now you are becoming a woman," I told her. She knelt on one knee, her right; her left leg was flexed; the tether was taken, in a turn, about her left thigh; her hands, too, were on her left thigh; her head was down, but turned toward me; her lip trembled. "Continue to dance, Slave," I told her.

"Yes, Master," she said.

I watched her, and marveled. It is interesting to note that such movements, those of slave dances, despite the inhibitions of rigid cultures, may occur in a girl's sleep, and may even occur, almost spontaneously, when she, nude, alone, passes before a mirror in her bedroom. How shocked she may be to suddenly see her body move as that of a slave. Could it have been she who so moved? Later, perhaps to her surprise, she finds herself standing before the mirror. She is naked, and alone. Then, perhaps scarcely understanding what is occurring within her, she sees the girl in the mirror has begun to dance. The movements are not dissimilar perhaps to those of women who, thousands of years ago, danced in firelit caves before their masters. Then, knowing well that it is she herself who is the dancer, she dances brazenly, boldly, before the mirror. Well does she present her bared beauty before it in the movements, the attitudes and postures of the female slave. Then perhaps she falls to the rug, scratching at it, pressing her belly to it. "I want a Master," she whispers.

I now stood up. My arms were folded.

The girl now was upon her knees at my feet, the tether on her neck slung back behind her to the slave stake. Still in her dance, she began to lick and kiss at my body.

I then took her by the upper arms and held her, half lifted from her knees, before me.

362

"Please do not whip me," she begged.

I then, by the upper arms, dragged her to the side of the slave stake. I put her on her knees there. She looked up at me. "You danced well as a slave," I said.

"Thank you, Master," she said. She looked up at me, trembling.

"What are you?" I asked.

"A slave," she said.

"Fully and only a slave?" I asked.

She regarded me. Her entire body began to shake.

The secret slave in her then was summoned forth. She crept from the dungeon, into the sunlight. She knelt then on the gravel of the courtyard, small, and beautiful and naked, at the feet of masters.

"Yes, Master," said the blond-haired barbarian. "I am fully and only a slave." Then, suddenly, she threw back her head and sobbed with joy. Then she put her head to my knees and, holding them, covered them with kisses. Then she put her head to my feet. She covered them, too, with kisses. I felt her hair on my feet. I felt the hot tears of her joy. "Yes," she whispered, "I am fully and only a slave."

The secret slave, I saw, was then free of her dungeon. Never again could she be put back in it.

The blond-haired barbarian raised her head. Tears were in her eyes. The secret slave, too, had raised her head. Tears, too, had been in her eyes. "Thank you, Master," said the blond-haired barbarian. "Thank you, Master," had breathed the secret slave.

"You are my slave," I said to the blond-haired barbarian. I took her by the hair. I looked into her eyes. "You are the slave of men," I said.

"Yes, my master," she said.

The secret slave then knelt joyfully in the sunlit courtyard, on the cruel gravel. She kissed the steel collar thrust to her lips. She closed her eyes, joyfully, as it was locked upon her small, fair throat. She wore then, locked upon her neck, that for which she had yearned in the long years of her imprisonment, the sweet, liberating, uncompromising collar of public bondage.

"I am free," breathed the blond-haired barbarian. "At last I am free!"

"Beware how you speak, Slave," I said.

"Yes, Master," she said.

She looked up at me, tears in her eyes. "I feel so free," she said.

"In a sense you are free and in a sense you are not free," I said. "The sense, or one of the senses, in which you are free," I said, "is the sense of emotional freedom. You, a slave, have now honestly admitted to yourself, in your own heart, fully, that you are truly a slave. This eliminates conflicts. This produces a sense of emotional joy and fulfillment. You are now at peace with yourself. You are now content with yourself. The sense in which you are not free is an obvious one. You are a slave, totally, and are fully at the mercy of your master, or masters."

"Yes, Master," she said.

I seized her hair and twisted her head to the side, cruelly. "Oh!" she cried.

"Do you think you are free?" I asked.

"No, Master," she wept.

I released her. I crouched back a bit, watching her. She lifted her head. "I am very happy," she said.

I did not speak.

"I love being under the total domination of a male," she said.

I moved more closely to her. I took her by the upper arms, crouching near her.

"Did I please my master by my dancing?" she asked.

"Yes," I said.

"How can I please my master more?" she asked.

I then, by her upper arms, my grip tight upon them, pressed her gently but forcibly backwards. She then lay beside the thick slave stake, her shoulder blades in the dirt. The tether was still upon her throat.

"Yes, Master," she whispered.

"I have never been so happy before in my life as this night, Master," she whispered.

She lay on her side, her back to me. I tied her hands behind her back.

"You are Janice," I told her, naming her.

"Thank you, Master," she said, putting her head back.

I had used her several times during the night. And several times she had, squirming in the helpless throes of the slave orgasm, screamed and sobbed herself mine.

"I had not known such sensations could exist," she had said.

"They are attainable only by the slave," I told her. "They are the surrender and submission spasms of the owned woman, the girl who must yield absolutely and totally, holding nothing back, to her master."

"I see, Master," she had said.

"They cannot, in the nature of things, be attained by the free woman," I said, "for she is her own mistress, not the slave of a master."

"Yes, Master," had said the girl.

"Did you like them?" I asked.

"I loved them," she said.

"Do you like being a slave?" I asked.

"I love it," she said. Then she had said, "Please, Master, rape me again," and I had done so.

I checked the knots on her wrists. The girl was secured.

"Thank you for naming me 'Janice'," she said.

"It is a pretty name," I said. "And it will give me a means by which to summon you, when I wish you to fetch and serve."

"Yes, Master," she said. Then she turned about, to lie on her right side, to face me. Her hands were tied behind her back. "I love wearing that name as a slave name," she said.

I looked at her.

"It was the name of that girl on Earth whom I was," she laughed, "that pretentious, foolish little slut, so haughty and smug, so proud of herself, so concerned to deny that anyone so lofty as herself could possibly be a slave. It gives me great pleasure to see that her master now puts her own name on her and forces her to wear it, openly and publicly, as a slave name."

"The name 'Janice'," I said, "apart from such considerations, is a beautiful name for a slave."

"I will try to be worthy of it," she said.

"If you are not," I said, "it may be soon changed."

"Yes, Master," she said. A free woman's name, of course, tends to remain constant. A Gorean free woman does not change her name in the ceremony of the Free Companionship. She remains who she was. In such a ceremony two free individuals have elected to become companions. The Earth woman, as a consequence of certain mating ceremonials, may change her last name. The first and other names, however, tend to remain constant. From the Gorean point of view the wife of Earth occupies a status which is higher than that of the slave but lower than that of the Free Companion. The case with slaves, of course, is much different from that of free women, either those of Gor or Earth. Their names are simply given to them, as the names of animals. They may be altered or changed at will. Indeed, sometimes a slave is not even given a name. The names a slave wears, of course, are functions of the master's pleasure. They can own a name no more than they can own anything else. It is they who are owned. Some masters have favorite names for girls. Some masters may reward a hard-working girl with a lovely name; others may torment a slave who has been insufficiently pleasing with a cruel or ugly name. Most girls, of course, are given beautiful and exciting slave names, for the masters wish the girl, too, to be beautiful and exciting. She is, after all, a slave. What names count as being beautiful and exciting, of course, is partly a cultural matter. For example, many women of Earth might be astonished to learn that their names, which they may regard as simple or common, names such as 'Jane' or 'Alice', are found extremely beautiful to the Gorean ear. To be sure, the Gorean commonly alters the pronunciation somewhat, to conform with phonemic variations with which he is more familiar. Further, as I may have mentioned, many Earth-girl names are found extremely provocative to the Gorean male. This probably has to do with emotive connotations resulting from his familiarity with such girls in his markets. Such names may suggest to him, usually correctly, that their lovely bearer is going to be an unusually helpless and delicious slave. I once saw a girl in her chains dragged from the very market block and raped in the aisle for no other reason, apparently, than that the auctioneer had mentioned that her name was Helen. Needless to say, a slave girl, as she changes collars, may change names. Most girls, in passing from the hands of one master into those of another, will have had various names.

"The name 'Janice', on Gor, is a slave name, isn't it?" asked the girl.

"Yes," I said. "Do you object?"

"No, Master," she said. "I find that delicious, and wholly appropriate."

She leaned to me, her hands tied behind her back, and kissed me, gently.

"Let us rest now, Slave Girl," I said.

"Yes, Master," she said.

I awakened, suddenly, startled for the instant. Then I realized what was happening.

It was perhaps an Ahn before dawn.

She lifted her head from my body. It was hard to see her in the light. The fire had burned down. "Please do not whip me, Master," she said, frightened.

"You may continue," I told her.

She again bent her head to my body. She knelt beside me in the darkness. Her hands were tied behind her back. The tether was on her throat.

"Stop for a bit," I told her.

"Yes, Master," she said. I felt her cheek against me. Then she put her head down, on my belly.

"Forgive me for disturbing your rest, Master," she said. "I know that I should not do that. Beat me, if you must."

"I am not angry," I said.

"I could not help myself," she said, "though I feared I might be beaten. You do not know what it is to be a female slave. I am so weak. I was so overcome with desire for my master."

"I am not angry," I told her. "But do not let it happen too often. It is I who will instruct you as to when to serve my pleasure."

"But what of my needs?" she asked.

"Your needs," I said, "will be satisfied if, and when, I please."

"Yes, Master," she said.

"It is perfectly acceptable for you to lie alone in the darkness, miserable, tormented by your needs," I said, "for you are a slave."

"Yes, Master," she said. "But may I not, upon occasion, beg to be used?"

"Of course," I said.

She then, lifting her head, began to lick and kiss softly at my body. I looked up at the stars. I listened to the noises of the jungle night. "How sweet, and strong and beautiful it is," she said.

I said nothing.

"Are you angry with me, Master?" she asked.

"No," I said.

"I love to kiss you," she said. Then she again put her head down on my belly.

"Do not stop, Slave," I said.

Again she lifted her head.

Then I took her by the hair and drew her close to me.

"Master?" she asked.

"Perform," I told her.

"Yes, Master," she said.

I then forced her head downward and held her in place, as is common with slaves.

"You are skilled," I told her.

She moaned softly.

"Quite skilled," I said.

She moaned again, a sweet, soft, piteous moan.

"Aiii," I whispered, softly, and, not releasing her, holding her head to me, reared to my feet, half crouching. She was gasping, sobbing. She was half lifted from her knees. I looked down at her. How incredibly beautiful she was in the jungle night, so small, so white and soft, her small hands tied behind her, the tether on her throat. I gasped, and put my head back, taking air into my lungs. Then I lowered her gently to the ground. She looked up at me. "I love you, Master," she whispered. I forced myself to remember that she was only a slave. Then I lay beside her. I wiped her mouth with the back of my forearm. I held her head in my hands and kissed her on the forehead. Then, shuddering, I clutched her. In a few minutes I was calm. In a quarter of an Ahn she felt me move against her thigh. "You are strong, Master," she said. "You are beautiful," I told her.

"You have told me," she said, "that I might, upon occasion, beg to be used."

"It is my intention to use you again," I said. "You need not beg."

"But may I not beg, if I wish?" she asked.

"Of course," I smiled.

"I beg to be used, Master," she whispered.

"You are an incredibly beautiful and desirable woman," I said. "How miserable it would be for men if you were not a slave."

"But I am a slave," she laughed. "And men may buy me, and do what they want with me."

I kissed her.

"Will you not accede to the plea of your aroused slave, Master?" she asked.

"Perhaps," I said.

"I must now be silent on the matter and await your decision," she said.

"That would be wise," I said.

368

"You could beat me, if you wished, couldn't you?" she asked.

"Of course," I told her.

"I desire you," she whispered.

"We shall see," I said.

"Oh," she laughed. Then she said, "It is well that I spoke the truth." She kissed me. "Do you customarily subject your girls to such an examination?" she asked.

"When it pleases me," I said.

"Of course, Master," she said. "We are slaves."

I again placed my hand upon her, and she put her head back. "You see that I did not lie, Master," she said.

"Yes," I said. I felt her small body move beneath my hand. She lifted her body, piteously. "Am I not ready for my master?" she asked.

"Yes, Slave," I said. "You are well ready."

"Ready as is an Earth woman for the penetration of an equal?" she asked.

"No," I said, "ready as is a Gorean slave girl, begging for the least touch of her master."

"It is true, Master," she said. "No longer am I an Earth woman. I am now only a Gorean slave girl, nothing more."

"Are you loving and obedient, Slave?" I asked.

"Yes, Master," she said.

I kissed her.

"If I dared," she said, "I would again beg to be taken."

"You may beg," I told her.

"Please take me, Master," she begged. "Please take me, Master."

"What a slave you are," I said.

"Yes, Master," she said.

"How do you wish to be treated?" I asked.

She pressed herself against me, kissing, half sobbing. "Treat me as the amorous, worthless slave I am," she said.

"You are not worthless," I said. "You have a market value. Indeed, it has been improved this night."

"But I am a total slave," she said.

"That is true," I said, "and a squirming, aroused, amorous one."

"Yes, Master," she said.

I held her head in my hands. I kissed her about the throat.

"Please take me, Master," she begged.

"With mercy?" I asked her.

"No," she whispered, "without mercy."

"How incredible was that experience," she said.

"There are many ways to take a woman," I told her, "even many ways to take her without mercy."

"Perhaps it is only the free who permit themselves to be imprisoned by routine," she said.

"Perhaps," I said. "I would not know." I kissed her, gently. "Sleep now," I said. "It is nearly light."

"Yes, Master," she said.

"It is light, Master," she said, softly.

I awakened. I rolled over and lifted myself on one elbow. I regarded her in the glistening, moist jungle dawn. She was lying beside me, the tether on her throat, her hands tied behind her back.

"We must soon be on our way," I said.

"Yes, Master," she said. I saw that she was very beautiful. Yesterday she had been a woman who had been enslaved. This morning she was a slave.

"Master?" she asked.

I took her ankles and threw them apart.

"Yes, my master," she whispered.

Later I stood over her, and looked down upon her. She looked up at me. "I love you, Master," she said.

"You will doubtless be bought and sold many times, Slave," I said, "and will have many masters."

"I will try to love my masters," she said.

"That would be wise on your part," I told her.

"Yes, Master," she smiled. I looked down upon her. Perhaps someday she would find her love master, he to whom she would be the perfect love slave. Sometimes such individuals know one another immediately, sometimes not. Sometimes a man simply sees a naked woman in her chains upon the block and knows suddenly that she is the perfect one, she who is destined to be the perfect love slave for whom he has always sought. Sometimes a girl, kneeling before a new master, is seized by a sudden wild emotion. Perhaps it is something in the way his steel is locked upon her body; perhaps it is something in the audacity and assurance with which he handles her. She lifts her head, meeting his eyes. Quickly she puts her head down, trembling. She knows then she has met one who may well be her love master, one to whom she can be but the most helpless of love slaves. I looked down at the girl, lying at my feet. Perhaps someday, I mused, she would find her perfect love master, he to whom she would be the perfect love slave. Until then let her be bought and sold, and passed from hand to hand, subject to exchanges, and vendings and barterings; let her know the joys and miseries of diverse bondages; it did not matter, for she was only a slave.

I kicked her with the side of my foot. "On your feet," I told her.

"Yes, Master," she said.

I let her stand there, tethered and bound, and naked, while I ate some of the roast tarsk. I brushed black ants from it. I then removed the one end of the tether from the slave stake and drew her to the tarsk. "Kneel and feed," I told her. She knelt and, putting down her head, bit at the tarsk. After a time I pulled her away from it and, again using the tether as a leash, led her to a fan palm. I tied the tether to the fan palm. "Drink," I told her. "Yes, Master," she said. While she quenched her thirst, and then knelt beside the fan palm, I destroyed the signs of our encampment. I even, slowly, painfully, drew up the slave stake and discarded it in some growth. It need not reveal that a slave, or slaves, had been tethered here. I then tied the pieces of roast tarsk together, in a heavy ring of meat. Then, fetching the lovely slave, my pretty beast of burden, I stood her in the clearing. I untied her hands and removed the tether from her throat. I threw her the bit of bark cloth for her hips. "Dress," I told her. "Yes, Master," she smiled. She wound the bit of cloth about her hips, and tucked it in. She then thrust it down further, well over her hips, that the loveliness of the slave belly be well revealed.

"Do I meet with the approval of my master?" she asked.

"Yes," I said.

She posed before me, smiling. "The morning garb," she said, "of the well-dressed slave girl."

"Often," said I, "slave girls are kept naked, save for their collar and brand."

"Ah," she said, "and I do not even have a collar. How deprived I am! But I am wearing my brand."

"You cannot take it off," I said.

"That is true," she smiled.

"It marks you well," I said.

She drew up the bark skirt. "Yes," she said, "it does."

"How did you get it?" I asked.

"Some cruel brute burned it into my flesh with a hot iron," she said.

"I recall," I said.

371

"I love my brand," she said.

"Most girls do," I said.

"It makes me prettier, doesn't it, as well as marking me as what I am, a slave?"

"Yes," I said, "a brand makes a woman a thousand times more beautiful. It is not just the aesthetic loveliness of the mark, of course, though that in itself incredibly enhances a woman's beauty; it is, of course, even more, its meaning."

"I understand, Master," she said.

"What is its meaning?" I asked.

"It means that I am a slave," she said.

"Yes," I said, "one of the most helpless, beautiful, exciting and desirable of women, she who is owned, she who is at the complete mercy of the master, she who must well serve and obey in all things."

She entered my arms and melted to me.

"We must be on our way," I told her. Then I lowered her to the ground.

"You're going to rape me, aren't you?" she asked.

"Yes," I said.

I threw the ring of tarsk meat about her neck, over her shoulders. She stumbled a bit under the weight. Then she straightened herself.

"I know why most slave girls do not desire to escape their masters," she said.

"Why?" I asked.

"Because we love them, and desire to please them," she said.

I turned her about, and thrust her in the direction of our main camp, where Kisu and the others awaited us.

I followed her.

I carried the long leather strap, that which had served as her tether, looped in my hand.

I looked up at the sun. We must hurry.

"Har-ta, Kajira!" I said. "Faster, Slave Girl!" I struck her with the straps, a sharp blow, that she might understand that she was not to dally.

"Yes, Master," she said.

35

THE SQUABBLES OF SLAVES

"Please do not tie me, tonight, Master," begged Tende.

"Be silent," said Kisu. He then threw her on her stomach and tied her hands behind her back and crossed her ankles and bound them. By a leather thong looped about her right forearm he fastened her to a small tree a few feet from our fire.

It had been a week since we had first, on the height of the falls, seen the flotilla of Bila Huruma pasangs behind us.

"Have you forgotten to tie me tonight, Master?" asked Janice.

"Yes, I have forgotten," I said.

"You forgot last night, too," she said.

"That is true," I said.

"Aren't you going to tie me?" she asked.

"No," I said. "Run away, if you dare."

"I neither dare to, nor do I wish to," she said.

"Lie here," I said.

She lay where I had indicated, her head at my thigh. She snuggled closely to me.

"Janice," whispered Tende.

Janice left my side to crawl to Tende. Tende had struggled to a sitting position. Janice knelt while Tende sat, for Tende was first girl. "Mistress?" asked Janice.

"May I speak with you?" asked Tende.

"Of course, Mistress," said Janice.

Tende then struggled to her knees. I knew then she wished to speak of her master.

"How can I please Kisu more?" she asked Janice.

"Do you feel, deep in your heart, that you are a slave?" asked Janice.

"Yes," said Tende, "in the most profound depths of my heart I feel that I am a slave."

"Then serve him as a slave, fully," said Janice.

"I will," said Tende.

The girls had spoken in Gorean. Kisu had asked that I have Janice and Alice help Tende with the language. I had complied. In the several weeks of our trip she had become

373

reasonably fluent. Tende was an intelligent woman. Kisu, too, of course, profited from these lessons. Indeed, perhaps it was partly from his own interest that he insisted on these instructions for Tende. But, too, doubtless, he thought it amusing that Tende, who had once been so proud, be forced under his will to acquire a new language. For my part, I was pleased at both Kisu's and Tende's growth in Gorean. Considering Ayari and myself, and Alice and Janice, it was clearly the most sensible choice for a common medium of communication.

Janice then crawled back to my side.

"He did not forget to tie me," said Alice. She knelt a few feet from us, her hands bound behind her, a line running from her bound wrists to the same tree to which Tende was tethered.

"Oh, be quiet, Bound Slave," said Janice.

"Untie me, Master," begged Alice. "Let me serve you."

"I will serve him," said Janice, not pleasantly.

"Let me serve you, Master," begged Alice.

"Be quiet," said Janice, "or I will scratch your eyes out!"

"If I were not bound," said Alice, "I would claw you to pieces!"

One of the aspects of the mastery, inconvenient at times, though it can be borne, is the competition among girls for the attentions of the master. Indeed, some masters keep more than one girl, just for this purpose, not merely to lessen the labors of each, but that each may, in the intensity of their rivalry, strive to please him more than the other. Each wishes, of course, to undermine the position of the other and to become the favorite. From the girl's point of view there are few slaves who would not rather do double the labor and be the only wench in the master's compartments. To be sure, the loser in such a competition generally becomes the master's work slave and the winner his pleasure slave. My own view on the matter, for what it is worth, is that a pleasure slave becomes even more marvelous when she is forced to function also as a work slave. The girl who launders, cleans and cooks for a master knows well she is owned. In my own house I see that my favorite pleasure slaves, girls such as lovely, dark-haired Vella, perform their full share or, if I please, much more than their full share of servile labors. It is not unusual to see her in a brief work tunic, sleeveless and white, sweating over the laundry tubs or, on her hands and knees, naked, scrubbing the corridors in chains. I recalled that she

374

had upon occasion displeased me. Once a guest at first refused to believe that the lovely wench in pleasure silk, a chain on her slave bracelets run to a ring on her serving collar, who served his viands at a feast was the same girl whom he had spurned to one side with his foot that afternoon in a corridor. I stripped her and put her on her hands and knees and he saw then that it was she. Even more astonished was he when I had her dance for him and the other guests. "You let such a superb slave scrub in your corridors," he asked. "Yes," I said. "Why?" he asked. "Because it pleases me," I told him.

"Master!" begged Alice.

"Be quiet!" said Janice.

Whereas rivalries among men can be serious and dangerous, the most that rivalries among slave girls can be is petty and vicious; that is to be expected; they are, after all, only small, lovely animals.

"I can please you more than she," said Alice.

"No, you cannot," said Janice.

"I can!" insisted Alice.

"No!" said Janice. Then she smiled. "If you are so pleasing," she said, "then why is it that it is you who are trussed and tethered like a domestic tarsk at the slave post and it is I who lie free by my master's side?"

Alice fought her bonds, and wept. Janice laughed.

"Do you think you are better than she?" I asked Janice.

"Am I not, Master?" she inquired.

"No," I said.

I then took a line and tied Janice's hands behind her back and threw her to her side at the slave post. By the free end of the line I tethered her, like Alice, to the post.

"Now see what you have done!" said Janice to Alice. "Now you have had us both tied!"

Alice did not seem displeased.

"Go to sleep now, Slaves," I told them.

"Yes, Master," said Alice.

"Yes, Master," said Janice, angrily.

"Are you angry?" I asked.

"No, Master," she said, quickly. "Please do not beat me."

"Slave," said Alice.

"Yes, slave," said Janice.

"I am a better slave than you," said Alice.

"No, you are not!" said Janice.

"Go to sleep," I said.

"Yes, Master," said Alice.

"Yes, Master," said Janice.

36

WRECKAGE;
AGAIN WE MOVE UPRIVER

"There, " said Ayari, pointing.

We put down the canoe we were carrying past the hurtling cataract.

We saw, shattered on rocks, the stern quarter of a river galley. Jagged planks, dry and hot, thrust up in the sunlight, and, lower, wedged in, pressed between rocks, wet and black, water foaming about it, was the stern itself with its splintered, side-hung rudder.

I waded out to it. There was nothing left in the wreckage.

"It could have been washed downriver for pasangs," said Ayari.

I nodded. Once before, long ago, we had recovered evidence of what had seemed to be another mishap on the river, a chest or crate of trade goods. We had managed to put them to good use. We had not seen wreckage, however. The chest, not lashed down properly, might have been jolted or washed overboard. Too, there might have been a capsizing. We had not seen wreckage, however. Shaba had not, at that time, as far as we knew, lost a galley.

I put my shoulder against the wreckage. I then put my back against it. I freed it, and, twisting, it plunged away, westward, downriver.

I returned to the rocks of the shore. Shaba now had but two galleys.

"It was wise of you to free it," said Kisu. He looked about. "The less evidence there is of strangers on the river the safer we shall all be."

I looked about, too, at the jungles. They seemed quiet. "Yes," I said. "But I would have freed it anyway."

"Why?" asked Kisu.

"It is what is left of a ship," I said. "It should be free."

376

How could I tell Kisu, who was of the land, of the feelings of those who had known the waves of Thassa?

"You will not free me, will you, Master?" asked Janice.

"Kneel," I said.

She knelt.

"You are a woman," I said. "You will be kept as a slave."

"Yes, Master," she said.

"Now pick up your burden," I said. She picked up her burden and held it on her head, with her two hands. "Straighten your back," I said.

"Yes, Master," she said.

I then, with Ayari and Kisu, lifted the canoe again, and again we moved upriver.

37

WE DO NOT TRADE TENDE

The chief, on his small stool, pointed at Tende. Kisu lifted beads before him, of purple glass, strung on wire. The chief shook his head, vigorously. He pointed again at Tende.

Tende knelt beside Kisu, her hands tied behind her back. In the weeks since her conversation with Janice she had become to him a superb love slave. This is hard for a woman to conceal. The chief's eyes glistened as he looked upon her.

Kisu shook his head, negatively.

In spite of the fact that Tende had now become to Kisu a superb love slave, he still kept her under the strictest security. Often she cried about this, but he was unrelenting. "I love you, Master," she would weep. "I love you!" But he continued to treat her unremittingly with the discipline and harshness commonly accorded a fresh capture, not with the authority and rough affection commonly given to a girl who is so enamored of her master that she can scarcely be beaten from his feet with whips. She would cry alone at night, secured to the slave post, until Kisu, by a word, or kick or blow, would silence her.

The chief again pointed at Tende.

Kisu again shook his head negatively.

"Let us go," said Ayari, nervously. "Yes," I said.

We rose to our feet and pushed through the villagers. The

377

chief called out behind us, but we continued on. I thrust a man away.

We hurried to the canoe and, quickly, thrust it into the river.

38

WHAT AYARI THOUGHT HE SAW IN THE FOREST

Ayari returned to the campfire.

Suddenly he seemed startled. "Janice is here," he said.

"Yes," I said. Janice looked up at him, and Alice.

"What is it?" asked Kisu.

"I thought I saw her in the forest, a moment ago," he said. "Was she not gathering wood?"

"No," I said. I leaped to my feet. "Take me to where you think you saw her."

"It was there," said Ayari, a moment later, pointing to a space between trees.

We investigated the area. I crouched down and studied the ground in the moonlight. "I see no tracks," I said.

"Doubtless it was a trick of the lights and shadows," said Ayari.

"Doubtless," I said.

"Let us return to camp," he said.

"Yes," I said.

39

WE ARE NOT PURSUED

"There is a village on the right," said Ayari.

We had, in the past six days, passed two other villages. In these two other villages the men, with shields and spears, had rushed out to the shore to threaten us. We had kept to the center of the river and had continued on.

378

"There are women and children on the bank," said Ayari. "They are waving for us to come in."

"It is pleasant to see a friendly village," said Alice.

"Let us take the canoe in," said Ayari. "We can perhaps trade for fruit and vegetables and you can obtain information on he whom you seek, he called Shaba."

"It will be pleasant to sleep in a hut," said Janice. There is often a night rain in the jungle, occurring before the twentieth Ahn.

We moved the canoe in toward the shore.

"Where are the men?" I asked.

"Yes," said Kisu. "Where are the men?"

The canoe was now about forty yards from the shore. "Hold the paddles," said Ayari. "Stop paddling."

"They are behind the women!" I said.

"Turn the canoe," said Kisu, fiercely. "Hurry! Paddle!"

Suddenly, seeing us turning about, the crowd of women and children parted. Streaming out from behind them, brandishing spears and shields, knives and pangas, crying out, plunging toward us in the water, were dozens of men.

Spears splashed in the water about us, bobbing under, then floating.

One man reached us, swimming, but I struck him back with the paddle.

"Paddle! Hurry!" said Kisu.

We looked behind us. But we did not see the men putting canoes into the river.

"They are not pursuing us," said Ayari.

"Perhaps they only wished to drive us away," said Alice.

"Perhaps," said Ayari, "they know the river better than us, and do not desire to travel further eastward upon it."

"Perhaps," I said.

"What shall we do?" asked Ayari.

"Continue on," said Kisu.

40

TENDE SPEAKS TO KISU

I looked up at the stars.

I listened to the jungle noises, and the small, quiet crackle of the burning wood in the campfire.

Tende knelt beside Kisu, bending over him. I could hear her licking and kissing softly at his body. Her hands were tied behind her, a line running to the small tree which served us in the camp as slave post. Her ankles, too, were crossed and tied.

Both Janice and Alice, now asleep, lay near me. Neither was secured.

"Ah, excellent, Slave," said Kisu. He then took her by the hair. "Excellent," he said.

He then released her hair, and she put her head down on his belly. "Find me pleasing, Master," she begged.

"I do," he said.

"I love you, Master," she said.

"You are the daughter of my hated enemy, Aibu," he said.

"No, Master," she said. "I am now only your conquered love slave."

"Perhaps," he said.

"Do you think me any the less conquered than Janice and Alice, my white sisters in bondage?" she asked.

"Perhaps not," said Kisu. "It is not easy to tell about such matters."

"I, too," she said, "am only a slave, lovingly and helplessly a slave."

"But you are black," he said.

"It makes no difference," she said. "I, too, am a woman. And you have made yourself my master, fully."

He did not speak.

"Do you hate me, Master?" she asked.

"No," he said.

"Do you not like me, just a little?" she asked.

"Perhaps," he said.

"I love you," she said.

"Perhaps," he said.

"Can you not trust me, just a little?" she asked.

"I do not choose to do so," he said.

"It is strange," she said. "The other girls sleep free beside their master and I, who am so helplessly yours, surely as much a slave as they, am kept in severe constraints."

He did not speak.

"Why, my master?" she asked.

"It pleases me," he said.

"How can I convince you of my love?" she asked. "How can I earn your trust?"

"Do you wish to be whipped?" he asked.

"No, Master," she said.

He rolled over and took her by the arms, and put her to her back.

"It seems a small thing," she said, "that a girl beg to be permitted to sleep at her master's feet." She lifted her lips and kissed him. Then she lay back. "Do you think me less than the white slaves?" she asked.

"No," he said. "You are neither more nor less than they. You are all alike in being slaves."

"But I am the only tied slave," she said.

"Yes," he said.

"Could you not at least unfasten my ankles?" she asked.

"Ah," he laughed. "You are a little slave, Tende."

When he had finished with her, he did not retie her ankles.

"You have not retied my ankles," she said. "Does this mean that you are now moved to treat me with a bit more kindness?"

"No," he said. "It is merely that I may want you again before morning."

"Yes, my master," she laughed. She then snuggled against him. Soon they were both asleep.

41

THE NET IN THE RIVER

"Look out!" cried Ayari.

It seemed to rip up from the water, extending across the river.

It rose before us, reticulated and wet, dripping, a net, a barrier of interwoven vines.

"Cut through!" shouted Kisu.

At the same time, behind us, we heard shouting. From each side of the river, about two hundred yards behind, we saw canoes, dozens, being thrust into the river.

"Cut through!" cried Kisu.

Ayari, with his knife, slashed at the vines.

We brought the canoe against the net, so that I and Kisu, too, each armed with a panga, might slash at the woven wall which had, on vine ropes, sprung from shore, lifted up before us.

The shouting behind us came closer.

The trap, weighted, just below the surface, is activated by two vine ropes, slung over tree branches, ropes which are drawn taut when two logs, to which they are attached, one on each shore, are rolled or dropped from a concealed scaffolding. A signal which we had failed to note had doubtless been given.

The keen steel of our pangas smote apart thick vines. Water from the wet vines, struck loose by our blows, showered upon us.

"Get the canoe through!" cried Kisu.

We turned the canoe. A spear splashed near us. Ayari lifted aside vines. The canoe, vines sliding against its side, slipped through.

"Paddle!" said Kisu. "Paddle for your lives!"

42

WE LEAVE A VILLAGE AT NIGHT

"Tarl," whispered Ayari.

"Yes," I said.

"We must leave this village," he said.

We had now been on the river four months since we had, first, on the looming height of the falls, observed the many ships and canoes of the forces of Bila Huruma far behind us. We did not even know, now, if they were behind us or not. Too, we had seen no new evidence of Shaba ahead of us. A month ago we had eluded the net of vines and, by paddling into the darkness, had escaped our pursuers. They would not remain on the river at night. It is impossible to convey, in

382

any brief measure, the glory and length of the river, and the hundreds of geographical features, and the varieties of animal and vegetable life characterizing it and its environs. The river alone seems a world of nature in its own right, let alone the marvels of its associated terrain. It was like a road to wonders, a shining, perilous, enchanted path leading into the heart of rich, hitherto unknown countries. It, in its ruggedness, its expanse, its tranquillity, its rages, was like a key to unlock a great portion of a burgeoning continent, a device whereby might be opened a new, fresh world, green, mysterious and vast. Not a geographer, I could scarcely conjecture the riches and resources which lay about me. I had seen traces of copper and gold in cliffs. The river and forests teemed with life. Fibrous, medicinal, and timber resources alone seemed inexhaustible. A new world, untapped, beautiful, dangerous, was opened by the river. I think it would be impossible to overestimate its importance.

"What is wrong?" I asked.

"I have been looking about the village in the darkness," he whispered.

"Yes?" I said.

"I have found the refuse dump," he said.

"Within the walls?" I asked.

"Yes," he said.

"That is strange," I said. Normally a village would have its refuse dump outside the walls.

"I thought it strange, too," said Ayari. "I took the liberty of examining it."

"Yes?" I said.

"It contains human bones," he said.

"That is doubtless why it is kept within the walls," I said.

"I think so," said Ayari. "That way strangers will not see it before, unsuspecting, they enter the village."

"They seemed friendly fellows," I said. They were, however, I admitted to myself, not the most attractive lot I had ever seen. Their teeth had been filed to points.

"I never trust a man," said Ayari, "until I know what he eats."

"Where are the men of the village?" I asked.

"They are not asleep," said Ayari. "They are gathered in one of the huts."

"I shall awaken Janice and Alice," I said. "Awaken Kisu and Tende."

"I shall do so," he whispered.

383

In a few Ehn, our things in hand, we crept from the village. By the time we heard men crying out in rage, and saw torches on the shore, we were safely on the river.

43

TALUNAS

"See the size of it," said Ayari.

"I do not think it will attack a canoe," said Kisu.

Ayari shoved it away from the side of the canoe with his paddle and it, with a snap of its tail, disappeared under the water.

"I have seen them before," I said, "but they were only about six inches in length."

The creature which had surfaced near us, perhaps ten feet in length, and a thousand pounds in weight, was scaled and had large, bulging eyes. It had gills, but it, too, gulped air, as it had regarded us. It was similar to the tiny lung fish I had seen earlier on the river, those little creatures clinging to the half-submerged roots of shore trees, and, as often as not, sunning themselves on the backs of tharlarion, those tiny fish called gints. Its pectoral fins were large and fleshy.

"Oh, men!" we heard cry. "Men! Men! Please help me! Take pity on me! Help me!"

"Look, Master!" cried Alice. "There, near the shore! A white girl!"

She was slender-legged and dark-haired. She wore brief skins. She ran down to the edge of the water. Her hands were not bound together but, from each wrist, there hung a knotted rope. It was as though she had been bound and, somehow, had been freed.

"Please save me!" she cried. "Help me!"

I examined the condition of the skins she wore. I noted, also, that she wore a golden armlet and, on her neck, a necklace of claws. She also had, about her waist, a belt, with a dagger sheath, though the sheath was now empty.

"Save me, please, noble sirs!" she wept. She waded out a few feet into the water. She extended her hands to us piteously. She was quite beautiful.

384

I considered the forest behind her. The trees were thick, the brush, near the river, heavy.

Kisu and I dipped our paddles into the water.

"Master!" cried Janice. "Surely you cannot leave her here?"

"Be silent, Slave Girl," I said to her.

"Yes, Master," she said. She choked back a sob. She again dipped her paddle into the water.

"Please, please help me!" we heard the girl cry.

Then we had left her behind.

"Master," sobbed Janice.

"Be silent, Slave Girl," I said.

"Yes, Master," she said.

"Look!" cried Alice. "There is another!"

Now, on the shore, standing at a post, chains about her body, we saw a blond girl. "Please help me!" she cried, straining against the chains. She, like the first, was dressed in brief skins and, like the first, was ornamented, with an armlet and necklace. Too, about her left ankle, there was a golden bangle.

We removed the paddles from the water.

"A beautiful wench," said Kisu.

"Yes," I said.

"Please help me!" cried the girl, straining against the chains. "Save me! Save me! Take pity on me! I have been left here to die! Take pity on me! Save me! Please, save me!"

"Have mercy on her, Master, please," begged Janice. "You cannot simply leave her here to die."

"I think we have lingered here long enough," said Kisu, looking about. "This is a dangerous place."

"Agreed," I said.

"Do not leave without her, please, noble masters," begged Janice. "Please, Master," begged Alice. "Please, Master," begged Tende.

"What little fools you all are," said Kisu. "Can you not see that it is a trap?"

"Master?" asked Tende.

Kisu threw back his head and laughed.

"Master?" asked Janice.

"They speak Gorean," I pointed out. "Thus they are not originally of the jungle. The color of their skins alone, white, should make that clear to you. Consider the first girl. The lengths of rope dangling from her wrists seemed rather long for any usual form of binding. Eighteen inches of rope is quite sufficient for tying a girl's hands either before her body or behind. Too, it is common to loop a wrist binding, and use a single knot, rather than tie each wrist separately."

"Perhaps she was tied about a tree," said Janice.

"Perhaps," I said. "But, too, the rope was cut, not frayed. How would it have been cut?"

"I do not know, Master," she said.

"Consider also," I said, "that she retained her belt and dagger sheath. A normal captor would surely have discarded these. What need has a captured woman for such accouterments?"

"I do not know, Master," she said.

"Too," I said, "she, like the girl at the post, there on the shore, wore clothing and ornaments. One of the first things a captor commonly does with a woman is to take away her clothing. She is not to be permitted to conceal weapons. Also, it helps her to understand that she is a captive. Also, of course, a captor commonly wishes to look upon the beauty of his capture. This pleases him. Also, of course, he may wish to form a conjecture as to its market value or the amount of pleasure he will force it to yield to him. At the very least it seems reasonable that her ornaments, and in particular those of gold, would be removed from her. One does not expect to find rich ornaments of gold on the body of a captured woman. Surely such things belong rather in the loot sack of her captor. She might, of course, wear them later, as her master's property, he using them then to decorate his slave. Consider, too, the nature and condition of their garments. The garments are not ripped or torn. They show no signs of a struggle or of the abuse of their owner. Too, they are skins, of the sort which might be worn by free women, huntresses, not rep-cloth or bark cloth, not rags, of the sort which might be worn by slaves."

"Their bodies, too," said Kisu, "showed no signs of lashings or bruises. Presumably, then, they were not fresh captures."

I nodded. Sometimes a free woman must be taught that she is now subject to discipline. Some women refuse to believe it until the whip is on them.

"Other clues, too," I said, "suggest that they are not what they seem. Consider the girl at the post. Her hands are not fastened over her head, which would lift and accentuate the beauty of her breasts. You must understand that a post is often used to display a girl, not merely to secure her. As it is, we do not even know if her hands are truly fastened behind her or not. We simply cannot see. Too, captors in the forests, natives of these jungles, would not be likely to have chains to secure their captures."

"Please help me!" called the girl, plaintively.

"How long have you been at the post?" I called to her.

"For two days," she wept. "Take pity on me! Help me, please!"

"Have you any doubt now?" I asked. "Consider her condition. It is prime. Does she truly seem to have been at the post for two days?"

"No, Master," said Janice.

"Too," I said, "had she been at the post overnight is it not likely that tharlarion would have discovered her and eaten her from the chains?"

"Yes, Master," said Janice.

"I am, too, made uncomfortable by the thickness of the brush and trees in these areas, both before and now. They seem fit to conceal the numbers of an ambuscade."

"Perhaps we should hurry on," said Tende, looking about.

"Take up your paddles," said Kisu. "Continue on."

"Please, stop!" begged the girl in chains. "Do not leave a poor woman here to die!"

"But can we truly leave her?" asked Janice.

"Yes," said Kisu.

"Yes," I said.

Janice moaned.

"Paddle," I told her.

"Yes, Master," she said.

As our canoe moved away we looked back. "After them!" cried the girl. She slipped from her chains and bent to the grass beside her, seizing up a light spear. From the brush about her appeared numbers of girls similarly clad and armed. We saw canoes being thrust into the water.

"Perhaps now you will paddle with a better will," I said.

"Yes, Master!" said Janice.

There were now some eight canoes behind us. In each canoe there were five or six girls. In the prow of the first canoe was the blond girl who had seemed to be chained at the post. In the prow of the second was the slender-legged, dark-haired girl whom we had seen earlier. She still had the dangling ropes knotted on her wrists.

"Will they overtake us?" cried Alice.

"It is unlikely," I said. "In no canoe are there there more

than six paddlers. In this canoe, too, there are six paddlers, and three of these are men."

In less than a quarter of an Ahn we had considerably lengthened our lead on our pursuers.

"Do you not recall, Janice," I asked, "in one of the villages long ago, one of the men inquired if you were a taluna?"

"Yes," she said.

"Those behind us," I said, "are talunas."

In half an Ahn the canoes of the pursuers had fallen far back. In a few Ehn more they ceased the pursuit.

"I am exhausted, Master," said Alice.

Janice and Tende, too, could no longer keep the stroke. They gasped for breath. They could scarcely lift their arms. "The paddle is like iron in my grasp," said Janice. Tende sobbed. "Forgive me, Master," she begged Kisu. Her paddle struck the side of the canoe. She almost lost it in the water. Then she put her head down, gasping. "Forgive me, Master," she begged.

"Rest," said Kisu to her.

"Rest," I said to Janice and Alice.

The girls, then, sick with the misery of their labor, placed their paddles in the canoe. Alice and Janice threw up into the water. Then, trembling and gasping, the girls lay down in the canoe.

Ayari, Kisu and I continued to paddle.

44

THE SMALL MEN;
OUR CAMP HAS BEEN ATTACKED

"Join me!" she laughed, splashing in the water.

It was a lagoon, opening off the river, some hundred yards away. I stood on the shore, with one of the raider's spears in my hand. There seemed no tharlarion or danger about, but it would not hurt to maintain a vigilance in such a respect.

She was very lovely, bathing in the water.

We were not now with the main group. We had separated off, as we did upon occasion, to hunt. Also, it is sometimes pleasant, you must understand, to be alone with a delightful slave.

"Clean yourself well, Slave," I called to her, "that you may be more pleasing to my senses."

"Yes, Master," she laughed. "What of you?" she called.

"It is you who are the slave," I told her.

"Yes, Master," she said.

I thought I heard a rustling in the forest behind me. It did not sound like the passage of a man or animal. It seemed more like a wind, moving among leaves. Yet there seemed to be no wind.

I turned and walked a few yards into the forest. I did not now hear the sound. It had been caused, I assumed, by an unusual current of air.

Suddenly the girl, from the lagoon, uttered a scream. Immediately I spun about and ran to the edge of the trees.

"Come to shore!" I called to her.

At the far end of the lagoon, where its channel leads to the river, I saw what had alarmed the girl. It was a large fish. Its glistening back and dorsal fin were half out of the water, where it slithered over the sill of the channel and into the lagoon.

"Come to shore!" I said. "Hurry!"

I saw the large fish, one of the bulging-eyed fish we had seen earlier, a gigantic gint, or like a gigantic gint, it now having slipped over the channel's sill, disappear under the water.

"Hurry!" I called to her.

Wildly she was splashing toward the shore. She looked back once. She screamed again. Its four-spined dorsal fin could be seen now, the fish skimming beneath the water, cutting rapidly towards her.

"Hurry!" I called.

Sobbing, gasping, she plunged splashing through the shallow water and clambered onto the mud and grass of the bank.

"How horrible it was!" she cried.

Then she screamed wildly. The fish, on its stout, fleshy pectoral fins, was following her out of the water. She turned about and fled screaming into the jungle. With the butt of the spear I pushed against its snout. The bulging eyes regarded me. The large mouth now gulped air. It then, clumsily, climbed onto the bank. I stepped back and it, on its pectoral fins, and lifting itself, too, by its heavy tail, clambered out of

389

the water and approached me. I pushed against its snout again with the butt of the spear. It snapped at the spear. Its bulging eyes regarded me. I stepped back. It lunged forward, snapping. I fended it away. I then retreated backward, into the trees. It followed me to the line of trees, and then stopped. I did not think it would wish to go too far from the water. After a moment or so it began to back away. Then, tail first, it slid back into the water of the lagoon. I went to the water's edge. There I saw it beneath the surface, its gills opening and closing. Then it turned about and, with a slow movement of its tail, moved away. Ayari and Kisu referred to such fish as gints. I accepted their judgment on the matter. They are not to be confused, however, that is certain, with their tiny brethren of the west.

"Help me!" I heard. it was the voice of Janice. I moved rapidly toward the sound of her voice. Some fifty yards into the jungle I stopped. There, ringing a depression, were more than a dozen small men. They wore loincloths with vine belts. From loops on the belts hung knives and small implements. They carried spears and nets. I do not think any of them were more than five feet in height. I doubt that any of them weighed more than eighty pounds. Their features were negroid but their skins were more coppery than dark brown or black. They did not seem to be one of the black races, which are usually tall, long-limbed and supple, but their racial affinities seemed clearly to be more aligned with one or more of those groups than any others.

"Help me!" I heard Janice cry.

I looked at the small men. They did not seem threatening. "Tal," said one of them.

"Tal," I said. "You speak Gorean."

"Master," cried Janice.

I went to the edge of the depression. There, a few feet below me, suspended in a gigantic web, was Janice. One of her legs was through the web, and an arm. It was not simply the adhesiveness of the web's strands which prevented her from freeing herself but, also, its swaying and elasticity, sinking beneath her as she tried to press against it.

I looked at the small men. They seemed friendly enough. Yet none of them made any move to help Janice.

"Master!" screamed Janice.

I looked down. The web was now trembling. Approaching her now, moving swiftly across the web, was a gigantic rock spider. It was globular, hairy, brown and black, some eight

390

feet in thickness. It had pearly eyes and black, side-hinged jaws.

Janice threw back her head and screamed with misery. I slid down the side of the depression to the edge of the net. I drew back the spear I carried. I flung it head-on into the spider. It penetrated its body and slid almost through. It reached up with its two forelegs and drew it out. It then turned toward me. As soon as it had turned in my direction, away from the girl, the small men, howling and shrieking, began to hurl their small spears into its body. It stood puzzled on the web. I scrambled about the side of the depression, slipping once, and retrieved the spear. It was wet with the viscous body fluids of the arachnid. It turned again and I, slashing with the spear blade, cut loose a jointed segment of its leg. It charged and I thrust the spear blade into its face. Some of the small men then hurried about the depression striking at the beast with palm leaves, distracting it, infuriating it. As it turned toward them I cut another segment of one of its rear legs from it. It then, unsteadily, again moved toward me. I slipped to the side and cut at the juncture of its cephalothorax and abdomen. It began to exude fluid. It retreated sideways from me. It turned erratically. The side-hinged jaws opened and shut. A strand of webbing from one of its abdominal glands began to emerge meaninglessly. I then, as it dragged itself backward on the web, cut away at its head. the small men then flooded past me, clambering on the web itself, and began to crawl upon the beast with their knives, cutting it to pieces. I went then to the height of the depression, the spear in hand, the fluids of the beast drying upon it. Janice lay naked, trembling, in the web. The great arachnid now lay on its back, the small men swarming over it. Some stood to their knees in its body. I cleaned the shaft and blade of the spear with moist leaves. When I returned the small men had rolled the carcass of the beast to one side. It reposed there, gigantic and globular, in the fashion of the rock spider, its legs tucked beneath it. The small men then stood again about the upper edge of the depression. "Tal," said their leader to me, grinning. "Tal," I said to him.

"Master," called Janice. "I cannot free myself."

I looked down at her. She was tangled and could get no footing.

I made as though to hold down to her, that she might grasp it, the shaft of the raider's spear.

Immediately the small men rushed to me, shaking their

heads. They tried to pull me away. "No," said their leader. "No, no!"

I was puzzled. The small men, I recalled, had originally stood about the upper edge of the depression, impassively observing Janice's predicament. They had made not the least effort to help her, even when the eight-legged monster had emerged to claim her as his trapped quarry. Yet when I had fought the monster, and when he had turned upon me, they had sprung vigorously to my aid. They had hurled their spears into the beast and had, helping me, distracted it in its ferocities. Then they had rushed past me and, with their knives, had boldly finished the creature. But now it seemed they, though obviously disposed to be friendly towards me, did not wish to free Janice, the slave. They wished me, for some reason, to leave her there, helpless, unable to free herself, lying there at the mercy of the jungle, surely either to starve or thirst to death, or, more likely, to fall victim to some new predator.

I brushed the small men back. "Get back," I told them. They moved back. They were not pleased but, too, it did not seem they would try to stop me. I extended the shaft of the spear to Janice and she, seizing it with one hand, her free hand, was drawn upward, out of the net, to the safety of the jungle floor.

Then, to my surprise, when she stood safe, trembling beside me, the small men crowded about her and knelt down, putting their heads to the ground.

"What does it mean?" she asked.

"They are showing you respect or obeisance," I said.

"I do not understand," she said, frightened.

"Of course!" I said. "Now it is clear!"

"What?" she asked, frightened.

"Stand! Stand!" I told the small men. "Get up! Get up!"

Terrified, the small men rose to their feet.

I looked at Janice, harshly. "Are you not a slave girl in the presence of free men?" I asked.

"Forgive me, Master," she cried. Swiftly she knelt. The small men regarded her, startled and frightened.

"Put your head to their feet," I said. "Kiss their feet. Beg their forgiveness for the affront you have shown them."

Janice put down her head and kissed the feet of the small men. "Forgive me, Masters," she begged.

They looked at her in wonder.

"Get up," I told the girl. I then, roughly, tied her hands together behind her back. The small men gathered around, seeing that her hands, truly, were tightly tied.

"This is a slave," I told them.

They spoke quickly among themselves. It was not in Gorean.

"We are the slaves of the talunas," said one of the men, their leader.

I nodded. I had thought so, from their behavior. It was from the talunas, too, doubtless, that they had learned their Gorean.

"We fish and hunt for them, and make cloth, and serve them," said one of the men.

"Men should not be the slaves of women," I said. "Women should be the slaves of men."

"We are small," said a man. "The talunas are too large and strong for us."

"They may be taken, and made slaves, as any women," I said.

"Help us to rid ourselves of the talunas," said the leader.

"I have business on the river," I said.

Their leader nodded.

I then turned about and, followed by the girl, my slave, made my way back to the lagoon. To my surprise the small men, in single file, followed me. At the lagoon I retrieved the girl's bark-cloth skirt and beads, which she had discarded while bathing. I slung the beads about her neck. I adjusted the bark-cloth skirt on her body. I made certain it was well down on her hips. I then looked about at the forest, and then up at the sun. I adjudged it too late to hunt further that day. I then turned about and, followed by the bound girl, my slave, made my way back towards our camp. To my surprise the small men, in single file, again followed me.

"Kisu!" I called, alarmed. "Ayari! Tende! Alice!"

Unmistakably in the small camp I saw the signs of struggle. Too, on the ground, I saw shed blood.

"They are gone," said the leader of the small men. "They were taken by the Mamba people, those who file their teeth."

The word 'Mamba' in most of the river dialects does not refer to a venomous reptile as might be expected, given its meaning in English, but, interestingly, is applied rather generally to most types of predatory river tharlarion. The Mamba people were, so to speak, the Tharlarion people. The Mamba people ate human flesh. So, too, does the tharlarion. It is thus, doubtless, that the people obtained their name.

"How do you know it was the Mamba people?" I asked.

"They came through the forest on foot," said the leader of the small people. "Doubtless they were following you. Doubtless they wished to surprise you."

"How do you know it was they?" I asked.

"We saw them," said one of the men.

"It is our country," said another. "We know much of what occurs here."

"Did you see the attack?" I asked.

"We did not wish to be too close," said another man.

"We are a small people," said another. "There were many of them, and they are large."

"We saw those of your party being led away," said another man.

"They were then alive," I said.

"Yes," said another man.

"Why did you not tell me of these things sooner?" I asked.

"We thought you knew of the attack," said one of the men, "and had fled, thus escaping."

"No," I said. "I was hunting."

"We will give you meat, if you wish," said one of the small men. "Our hunting earlier today was successful."

"I must attempt to rescue those of my party," I said.

"There are too many of the Mamba people," said one of the small men. "They have spears and knives."

"I must make the attempt," I said.

The small men looked at one another. They spoke swiftly in a language I could not follow. Certain of the words, but very few of them, were recognizable. There are linguistic affinities among most of the lake and river dialects. The language they spoke, however, was far removed from the speeches of Ushindi or Ukungu.

In a moment the small men turned to regard me. "Let us exchange gifts," said their chieftain. "Rid us of the talunas, and we will help you."

"You must be very brave," I told them.

"We can be brave," said one of the men.

"You are spear and net hunters," I said. "This is my plan."

45

I CAPTURE THE CHIEF OF
THE TALUNAS

Lightly I dropped down within the stockade of the talunas. It contained several small, thatched huts. It was not difficult to see in the light of the three moons.

I made my way quietly, crawling, stopping upon occasion to listen, toward the more central huts. In one of the huts, one with a door tied shut from the outside, I heard a rustle of chain.

I picked that hut which seemed the largest and most impressive, one in the center of the camp.

On my belly, quietly, I entered it. Moonlight filtered in through the thatched roof and between the sticks which formed the sides of the hut. She was sleeping within, in her brief skins. Her weapons were at the side of the hut. She lay on a woven mat, her blond hair loose about her head. I examined her thighs, moving back the skins she wore. They had never been branded. She turned, restlessly. She was the girl who had feigned being chained at the post, to lure us into a trap. She was, I was sure, the leader of the talunas. She had given commands in our pursuit. She did not share her hut with another girl. She threw her arm restlessly over her head. I saw her hips move. I smiled. She was a woman in need. She moaned. I waited until her arms were again at her sides, and she lay upon her back. I saw her lift her haunches in her sleep. She was starved for a man's touch. Such women, in their waking hours, are often tense and restless; it is not unusual, too, for them to be irritable; and many times they are hostile toward men; many times they are not even fully aware of the underlying causes of their uncomfortable conscious states; how horrified they might be if they were told that they were women, and desired a master; yet must they not, on some level, be aware of this; would not their hostility toward the male who does not understand their needs or is too cowardly or weak to satisfy them not be otherwise inexplicable; what other hurt could the uncooperative male be inflicting upon them; the more he tries to please them the more they demand; the more he tries to do what they claim to wish the more he finds himself disparaged and despised; can he not see that what they really want is to be thrown to his feet and subjected, totally, to his will? They wish to be women, that is all. But how can they be women if men will not be men? How cruel a man is to deny to a woman the deepest need of her womanhood. Can they not care for them? Can they not see how beautiful they are, and how marvelous?

But I steeled myself against thoughts of mercy for the blond beauty. She was an enemy.

Her head was then turned to the side. She twisted restlessly in her sleep.

I waited until her head was back, and she lay upon her back, her arms at her side. Her small fists were clenched. She whimpered, needing a man.

She was indeed beautiful. I thought she would look well naked, on a slave block.

Swiftly I knelt across her body, pinning her down, pinning her arms to her sides. Almost instantly, frightened, she wakened. The trapped girl's first impulse is to scream. This may be depended upon. As her mouth opened I, with my thumb, thrust the rolled-cloth wadding deep into it. In a moment I had lashed it in place. I then threw her to her stomach and tied her hands behind her back. I then put her again on her back. Her eyes were wild, terrified, over the gag. With my knife I cut the skins from her. "You will not be needing these," I told her. I regarded her. Such women bring high prices. I took her in my arms. Her eyes were frightened. She shook her head fiercely, negatively. But her body, as though in sudden relief, desperately clasped me. She twisted her head to the side, and then, again, looked at me. She shook her head, negatively. But her body thrust itself against me, asking no quarter, piteously and helplessly soliciting its full impalement. "Very well," I told her. She looked at me in fury. "Your eyes say, 'No,'" I told her "but your body says 'Yes.'" Her hips and thighs then began to move. She put back her head in misery on the mat. Then, in a moment, there were tears in her eyes, and she tried to lift her head and gagged mouth to touch me. When later I crouched over her she sat up, shuddering, and put her cheek to my left shoulder. I felt the lashings of the gag against my shoulder.

I thrust her to her back on the mat. "You are only bait," I told her. I then tied her ankles together and, putting her over my shoulders, her head hanging down over my back, left the hut. I left by way of the stockade gate. I would leave an obvious trail.

46

THE BALANCE OF THE TALUNAS HAVE NOW BEEN CAPTURED; I HEAR OF THE MARCHERS

"There they are! We have them now!" cried the slender-legged, dark-haired girl.

I plunged through brush, dragging the bound, gagged blond girl, running and stumbling, bent over, by the hair at my side.

The talunas, more than forty of them, plunged after us, brandishing their weapons, in hot pursuit.

I turned when I heard their sudden cries of surprise, and then of rage, and then of fear.

I tied the blond girl by her hair to a slender palm and strode back to the nets.

Some of the talunas lay upon the ground, tangled in nets, the spear blades of the small men at their throats and bellies. More than twenty of them struggled, impeding one another's movement, in a long vine net about them.

The first girl I pulled from a net was the slender-legged, dark-haired girl. I cuffed her, and then threw her on her belly and bound her hand and foot. I then drew forth another girl and treated her similarly. Then, in a row, lying on the jungle floor, there were forty-two captives. I then released the blond girl from the palm tree and, tying her ankles, threw her with the rest. I did not bother to ungag her.

"Release us," said the dark-haired girl, squirming in her bonds.

"Be silent," said the leader of the little men, jabbing his spear blade below her left shoulder blade.

The girl gritted her teeth, frightened, and was quiet.

"Remove their clothing and ornaments," I told the little men.

This was done. The little men then tied a vine collar on the throat of each girl and, by the arms, dragged them, one by one, to a long-trunked, fallen tree. About this tree, encircling it, were a number of vine loopings. The little men then knelt each girl at one of the vine loopings. Pushing down their heads, they then, with pieces of vine rope, fastened both under the vine collars on the girls, tied down their heads, close to the trunk. The forty-three girls then knelt, naked, hands tied behind them, ankles crossed and bound, at the trunk of the fallen tree, their heads tied down over it. They could not slide themselves free sideways, moving the vine loopings, because of the roots of the tree at one end and its spreading branches at the other. They were well secured in place, their heads over the tree trunk. One of the little men then, with a heavy, rusted panga, probably obtained in a trade long ago, walked up and down near them. They shuddered. They knew that, if the little men wished, their heads might be swiftly cut from them.

"There are the mighty talunas," I said.

Many of the little men leaped up and down, brandishing their spears and singing.

"At the stockade of the talunas," I said, "there was a prison hut. Within it I heard the chains of a prisoner. The chains were heavy. It is probably a male. Women such as talunas sometimes keep a male salve or two. They are useful, for example, in performing draft labors. I would keep him chained until a determination can be made of his nature. He may be a brigand. I then suggest that the stockade be examined for any other slaves, or objects of interest or value. Then I would, if I were you, burn the stockade."

"We will do these things," grinned the leader of the small men.

"I now," I said, "must address myself to the attempt to rescue those of my party."

"We must move quickly," said the leader of the small men, "for there is going to be war on the river."

"War?" I asked.

"Yes," he said, "a great force of men is coming up the river, and the peoples of the river are joining, that they may be stopped." He looked up at me. "There will be great fighting," he said, "like never before on the river."

I nodded. I had thought that it would be only a matter of time until the peoples of the river would mass in an attempt to stop the advance of Bila Huruma. Apparently they were now on the brink of doing so.

"How many men may I have?" I asked.

"Two or three will be sufficient," said the leader of the small men, "but because we are so fond of you, I, and nine others, will accompany you."

"That is perhaps generous," I said, "but how do you propose that the camp of the Mamba people be stormed with so few men?"

"We shall recruit allies," said the small man. "They are nearby even now."

"How many do you think you can recruit?" I asked.

"So high I cannot count," he said.

"Can you not give me some impression?" I asked. I knew that the mathematics of these men, who had no written tradition, who had no complex cultural accumulation of intricate tallyings and abstract inventions, would be severely limited.

"They will be like the leaves on the trees, like the bits of sand at the shore," he said.

"Many?" I asked.

"Yes," he said.

"Do you jest with me?" I asked.

"No," he said. "This is the time of the marchers."

"I do not understand," I said.

"Come with me," he said.

47

THE ATTACK OF THE MARCHERS; WE CONCLUDE OUR BUSINESS IN THE VILLAGE OF THE MAMBA PEOPLE

Within the stockade of the Mamba people there was much light and noise. I could hear the sounds of their musical instruments, and the pounding of their drums. Within the stockade, too, we could hear the chanting of the people and the beating of sticks, carried in the hands of dancers.

I knew the stockade, for it was the same from which we had, earlier, stolen away in the night.

Two days ago the leader of the small people had led me into the jungle, leaving behind the clearing where we had secured the lovely talunas, their necks at the mercy of the panga.

We had trekked but a short way into the jungle when the leader of the small men held up his hand for silence. I had then heard, as I had once before, but had been unable to place the noise, the sound, that strange sound, as of a small wind moving leaves. I had heard it before on the edge of the lagoon, but had not understood it.

Soon, as we approached more closely, quietly, the sound became much louder. It was now clearly distinguishable as a quite audible rustling or stirring. But there was no wind.

"The marchers," said the leader of the small men, pointing.

The hair on the back of my neck rose.

I saw now that the sound was the sound of millions upon millions of tiny feet, treading upon the leaves and fallen debris of the jungle floor. Too, there may have been, mixed in that sound, the almost infinitesimal sound, audible only in its cumulative effect, of the rubbings and clickings of the joints of tiny limbs and the shiftings and adjustments of tiny, black, shiny exoskeletons, those stiff casings of the segments of their tiny bodies.

"Do not go too close," said the leader of the small men.

The column of the marchers was something like a yard wide. I did not know how long it might be. It extended ahead through the jungle and behind through the jungle farther than I could see in either direction. Such columns can be pasangs in length. It is difficult to conjecture the numbers that constitute such a march. Conservatively some dozens of millions might be involved. The column widens only when food is found; then it may spread as widely as five hundred feet in width. Do not try to wade through such a flood. The torrent of hurrying feeders leaves little but bones in its path.

"Let us go toward the head of the column," said the little man.

We trekked through the jungle for several hours, keeping parallel to the long column. Once we crossed a small stream. The marchers, forming living bridges of their own bodies, clinging and scrambling on one another, crossed it also. They, rustling and black, moved over fallen trees and about rocks and palms. They seemed tireless and relentless. Flankers marshaled the column. Through the green rain forest the column moved, like a governed, endless, whispering black snake.

"Do they march at night?" I asked.

"Often," said the small man. "One must be careful where one sleeps."

We had then advanced beyond the head of the column by some four hundred yards.

"It is going to rain," I said. "Will that stop them?"

"For a time," he said. "They will scatter and seek shelter, beneath leaves and twigs, under the debris of the forest, and then, summoned by their leaders, they will reform and again take up the march."

Scarcely had he spoken but the skies opened up and, from the midst of the black, swirling clouds, while lightning cracked and shattered across the sky and branches lashed back and forth wildly in the wind, the driven, darkly silver sheets of a tropical rain storm descended upon us.

"Do they hunt?" I shouted to the small man.

"Not really," he said. "They forage."

"Can the column be guided?" I asked.

"Yes," he grinned, rubbing the side of his nose. Then he and the others curled up to sleep. I looked up at the sky, at the sheets of rain, the lashing branches. Seldom had I been so pleased to be caught in such a storm.

Within the stockade of the Mamba people there was much light and noise. I could hear the sounds of their musical instruments, and the pounding of the drums. Too, we could hear, within, the sounds of chanting and the beatings of the sticks carried in the hands of the dancers.

It is not so much that the column is guided as it is that it is lured.

This morning, early, the small men, with their nets and spears, had killed a small tarsk.

"Look," had said the leader of the small men this morning, "scouts."

He had thrown to the forest floor a portion of the slain tarsk. I watched the black, segmented bodies of some fifteen or twenty ants, some two hundred yards in advance of the column, approach the meat. Their antennae were lifted. They had seemed tense, excited. They were some two inches in length. Their bite, and that of their fellows, is vicious and extremely painful, but it is not poisonous. There is no quick death for those who fail to escape the column. Several of these ants then formed a circle, their heads together, their antennae, quivering, touching one another. Then, almost instantly, the circle broke and they rushed back to the column.

"Watch," had said the small man.

To my horror I had then seen the column turn toward the piece of tarsk flesh.

We had further encouraged the column during the day with additional blood and flesh, taken from further kills made by the small men with their nets and spears.

I looked up at the stockade. I remembered it, for it was the same from which we had, earlier, slipped away in the darkness of the night.

I rubbed tarsk blood on the palings. Behind me I could hear, yards away, a rustling.

"We will wait for you in the jungle," said the leader of the little men.

"Very well," I said.

The rustling was now nearer. Those inside the stockade, given their music and dancing, would not hear it. I stepped back. I saw the column, like a narrow black curtain, dark in the moonlight, ascend the palings.

I waited.

Inside the stockade, given the feast of the village, the column would widen, spreading to cover in its crowded millions every square inch of earth, scouring each stick, each piece of straw, hunting for each drop of grease, for each flake of flesh, even if it be no more than what might adhere to the shed hair of a hut urt.

When I heard the first scream I hurled my rope to the top of the stockade, catching one of the palings in its noose.

I heard a man cry out with pain.

I scrambled over the stockade wall. A woman, not even seeming to see me, crying out with pain, fled past me. She held a child in her arms.

There was now a horrified shouting in the camp. I saw torches being thrust to the ground. Men were irrationally thrusting at the ground with spears. Others tore palm leaves from the roofs of huts, striking about them.

I hoped there were no tethered animals in the camp. Between two huts I saw a man rolling on the ground in frenzied pain.

I felt a sharp painful bite at my foot. More ants poured over the palings. Now, near the rear wall and spreading toward the center of the village, it seemed there was a growing, lengthening, rustling, living carpet of insects. I slapped my arm and ran toward the hut in which, originally, our party had been housed in this village. With my foot I broke through the sticks at its back.

"Tarl!" cried Kisu, bound. I slashed his bonds. I freed, too, Ayari, and Alice and Tende.

Men and women, and children, ran past the doorway of the hut.

There was much screaming.

"Ants!" cried Ayari.

Alice cried out with pain.

We could hear them on the underside of the thatched roof. One fell from the roof and I brushed it from my shoulder.

Tende screamed, suddenly, bitten.

"Come this way," I told them. "Move with swiftness. Do not hesitate!"

We struck aside more sticks from the rear of the hut and emerged into the rustling darkness behind it.

People were fleeing the village. The stockade gate had been flung open. One of the huts was burning.

"Wait, Kisu!" I cried.

Alice cried out with misery.

Kisu, like a demented man, ran toward the great campfire in the center of the village. There, in the midst of people who did not even seem to notice him, he wildly overturned two great kettles of boiling water. Villagers screamed, scalded. The water sank into the earth. Kisu's legs were covered with ants. He buffeted a man and seized a spear from him.

"Kisu!" I cried. "Come back!" I then ran after him. A domestic tarsk ran past, squealing.

Kisu suddenly seized a man and hurled him about, striking him repeatedly with the butt of his spear, beating him as though he might be an animal. He then kicked him and drove him against the fence. It was the chieftain of the Mamba people. He drove the butt of the spear into the man's face, breaking his teeth loose. Then he thrust the blade of his spear into his belly and threw him on his face beside the wall. Again and again Kisu, as though beside himself with rage, drove the spear blade down into the man's legs until the tendons behind the knees were severed. He then, almost black with ants himself, shrieking, bit from the man's arm a mouthful of flesh which he then spat out. The chief, bleeding, cried out with misery. He lifted his hand to Kisu. Kisu turned about then and left him by the wall. "Hurry, Kisu!" I cried. "Hurry!" He then followed me. We looked back once. The chieftain of the Mamba people rolled screaming at the wall,

403

and then, scratching and screaming, tried to drag himself toward the gate. The villagers, however, in their departure, had closed it, hoping thereby to contain the ants.

48

WE ACQUIRE THREE NEW MEMBERS FOR OUR PARTY, TWO OF WHOM ARE SLAVE GIRLS

I kicked her. "I will take this one," I said.

The leader of the small people then untied the ankles of the blond girl and unbound the fastening that held her, by her vine collar, to the loop tied about the log.

"Stand up," he told her. She stood up. She still wore her gag. It had been removed only to feed and water her.

The leader of the talunas stood before me, a vine collar on her throat, her hands tied behind her back.

"Put your head down," I told her. She lowered her head.

I then went to the white male, who had been the captive of the talunas, released by the small people from his prison hut before they burned the taluna village.

He knelt in the clearing, in the chains of the talunas, shackles on his ankles and wrists, connected to a common chain depending from a heavy iron collar.

"You were with Shaba," I said.

"Yes," he said, "an oarsman."

"Do I not know you?" I asked.

"Yes," said he. "I am Turgus, who was of Port Kar. It was because of you I was banished from the city."

"The fault," I smiled, "seems rather yours, for it seems it was your design to do robbery upon me."

It had been he, with his confederate, Sasi, who had attempted to attack me in Port Kar, along the side of the canal leading to the pier of the Red Urt.

He shrugged. "I did not know you were of the Warriors," he said.

"How came you upon the river?" I asked.

"When banished from Port Kar," he said, "I must leave the city before sundown. I took passage on a ship to Bazi, as an oarsman. From Bazi I went to Schendi. In Schendi I was contacted by an agent of Shaba, who was secretly recruiting oarsmen for a venture in the interior. The pay promised to be good. I joined his expedition."

"Where now is Shaba?" I asked.

"Doubtless, by now," said he, "he had been destroyed. Our ships were subjected to almost constant attack and ambush. There were accidents, a wreck, and several capsizings. We lost supplies. We were attacked from the jungles. There was sickness."

"Shaba did not turn back?" I asked.

"He is dauntless," said the man. "He is a great leader."

I nodded. It was a judgment in which it was necessary to concur.

"How came you to be separated from him?" I asked.

"Shaba, lying ill in a camp," he said, "gave permission that all who wished to leave might be free to do so."

"You left?" I said.

"Of course," he said. "It was madness to continue further on the river. I, and others, making rafts, set out to return to Ngao and Ushindi."

"Yes?" I said.

"We were attacked the first night," he said. "All in my party were killed save myself, who escaped. I wandered westward, paralleling the river." He cast a glance at the talunas, trussed kneeling by the log, their heads down, fastened to it, their necks helpless to the blow of the panga, should it descend. "I fell to these women," he said. He lifted his chained wrists. "They made me their work slave," he said.

"Surely they forced you to serve their pleasure, as well," I said.

"Sometimes they would beat me and mount me," he said.

"Unchain him. He is a male," I said.

Ayari, with a key taken from a pouch found in the hut of the taluna leader, unlocked the chains of Turgus, who had been from Port Kar.

"You are freeing me?" he asked.

"Yes," I said, "you are free to go."

"I would choose to remain," he said.

"Fight," I told him.

"What?" he asked.

"Strike at me," I said.

405

"But you have freed me," he said.

"Strike," I told him.

He struck out at me and I blocked the blow and, striking him in the stomach and then across the side of the face, sent him grunting and sprawling to the debris of the jungle floor.

He sprang to his feet, angrily, and I struck him down again. He was strong. Four more times he rose to do combat, but then he could not again climb to his feet. He tried to do so, but fell back.

I then pulled him to his feet. "It is our intention to go up-river," I told him.

"That is madness," he said.

"You are free to go," I told him.

"I choose to remain," he said.

"Kisu and I," I said, indicating the former Mfalme of Ukungu, "are before you. You will take your orders from us. You will do what we tell you, and well."

Kisu lifted a spear, and shook it.

Turgus rubbed his jaw, and grinned. "You are before me, both of you," he said. "Have no fear. I will take my orders, and well."

"Insubordination," I said, "will be punished with death."

"I understand," said Turgus.

"We are not gentlemen like Shaba," I said.

Turgus smiled. "On the river," said he, "Shaba is not a gentleman either." On the river, he knew, and all knew, there must be strict discipline.

"We now well understand one another, do we not?" I asked.

"That we do," said he, "—Captain."

"Examine these women," I said, indicating the line of kneeling, trussed talunas. "Which among them pleases you most?"

"That one," said he, indicating the slender-legged, dark-haired girl who had been, as we had determined, second in command among the talunas. There was a menace in his voice.

"Perhaps you remember her well from your enslavement?" I asked.

"Yes," he said. "I do well remember her."

"She is yours," I said.

The girl began to involuntarily shudder. "No," she begged, "please, do not give me to him!"

"You are his," I told her.

"He will kill me," she cried.

"If he wishes," I said.

"Please do not kill me," she cried to Turgus. "I will try to please you totally, and in all ways!"

He did not speak.

"I will be the most loving and lowly slave a man could ask," she wept. "Please, let me try to earn my life!"

He untied her ankles and freed her vine collar from the loop on the trunk of the tree. He threw her to her feet and pushed her head down, submissively. She then stood, hands tied behind her, beside the blond girl, the leader of the talunas.

I took two pair of slave bracelets from the loot of the taluna camp. Girls such as talunas keep such things about in case slave girls should fall into their hands. They are extremely cruel to slave girls, whom they regard as having betrayed their sex by surrendering as slaves to men. Actually, of course, it seems likely that their hatred of slave girls, which tends to be unreasoning and vicious, is due less to lofty sentiments than to their own intense jealousy of the joy and fulfillment of their imbonded sisters. The joyful slave girl, obedient to her master's wishes, is an affront and, more frighteningly, an unanswerable and dreadful threat to their most cherished illusions. Perhaps they wish to be themselves slaves. Why else should they hate them so?

I slipped the straps on the wrists of the blond girl a bit higher on her wrists. I then, below the straps, snapped her wrists into one of the pairs of slave bracelets from the loot of the taluna camp. I then untied the straps which had, hitherto, confined her wrists. Her hands, then, were still fastened behind her, but now in slave bracelets.

I loosened the gag from the mouth of the blond girl and let it fall, its wadding looped about it, before her throat.

She threw up on the jungle floor. The wadding smelled. She threw back her head, gasping for air. I cleaned her mouth with a handful of leaves.

"Do you wish to be a slave girl?" I asked her.

"No," she said. "No!"

"Very well," I said. I threw the other pair of slave bracelets to Turgus. He snapped them on the dark-haired girl and then, as I had, freed her wrists of the earlier binding, which had been, in her case, a length of vine rope from the small people.

She looked at him, puzzled.

"Do you wish to be a slave girl?" he asked.

"No," she said, "no, no!"

"Very well," he said.

I grasped the hand of the leader of the small people in friendship. "I wish you well," I said. "I wish you well," he said.

Then I, and Kisu, followed by Turgus, and by Janice, Alice and Tende, turned about to leave the clearing. We would return to our hidden canoe, beached near the river, near which we had concealed many of our supplies.

"What shall we do with these?" called the leader of the small people. We turned about. He indicated the line of miserable, trussed talunas.

"Whatever you wish," I told him. "They are yours."

"What of those?" he asked. He indicated the blond girl who had been the leader of the talunas and the dark-haired girl, who had been her second in command. They stood, their hands braceleted behind them, confused, in the clearing.

"They were ours," I said. "We let them go. Let them go."

"Very well," he said.

Kisu and I, and Turgus, and our girls, Alice, Janice and Tende, then left the clearing.

"Unlock our bracelets," begged the blond girl. She and the dark-haired girl had followed us to the edge of the river.

Kisu and I, and Ayari, were sliding our canoe, from which we had removed its camouflage, toward the water. The girls, Janice, Alice and Tende, with the paddles and supplies, accompanied us.

Then we were at the edge of the water.

"Please," begged the blond girl. She turned, that her wrists, inclosed snugly in the linked, steel bracelets, might be exposed to me. "Please unlock our bracelets," she begged. "Please, please!" begged, too, the dark-haired girl.

Kisu and Ayari thrust the canoe into the water. Janice, Alice and Tende, wading, placed the paddles and supplies in the canoe, and then, entering the narrow vessel, assumed their places.

"Please free us," begged the blond girl.

"They are only slave bracelets," I said. "Free yourselves."

"We cannot do so," said the blond girl. "We are women, and have only women's strength."

I shrugged.

"Please," she begged again.

"Did you think, noble free women," I asked, "that you

408

might do fully as you wished, that no penalties would be inflicted upon you?"

"You cannot leave us here!" she wept. She looked behind her, fearfully, at the jungle.

Turgus and I waded to the canoe, which Kisu and Ayari held steady in the water.

"Please," begged the blond girl. "You cannot leave us here!"

I turned to face her. "You have lost," I told her. I turned away.

"There is another penalty which may be inflicted upon free women," cried the blond.

I turned again to face her. "Do not even speak of it," I said. "It is too degrading and horrifying. Surely death is a thousand times more preferable."

"I beg that other penalty," said the blond, kneeling in the mud on the shore. "I, too," cried the dark-haired girl, kneeling, too, in the mud. "I, too!"

"Speak clearly," I said.

"We beg enslavement," said the blond. "Enslave us, we beg of you!"

"Enslave yourselves," I said.

"I declare myself a slave," said the blond, "and I submit myself to you as my master." She put her head down to the mud. "I declare myself a slave," said the dark-haired girl, and then she turned to face Turgus, "and I submit myself to you as my master." She then put her head down, like the blond, to the mud.

"Lift your head," I said to the blond. "Lift your head," said Turgus to the other girl. The two girls lifted their heads, anxiously.

"You are now only two slaves," I said.

"Yes, Master," said the blond. "Yes. Master," said the dark-haired girl. They had declared themselves slaves. The slave herself, of course, once the declaration has been made, cannot revoke it. That would be impossible, for she is then only a slave. The slave can be freed only by one who owns her, only by one who is at the time her master or, if it should be the case, her mistress. The legal point, I think, is interesting. Sometimes, in the fall of a city, girls who have been enslaved, girls formerly of the now victorious city, will be freed. Technically, according to Merchant Law, which serves as the arbiter in such intermunicipal matters, the girls become briefly the property of their rescuers, else how could they be freed? Further, according to Merchant Law, the rescuer has no obligation to free the girl. In having been enslaved she has lost all claim to her former Home Stone. She has become an animal. If, too, she is sufficiently desirable, it is almost certain she will not be freed. As the Goreans have it, such women are too beautiful to be free. Too, as often as not, city pride enters into such matters. Such girls, with other slave girls, both of various cities and with the former free women of the conquered city, now collared slaves, too, will often be marched naked in chains in the loot processions of the conquering cities. It is claimed they have shamed their former city by having fallen slave, and if they were good enough to be only slaves in the conquered city then surely they should be no more within the walls of the victorious city. Such girls usually are marched in a special position in the loot processions, behind and before banners which proclaim their shame. The people much abuse them and lash them as they pass. Such girls usually beg piteously to be sold to transient slavers. It is hard for them to wear their collars in their own city.

Kisu and Ayari, and Turgus and I, entered the canoe. "Masters!" cried the blond, kneeling in the mud, her hands braceleted behind her. "Wait!" cried the dark-haired girl.

"You are slaves," I told them. "You may be left behind." The prow of the canoe swung slowly toward the center of the river.

"Do not leave us!" cried the blond. She struggled to her feet and, slipping slipping, waded splashing to the side of the canoe. So, too, did the dark-haired girl.

The canoe was now in waist-deep water.

The blond, wading beside it, crying, thrust her body against its side. "Please," she begged, "please!" Both the girls still wore the vine collars on their throats, which the small people had affixed on them, that they might be fastened more easily at the fallen tree. The blond, too, still had looped about her neck her gag lashing with its unrolled, dependent wadding looped about it.

"Let us serve you as work slaves!" cried the blond. "Yes, Master, please!" cried the dark-haired girl. The canoe continued to move, and the two girls waded, weeping, beside it. "Let us serve you as work and pleasure slaves!" cried the blond. "Yes, Masters," cried the dark-haired girl. "Please, please!"

"Do you have the makings of a pleasure slave?" I asked the blond. I held her by the vine collar at the side of the canoe.

410

"Yes, Master," she wept. "Yes, Master!" "I, too," cried the dark-haired girl.

I pulled the blond into the canoe, kneeling before me, her back to me. She was shuddering. Turgus drew the weeping trembling dark-haired girl, too, into the canoe. She fainted, overcome, and he placed her on her side, knees drawn up, before him.

"Where are you from?" I asked the blond girl.

"I, and Fina," she said, indicating with her head the dark-haired girl, "are from Turia. The other girls are from various cities in the south."

"Did you spy upon us once," I asked, "further down the river?"

"Yes," she said. "It was I. We then determined to try and trap you, for slaves." Ayari, then, long ago, had, as I had suspected, seen a taluna in the forest. He had thought it might have been Janice, gathering wood.

"How came you to the rain forests?" I asked.

"I, and Fina, and the others," she said, "fled undesired companionships."

"But now you have fallen slave," I said.

"Yes, Master," she said.

"Your entire band," I said, "will doubtless know no nobler fate."

"Yes, Master," she said. She shuddered. "We now, all of us, belong to men."

"Yes," I said.

"You left our vine collars on," she said. "You knew, did you not, that we would beg slavery?"

"Yes," I said.

"But how could you know?" she asked.

"Though you and the others have fought your femininity," I said, "yet you and they are both beautiful and feminine."

"You knew that we were natural slaves?" she said.

"Of course," I said.

"I will no longer be permitted to fight my femininity, will I?" she asked.

"No," I said. "You are now a slave girl. You will yield to it, and fully."

"I'm frightened," she said.

"That is natural," I said.

"It will make me so loving and helpless," she said.

"Yes," I said.

"Can I dare, too, now," she asked, "to be sensuous?"

411

"If you are not fully pleasing in all the modalities of the slave girl, sensuous and otherwise," I said, "you will be severely punished."

"Yes, Master," she said.

"Or slain," I said.

"Yes, Master," she whispered.

The canoe moved into the center of the river. "I do not know how to be a slave girl," she suddenly wept. I thrust her head down, "You will begin," I said, "by learning to be docile and submissive." I then rewound the wadding and, dragging her head up briefly, by the hair, from behind, pushed it into her mouth and lashed it in place. I then again thrust her head down. "Also," I said, "you will consider whether or not, at a given time, your master wishes to hear you speak. If you are in doubt, you may ask his permission to speak, which may then be granted or denied, as he pleases."

She nodded, piteously signifying her slave's assent.

We then continued our journey eastward.

In a few moments she began to tremble. Tears fell from her eyes, staining her thighs and the wood of the canoe bottom. I put her then gently on her stomach, her head turned to the left. She shuddered and then, exhausted by her ordeal, fell asleep.

We paddled on.

We would let the new slaves sleep for a time. Then, in an Ahn or so, we would put our hands upon them and, holding them by the hair and the braceleted wrists, thrust them half over the side, immersing their heads and torsos in the river, that they might be awakened. We would then pull them back into the canoe, tie their ankles to a thwart and remove their slave bracelets. Paddles would be thrust into their hands. Janice, Alice and Tende might then rest, and the new girls, fresh, raw slaves, but now more cognizant than before of their condition, might contribute to our progress on the river.

49

THERE IS TO BE WAR UPON THE RIVER; TENDE WILL NOT BE TIED TONIGHT

"Can you read the drums, Ayari?" I asked. "Kisu?"

"No," said Ayari.

"No," said Kisu.

"The drums have the rhythm of neither the Ushindi nor Ukungu speech," said Ayari.

Two days ago we had left the country of the small people, where we had made the acquaintance of Turgus and acquired two new slaves.

An Ahn later we could still hear the drums, both behind us and before us.

"Keep paddling," I told Janice.

"Yes, Master," she said.

We had cut new paddles, carving them into shape, that each member of our party, free and slave, might have his own lever. If it became necessary to expedite our passage we wished each member of our party, whether free or bond, to be able to lend his strength to this work. Commonly, however, only four or five of us, two men, and two or three women, paddled at a given time. That way we were not only usually assured of a crew in readiness but we could spend longer hours on the river. Kisu had placed the finishing touches on the new paddles, making them fit, in grip and weight, for Turgus and the two new slaves, the blond who had been the leader of the talunas and the dark-haired girl, who had been her second in command. We had also, incidentally, cut an extra paddle, to go with the extra paddle we were already carrying. The carrying of an extra paddle, or paddles, as I may have mentioned, is a not uncommon precaution on the river.

Ayari looked about himself. He listened to the drums. "The jungle is alive," he said.

Suddenly Alice screamed. "Look!" she cried, pointing. We saw, dangling over the water, hung there by the neck, the

413

body of a man. There was upon his body, half torn away, the blue of the scribe.

"Is it Shaba?" asked Kisu.

"No," I said.

"It is one of his men," said Turgus, grimly.

"There is another!" cried Alice. About a hundred yards beyond the first body, on the same side of the river, it, too, suspended from a tree branch, hung by the neck, dangling over the water, was a second body. This one wore tattered brown and green.

"It is another of Shaba's men," said Turgus. "I think it would be wise to turn back."

The drums pounded from the jungle, both before us and behind us, along the river.

"Continue on," I said.

In a few Ehn we had passed some six more bodies.

"Look, over there," said Ayari. "On the shore."

We took the canoe to the shore and drew it up among the roots and brush.

"It is one of the galleys of Shaba, is it not?" I asked Turgus.

"Yes," he said.

It was partially burned. Its sides wore weapon cuts. The bottom had been hacked out of it with pangas or axes. Splintered oars lay about.

"I do not think Shaba continued further on the river," said Turgus.

The two new slaves, the blond girl and the dark-haired girl, remained in the canoe. Their ankles were fastened to two thwarts. They had placed their paddles across the canoe and, weary, were bending over them.

"There were three galleys," I said.

"I do not like the sound of the drums," said Ayari.

"Yes," said Turgus, thoughtfully. "There were three galleys."

"We found the wreckage of one earlier," I said, "and now the wreckage of this one."

"Surely Shaba could not have proceeded further," said Turgus. "Hear the drums."

"There was a third galley," I said.

"Yes," said Turgus.

"Do you think Shaba would have turned back?" I asked.

"He was ill," said Turgus. "Doubtless he has lost many men. What hope could he have had?"

414

"Do you think he would have turned back?" I asked.

"No," said Turgus.

"We shall then continue on," I said. We returned to the canoe and thrust it again into the muddy waters of the wide Ua.

Within the next Ahn we passed more than sixty bodies, dangling at the side of the river. None was that of Shaba. About some of these bodies there circled scavenging birds. On the shoulders of some perched small, yellow-winged jards. One was attacked even by zads, clinging to it and tearing at it with their long, yellowish, slightly curved beaks. These were jungle zads. They are less to be feared than desert zads, I believe, being less aggressive. They do, however, share one ugly habit with the desert zad, that of tearing out the eyes of weakened victims. That serves as a practical guarantee that the victim, usually an animal, will die. Portions of flesh the zad will swallow and carry back to its nest, where it will disgorge the flesh into the beaks of its fledglings. The zad is, in its way, a dutiful parent.

"The drums," I said, "may not have us as their object."

"Why do you say that?" asked Ayari.

"We heard them, first," I said, "far upriver of us. The message, whatever it is, was then relayed downstream."

"What then could be the message?" asked Ayari.

"I fear," said Turgus, "that it signifies the destruction of Shaba."

"What think you, Kisu?" I asked.

"I think you are right about ourselves not being the object of the drums' call," said Kisu, "and for the reason which you gave. But I think, too, that if the destruction of Shaba was the content of the message that we might well have heard drums yesterday and the day before, when perhaps the second galley was destroyed. Why would the drums sound just now?"

"Then Shaba may live," I said.

"Who knows?" asked Kisu.

"What then is the meaning of the drums?" pressed Ayari.

"I think that I may know," I said.

"I suspect that I, too, know," said Kisu, grimly.

"Listen," said Ayari. We ceased paddling.

"Yes," I said. "Yes," said Kisu.

We then heard, drifting over the waters, from upstream, singing.

"Quickly," I said, "take the canoe to the left, take shelter upon that river island!"

We took the canoe quickly to a narrow river island, almost a wooded bar, on either side of which, placidly, flowed the Ua.

Scarcely had we beached the canoe and dragged it into the brush than the first of the many canoes rounded the southern edge of the island.

"Incredible," whispered Ayari.

"Get down, Slaves," I said to the blond girl and the dark-haired girl, who were tied by their ankles in the canoe. They lay then on their stomachs in the canoe, not daring to raise their heads. The rest of us lay in the grass and brush and watched.

"How many can there be?" asked Ayari.

"Countless numbers," I said.

"It is as I had hoped," said Kisu.

Hundreds of canoes were now passing the small island. They were, many of them, long war canoes, containing as many as fifteen or twenty men. They paddled in rhythm and sang. They were bright with feathers. Their bodies, in white and yellow paint, were covered with rude designs.

"I was told of this by the leader of the small people," I said. "It is the massing of the peoples of the river for war."

Still the canoes streamed past us. We could hear the drums in the background, behind the singing, throbbing and pounding out their message.

Finally, after a half of an Ahn, the last of the canoes had disappeared down the river.

Kisu and I stood up. Tende, too, stood up.

"Well, Kisu," said I, "it seems you have lured Bila Huruma to his destruction. He will be outnumbered by at least ten to one. He cannot survive. Your plan, it seems, has been fulfilled. In your battle with the Ubar it is you, Kisu, who seems to have won."

Kisu looked down the river. Then he put his arm about the shoulders of Tende. "Tonight, Tende," he said, "I will not tie you."

416

50

THE LAKE;
THE ANCIENT CITY;
WE WILL ENTER
THE ANCIENT CITY

"It is so vast," said Ayari.

"It is larger than Ushindi or Ngao," said Turgus.

We guided our canoe over the shining, placid waters of a broad lake.

"It is, I am confident," I said, "the source of the Ua."

"Into it must flow a thousand streams," said Kisu.

Two weeks ago we had come to another high falls, even higher than that from which we had, long ago, caught sight of the following forces of Bila Huruma, pasangs behind in the distance. We must be thousands of feet Gorean, given the length of the river, the numerous plunging cataracts, and the plateaus and levels we had ascended, above sea level, above the entrance points, west of Ngao and Ushindi, of the brown Kamba and Nyoka into the green waters of Thassa. From the falls at the edge of this unnamed lake we had been able to see far behind us. The river had been clear.

Here and there, emerging from the lake, were great stone figures, the torsos and heads of men, shields upon their arms, spears grasped in their hands. These great figures were weathered, and covered with the patinas of age, greenish and red. Lichens and mosses grew in patches on the stone; vines clambered about them. Birds perched on the heads and shoulders of the great figures. On ridgework near the water turtles and tharlarion sunned themselves.

"How ancient are these things?" asked Janice.

"I do not know," I said.

I looked at the huge figures. They towered thirty and forty feet out of the water. Our canoe seemed small, moving among them. I studied the faces.

"These men were of your race, or of some race akin to yours, Kisu," I said.

"Perhaps," said Kisu. "There are many black peoples."

"Where have the builders of these things gone?" asked Ayari.

"I do not know," I said.

"Let us continue on," said Kisu, thrusting with his paddle against the calm water.

"How beautiful it is," said Janice.

"There, at the landing, moored," said Ayari, "is a river galley."

"It is the third galley," said Turgus, "the last galley of Shaba."

Before us, more than four hundred yards in width, was a broad expanse of stone, at the eastern edge of the huge lake. It was a landing, a hundred yards deep. On it were huge pillars, with iron rings, where vessels might be moored. At the back of the landing, leading upward were flights and levels of steps, extending the full length of the four hundred yards of the landing. At the height, on that level, set far back, was a great, ruined building, with stairs and white columns. Behind it, extending backward, was a ruined city, with crumbling walls. We could not, from where we were, conjecture its extent. A tharlarion splashed from the landing into the water. The landing was covered with vines.

At places, and flanking the huge building at the top of the flights of stairs, were more of the huge figures of warriors, with shields and spears.

"Shaba must be here," said Turgus.

"He was first to the source of the Ua," said Kisu.

I unwrapped a panga from near my place in the canoe. I freed a spear, one that we had taken from the raiders so long ago.

"Take the canoe in," I said. "Moor it near the galley."

"Your long quest, Tarl, my friend," said Kisu, "has now come to an end."

I stepped out onto the landing. I slung the panga at my waist. I carried the spear.

"Why do you seek Shaba?" asked Turgus. "Your eyes have in them the look of one who embarks upon the business of the warrior."

"Do not concern yourself," I told him.

"Do you mean harm to Shaba?" he asked.

"It will be necessary, I presume," I said, "to kill him."

"I cannot permit that," said Turgus. "I was in service to Shaba."

"You are in service now," I said, "to Kisu and myself."

"Shaba treated me well," said he. "He gave me, and others, full liberty to take our leave of him when we did."

"Have you, a brigand, honor?" I asked.

"Call it what you will," said he, angrily.

Kisu struck Turgus between the shoulder blades with the butt of one of the spears.

We dragged Turgus, half stunned, to the landing. There Kisu threw him on his belly and tied his hands behind his back. He then gagged him. He then put a rope on his throat.

I regarded the slave girls. "Onto the landing, and onto your bellies," I said.

Alice and Janice, and the blond girl who had been the leader of the talunas, and her second in command, the slender-legged, dark-haired girl, and Tende, all, left the canoe and lay on their bellies on the landing. One by one we tied their hands behind their backs, and then, with a long strap, put them in throat coffle. I gagged the dark-haired girl, for she was the slave of Turgus. She looked at me in misery. I smiled. She would be given absolutely no opportunity whatsoever to attempt to give an alarm to Shaba, should we come upon him, thinking such an action on her part might please her master. I think this was wise on my part. I had seen her squirming with joy in the arms of Turgus. She had been well conquered and certainly might now strive to serve him in just such a harrowing detail, even though it might be at the risk of her own life. The gag, preventing her from acting in such a contingency, could well save her life. It would not be necessary, then, for Kisu or I to cut her throat.

"Follow me," I said.

"Get up, Turgus," said Ayari, holding to his neck rope. Turgus, unsteadily, staggered to his feet.

I started up the stairs, Kisu a step behind me. Then came Ayari and Turgus. Behind them, single file, their hands tied behind them, came five slave girls. Tende was first, for she was first girl. Then came Janice and Alice, and then the blond girl and, lastly, the slender-legged, dark-haired girl. I had, some days ago, removed the gag from the blond-haired girl. The formerly proud leader of the talunas was now well tutored in docility and deference, and already she was showing early signs of emergent growth in vitality and sensuousness. Too, she was becoming happy. Her gag, no longer necessary on her as an instructional or disciplinary device, was that which now packed the pretty face of the dark-haired girl, she who had been her second in command, who now brought up the rear of the coffle.

51

BILA HURUMA

"Like this?" asked the blond girl of Janice.

"Crouch down further," said Janice. "Take the tether in both hands, one above and one below your left thigh. Hold the tether tightly against your left thigh. Feel it there. Now move your hips like this."

"Like this?" asked the blond girl.

"Yes," said Janice.

I watched the blond girl. How flushed and excited was her face, how free of tension and tightness, how free of anxiety and stress. There is an incredible, effusive release of energy and happiness when a woman stops fighting herself. It requires an inordinate amount of energy, of course, to maintain the stern rigidities of self-suppression and constriction. Self-denial, self-torture, pretense, hypocrisy and conformance to external, alien standards must exact their inevitable costs. Their damage and toll is torn not only from the heart, but from the tissues of the body as well. The laws are implacable, the consequences inexorable. The equations of misery are registered not only in the conscious annals of pain but, too, are tallied no less in the very chemistry of the body. The human being is the only animal we know who tortures itself. It need not do so. Yet how few human beings understand that, and how few believe it, truly.

"Should this not be done, really, with a chain?" asked the blond girl.

"I have done it myself only with a tether," said Janice. "A chain, however, might be nice."

"Surely this drilling in the stone at my feet," said the blond, "was for a chain."

"Probably," said Janice.

The blond stopped, and straightened up. She was covered

420

with sweat. "If I learn to do this well," she asked, "do you think my master might permit me a garment?"

Janice shrugged. "If your performance merits it, and if you are sufficiently pleasing to him in all ways, he might deign to throw you a rag to cover your prettiness."

"I will try to be pleasing to him," said the blond.

"See that you do," said Janice, "but remember that he is my master before he is yours."

"Yes, Mistress," said the blond. The two new slaves addressed our older girls as 'Mistress.' Kisu and I thought that would be useful in keeping order among them. In any training situation, of course, it is common for the girl being trained to address a female trainer, whether the trainer is bond or free, as 'Mistress.' Strict discipline is essential in slave instruction.

"You are not really much larger than I," said Janice.

"No, Mistress," said the blond. The blond was about five and a half feet tall, and would have weighed, I conjecture, about twenty-nine stone, Gorean, about one hundred and sixteen pounds.

"Now sit down and cross your ankles," said Janice. "Loop the tether about them, as though they were bound. When I give the signal, unloop the tether as though it were unbound. Rise then, and stretch, as a slave girl, before your master."

"Yes, Mistress," said the blond.

I smiled to myself. Never when she was on Earth, I conjectured, had Janice thought that she would one day be giving instruction in, of all things, the arts of pleasing a man. Earth women, it is well known, are above such things, unless perhaps they are brought naked to Gor and placed in steel collars. They then, quickly enough, become desperately eager to learn the delightful and sensuous arts. This makes sense. Their lives depend on it.

"Not bad," said Janice.

"You will teach me things to do with my mouth and tongue, won't you?" begged the blond.

"Perhaps," said Janice, "if you gather wood for me, and wash clothing for me, with the exception of that of my master."

"I will, I will," said the blond. Girls seek eagerly to learn from one another.

"That is enough," said Kisu. He pulled apart Turgus and the dark-haired girl. They were still gagged, and had their hands tied behind them. Kisu then crossed and bound the ankles of each.

I looked about the great room. It was perhaps two hundred feet in width and depth, with tall columns. It was filled with great blocks of stone, which had fallen, perhaps centuries ago, from the roof. The walls were still, generally, intact. The floor, save where it was cluttered, was generally smooth, save for certain drillings, through which chains might be passed. Some chains, little more than fragile collections of rust, ready to crumble at a touch, lay about. The room was reached by a broad flight of stairs. And, in the rear of the room, there was another broad flight of stairs, leading upward to another landing and walk. On the walls, which circled about, still largely standing, there were dim mosaics. The chamber had, apparently, long ago, been used in the enslavement and training of women, doubtless taken in the raids and wars of those who had built these mighty halls. Some of the mosaics showed the clothing of miserable captives being taken from them; others showed them being tied and whipped, doubtless to introduce them quickly and mercifully to the concept of being under discipline; others showed them being marked by hot irons and placed in collars; others showed them kneeling, head down, in submission, before their masters; others showed them being danced before their masters; others showed them serving the intimate pleasures of their masters.

We had chosen this room in which to camp, because of the girls. They had been thrilled with the mosaics. Almost fainting they had begged to dance and be used. Women learn from example. If one presents them only with masculine images, presented in approval contexts, they will often attempt dutifully to conform to these alien models. If one, on the other hand, permits them to be aware of genuine female images, presented within contexts of honesty, openness and permissibility, it is natural for them to feel deep biological affinities for what is portrayed. For what it is worth women tend on the whole to be unsuccessful in conforming to masculine images, and tend to take gracefully and naturally to feminine images, toward which they seem to have genetic predispositions. Perhaps that is because that is what they really are, not men but women. Sex is not superficial. Not one cell in the body of a woman is the same as that in the body of a man.

I saw Tende in the arms of Kisu. He had not tied her at night since we had seen the forces of the river peoples pass the island on which we had hidden, those forces of incredible numbers which had doubtless wiped out Bila Huruma, his flotilla and his battalions of askaris.

I approached the blond and she knelt, swiftly, head down.

I had her stand and lashed her wrists behind her back. She was already tethered.

"Lie down," I told her. She lay down on the stone floor.

"Are you going to tie me?" asked Alice.

I tied her hands behind her back. Then I tied her neck to the neck of the dark-haired girl, using the coffle strap. "Lie down," I told her. She lay down.

"Prepare to be bound," I told Janice.

"Please do not bind me," wheedled Janice, approaching me, looking up at me, running her finger on the left shoulder of my tunic.

"Do you question my will?" I asked.

Swiftly she knelt, her head to my feet. "No, Master," she said. "Please do not whip me." She lifted her head, and held to my legs. "Please, Master, let me serve your pleasure instead."

"You have already this evening," I said, "as the others, danced and served well."

"I have only begun to be aroused, Master," she said.

I took her by the hair and pulled her, she half crawling, then half crouching and walking, to where lay the dark-haired girl and Alice. I put her on her knees there and tied her hands behind her back. I then added her to the coffle strap.

She looked up at me, the coffle strap dangling from her throat, attaching her to Alice, and then to the dark-haired girl. "Please, Master," she said.

"Lie down," I told her. She lay down, first on her left shoulder and then on her back.

I looked down upon her, and considered putting her under the whip.

"Let me placate you," she begged. She lifted her body to me. "Please, Master," she begged.

I looked down at her. "You are a beautiful slave," I said.

"Please, Master," she begged.

"Very well," I said. Her offense, that of questioning my will, required discipline. But the whip of the furs, I decided would be sufficient.

"You made her moan well," said Kisu.

"She is a sweetly hipped, hot slave," I said. I joined Kisu at the small fire in the ruins of the great building. He was sitting near it, cross-legged. Tende lay beside him, unbound, her head on her hands.

I looked back at Janice who, hands tied behind her back, fastened in the coffle, lay on her side. I smiled. I think there is no music more pleasing to a man's ears than the moans of a yielding slave girl.

"You see, Tende," asked Kisu, "you are the only slave here who is not bound."

"Yes, Master," she smiled. "Thank you, Master."

"Put wood on the fire," said Kisu.

She laughed. "You are a beast, Master," she said. She rose to her feet and fetched wood, which she placed on the fire. Then she lay as before, beside Kisu.

"May I face my master?" asked Janice, who lay, as I had placed her, facing away from us.

There were bruises on her body, for I had taken her on the stones.

"Yes," I said.

She struggled about, that she might face us. Her eyes were moist. She pursed her lips, and then, delicately, kissed with them, as though her mouth might be upon my body. I blew her a kiss, brushing it from the side of my face towards her in the Gorean fashion. I then looked away from her. "Master," she said, "I love you." "Be silent, Slave Girl, " I said, not looking at her. "Yes, Master," she said, sobbing. She was an excellent slave, and would doubtless know many loves, until she, a superb love slave, might at last find herself fallen helplessly and totally into the absolute power of such a man as she had never dreamed might exist, he who to her, in the personal and intricate chemistry of couples, would be her ideal master, one powerful, and uncompromising and strict, one capable of seeing that she served well, one capable of whipping her, if need be, but yet one loving and tender, one who would be to her the perfect love master. It did not seem likely that she would be again sold. What would be the point of it?

"The city is large," said Kisu. "It is quite possible that we will never find Shaba within it."

"We must continue the search," I said. "I am certain he is here somewhere."

Suddenly Janice screamed and we leaped to our feet. Askaris had entered the room, perhaps two hundred of them, armed. Msaliti was with them. And with them, too, at their head, was an unmistakable figure, black and huge, with shield and spear.

"Bila Huruma!" cried Kisu.

52

THE SCRIBE

Tende fled from the feet of Kisu, running to Bila Huruma. She knelt at his feet, weeping. "I will go with you!" she cried. "Do not hurt them! Do not kill them! I will come willingly with you! You have found me! Please, I beg of you to let the others go! Let them be free, great Ubar!"

"Who is this woman?" asked Bila Huruma.

Kisu stepped back, startled. Tende looked up at Bila Huruma, stunned.

"Have you not sought me, great Ubar?" she asked. "Was it not for me that you journeyed upon the river?"

"Where is Shaba?" asked Bila Huruma.

"I do not know," I said.

"Great Ubar," cried Tende.

"Who is this?" asked Bila Huruma.

"I do not know," said Msaliti. "I have never seen her before."

Bila Huruma looked down at the half-naked slave suppliant at his feet. "Have I ever seen you before?" he asked.

"No, Master," she said.

"I thought not," he said. "Had I done so, doubtless I would have recalled the lines of your body."

"I was Tende of Ukungu," she said.

"Who is Tende of Ukungu?" asked the Ubar.

"Ah," said Msaliti. "She was to be sent to you by Aibu, chieftain in Ukungu, that the alliance between the empire and Ukungu be consolidated."

"Ukungu is part of the empire," said Bila Huruma.

"No!" cried Kisu, seizing up a spear.

Bila Huruma paid Kisu no attention. He looked down at Tende, kneeling at his feet, looking up at him.

"A lovely slave gift," said Bila Huruma, "a lovely token of

425

esteem and good will, but scarcely sufficient to consolidate a matter as weighty as a political alliance."

"She was the daughter of Aibu," said Msaliti. "She was to have been companioned to you."

"Companioned?" inquired Bila Huruma.

"Yes," said Msaliti.

"This exquisite slut was once a free woman?" asked Bila Huruma.

"Yes," said Msaliti.

"Is that true, my dear?" asked Bila Huruma.

"Yes, Master," she said.

"Tende of Ukungu?" he asked.

"I was once Tende of Ukungu," she said. "I am now only Tende, the slave, and am called Tende only because my master was pleased to put that name upon me."

"Did you once wear the regalia of the free woman?" asked Bila Huruma.

"Yes, Master," she said.

"You wear now the rags and beads of a slave," he said.

"Yes, Master," she said.

"They become you," he said.

"Thank you, Master," she said.

"Rags and beads are more attractive on a woman than gowns, are they not?" he asked.

"Yes, Master," she said. It was true.

"It is fitting that you were enslaved, Tende," he said, "for your body is lovely enough to be that of a slave."

"Thank you, Master," she said.

"I do not understand one thing here," he said.

"Master?" she asked.

"My reports were apparently mistaken," he said.

"Master?" she asked.

"Tende of Ukungu was said to have been proud and cold."

"Your reports were not mistaken, Master," she said. "They were correct. Tende of Ukungu was a proud, cold woman."

"But you are not she," he said.

"No, Master," she said. "I am now only Tende, the slave of Kisu, my master."

"Are you responsive and hot?" he asked.

Tende put down her head. "Yes, Master," she said.

Bila Huruma smiled.

Tende did not raise her head. "My master has conquered me," she said.

"Excellent," said Bila Huruma.

"Please, great Ubar," begged Tende, suddenly lifting her head, tears in her eyes, "do not do harm to my master, Kisu."

"Be silent, Slave!" snapped Kisu.

"Yes, Master," she wept.

"You are now only a worthless slave, Tende," said Msaliti. "If my Ubar chooses to take you to please his senses, he will. Otherwise he will not."

"Yes, Master," she said.

"I have many slaves," said Bila Huruma, "and many of them are more beautiful than you. On your belly."

"Yes, Master," said Tende, frightened.

"Now crawl back to your master," said Bila Huruma.

"Yes, Master," said Tende.

There were some two hundred askaris in the room, and Msaliti and Bila Huruma. Kisu and I stood facing him, Kisu with a spear in hand. Ayari was behind us, and to the left. The girls in the coffle were now all awake. The dark-haired girl could not rise to her feet for her ankles were tied. Alice and Janice, however, were on their feet. Too, the blond-haired girl, who had been the leader of the talunas, was on her feet, where she was tethered, the strap going through the drilled stone at her feet. Turgus, in his gag, and bound hand and foot, lay on his side.

"Let us fight!" called Kisu to Bila Huruma.

Tende lay on her belly at his feet.

"We did not expect to see you again," I said.

"I fought my way through," said Bila Huruma. "I retain two hundred and ten men, three galleys and four canoes."

"I salute your generalship, and your indomitable will," I said. "You did well."

"Let us fight!" called out Kisu, lifting and clutching his raider's spear.

"Who is that fellow?" asked Bila Huruma.

"Kisu, the rebel of Ukungu," said Msaliti. "You saw him once in your court, kneeling before you in chains. It was at much the same time that you first saw, too, Mwoga, the high wazir of Aibu, chieftain of Ukungu. He discussed with you at that time, if you recall, my Ubar, the girl, Tende, daughter of Aibu, she who was to have been companioned to you, she who now lies upon her belly, a slave, at his feet."

"Ah, yes, I recall," said Bila Huruma. He looked at Kisu. "The one with the size and temper of a kailiauk," he said.

"Yes," said Msaliti.

"Prepare to do battle," said Kisu to Bila Huruma.

"Our war is done, and you have lost," said Bila Huruma.

"My war is not done, while I still have the strength to clutch a spear," said Kisu grimly.

"There are over two hundred askaris, Kisu," I said.

"Do battle with me singly, if you dare," called Kisu to Bila Huruma.

"Ubars," I pointed out to Kisu, "seldom see much point in engaging in single combat with common soldiers."

"I am Mfalme of Ukungu!" said Kisu.

"You were deposed," I said. "With all due respect, Kisu, you are not of sufficient political importance to warrant a duel with a Ubar."

"Appoint me again Mfalme of Ukungu," said Kisu to Bila Huruma, "if you find that necessary."

"Really, Kisu," said Ayari.

"What sign have you seen of Shaba?" inquired Bila Huruma.

"Like yourself, doubtless, only his galley. We, too, search for him."

"I do not think he is far," said Bila Huruma.

"That is my hope," I said.

"Where is the golden chain I gave you in my chambers?" asked Bila Huruma.

"In the supplies, in our canoe," I said.

"No longer," he said. He gestured to an askari, who threw me the chain.

"I thought I would find you here," said Bila Huruma. "I recognized the chain."

"Thank you, Ubar," I said. I again looped the chain about my neck.

"Fight!" challenged Kisu.

"I seek Shaba," said Bila Huruma. "I do not wish to be distracted by this brash malcontent."

"Fight!" cried Kisu, shaking the raider's spear.

"I could be behind the guard of that clumsy weapon in a moment," said Bila Huruma to Kisu. "Why do you think I adopted the stabbing spear for my soldiers?"

"We have such weapons!" cried Kisu. We had two such weapons. Ayari held one. The other was behind in the canoe.

"Do you know their techniques," asked Bila Huruma, "their utilities and tricks, the subtleties of their play?"

"No," said Kisu. "But I will fight you anyway!"

"You are a strong man, and a good and brave man, Kisu,"

I said, "but Bila Huruma and his men are trained fighters. Desist in your madness."

"If I slay Bila Huruma," said Kisu, "I slay the empire."

"That is highly unlikely," I said. "The empire, like gold, is valuable. Should it fall from the hand of one man it would likely be seized up by the hand of another."

"I do not choose to meet you in battle," said Bila Huruma. "And if you attack me, then I must either slay you or have you slain."

"He is a trained fighter, Kisu," I said. "Do not fight him."

"What am I to do?" asked Kisu.

"My recommendation," said Ayari, "would be to stab him when he is not looking, or perhaps to poison his palm wine."

"I cannot do such things," cried Kisu. "What then am I to do?"

"Put up your spear," I told him.

With a cry of rage he drove the butt of the spear down on the stone.

We all, all in that room, regarded Kisu.

He stood there, the butt of the spear on the stone, the blade over his head. He held the spear under the blade, his hands over his head. His head was down. His shoulder shook. He wept. Tende crept to his feet and kissed him, sobbing, too.

"Why do you seek Shaba?" asked Bila Huruma.

"Doubtless for the same reason you, too, seek him," I said.

Msaliti twitched nervously at the side of Bila Huruma. "We have come far, great Ubar," he said. "We have endured many hardships and dangers. These few men constitute but one last obstacle in your path. We outnumber them considerably. Clear them away. Give orders to your askaris to do away with them."

Bila Huruma looked at me. For the moment he seemed lost in thought.

"Bila Huruma," we heard. The voice came from the height of the stairs behind me, and to my left, that leading to a higher level in the building, an open court, which lay above us.

We all looked to the height of the stairs.

There, in blue rags, yet standing proudly, was a scribe.

"I am Bila Huruma," said the Ubar.

"That is known to me," said the scribe. He looked about, down at us. "Is one called Tarl Cabot among you?" he asked.

"I am he," I said.

Msaliti reacted suddenly. It was a name, apparently, not

429

unknown to him. His hand darted to the hilt of the dagger sheathed at his hip, but he did not draw the weapon.

"I will take you to Shaba," said the scribe.

53

THE BATTLE; BLOOD AND STEEL; WE SURVIVE

"I had hoped that you would follow," said Shaba. "When you were put upon the rogues' chain I feared it might be the end of you. I cannot tell you how overjoyed I am to find that you are here."

Shaba, drawn and worn, lay upon a couch, blankets behind his head. His left arm seemed useless and he was haggard with disease.

"Then," said I, "remove these manacles in which I have been placed." The scribe had led us through the city, ascending and descending streets, making our way through various buildings, following various ancient avenues, flanked by the ruins of what must once have been an impressive grandeur. Bila Huruma and I had followed the scribe most closely. Then had come the members of our various parties. Kisu had kept our girls, with the exception of Tende, in coffle. We had unbound the ankles of the dark-haired girl and of Turgus. We had kept them gagged. The neck rope of Turgus had been in the keeping of Ayari. Then we had come, more than two hundred of us, to a fortresslike ruin, on a raised level. We had been requested to wait within the ancient threshold, which had once held a gate. Shaba's men had, to some extent, refortified the ruin, placing stones within the threshold so that only one man at a time might enter. Too, between the edges of the walls, over the stones, they had erected a barrier of lashed poles. Shaba had still with him some fifty men. While the rest of our two parties, including Bila Huruma, had waited within the threshold, I was conducted across the broad stone court to its center, where, on a huge stone couch, of ancient design, lay Shaba. Before being allowed to approach him closely Shaba's men, ringing me with spears, placed me in manacles, locking my hands behind my back. It was thus that I stood now before the geographer of Anango.

"Shaba is dying," had said the scribe who had conducted us to this place. "Do not speak long."

I regarded Shaba.

"Please, my friend," said Shaba to me, "forgive the manacles. But surely you must understand that they constitute a sensible precaution of my part."

About Shaba's neck, on a thin golden chain, hung a ring. It was heavy and golden, much too large for the finger of a man. In the ring was a silver plate. Opposite the bezel, on the outside of the ring, was a circular, recessed switch.

"You display the ring boldly," I said.

Shaba touched the ring. On his right hand, now, he wore another ring, the fang ring, which, filled with kanda, I had seen earlier in Schendi. A scratch from that ring would destroy a kailiauk in a matter of seconds. "Do you think ill of me, Tarl Cabot?" he asked.

"You are a traitor to Priest-Kings," I said. "You have stolen the Tahari ring."

"I am a scribe, and a man of science and letters," said Shaba. "Surely you can understand the importance of the ring to me."

"It can bring wealth and power," I said.

"Such things are not of interest to me," said Shaba. The tribal stitching of tattoo marks on his dark face wrinkled with a smile. "But I do not expect you to believe that," he said.

"I do not," I said.

"How hard it is for two who do not share caste to understand one another," he said.

"Perhaps," I said.

"I took the ring for two reasons," he said. "First, it made possible the ascent of the Ua. Without it we should not have come this far. In many villages, and among hostile peoples, the demonstration of the power of the ring, as I had hoped, permitted us safe passage. On the river, I am afraid, I am regarded as something of a wizard. Had it not been for the ring I and my men would have been slain many times." He smiled at me. "My exploration of the Ua," he said, "would not have been possible without the ring."

"Surely you are aware that possession of the ring is dangerous," I said.

"I am well aware of that," he said. With his right hand he gestured about himself. He indicated the walls of the fortresslike enclosure within which he had ensconced himself and his men. Too, about this enclosure, at the foot of stairs leading from it, was a broad, shallow moat. Waters from the lake circulated through the city and fed this moat. In it, as had been demonstrated, by the hurling of a haunch of tarsk into the waters, crowded and schooling, were thousands of blue grunt. This fish, when isolated and swimming free in a river or lake, is not particularly dangerous. For a few days prior to the fullness of the major Gorean moon, however, it begins to school. It then becomes extremely aggressive and ferocious. The haunch of tarsk hurled into the water of the moat, slung on a rope, had been devoured in a matter of Ihn. There had been a thrashing frenzy in the water and then the rope had been withdrawn, severed. The moat had been crossed by a small, floating wooden bridge, tied at each end. This had been built, being extended outward from the opposite shore, by Shaba's men. The effectiveness of the moat, aside from the barrier of the water itself, would become negligible with the passing of the full moon, until the next. The grunt, following the mating frenzy, synchronized with the full moon, would return to the lake. Given the habits of the fish I had little doubt but that this place was an ancient mating ground for them, for the grunt populations tend to return again and again to the places of their frenzy, wherever, usually in a lagoon or shallow place in a river, they may be. The grunt now schooling in the open moat, come in from the lake, could well be the posterity of grunt populations dating back to the time when the city was not in ruins but in the height of its glory and power. The grunt in the moat were for a time an effective barrier, but surely Shaba and his men realized that it must be temporary. Suddenly the hair on the back of my neck rose. I now understood the practicality of their present situation.

"You were waiting for us," I said.

"Of course," said Shaba. "And if you had not come by today, I do not know what we would have done."

"The wall of the grunt," I said. "It has protected you for some four or five days."

"It proved enough," said Shaba. "It gave you time to arrive."

"You have been followed by Kurii," I said.

"Yes," said Shaba. "That is our belief. We have, however, seen only tracks. I fear, even now, however, they may be gathering. They must be somewhere in the city."

"Your man was courageous to come and fetch us," I said.

"He is Ngumi," said Shaba. "He is courageous, indeed. We did not know if he would get through."

"I did not know a scribe could be so courageous," I said.

"There are brave men in all castes," said Shaba.

"We may have been permitted, however, to come through," I said.

"That Msaliti gain entrance to the fortification?" asked Shaba.

"Of course," I said.

"Perhaps," he said.

"You said," I said, "that you took the ring for two reasons, but you mentioned only one, that it facilitated your journey upon the Ua."

"Look there," said Shaba, indicating a table to one side, on which there lay a cylindrical leather case, with a leather cap, and four notebooks, heavy and bound with leather.

"I see," I said.

"There is a map case there," he said, "and my notebooks. I have, in my journey, charted the Ua, and in the notebooks I have recorded my observations. Those things, though you, of the warriors, may not understand this, are priceless."

"Your records would doubtless be of value to geographers," I said.

"They are," said Shaba, "of inestimable value to all civilized men."

"Perhaps," I said.

"The maps, those records," said Shaba, "open up a new world. Think not only in terms of crass profit, my friend, of the bounties there to hunters and trappers, to traders and settlers, to planters and physicians, but to all men who wish to understand, who wish to know, who wish to unveil hidden secrets and penetrate hitherto unsolved mysteries. In these maps and records, for those who can understand them, lie the first glimpses of new and vast countries. In these maps, and in these notes and drawings, there are treasures and wonders." He looked at me, intently. "And that," he said, "is the second reason I took the ring."

"I do not understand," I said.

"I did not expect to survive this journey, nor to return," he said. "I am pleased that I have come this far, that I have found the source of the Ua."

"Yes?" I said.

"I took the ring," he said, "not only to facilitate my journey, but that you, or another, would follow, that there would be someone who could bring my maps and notes back to civilization."

"You fled," I said, "fearing me."

Shaba smiled. "The Ua," said he, "seems a strange avenue of escape. No, my friend, I did not flee. Rather I began my voyage of exploration, my expedition into the interior."

"What of the moneys, those vast sums wrought from the Kurii, the notes negotiated in Schendi?" I asked.

"They were to defray the costs of outfitting the expedition, of hiring the men," he said. "Surely you do not object to my making use of the funds of Kurii for such a purpose. They should be pleased to have made their contribution to so noble a project."

"You distribute your treacheries impartially," I said. "Doubtless that is to your credit."

"Do not think too poorly of me, Tarl," said Shaba. "This was to me the opportunity of a lifetime. If I have erred, I have erred in the cause of my caste and in that, more generally, of humankind." He regarded me, a little sadly. "What do you think Priest-Kings would do with the ring?" he asked. "It would not be important to them. But to me, to men, it is momentous. Indeed, I doubt that Priest-Kings would even wish to permit the use of the ring to men. It seems possible to me they would regard its use as contravening their structures on human technology."

"Perhaps," I said. "I truly would not know how they might view the matter."

"So," said Shaba, "I took the ring. With it I have explored the Ua. I have found her source. With it, too, I have lured you after me, that my maps and notes might be returned safely to civilization."

I looked down at the map case and the notebooks.

"Yes," said Shaba, "it is those things which I have purchased with the theft of the ring, and my life." He suddenly tensed. I saw that he was in pain. "Guard them well, my friend," he said.

"Why did you flee the palace of Bila Huruma?" I asked. Shaba had fled, I recalled, with three galleys. Bila Huruma, with the balance of his ships and supplies, had followed him.

"It is perhaps he whom I have most wronged," said Shaba, sadly, "and yet I think that in fleeing his palace I may have saved his life."

"I do not understand," I said.

434

"Bila Huruma, my patron and protector," said Shaba, "stood between Msaliti and myself. Msaliti had already attempted one attack on his life, that in which Jambia, the assassin, died by the osts, that same attack in which he sought to implicate you."

"Yes," I said.

"As long as I remained in the palace, Bila Huruma was in danger," he said. "When I fled there would be no reason for Msaliti to plot his death. Yet I knew well that when I fled Bila Huruma would follow me."

"Of course," I said. "Msaliti would then have no alternative but to tell Bila Huruma of the ring, and then join with him in Bila Huruma's attempt to seize it, hoping later to secure it for himself."

"I do not think Bila Huruma has followed me for the ring," smiled Shaba.

"Why else?" I asked.

Shaba said nothing.

"No other motivation could bring him to this place," I said, "other than to kill for the ring. Its power would make him absolute and invincible."

"Perhaps," smiled Shaba.

"How is it," I asked, "that you fear you may have wronged Bila Huruma?" That seemed as unlikely to me as a fellow worrying about wronging a larl who was padding along upon his trail.

"By using him for my purposes," said Shaba.

"What purposes?" I asked.

Shaba lay back on the blankets for a moment. He shut his eyes in pain.

I watched the ring on the chain about his neck.

Shaba, weary, opened his eyes. He looked at me. He was weak.

"I have no interest in your maps and notebooks," I said. "I have come for the ring. Have these manacles removed. Give me the ring."

There was suddenly a scream from the height of the wall. I spun about to see one of Shaba's men reel about and then plunge bloody from the wall's height to the stones below. Then, rimmed against the blue tropical sky I saw, arms upraised, a red-spattered panga in its right paw, the huge, towering shaggy figure of a Kur. There were screams from below. Then I heard the screams of wild Kurii from all about, encircling the walls. I saw the height of a slender tree

435

trunk suddenly protruding against the sky, leaning against the wall from the outside. A Kur scrambled up the trunk and leaped down over the wall. At other places, too, I saw the heads of Kurii, broad and fanged, eyes blazing, arms and paws thrust over the wall.

One of the Kurii screamed, a stabbing spear thrust in its chest. Bila Huruma swiftly deployed his askaris. I saw Kisu, a raider's spear over his head, held in both hands, rush toward a crouching Kur, one just leaped into the courtyard.

"Remove these manacles!" I cried to Ngumi, the scribe at the side of Shaba, he who had conducted us to this place.

Eight or ten more Kurii dropped inside the wall, lightly for their weight, and crouched there for the moment, pangas in their fangs, the knuckles of their paws on the stones.

I saw Msaliti draw his knife and slip to the side.

Askaris rushed up stone stairs to the height of the walls, where the lateral walkways had not crumbled. I saw one thrust back another tree trunk. Then I saw four of them cut from the top of the wall by a charging Kur, one wielding a giant panga. I saw Kurii, too, thrusting their arms through the barrier of lashed poles mounted over the stones at the threshold. Ayari, small Ayari, joined the askaris there, thrusting with a stabbing spear through the poles.

"Free me!" I cried, maddened, to the scribe. I fought the manacles. I saw more Kurii clambering over the walls.

The scribe threw a wild look at Shaba. "Free him," said Shaba.

I saw two Kurii, on all fours, pangas in their fangs, look towards us.

I heard screams at the threshold. I saw the poles being splintered and smote apart by pangas.

One of the slave girls, somewhere, screamed. A manacle, its double bolt thrust back by the key, opened. Many of the Kurii, I suspected, were Gorean Kurii, wild, degenerate Kurii, descendants of marooned Kurii or survivors of crashed ships. Others, I feared, were ship Kurii. "Hurry!" I cried. One of the two Kurii who had been looking at us suddenly lifted his arm and pointed towards us. On all fours, moving with an agility and speed frightening in so large a beast, they charged. The other manacle snapped free. I saw one of the beasts throw itself, panga still in its fangs, toward Shaba, reaching for the ring on its chain. I hurled the loosened manacles into the face of the other Kur. The beast who had attacked Shaba suddenly drew back, startled. Puzzled it looked at its paw, where there was a flash of bright blood. The panga fell from its fangs. The beast who confronted me, howling, tore the manacle from its slashed, moonlike eye. Its mouth was bloody where it had bitten on the steel of the panga. I scrambled, leaping, half crawling, to the place on the stones where Ngumi had, after putting me in manacles, dropped my belt, sheath and dagger. I rolled wildly to the side. The panga of the beast who followed me, with a great ringing sound, and a flash of sparks, smote down on the stone. The beast who had attacked Shaba lay dead by his couch. Shaba was coughing and spitting blood. The blade of his fang ring, that containing kanda, was exposed, and bloody. I threw myself to the side again and again the great panga fell. The table on which reposed the map case and notebooks of Shaba seemed to explode in two, wood splintering and flying to the sides, the map case and notebooks, scattering, showering upward.

The Kur, roaring and snarling, looked about. For the moment it had lost me. I kept to its blind side. Then, uttering the war cry of Ko-ro-ba, I leaped upon its back, and, an arm about its throat, plunged the dagger to its heart. I felt the great body shuddering under me and I leaped away from it.

I spun about. I saw another Kur at Shaba. Again Shaba interposed the fang ring. I saw the six digits of the paw close on the chain about Shaba's neck, and then the digits released the chain and the beast slipped back, limply. It sat for a moment, and then, unsteadily, fell to the side.

I thrust the bloody dagger between my teeth. On it I tasted the blood of Kur.

I seized up the panga which had been carried by the beast I had slain. It was heavy. I must needs use two hands to wield it.

I looked back once to Shaba, who, head down, was clutching at the blankets of the couch. They were covered with blood. Ngumi ran to him. Shaba lifted his head. "Fight," he said. "Save yourselves."

"I will never leave you!" cried Ngumi. Then he cried out, half cut in two. I leaped forward and, frontally, struck the Kur which had slain Ngumi. Its broad head was cut open to the neck. I looked down at Ngumi. The tribal stitching on his face, so startling and paradoxical in a scribe, a man of civilization, was identical to that on the face of Shaba.

"Help!" I heard. "They are breaking through!"

I ran to the threshold and, leaping upon the stones, screaming, struck at the arms and paws which were thrusting back the barrier of lashed poles. Paws and arms, severed, flew bloody from the blade. Kurii, howling, drew back.

"Others are coming over the walls!" I heard.

"Free me!" I heard. I ran to Turgus and slashed his bonds. He seized up a stabbing spear from a fallen askari and ran to fight. I then slashed away the bonds of the huddled, crouching slave girls. "Master!" cried Janice. They might now have some chance to flee. Yet they were enclosed within the walls. A human female who falls to a male conqueror may sometimes, by submitting herself totally to him as a slave, save her life, at least until he determines whether or not she is sufficiently pleasing. Kurii, on the other hand, generally have little interest in human females except as food.

I turned to meet the attack of another Kur. I blocked his blow with the panga and was, from the force of it, thrown back a dozen feet. He struck again and I was hurled back to the wall. The panga had almost been ripped away from me. My hands stung. He struck again and stone showered out from the wall, to the right of my head. I slipped to the side and caught him with the panga, striking across the hip and lower abdomen. He grunted and stepped back, holding splinters of bone and loops of intestine in its paw. I then struck its head away.

"Kisu, watch out!" I cried.

Kisu turned but a figure interposed itself between him and the attacker. A stabbing spear was thrust into the belly of the Kur, and then, stabbing five times more, in the belly and chest, and throat, the interposing figure forced back the bewildered, enraged beast. An askari then struck the beast from behind, thrusting his stabbing spear deep into its back, below the left shoulder blade. The beast turned to attack its new menace, and he who had been the interposing figure, now behind it, as it had turned, thrust his own stabbing spear deep into its back, as had the askari. The beast sank to its knees and snapping crawled toward the retreating askari for more than a dozen feet until it collapsed on the stones.

Kisu glared at he who had been the interposing figure. "My thanks, Ubar," he then said. Then each, Kisu, the rebel, and Bila Huruma, Ubar of the equatorial empire, side by side, addressed themselves to thwarting the attack of new Kurii. I held the panga in two hands. My mouth was bleeding, as I had cut myself on the dagger clenched between my teeth. I looked about. I thrust the dagger through my tunic, it held in place, in the pierced cloth, by its hilt. I wiped blood from my face. I rejoined the fray. I struck a Kur from behind that was towering over a fallen askari, opening the shaggy skull to the nape. Another I struck, too, from behind, severing the spinal column. It had been bent over, pausing to feed. I saw yet more Kurii clambering over the wall. Others pressed again now at the lashed poles over the stones at the threshold. I ran toward the threshold. I hacked them back. They drew back, a leader roaring and gesticulating. Then others brought forth two of the slender tree trunks they had been using to scale the walls. I threw back my head to breathe. I checked that the dagger was still caught in my tunic. I thrust it through another place, too, in the tunic. Too easily, earlier, it might have been lost.

"How have we been surprised?" I asked Ayari, who was at the threshold.

"The guards at the small bridge were surprised and killed," he said. "They took the bridge and crossed the moat."

"It is a slaughter," I said.

I looked about. The oval leather shields and the stabbing spears of the askaris might have been ideal armament for invincibility in tribal warfare but they afforded little in the way of martial equity when compared to the weighty, slashing pangas of the Kurii. They were not the mighty axes and heavy shields of Torvaldsland.

Bila Huruma was screaming at his men. He himself had discarded his shield, or it had been struck from him. "Single them out," he cried. "Attack in fives, one engage, four strike!"

"He is improvising tactics," said Ayari.

"He is a Ubar," I said.

One askari might fend a committed blow of the panga with the iron blade of his stabbing spear. Four others might then, swarming upon the beast, drive their weapons repeatedly into it. These Kurii were, on the whole, wild Kurii, not ship Kurii. Each would be used to fighting alone, terrible and solitary, hunting its own kills in the ancient manner. They might be in proximity to one another, but each functioned, in effect, as an isolated unit. They were horrifying and ferocious, but were not trained.

"There are too many," I said.

"It is true that we are lost," said Ayari, "but we shall make a good fight of it."

"Well said," said I, "small rogue."

I saw Bila Huruma slip to one knee. A mighty Kur stood

439

over him, his panga raised over his head. Then, from behind Bila Huruma, there was a wild cry of Ukungu, and a raider's spear, in its length, thrust past the Ubar and buried itself in a red wound in the Kur's heart.

"My thanks, Rebel," said Bila Huruma, regaining his feet. Kisu pulled his weapon free, and grinned. "I now owe you nothing," he said.

"True," said Bila Huruma, and then again, side by side, rebel and Ubar, they fought.

One of the Kur leaders, then, marshaling his forces, formed them in loose lines, that they might no longer be singly attacked. I had little doubt but what he was a ship Kur. I admired his ability to control the degenerate, recruited Kurii he commanded. There was perhaps in them the vestige, or memory, perhaps passed on in an oral tradition, of the disciplines and dignities in their past, notably, doubtless, that of ship loyalty.

"We are finished now," I said. "They will fight together."

Bila Huruma now gathered his men about him. Many were covered with blood. There were probably no more than a hundred left then with him.

I saw more Kurii dropping over the wall.

Suddenly, behind us, there was a splintering of lashed poles, and bindings, too, tore loose. Again and again, then, the trunks of small trees struck at the barrier fending us from the main forces of the attacker.

"We must hold them," cried Ayari.

"It cannot be done," I said. The framework of lashed poles, suddenly, broke half apart and Kurii swarmed within, some with pangas, some with clubs and sharpened sticks. We fell back from the stones, literally swept from our rampart by the irruption of the wood and the flood of massive, charging bodies.

The panga then was gone from my hands, wrenched away, lost in the body of the Kur in which I had buried it.

"Form!" I cried. "Get the wall to your backs!"

Men streamed past me to take a stand by the wall. I leaped upon a Kur's chest, holding to him by my left hand, clenched in fur behind its shaggy neck. I drove the dagger, torn from my tunic, again and again into its chest. The Kur had worn rings of gold in its ears. I had little doubt it was a ship Kur. I slipped free as the animal screamed and reeled about, then fell, falling among the stones and wood, scratching at the stone.

I saw Turgus drive a stabbing spear into the chest of a maddened Kur.

Then it seemed Kurii were all about me, yet scarcely aware of me, intent rather on the men at the wall. I drove my dagger into the belly of one which was pressing past me, and in its rush, it hardly understanding that it was wounded, was carried, dragged, holding to the beast and dagger, for fifty feet among the Kurii. I wrenched the dagger free and, as another Kur, suddenly seeing me among them, truly seeing me, reached for me I thrust the dagger upward. It is difficult to reach the Kur's brain with so small a weapon. It may be done, however, with the proper angle of elevation, through the socket of the eye. It may also be done through the ear and, where the skull is thinner, the temple. The Kur roared with pain and I lost the dagger, it wrenched away as the Kur threw its claws to its face. It pulled loose the dagger howling. Then it reached for me. I backed away. It died before it reached me. I pressed back and then, on either side of me, was with men. Weapons clashed at the line of war. The golden chain I had received from Bila Huruma, which he had returned to me, retrieving it from our raiders' canoe, was covered with blood. I saw a Kur reaching over the wall, behind our men. I sprang upon the worn stone stairs leading at this point to the wall. I kicked it back over the wall. Another, finding footholds in the ancient stone, clambered upward. I removed the golden chain and lashed it in the face and it fell backwards from the wall, to the stones some twenty feet below. I raced along the wall's top and thrust back one of the tree trunks put against it. Two Kurii leaped from it as it toppled. I then saw a Kur below, within the wall. It was behind our line of men. It drew back the panga. I leaped from the wall's height to its shoulders and looped the golden chain about its neck. It reached for me but could not dislodge me. I kept my head low, and my body away from the panga. I tightened the chain. It flung itself against the wall and I was half crushed. My back felt wet and bits of rock stung in my back. I tightened the chain, tenaciously. I felt the claws of the Kur tearing at my back. I then felt the sudden rupture of the cartilage of its throat. Still it clawed at me. It could make no sound. Its tongue was half bitten through. The panga fell to the ground. It stood unsteadily. My hands were bloody on the golden chain, its links deep, almost unseen, in the throat of the Kur. Then it fell. I leaped free of it and tore loose the chain, looping its bloody links about my own neck. I picked up the fallen panga. To my horror the beast reached for me. I saw its great lungs expand and its eyes looking at me. It sucked air into its body through its ruptured throat, blood emerged from its mouth. It is not easy to kill a Kur. It reached again for me. I struck it with the panga, and then struck it again. "Forgive me, my friend," I said. The blows had not been those of a warrior, but of a butcher. I was unsteady, and weak, my hands had trembled. I hoped that it would not regard itself as dishonored by my clumsiness.

I heard Bila Huruma rallying his men by the wall. Then he cried, "Charge!"

His audacity had taken the Kurii by surprise. But, in moments, viciously, Bila Huruma, Kisu, Turgus, Ayari and the askaris had been forced back again.

The situation was hopeless and yet, I think, the Kurii had been taught respect for men.

I saw a Kur leader, quickly and methodically, aligning his beasts. I doubted but what it would take more than one charge by the massed forces of the Kurii. To my surprise I saw the Kur leader, a huge, brown Kur, doubtless from one of the far ships, lift his panga in salute to the black Ubar. Bila Huruma, then, breathing heavily, raised his stabbing spear in his dark and bloody fist. "Askari hodari!" he cried. I shook with emotion. It was much honor he had done the beast, not even human, confronting him. The salute of the Kur commander had been acknowledged and returned. The words Bila Huruma had uttered were of course in the native tongue of Ushindi. One might translate them, in the context, I suppose, as 'Brave Soldier'. A better translation, however, I think, especially since there is no other way to say this in the Ushindi tongue, is doubtless the simpler one, 'Warrior.'

"I have it," we heard cry. We looked to the stones at the threshold. There stood Msaliti, an upraised bloody dagger in one hand, and, in the other, held high over his head, on its chain, a dangling ring.

"He has the ring!" I cried.

Msaliti shook the chain over his head. "I have it! I have it!" he cried.

I looked to the couch of Shaba. About it lay dead Kurii and slaughtered askaris. Shaba, coughing, held his chest. The poison ring, the fang ring, had been emptied. Msaliti had awaited his opportunity. He had then fallen upon Shaba. From the wounds I adjudged Shaba had been struck at least four or five times. He had then seized the chain and ring, and run to the threshold. The Kurii were between us and Msaliti.

The Kur commander raised his paw. His lips drew back over his fangs. It was a sign of Kur triumph, or pleasure. Then he swiftly communicated commands to his beasts. Msaliti leaped down from the stones and withdrew from the fortresslike enclosure. The Kurii facing us then, snarling, watching us, not turning their backs, began to withdraw. They obeyed their commander. He had won. He would not now risk more of his beasts. Too, he would wish to use them to guarantee the safe passage of the ring to his prearranged rendezvous, from whence it would be eventually returned to the steel worlds, or, on this planet, used devastatingly against men and Priest-Kings.

I, panga clutched in two hands, lunged after the beasts. Kisu seized me, holding me back. Bila Huruma, too, interposed himself between me and our shaggy adversaries. "No!" cried Kisu. "No!" cried Bila Huruma. "It is madness to follow!" "Stay with us, Tarl!" cried Ayari. Turgus, too, seized an arm. I could not free myself from Kisu and Turgus.

"Release me!" I said.

"You can do nothing now," said Kisu.

"They will destroy the bridge," I said. "We will be prisoners here!"

"Tonight is the full moon," said Ayari. "Tonight, if you wish, you may wade through the fish unharmed. Tomorrow they will have returned to the lake."

"Release me!" I cried.

"You can do nothing now," said Kisu.

I, held, watched the departure of the Kurii. They, obedient to their orders, withdrew. I admired the Kur commander, that he had been able to instill in his fierce beasts such discipline. As they withdrew some dragged with them the fallen bodies of askaris.

Bila Huruma hurried to the side of Shaba.

I shook loose of Turgus and Kisu and ran to the stones at the threshold. As I ascended to their height I saw the floating bridge cut free at our end. It was then dragged to the opposite side and hauled onto the level. Between myself and the beasts there lay the broad, uneasy moat, some forty feet across, stirring with the movements of the crowded fish.

I descended from the stones which had been piled in the threshold by Shaba's men, the better to fortify the walled area.

I looked across the moat at the Kurii. Kisu and Turgus, and Ayari, stood behind me.

On the other side of the moat Msaliti lifted the chain and ring over his head. "I have won!" he cried.

The Kur commander took the chain from him and looped it over his head.

"I have won!" cried Msaliti.

The Kur commander than gave orders to one of his beasts. Msaliti screamed with misery as the animal lifted him high over his head and then threw him into the moat.

Almost instantly Msaliti was on his feet and then he screamed, and fell, and again regained his feet, and fell again. There was a thrashing about him, a churning in the water, and it seemed the water exploded with blood and bubbles. Msaliti, as though moving through mud, howling, waded through the packed, slippery, voracious bodies. I tore the raider's spear from Kisu and extended it to Msaliti who, screaming, grasped it. We drew him from the water. His feet and legs were gone. We struck tenacious fish from his body. He then lay on the level and we, with strips of cloth, tried to stanch his bleeding.

The Kurii, on the other side of the moat, single file, then padded away.

We fought to save Msaliti. Finally, with tourniquets, we managed to slow, and then stop, the bleeding.

Bila Huruma then stood beside me, on the level near the moat. "Shaba is dead," he said.

Msaliti lifted his hand to the Ubar. "My Ubar," he said.

Bila Huruma looked down at Msaliti sadly. Then he said to his askaris, "Throw him to the fish."

"My Ubar!" cried Msaliti, and then he was lost in the moat, the fish swarming about him.

I suddenly felt Janice clinging to my arm weeping. There was leather on her throat, and, on her wrists and ankles were the deep marks of freshly slashed binding fiber. She and the other girls, during the action, had, one by one, been caught by Kurii and put in throat coffle. The coffle had then been dragged to a corner of the fortresslike enclosure. There the girls, without being removed from the coffle, had been thrown on their bellies and bound hand and foot. They had then been left there, left for later, squirming and helpless, tied as fresh meat. An askari, after the withdrawal of the Kurii, had freed them.

"Oh, my master," wept Janice, holding me. "We are alive, my master!"

I looked bitterly across the moat. I had failed. Then I held the girl's head to my shoulder and, as she wept, I considered the fortunes of war.

I saw the narrow column of Kurii disappear among the distant buildings.

I clasped the slave closely to me. "Do not cry, sweet slave," I told her. Then I, too, but in bitterness and misery, shed tears.

54

WE WILL LEAVE
THE ANCIENT CITY

"I have examined the maps and notebooks," I said to Bila Huruma.

"Were all recovered?" he asked.

"Yes," I said.

We stood now on a broad level. To it led the several flights of broad stairs, ascending from that vast marble landing, with its marble mooring posts, which lies at the western edge of the ancient city, that landing to which we had first come, days ago, after our crossing of the lake. The great building, with its tall columns, some broken, fallen aside, in its ruins, lay behind us. Flanking it, on each side, were the towering figures of stone warriors, their stern gaze facing westward. Shaba's galley, and the three galleys and canoes of Bila Huruma, and our raiders' canoe, which had served us so long and faithfully, could be seen far below us, where they were moored at the landing.

We looked out over the placid, vast lake.

On the level, to one side, we had built a great pyre. Bila Huruma himself, with his own hands, had cast the ashes of Shaba high into the air where the wind would catch them and carry them over the city, and to the jungles beyond. A part of Shaba, thus, would continue his geographer's trek, a bit of white ash blown on the wind, evanescent but obdurate, brief but eternal, something irrevocably implicated in the realities of history and eternity.

"This lake, forming the source of the Ua," I said, "he named Lake Bila Huruma."

"Cross that out," said Bila Huruma. "Write there, instead, Lake Shaba."

"I will do so," I said.

For a time Bila Huruma and I watched the galleys and canoes being readied for casting off. Hunting had been done. Supplies had been gathered. Of his forces Bila Huruma retained some ninety askaris. Of Shaba's men some seventeen survived.

"I am a lonely man," said Bila Huruma. "Shaba was my friend."

"Yet you pursued him," I said, "that you might overtake and slay him, doing robbery upon him."

Bila Huruma looked at me, puzzled. "No," he said. "I followed him to protect him. He was my friend. In our plans he was to take one hundred galleys and five thousand men. But he fled with three galleys and perhaps not even two hundred followers. I wished to lend him the support and defense of ships and numbers."

"You were not to accompany him on the originally projected expedition," I said.

"Of course not," he said. "I am a Ubar."

"Then why did you follow him?" I asked.

"I wanted the forces to get through," he said. "Shaba might have brought them through. I might have brought them through. I was not certain others could do so."

"But you are a Ubar," I said.

"I was also his friend," said Bila Huruma. "To a Ubar a friend is precious," he said. "We have so few."

"Shaba told me," I said, "that he had wronged you."

Bila Huruma smiled. "He regretted bringing me out upon the river by subterfuge," he said. "Yet he may have saved my life by fleeing the palace. One attempt already had been made upon my life. He thought that if he had fled I would no longer be in any immediate danger."

I nodded. Msaliti, needing the protection of the Ubar and his men on the river, would surely desist, at least temporarily in plotting against his life. To be sure, Msaliti had no interest in slaying the Ubar for its own sake. Such a murder was to be only a method for removing an obstacle in the path to the Tahari ring.

"Did Msaliti not encourage you to venture in pursuit of

Shaba?" I asked. "Did he not inform you of something of great value which lay in the possession of Shaba?"

"No," said Bila Huruma. "An effort of such a nature was not necessary of his part. I was determined. He only begged to accompany me, which permission I, of course, granted."

"It seems," I said, "that Shaba expected me, or another, to follow him upon the river."

"Yes," said Bila Huruma. "He did not expect to survive, for some reason. He wanted you to follow, or another, perhaps, that his maps and notebooks might be returned safely to civilization."

"It seems so," I said.

"Why did he not expect to survive?" asked Bila Huruma.

"The river, the dangers, illness," I speculated.

"The beasts, surely," said Bila Huruma.

"Yes," I said, "the beasts, too."

"And you, too," said Bila Huruma. "Surely you would have killed him to obtain whatever it was you sought."

"Yes," I said. "Had it been necessary, I would have killed for what I sought."

"It must be very precious," said Bila Huruma.

I nodded. "It was," I said.

"Was?" he asked.

"The Kurii took it," I said, "those who attacked us, the beasts."

"I see," he said.

"Shaba," I said, "told me that he had used you for his purposes. I think it was in that sense, rather than in simply having brought you upon the river, that he felt he had wronged you."

"Of this he spoke to me before he died," said Bila Huruma.

"I do not understand," I said, "how you were used for his purposes."

"Is it not now clear?" he asked, smiling.

"No," I said.

"I was to protect you," he said, "on your return downriver, that the maps and notebooks might safely reach the environs of civilization."

I stood on the landing, stunned. Kisu climbed the stairs to where we stood. "The galleys, the vessels, are ready," he said.

"Very well," said Bila Huruma.

"We will join you momentarily," I said.

Kisu nodded and returned down the stairs to where the galleys and canoes were moored.

"We were both tricked," said Bila Huruma.

"You do not seem bitter," I said.

"I am not, he said.

"We may burn the maps and notebooks," I said.

"Of course," he said.

"I cannot do so," I said.

"Nor I," smiled the Ubar. "We shall take them back to Ushindi, and you may then, with a suitable escort, convey them down the Nyoka to Schendi. Ramani of Anango, who was the teacher of Shaba, awaits them there."

"Shaba planned well," I said.

"I shall miss him sorely," said Bila Huruma.

"He was a thief and a traitor," I said.

"He was true to his caste," said Bila Huruma.

"A thief and a traitor," I said, angrily.

Bila Huruma turned away and looked back at the ruins of the huge building, at the great stone statues, worn and covered with vines, and at the city, lost and forgotten, lying to the east.

"There was once a great empire here," he said. "It is gone now. We do not even know who raised and aligned these stones, forming walls and temples, and laying out gardens and broad avenues. We do not even know the name of this empire or what the people may have called themselves. We know only that they built these things and, for a time, lived among them. Empires flourish and then, it seems, they perish. Yet men must make them."

"Or destroy them," I said.

"Yes," said Bila Huruma, looking down then at the galleys and canoes. Kisu was there, waiting for us. "Yes," he said, "some men make empires, and others would destroy them."

"Which is the noblest?" I asked.

"I think," said Bila Huruma, "it is better to build than it is to destroy."

"Even though one's work may fall into ruin?" I inquired.

"Yes," said Bila Huruma. "Even though one's work may fall into ruin."

"Do you know," I asked, "what I, and Msaliti, sought from Shaba?"

"Of course," he said. "Shaba, before he died, told me all."

"It was not rightfully his," I said. "He was a thief and a traitor."

"He was true to his caste," said Bila Huruma.

I turned away from the Ubar, and began to descend the steps to the waiting vessels.

"Wait," said Bila Huruma.

I turned to face him, and he descended the stairs until he reached where I stood.

"Shaba," he said, "asked me to give this to you. It was concealed upon his person." He pressed into my hand a large ring, one too large for a human finger. It was golden, with a silver plate. On the outside of the ring, opposite the bezel, was a circular, recessed switch. On the ring itself there was a tiny, unmistakable scratch.

My hand trembled.

"Shaba," said Bila Huruma, "asked me to extend to you his thanks and apologies. He had need of the ring, you see. On the Ua, as you might expect, he found it of great utility."

"His thanks?" I asked. "His apologies?"

"He took the ring on loan, so to speak," said Bila Huruma. "He borrowed it. He hoped you would not mind."

I could not speak.

"It was his intention to return it himself," said Bila Huruma, "but the attack of the beasts, so sudden and unexpected, intervened."

I closed my hand on the ring. "Do you know what you are giving me?" I asked.

"A ring of great power," said Bila Huruma, "one which can cast upon its wearer a mantle of invisibility."

"With such a ring," I said, "you could be invincible."

"Perhaps," smiled Bila Huruma.

"Why do you give it to me?" I asked.

"It was the wish of Shaba," said Bila Huruma.

"I had scarcely known such friendship could exist," I said.

"I am a Ubar," said Bila Huruma. "In my life I have had only two friends. Now both are gone."

"Shaba was one," I said.

"Of course," said Bila Huruma.

"Who was the other?" I asked.

"The other I had killed," he said.

"What was his name?" I asked.

"Msaliti," he said.

449

55

THE EXPLOSION;
WE LEAVE THE ANCIENT CITY

"Let us leave," called Kisu.

The Ubar and I descended the steps together, that we might make our departure from the landing, from the eastern shore of Lake Shaba.

It was then that the explosion occurred. It took place several pasangs away. There was a blast of light. A great towering blade of fire stormed upward against the tropical sky. There was a vast, spreading billowing cloud of dust and leaves. The earth shook, the waters of Lake Shaba roiled. Men cried out and girls screamed. We felt a shock wave of great heat and saw trees falling. There was a rain of rocks, branches and debris.

And then it was quiet, save for the water lapping against the landing and the sides of the wooden vessels. To the southwest there was a darkness in the sky. In places the tops of standing trees still burned. Then the fires, no longer sustained by the heat of the blast, one by one vanished, unable to overcome the living freshness of the wood.

"What was that?" asked Kisu.

"It is called an explosion," I said.

"What is its meaning?" asked Bila Huruma.

"It means, I think," I said, "that it is now safe to descend the river."

I smiled to myself. The false ring would never be delivered to the Sardar.

"Let us proceed," said Bila Huruma.

"Cast off the lines," I called to the men.

Soon the four galleys and the canoes, including our raiders' canoe, were upon the lake.

I tied the Tahari ring about my neck, where it hung, with the golden chain of Bila Huruma, on my chest. Near me in the canoe, wrapped in waterproof, oiled skins, and tied to a floatable frame, were the map case and notebooks of Shaba.

I looked back once at the city, and once at the darkness in the sky to the southwest.

I then lowered my paddle and thrust back against the waters of the lake.

56

WHAT OCCURRED IN NYUNDO, THE CENTRAL VILLAGE OF THE UKUNGU REGION

"Where is Aibu?" cried Kisu.

We stood in the clearing of Nyundo, the central village of the Ukungu region.

Mwoga, spear in hand, a shield on his arm, came out to greet us. "He is dead," said Mwoga.

Tende, behind Kisu, cried out with misery.

"How did he die?" asked Kisu.

"By poison," said Mwoga. "I, now, am chieftain in Ukungu."

"My spear says it is not true," said Kisu.

"My spear," said Mwoga, "says that it is true."

"We shall, then, let them decide," said Kisu.

Small leather strips customarily sheath the blades of the spears of Ukungu. Both Mwoga and Kisu had now removed these tiny strips from their weapons. The edges of the blades gleamed. Each man carried, too, a shield. On the Ukungu shield there is, commonly, a tuft of feathers. This is fastened at one of the points of the shield. When the tuft of feathers is at the bottom of the shield, the shield being so held, this is an indication that the hunter seeks an animal. When the tuft of feathers is at the top of the shield, the shield so held, it is an indication that the quarry is human. On both the shield of Kisu and Mwoga the tufts were now at the top.

"I would make a better Mfalme than Aibu," said Mwoga. "It was thus that I had him killed."

The fight was brief, and then Kisu withdrew the bloodied point of his weapon from the chest of Mwoga, who lay at his feet.

451

"You fight well," said Bila Huruma. "Will you now see to the slaughter of those who supported Mwoga?"

"No," said Kisu. "My quarrel is not with them. They are my fellow tribesmen. They may remain in peace in the villages of Ukungu."

"Once, Kisu," said Bila Huruma, "you were little more than a kailiauk, with the obstinacy and crudity of the kailiauk's power, quick to anger, thoughtless in your charges. Now I see that you have learned something of the wisdom of one worthy to be a Mfalme."

Kisu shrugged.

"Proceed with us further to Ushindi," said Bila Huruma. "Msaliti is gone. I shall have need of one to be second in my empire."

"Better to be first in Ukungu," said Kisu, "than second in the empire."

"You are first in Ukungu," said Bila Huruma, naming Kisu to power.

"I shall fight you from Ukungu," said Kisu.

"Why?" asked Bila Huruma.

"I will have Ukungu free," said Kisu.

Bila Huruma smiled. "Ukungu," he said, "is free."

Men cried out in astonishment.

"Clean now the blade of your spear, Kisu," said Bila Huruma. "Put once more upon it the sheathing strips of guarding leather. Turn your shield so that the feathers lie again at its base."

"I will clean and sheath my spear," siad Kisu. "I will turn my shield."

Kisu handed his weapons to one of the villagers. He and Bila Huruma embraced.

It was thus that peace came to Ukungu and the empire.

57

I BOARD AGAIN THE PALMS OF SCHENDI; I WILL TAKE SHIP FOR PORT KAR

"It is not necessary to chain me like this, Master," said Janice.

She knelt on the hot boards of the wharf at Schendi. Her ankles were shackled, and her small wrists locked behind her in slave bracelets. A tight belly chain, locked on her, running to a heavy ring in the wood, about a foot from her, secured her in place. She was stripped. On her throat, locked, was a steel collar. It read 'I am owned by Bosk of Port Kar'. That is a name by which I am known in many parts of Gor. It has its own history.

"Before," said Janice, looking up at me, in my collar, "when I might have fled, and did, in Port Kar, I was not even secured. Now, when I know what I do, what it is to be a slave girl on Gor, and would be terrified to so much as move from this place without permission, I am heavily chained."

"It is common to secure female cargo before loading," I said. "It should have been done before."

"Yes, Master," she said.

I looked down at her. "Even if you were not chained, and wished to escape," I said, "I do not think such a venture would now be practical."

"No, Master," she said. "I am now branded. I am now collared."

"Greetings," said Captain Ulafi to me.

"Greetings," said I to him.

"Is this the little troublemaker?" he asked, looking down at Janice.

"I do not think she will cause you trouble now," I said.

Janice put her head down to the boards of the wharf. "Forgive me, Master," she said, "if I once displeased you."

"Lift your head," said Ulafi.

Janice looked up at him.

453

"How beautiful she has become," said Ulafi. "It is difficult to believe that she is the same girl." He regarded her. "She has become a sensuous dream," he said.

"She is a slave," I said. I shrugged.

"What fools men are to let any woman be free," he said.

"Perhaps," I said.

"You wish to take passage again on the *Palms of Schendi,*" he asked, "for return to Port Kar?"

"With your permission, Captain," I said.

"The arrangements have been made," he said. I pressed into his hands the coins on which we had agreed.

"We sail shortly," he said, "with the tide."

When I had returned to Schendi I had borne with me notes from the court of Bila Huruma. The moneys which I had lost when apprehended in Schendi, for seizure and transportation to the canal, had been returned to me. I had obtained again, too, my sea bag and its enclosed articles. I had received these back from the woman who had rented me the room off the Street of Tapestries. The sea bag lay at my feet. In it, with my other things, was a chain of gold, which I had received, long ago, from Bila Huruma. It had shared much of my equatorial odyssey. About my neck, on a leather string, inside my tunic, I wore the Tahari ring.

I thought of Bila Huruma, and the loneliness of the Ubar. I thought of Shaba, and his voyages of exploration, the circumnavigation of Lake Ushindi, the discovery and circumnavigation of Lake Ngao, and the discovery and exploration of the Ua, even to the discovery of its source in the placid waters of that vast lake he had called Lake Bila Huruma. But by the wish of Bila Huruma I had changed its name to Lake Shaba. He was surely one of the greatest, if not the greatest, of the explorers of Gor. I did not think his name would be forgotten.

"I am grateful," had said Ramani of Anango, who had once been the teacher of Shaba. I had delivered to him, and to two others of his caste, the maps and notebooks of Shaba. Ramani and his fellows had wept. I had then left them, returning to my lodgings. Copies would be made of the maps and notebooks. They would then be distributed by caste brothers throughout the cities of civilized Gor. The first copies that were made by anyone had already, however, been made, by the scribes of Bila Huruma in Ushindi. Ramani need not know this.

"Will you continue work on the canal?" I had asked Bila Huruma.

"Yes," he had said.

When Lakes Ushindi and Ngao had been joined by the canal a continuous waterway would be opened between Thassa and the Ua. One might then, via either the Kamba or the Nyoka, attain Lake Ushindi. One might then follow the canal from Ushindi to Ngao. From Ngao one could enter upon the Ua. One could then, for thousands of pasangs, follow the Ua until one reached its terminus in Lake Shaba. And Lake Shaba itself was fed by numerous smaller streams and rivers, each giving promise, like the tributaries of the Ua itself, to the latency of new countries. The importance of the work of Bila Huruma and Shaba, one a Ubar, the other a scribe and explorer, could not, in my opinion, be overestimated.

I thought of small Ayari, with whom I had shared the rogues' chain and my adventures upon the Ua.

He wore now the robes of the wazir of Bila Huruma. It was a wise choice, I thought, on the part of Bila Huruma. Ayari had proved his hardiness and worth in the journeys upon the Ua. He was facile with languages, and had connections with the villages of Nyuki on the northern shore of Ushindi, which was the territory of his father's birth, and, because of his connections with Kisu, with the Ukungu districts on the Ngao. Beyond this he had been born and raised in Schendi and, accordingly, spoke Gorean fluently. Adding to these things his intelligence, and his shrewdness and humanity, he seemed to me ideally suited for his work. Such a man might profitably be employed by a Ubar who wished to improve his relations not only with the interior but, too, with the city of Schendi, one of the major ports of civilized Gor. Too, Ayari was one of the few men who had ascended the Ua and lived to speak of it. He would doubtless figure prominently in the long-range programs and plans of Bila Huruma. In time I had little doubt that Ayari would become one of the most important men in the equatorial regions of Gor. I smiled to myself. There were probably few who thought that the little rogue of Schendi, the son of a lad who had once fled a village for stealing melons, would one day stand at the side of a throne.

But I thought most fondly of Kisu, he who was now again Mfalme in Ukungu.

To this day, as one may see upon the map, the land of

Ukungu stands as a sovereign free state within the perimeters of the empire of Bila Huruma.

Before Bila Huruma had left the village of Nyundo, central village of the Ukungu villages, he had spoken to Kisu. "If you wish," he had said, indicating Tende, who knelt beside them, "I will take this slave and arrange for her sale in Schendi. I will then have whatever moneys she brings returned to you."

"Thank you, Ubar," had said Kisu, "but I will keep this woman in Ukungu."

"Is it your intention to free her?" asked Bila Huruma.

"No," had said Kisu.

"Excellent," had said Bila Huruma. "She is too beautiful to be free."

Tende had looked up at Kisu. "I will try to please my master well," she had said.

We had remained that night in the village of Nyundo. I remembered the feast well. In addition to its political importance it had given the talunas an opportunity to learn to dance and serve. Their progress in femininity had not been much advanced by their work at the oars of a galley.

I smiled.

In our journey downriver we had found the small people marching the talunas westward, to sell them. The talunas, stripped, were being marched in tandem pairs, each pair fastened in the long coffle. Two forked sticks are lashed together. The fork of the first stick goes to the back of the neck of the first girl. Another stick then is thrust crosswise under the chin of the first girl and tied on the fork, holding her in the fork. The fork of the second lashed stick is before the throat of the second girl. Another stick then is thrust crosswise behind the neck of the second girl and lashed in place. The hands of each girl are tied behind their backs. Each pair, bound and fastened in the sticks, is then added as a unit to the coffle. The second girl in one pair, unless she is the last in the long line, and the first girl in the succeeding pair, unless she is the first in the long line, are fastened together by neck ropes. Thus is the coffle formed.

When we found the talunas being herded along by the small people we had brought our vessels to shore.

We bought the entire band of captive talunas for a crate of beads and five pangas.

We relieved the caught beauties of the coffle and chained them, four to a bench, to certain of the thwarts of one of the

456

galleys. Oars were then thrust in their hands, four girls to one oar, that they might be able to move the levers. There were enough girls, in this arrangement, for five oars to a side with one girl left over, who could carry food and water to her laboring sisters. A long chain was run lengthwise in the galley and fastened to rings at both stem and stern. The left ankle of the extra girl, the fetch-and-carry girl, who was already in wrist rings, joined by a foot of chain, was then locked in one of two ankle shackles, joined by about eighteen inches of chain. The right ankle shackle was then passed under the long chain and snapped shut about her right ankle. She was thus, by her lovely legs and body, and shackled ankles, literally fastened about the long chain, which served then as a slave's run-chain, permitting her movement, but strictly, by intent, controlling its scope. She might move back and forth, lengthwise in the galley, and to the benches, performing her labors, but could not leave the vessel or, indeed, even touch its bulwarks. Too, it did not permit her to move as far as its rudder. On this galley, the floating prison for the talunas, both those on the benches, chained to the thwarts, and the fetch-and-carry girl, we put five askaris, one for the rudder, for the river galley is single ruddered, and four, should the girls at the oars require encouragement, or the fetch-and-carry girl be in any way not completely pleasing, with whips.

"The river must be made safe," had said Bila Huruma, when the right ankle of the fetch-and-carry girl, the last girl to be chained, had been snapped in its shackle, fastening her by chain and body about the run-chain.

"What will you do with them?" I asked.

"I will have them sold in Schendi," he said.

I think that many of the talunas did not realize that their labors at the oar were intended to be temporary. Before the first Ahn was out many were sweating and moaning with pain, begging that they might be released, to be taught the more typical, softer labors of the female slave. It was hard to blame them for the oar of a river galley is normally drawn by a strong man. If the journey had not been downriver I do not think it would have been practical to put them at oars at all. The fetch-and-carry girl, of course, scolded the talunas for their weakness. The next day, however, it was she herself who sweated at an oar, crying out in pain under the whips of the vigilant askaris, while another took her place. She had not realized that the fetch-and-carry girl would be changed daily. In this way no taluna would have to spend more than forty

457

consecutive days at an oar. It had not taken the original fetch-and-carry girl more than an Ahn at the oar, incidentally, before she, too, had begged to be relieved of its pain, that she might be taught lighter duties, even those involving perfumes and silks, more fitting, more suitable, to the bodies and dispositions of female slaves.

The wharves were busy. I saw two slave girls, nude and chained, being delivered to a ship.

The talunas, last night, in a lot, had been sold to the black slavers of Schendi. The entire lot had gone for only two silver tarsks. I had then seen them, one by one, heads down, crawl to the slave circle. There they had rendered submission to men. They were then placed in wrist and throat coffle, their left wrists linked by one chain, their fair throats by another, and led away. They would be kept for a time in one of the underground pens beneath one of the fortresses of the black slavers. They would be given balms for their backs and oils for their blistered hands, and taught the duties of slaves. In a few weeks they would be ready, healed and cleaned, and to some extent trained, for the northern markets. Girls such as talunas, silked and perfumed, and placed under the iron will of a man, make superb slaves.

Two, however, who had once been talunas would not be with them. These were the blond-haired girl who had once been their leader, whom I decided to name Lana, and the dark-haired girl who had been her second in command, now the slave of Turgus. He had named her Fina.

I looked to my left, on the wharf. The blond-haired girl who had been the taluna leader, now the slave girl Lana, knelt there. Near her, too, was Alice. Both girls were stripped and had their hands braceleted behind their back. They were chained by the neck to the same ring.

"Master," said the girl who had been the taluna leader, Lana.

"Yes," I said.

"You are taking me to Port Kar," she said.

"Yes," I said. It is natural for a girl to fear the very name of that city.

"Will men be cruel to me in Port Kar?" she asked.

"You will be treated as the slave you are," I said.

She shuddered.

There is a saying in Gorean, that the chains of a slave girl are heaviest in Port Kar. I did not think, truthfully, however, that Port Kar was unusual in its treatment of female slaves.

Gorean men, generally, are not easy with them. The saying is probably motivated not so much by an objective analysis of the treatment of enslaved women in that city as by the fear and distrust which Port Kar has historically precipitated in the hearts of its enemies. If I had to make a choice I would suspect that it might be most difficult for a woman to wear her chains in the city of Tharna. There are complex historical reasons for this. Tharna is one of the few Gorean cities in which the great majority of its women are enslaved. Normally only about one in forty or so Gorean women in the cities is enslaved. Free Gorean women, incidentally, enjoy a prestige and status which, it seems to me, is higher than that of the normal Earth woman.

"What is done in Port Kar," asked Lana, "to a girl who is not found to be fully pleasing?"

"Commonly," I said, "she is bound hand and foot and thrown to the urts in the canals."

She looked at me, aghast. The chain was lovely on her throat, fastening her, kneeling, to the ring on the wharf. She pulled against the slave bracelets, confining her hands behind her back, but could not, of course, free herself.

"I would try, if I were you," I said, "to please my master."

"I will try desperately to please him," she said.

"See that you do," I said.

"Yes, Master," she said.

Alice put her cheek to my thigh. I then felt her lips at my thigh, as she kissed me. I put my hand in her hair, and, roughly, affectionately, shook her head. She looked up at me. "Please keep me, at least for a little time," she said. "Perhaps," I said. "Thank you, Master," she said. I looked down at her. She, like Janice, I thought, would somewhere, sometime, make someone a superb love slave. Until that time let her be put out again and again on the market.

Ngoma, who was of the crew of Ulafi, and two other crew members, then came up to me. "We shall be sailing soon," he said. "The cages are ready."

I nodded. I freed Janice of her shackles, bracelets and belly chain. She remained kneeling. She had not been given permission to rise. Ngoma put his hand in her hair. I then freed Alice and Lana of their bracelets and neck chains. They, too, remained kneeling, for they, too, had not received permission to rise. The two other crew members then put their hands in their hair.

Ngoma looked at me. I nodded. "Put them in their cages,"

I said. He pulled Janice to her feet, holding her head at his hip, and then, leading her behind him, bent over, conducted her up the gangplank to the deck of the *Palms of Schendi*.

"It will soon be time to board!" called Ulafi to me. He was on the stern castle of his vessel.

"Very well," I said.

His first and second officers, Gudi and Shoka, were near him.

I looked about.

There were as yet two empty slave cages on the deck of the *Palms of Schendi*, cages for which I had arranged.

"Ho, here!" I called, to the man from the tavern of Pembe.

He saw me and hurried toward me, dragging a leashed, blindfolded, sweetly hipped, naked slave with him. Her hands were braceleted behind her back. When he reached me he kicked her legs from beneath her and she knelt, trembling, at my feet. He removed her leash and bracelets. He then, roughly, removed the collar of the tavern of Pembe from her throat.

"Ngoma," I called.

The man from the tavern of Pembe then unknotted her blindfold and tore it away from her head.

"Oh!" cried she who had been Evelyn Ellis, looking up at me, blinking, startled.

"I own you now," I said. It had been she who had once served Kurii in this city.

"Yes, Master!" she said.

Ngoma, coming down the gangplank, arrived at my side.

I recalled her well from before, when she had served Shaba, Msaliti and myself. I recalled her well, too, from the tavern of Pembe. I was the first, months ago, to have taught her something of the meaning of a collar. I had purchased her last night, unknown to herself, when she had not been on the floor of the tavern. She had cost two silver tarsks.

"Oh, Master!" she cried, overjoyed.

"Submit," I said.

Swiftly she knelt back on her heels, her knees wide, and lifted and extended her arms, wrists crossed, as though for binding. Her head was down, between her arms.

"I submit myself, fully, and as a slave," she said.

I tied her wrists together and locked a collar on her, drawn from my sea bag.

"I am yours," she said.

"You are Evelyn," I said.

460

"Yes, Master," she said. "Thank you, Master."

"Put her in a cage," I said to Ngoma.

"It will be done," he said.

Evelyn was led away, drawn by the hair, bent over, to be thrust in one of the small slave cages on the deck. These cages, at their corners, by chains, are fastened to cleats. This prevents their movement in rough weather.

I thought of Janice. I smiled. Yesterday afternoon, for the first time, I had spoken in English to her.

"You speak English," she had cried, startled.

"Of course," I had said.

"But," she moaned, "I spoke in English before you, when I thought you could not understand. I revealed my inmost thoughts and feelings to you, totally."

"Yes," I said.

"Oh," she wept, "what an exposed slave you made me!"

"Of course," I said.

"Are you of Earth?" she asked. "No," she said, "a man such as you could never have been of Earth!"

"I was once of Earth," I said, "long ago." I looked at her. "I am now, however, like yourself, only of Gor."

She had then knelt before me. "I beg to be used by my Gorean master," she said.

I then took her by the arms and threw her to the furs.

"Master! Master!" cried Sasi, running toward me, her hands braceleted behind her back. I took her in my arms. "You are looking well, pretty little slut," I said.

The man from the tavern of Filimbi, to which she had been sold after I had been taken from Schendi, some months ago, was but a few feet behind her. He had unleashed her that she might run to me. She still wore a brief work tunic from the tavern, with the sign of the tavern, a flute, on its back. Filimbi was the name of the proprietor, but it is also an inland word for flute. In the morning tavern girls sometimes wear work tunics, as certain labors, such as laundering and scrubbing, may be set them. In the afternoon and evening, of course, they are dressed, if they are dressed at all, for the pleasure of the proprietor's customers. Sometimes, particularly in low paga taverns, the girl will be permitted to wear, besides her brand and collar, only perfume, or, if the proprietor wishes, perfume and chains. Like Evelyn I had bought Sasi yesterday, without her knowledge, for delivery to the

461

wharf this morning. She cost me two and five, two silver tarsks and five of copper.

"You did not forget me!" she cried.

"You are too pretty to forget," I told her.

The man from the tavern of Filimbi removed the bracelets from her wrists. Then, as she looked down, shyly, an unexpected modesty in a slave, he unsashed, parted and drew away the work tunic she wore. It was, after all, the property of the tavern.

She was exquisite.

"Kneel and submit, Slave," I said.

Swiftly then did she kneel and submit herself, totally, as a slave to me. Swiftly then were her wrists bound and her throat encircled in my collar.

"It is time to board!" called Ulafi.

"Greetings, Turgus," I said, as he came up to me. "It was nice of you to come to see me off."

"Who is this marvelous little slave who kneels at your feet?" he asked, looking down at Sasi.

"Surely you recognize your former accomplice of Port Kar?" I asked.

"She?" he asked. Then he said, "Lift your head, Girl."

Sasi lifted her head. "Yes, Master," she said.

"Is it you, Sasi?" he asked.

"Yes, Master," she said.

"Marvelous!" he said.

"Your own slave, Fina," I said, referring to the dark-haired girl kneeling behind him and to his left, "has also shown considerable improvement in beauty." She put down her head, happily. She was in a brief tunic. She was collared. Once, I recalled, she had been second in command among the talunas. Turgus had picked her out from among them, some forty girls, to be his personal slave. His choice had been excellent. Once a cold and arrogant taluna the girl knelt now, happily at his heels. She had been taught submission, and love.

From my sea bag I handed Turgus a letter. "In this letter," I said, "I have inscribed a petition that you be pardoned for your offenses in Port Kar. It is addressed to the council of captains, that body sovereign in Port Kar, of which I am a member. With this letter you may, if you wish, return to the city. It is my expectation that the council will rule favorably on the pardon. If they do not you will, at least, have ten days in which to take your departure from the city."

462

He took the letter. "I am grateful," he said. "But why would the council rule favorably?" he asked.

"We have fought together," I said.

"That is true," he said.

"Will you return to Port Kar?" I asked.

"I have moneys here in Schendi," he said, "notes which I have drawn upon my return from the Ua, moneys connected with my fees for accompanying Shaba's expedition. They will last me many months."

"It is less dangerous now for an outlander to remain in Schendi," I said, "since Ayari became wazir to Bila Huruma."

"Yes," he grinned. No longer now did Bila Huruma demand men from Schendi for the canal. This alteration in policy in itself had inaugurated a new era and climate in the relations between Schendi and the empire of Bila Huruma. I had little doubt but what Ayari had clarified to Bila Huruma the value of the friendship and facilities of the men of Schendi.

"With this letter," I said, indicating the document, "you may return when you wish. I would advise you, however, should the ruling, as I would expect, be in your favor, to consider the adoption of an honest occupation. If the magistrates do not apprehend you you might, in Port Kar, run afoul of the caste of thieves. They are sometimes jealous of their prerogatives."

He smiled. "I think I may go to a new city," he said. "I think I may make a new beginning somewhere. Perhaps I will go to Turia or Ar."

"They are great cities," I said, "rich in opportunities for the shrewd and ambitious." I looked at him. "Do you regret," I asked, "what has occurred to you in these past months?"

"No," he said, "I have had the honor of serving with Shaba, and with yourself. I have traveled the Ua. I have witnessed her source. These things are grand." He then looked back and down at the girl kneeling near him. "And, too," he said, "I have found a wondrous slave." She put down her head, smiling, joyful that her master had spoken highly of her, though she was only a slave. Then again he looked at me. He smiled. "I have no regrets," he said. "I am not dissatisfied. I am well pleased."

We clasped hands.

"I wish you well," I said.

"I wish you well," he said.

"It is time to board!" called Ulafi.

I lifted Sasi to her feet and then threw her over my shoulder. I reached down with my free hand and picked up my sea bag. I then ascended the gangplank and boarded the *Palms of Schendi.*